Patricia Scanlan lives in Dublin. Her books, all Number One bestsellers, include *Two For Joy*, *Double Wedding*, *Divided Loyalties* and *Forgive and Forget*.

Although Patricia loves writing fiction, she's *really* longing to be asked to research a book on Great Luxury Spas of the World or the Poshest Boutiques in Paris . . . she doesn't mind which!

www.transworldireland.ie

www.rbooks.co.uk

PATRICIA SCANLAN

HAPPY EVER AFTER?

TRANSWORLD IRELAND

TRANSWORLD IRELAND
an imprint of The Random House Group Limited
20 Vauxhall Bridge Road, London SW1V 2SA
www.rbooks.co.uk

HAPPY EVER AFTER?
A TRANSWORLD IRELAND BOOK: 9781848270466

First published in Great Britain
in 2009 by Transworld Ireland
Transworld Ireland paperback edition published 2010

Addresses for Random House Group Ltd companies outside the UK
can be found at: www.randomhouse.co.uk
The Random House Group Ltd Reg. No. 954009

The Random House Group Limited supports The Forest Stewardship
Council® (FSC®), the leading international forest-certification organisation.
Our books carrying the FSC label are printed on FSC®-certified paper.
FSC is the only forest-certification scheme supported by the leading
environmental organisations, including Greenpeace. Our
paper procurement policy can be found at
www.randomhouse.co.uk/environment

Typeset in 11.5/14.75pt by
Falcon Oast Graphic Art Ltd.
Printed and bound in Great Britain by Clays Ltd, St Ives plc

To my dear and precious Dad, who has been so strong for us and minded us all so well and kept us going this past eighteen months.

You're the best father in the world and we love you so much.

The great question ... which I have not been able to answer ... is, 'What does a woman want?'

Sigmund Freud

PROLOGUE

PROLOGUE

DEBBIE

It was hard to believe the honeymoon was over, Debbie Kinsella thought ruefully as she surveyed the shambles that was their bedroom. Bryan had half a dozen art-gallery catalogues strewn over the floor on his side of the bed. Three cool T-shirts she'd bought in Gap for her half-sister, Melissa, lay on top of the chest of drawers. Who would have ever thought she would end up buying a present for the teenager she'd despised for so long, she mused, putting the T-shirts on hangers so they wouldn't crease. Debbie felt an unwelcome pang of conscience, remembering how unfriendly and unkind she'd been to Melissa over the years. She'd been so angry and bitter at her father for leaving that she hadn't been able to bear to see him happy with his new family. When Melissa was born, Debbie had finally given up on the wistful notion that Barry and Connie would reunite. Melissa had been a focus for her anger for a long time. It had been undeserved, and Debbie was ashamed of herself and anxious to make amends. Hopefully, her half-sister would like the T-shirts she'd chosen for her, thought Debbie as she placed the hangers on the wardrobe door-knob.

The linen basket was overflowing, and their cases were still unpacked, full of clothes that needed to be washed. At this rate, she'd be washing for a week. Once, she would have gathered everything up and brought a bag full of clothes to the launderette and had them washed and ironed. It would have cost her. Ironing was expensive, but she wouldn't have cared; it was money well spent, in her eyes.

Now that they were saddled with a mortgage, loan repayments from the credit union for their wedding and honeymoon expenses, and a massive Visa bill, cashflow was a big issue, and the little luxuries that she and Bryan had taken so much for granted were going to have to fall by the wayside. Debbie had suggested going back to work on a Friday, as it was payday, and it would help them adjust to 'normal life' after all the excitement of the wedding and honeymoon. They'd only be in work one day, they'd have the weekend to recover, and they'd have money in their wallets. It had seemed like a good idea at the time, but now, studying the disarray surrounding her, she wasn't so sure.

She let her wet towel fall to the floor and began to dress. At least she didn't have to worry about what to wear, which was just as well, as she would have had to delve deep in their crammed, bulging wardrobe for something clean, and that, right at this moment, was not for the faint-hearted. Her uniform suit, neatly pressed, hung on the back of the door, and she gave herself a mental pat on the back for at least being that little bit organized. She brushed her shoulder-length copper hair, twirled it around and fastened it with a comb, loose tendrils escaping, framing her heart-shaped face. Her blue eyes, flecked with hazel, needed nothing more than a touch of grey, smudged eyeliner, which she applied with practised ease.

It was weird getting dressed to go back to work. This day last week, she and Bryan had been strolling arm in arm through the Met in New York, admiring the work of the American photographer Walker Evans, part of the museum's massive photography collection.

That had been a particularly nice day, reflected Debbie as she dusted shimmer powder over her cheeks, wishing she could disguise the smattering of freckles on her nose and cheekbones. They had breakfasted in a little deli on East 52nd and then ambled the few blocks up Fifth Avenue, to Tiffany's, where they'd bought each other a Heart Tag keyring as a memento of their honeymoon. They had carried on to the Met, where they spent a thoroughly enjoyable morning browsing the collections. Hunger had eventually forced them to drag themselves away that afternoon, and they had headed for Central Park and the Boathouse Restaurant on the lake. Sitting on the sun-drenched deck waiting for their prawns and salads to arrive, they watched the row-boats drifting by, the ducks and swans looking for titbits, as the sun glistened on the lake and the Manhattan skyscrapers soared above the trees on the opposite shore.

Debbie had remembered the scene in *Sex and the City* when Big and Carrie fell into the lake, and almost had to pinch herself to make her realize that she was honeymooning in New York and she was now Mrs Bryan Kinsella. Oh yes, it had been a glorious and happy day, she smiled, fingering the gleaming gold wedding band that encircled the fourth finger of her left hand.

She might have come down to earth with a bang, but at least she and Bryan had overcome their rocky times, and she couldn't be happier. And bad enough as it was going back to work, at least she wouldn't have to deal with her bullying boss, Judith Baxter, who was in hospital following a car accident. Word was she wouldn't be in the office for a while, which was a huge relief to most of the staff and to Debbie in particular. Judith was a tyrant and had given Debbie a rough ride in the run-up to her wedding. She'd been down on her like a ton of bricks for any mistake. Even Debbie being a few minutes late had incurred Judith's wrath, and she had stopped her pay increment for six months. Debbie had been shocked. That was uncalled for. She had been counting on her rise to help pay off her loans.

She didn't wish her boss ill, but there was no love lost between them and she'd be the first to admit that if she never saw the woman again she wouldn't give a toss. Hard enough as it was returning to work, it would have been a thousand times harder if Judith had been waiting, hawk-like, to see that she was on time.

She had to be thankful for small mercies, Debbie supposed as she raced downstairs, anxious not to be late on her first day back, Judith or no Judith. The post had come and, as she picked up what were mostly bills, her heart sank as she saw their Visa bill. She and Bryan were well maxed out on their credit card, and they really were going to have to tighten their belts big time in an effort to pay off their spiralling debts. Bryan would hate it, he was moaning about it already, but it was something they had to address before things got seriously out of hand.

Debbie pulled the door behind her and hurried along the path. It was going to be a scorcher – how nice it would have been to take her lounger out on to their deck and flick through magazines and drink coffee. Would she ever be able to give up work? Or even work part time, job sharing, like some of the married women in her office did? Not unless she won the Lotto, she thought glumly. It was eight million this week – she must remember to buy a few Quick Picks. She'd do it at lunchtime. She tried to cheer herself up: she had as much chance of winning as anyone else had.

She crossed the street, weaving in and out of traffic. Real life was back with a vengeance. At least she didn't have the usual knot of tension in the pit of her stomach from worrying about Judith Baxter, she comforted herself as the noisy stop-start of car engines and squealing brakes and children crying in buggies as their mothers rushed to crèches grated on her ears. Although Sandymount wasn't far from the city, driving in the rush hour was chaotic, and she and Bryan far preferred to take the train. But, sometimes, Bryan needed the car to travel to clients. At least she could walk to her office from the Dart and it kept her fit.

Debbie quickened her pace and joined the morning commute.

BRYAN

'Come on, come on, come on!' Bryan Kinsella sat behind the steering wheel of his Audi soft-top as the traffic inched along the Strand Road. He should have taken his chances and gone through the village and turned right for the East Link. He could see across to the Sean Moore road in the distance, and the traffic snaked along, bumper to bumper, hardly moving. Some mornings, if he went to work very early, he could get to the IFSC in less than ten minutes. It was easily going to take the guts of an hour today.

Was this what his life was going to be like, apart from his few precious weeks' holidays? He groaned as the lights went red again. It was incredible to think that the wedding was over. The reception, which he'd looked forward to more than the ceremony, was a blur, and the honeymoon, which had been the trip of a lifetime, when he'd got to see as many of the cultural sights and scenes of New York as he possibly could, was now just a lovely dream. How he'd enjoyed strolling through myriad art galleries and studios, sipping lattes on sidewalk cafés, taking in shows, browsing in Borders and buying treasured books with not a care in the world.

Now he was back to real life, with all its worries and pressures. He couldn't even think about the amount of debt they were in after the honeymoon. Both their credit cards were up to their limits, as was the one he had himself on the sly, which Debbie knew nothing about. He had a credit union loan that she knew nothing about either, he thought guiltily, and he was barely managing to pay the interest on *that*. It looked as though their hefty mortgage was going to increase by another half a per cent, and he hadn't paid the last telephone bill, even though he'd told Debbie he had.

This was what being married did to a fella, he thought gloomily as he stared unseeingly out the car window. Why were women so anxious to get married? He didn't understand it at all. He'd have been quite happy to mosey along in a smart, rented apartment in a good area, with no mortgage, for another few years, but Debbie had insisted they buy a house, saying that rent was money down the drain. He shouldn't have bloody well listened to her. They'd bought their townhouse in Sandymount at the height of the property boom, when prices had rocketed, and paid mad money for it. Sandymount was an undeniably chic address, and he liked living there. He liked the village ambience, the upmarket delis, bistros and restaurants, the quirky shops. It was enjoyable to stroll along the seafront on Sunday, buy the papers and have lattes and eggs Florentine in Itsa4 for brunch. Or to go to Brownes on a Saturday night and indulge in their famous fresh salmon rillettes wrapped in smoked salmon or their to-die-for flaked crab. His mouth watered as he thought of his favourite dishes. He hadn't eaten breakfast, and he was hungry.

Now, a slump had hit, and there was no way they'd ever get the price they bought their house for if they went to sell it, so they were in negative equity on that front. If Debbie hadn't been so impatient, they could have bided their time, rented and bought when prices dropped and it was a buyers' market. He'd make sure to say that to Debbie's mother, Connie, he thought grimly. She'd been pushing for them to get a house. She should have minded her own bloody business. He scowled, looking for someone to blame for his woes and thinking that Connie, his pushy mother-in-law, would fit the bill perfectly.

Connie wasn't his favourite person in the world. He always felt that she was judging him and finding him lacking – just because he didn't spend every precious weekend stripping wallpaper or doing DIY. She'd obviously hoped for better for her only daughter. *She* hadn't been able to keep a husband, so she needn't bother looking down her nose at him, he decided, conveniently forgetting the very generous cheque she'd given to himself and Debbie, money she had worked hard to earn.

The lights turned green, and the traffic moved a

19

couple of yards before stopping again. He glanced in the mirror, approving of the way his tan made his eyes look a deeper shade of brown. He was a good-looking guy, he had to admit, and he turned this way and that, noting with dismay that he was beginning to get lines at the corners of his eyes. Hell, before he knew it he'd be thirty and Debbie would want children, and his life would be well and truly over. It was a daunting thought. Did other new husbands think like he did, or was it just him? He'd never been one for taking on responsibilities; it made him feel smothered. He would have quite happily lived with Debbie for the rest of his life with no marriage and no kids. Just the two of them, enjoying their freedom and having fun.

Debbie would be well into the city on the Dart by now, even though he'd left much earlier than she had. Bryan wondered how she would react if he told her he'd like to quit his job and open up an art gallery. Not too well, he figured as he surfed the radio channels, coming to Lyric FM. The strains of 'Lara's Theme' from *Doctor Zhivago* floated across the airwaves, and he sat imagining how his art gallery would look until an impatient beep from the car behind brought him back to reality and he inched another few yards towards work.

CONNIE

Oh God, let me win the Lotto, Connie Adams prayed silently as she knelt at the feet of Miss Eunice Bracken and eased a pair of tights over her spindle-thin, purple, varicose-veined legs.

'Make sure they're straight, Nurse. I don't like wrinkles around the ankles. I'm not Nora Batty,' Miss Bracken instructed bossily. She was an ex-headmistress, and she treated the staff in Willowfield Nursing Home like schoolgirls. Connie manoeuvred the tights up over Miss Bracken's girdle and straightened the nylon slip down over her patient's knees. She then slithered another nylon slip down over the old lady's shoulders. Miss Bracken liked to wear two slips to keep out the cold, despite the fact that it was mid-summer.

'My beige skirt, cream blouse and mint-green cardigan are hanging up in the wardrobe. I'll wear them today.' Eunice gave an imperious wave in that direction. 'Lay them out neatly on the bed first.'

'*Yes, Miss Bracken, no, Miss Bracken. Three bags full, Miss Bracken,*' Connie thought irritably as she stood up and went to fetch the required clothes. What the hell was she doing being bossed around by a cantankerous old shrew at this stage of her life? Forty-eight years of age, twenty-nine of them a nurse, divorced mother of a newly wed twenty-five-year-old. Surely she was entitled to *some* respect?

'And pass me over my amethyst brooch – it's on the dressing table,' came the next haughty instruction. Clearly, her patient thought she was there to wait on her hand and foot.

'Certainly, Miss Bracken,' Connie responded, amused in spite of herself. There was no point in going down the road of standing on her dignity. She had nursed the old trout before and knew the best way to deal with her was to ignore her bossiness and not let her get a rise out of her.

A box of Terry's All Gold chocolates lay open beside the antique brooch, and Connie gazed at them longingly. She was dying for her tea break. She had her period, and salt and chocolate cravings had kicked in. She'd bought herself a packet of King crisps for her break; a chocolate would be lovely with them. But she knew better than to nick one. Miss Bracken was notoriously mean. She counted her chocolates daily, and woe betide the staff if any of them were eaten.

'Stop dawdling, Nurse,' Miss Bracken ordered brusquely, and Connie had to fight hard to restrain herself from giving a sharp retort. She didn't know if it was a menopausal thing or not, but lately she was feeling thoroughly grumpy and exasperated,

22

going so far, one Sunday morning, as to send in a furious email to a panellist on a radio show who had made light of the overcrowding problems in A&Es. It hadn't been read out, and she hadn't known whether to be amused or irritated by her behaviour. Miss Eunice Bracken was pushing her luck, if only she knew it. Connie's patience was hanging by a thread. Thank God her days doing agency nursing were coming to an end for the foreseeable future. She was looking forward to her new job as a part-time nurse to an elderly lady in Greystones, not far from where she lived. And, before that, she had a week in Spain with her sister-in-law, Karen, to look forward to. It was badly needed; she felt whacked.

The stress of her daughter Debbie's wedding had taken a lot out of her, more than she realized, she thought, stifling a yawn and sliding Miss Bracken's beige skirt over her head. 'Would you be careful what you're doing, you've messed my hair,' the elderly woman scolded, as her head emerged, hair slightly mussed, glasses awry, as Connie pulled the elastic-waisted skirt down over her thin frame. Miss Bracken suffered from arthritic hips and bad knees and couldn't lift her right leg to step into a skirt.

'Sorry,' Connie apologized. 'I'll brush your hair for you when you've finished dressing.'

'You needn't bother. I can do it myself, thank you,' Eunice Bracken snapped irritably as a dart of pain shot through her. 'Get me my tablets, and be quick about it. I'm tormented with my arthritis today.'

'It must be the rain we've had the past few days,' Connie said kindly, suddenly feeling sorry for the old lady in front of her. What sort of a life did she have? An intensely proud and independent woman like her, having to be helped to get dressed – it must be humiliating – and then she had to contend with a life of chronic and disabling pain. No wonder the poor thing was crabby.

She handed the tablets and a glass of water to her patient and then resumed dressing her, closing the buttons on her blouse, a task Miss Bracken was unable to undertake because of her arthritic fingers.

'You're not the worst of them,' her patient said grudgingly when Connie had finished her ministrations.

'Thank you, Miss Bracken.' Connie smiled, knowing she'd been paid quite a substantial compliment. 'Let me walk you down to the day room and get you a nice cup of tea.' She took the elderly lady's arm, and they walked slowly from the room, down the hall, to a bright, airy, comfortable drawing room that looked out on to verdant lawns and massed beds of shrubs and flowers.

'The chair by the window, quick now, before Mr McCall comes. He hogs it, you know. You'd think he owned it, the way he goes on,' Miss Bracken declared, managing a little spurt as she triumphantly laid claim to the comfortable arm-chair. 'Now you may get me my tea, and my *Irish Times*,' she instructed, settling in comfortably and gazing with longing at the lovely garden. She'd been an avid gardener once, but her arthritis had put a stop to that. Now, all she could do was look and criticize the planting strategy of the lazy lump who looked after the gardens but was more often to be seen smoking and chatting to anyone who would listen to him. He could do with a haircut too. 'That fellow looks like Worzel Gummidge,' she sniffed when Connie handed her the newspaper, and couldn't understand why she guffawed.

'I'm glad I amused you,' Miss Bracken said dryly.

'If you didn't have a sense of humour in this job, you'd be in trouble, believe me.' Connie couldn't keep the faint edge out of her voice.

'Indeed,' Miss Bracken agreed. 'I suppose you're right.' Their eyes met, and there was the tiniest hint of a twinkle lurking in Eunice's. It was a triumph of sorts, Connie felt as she made her way to the staff dining room to have the much-longed-for cuppa and crisps.

Connie was bone weary when she finally got home. Her eyes were gritty with tiredness, and her lower back ached, a dull, nagging pain which always accompanied her period. The early shift was a killer, but at least she had a long afternoon to herself. She was greeted lovingly by her little black cat, Miss Hope. 'Hello, my little pet.' Connie scooped her up and buried her nose in her soft, silky black fur. 'Let's have a bite to eat and a snooze,' she murmured, heading for the kitchen.

Working weekends as well as weekdays really

took it out of you, she reflected as she boiled the kettle, buttered a slice of brown bread and cut a wedge of red cheddar. She was trying to get her finances back on track after the expense of the wedding and her cash gift to Debbie and Bryan. And she didn't want to be scrimping and saving on her trip to Spain.

Once, working seven days straight had been no problem to her, but her energy levels weren't as good as they used to be, hard as it was to accept it. 'Ah, stop acting like an ould wan, you're in your prime,' she muttered, dipping her teabag up and down in her mug. 'Even if you are talking to yourself and sending off ratty emails.' She grinned.

She headed out to the deck with the mug of much-needed tea and sat down gratefully at the table, kicking off her shoes. Her mobile rang, and she frowned. Was ten minutes' peace too much to ask, she wondered crossly as she took it out of her pocket. She was surprised to see her ex-husband's phone number come up.

What did he want? The wedding was over, and she wasn't too anxious to be in constant contact with Barry. She didn't want to be reminded of their night of passion. She didn't exactly regret it, but it was a one-off, and he didn't seem to realize that. Both of them had been shattered after Debbie's showdown with him about her feelings towards him. Connie had been very shocked that she'd not realized how deep Debbie's hurt went. Their kiss of comfort had turned into much more than a kiss, but it was emphatically *not* going to happen again.

'Yes, Barry,' she said briskly, wishing the sun would come out from behind a bank of cloud which was casting shadows over her back garden.

'Hi Connie,' he said cheerfully. 'How are things?'

'Things are good. Off to Spain next week with Karen. I'm looking forward to it.' She kept her tone light, offhand almost. Barry seemed to think that, because they'd had a quick shag, in a moment of weakness for her, prior to the wedding, he was now her best friend and confidant. It was an assumption Connie was eager to dispel.

'Yeah, so I heard. I bumped into her the other day. My sister told me she plans to sleep, eat, drink and read. Sounds deadly boring to me.'

'Sounds perfect to me,' Connie riposted.

'If that's what you want, enjoy it. You deserve it, that's for sure.'

'Thanks,' she murmured. Barry had just made her forthcoming holiday sound dull and dreary.

'Listen, I hope you don't think I'm being pushy, but I'd really like to build on the momentum of the progress myself, Debbie and Melissa made coming up to the wedding. I don't want to let things drift.'

'Sure, I understand,' Connie agreed with a hint of warmth. She'd been so happy that Debbie and her father had finally, after years of bitterness, reconciled, and it had given her great joy to see the two half-sisters take those first faltering steps towards real sisterhood.

'I was thinking it would be nice if we could get

together for a coffee or a brunch or something but ... er ... I know you and Debbie and Aimee aren't exactly hitting it off, so that would be awkward. And I don't want Melissa picking up on it. She's very loyal to her mother, so I was wondering if we could sort of "bump" into you?'

'That would be nice, Barry,' Connie approved, ashamed of her earlier irritability at his call. Barry had become a good father over the years, she'd give him that. Her ex-husband was right: these new, unprecedented relationships should be nurtured. It was just such a nuisance that Aimee and her bad behaviour was now the cause of awkwardness and had to be pussyfooted around. Until the wedding, Connie had got on reasonably well with Barry's second wife, but after Aimee's strop outside the church, when she'd complained about the cost and said that it was *her* hard-earned money that was paying for it, relations were at an all-time low.

'Melissa and I often go for coffee and a Danish on Saturday mornings. How about if we go to one of the outdoor cafés along the Pavilion, and you and Debbie casually wander by? Or is that too obvious?' Barry asked.

'Um ... I could ask Debbie to meet me in Meadows and Byrne – I could let on I was thinking of changing my sofa or something and would like her advice,' suggested Connie helpfully.

'Would you, Connie? That would be great,' Barry said enthusiastically, and she had to smile. Barry was so naive really. He thought all the past hurts could be made better in an instant. He wanted them all to be one big, happy family.

Maybe he was right to be like that, she sighed. Maybe it *was* that easy to let go. She wouldn't stand in the way of it. 'I'll give Debbie a buzz and try and sort things,' she assured him. 'See you.'

'Thanks, Connie, really appreciate it.'

'You're welcome, Barry,' she said and hung up. She supposed she should be glad he was making the effort. God knows it had taken him and Debbie long enough to sort their differences. She'd do what she could to foster good relations between father and daughter. And, besides, she'd grown fond of Melissa, having eventually got through that prickly teenage façade. It was important that Debbie and Melissa developed their friendship. A close relationship with a sister was more precious than gold. Connie would have loved a sister. She hated being an only child. In days to come it would be good to know the two girls would have each other to lean on. Connie gave a wry smile. There she was again, trying to sort everybody out. Some things never changed. Once Debbie and Melissa were on track she was giving it up, she decided as she gave up on the sun and went inside and lay down on her sofa. She had her own life to lead. She was asleep in minutes.

BARRY

'Excellent game, Barry, most enjoyable. And I'm delighted we'll be able to do business. A quarterly publication advertising our wine selections, gift hampers and special offers will undoubtedly increase sales and consumer awareness. Your package was competitive and high quality – my sales people were impressed, and so was I. We'll let our people work out the finer details.' Desmond Donnelly shook Barry's hand before taking his leave.

Barry watched him stride out of the clubhouse and gave a deep sigh of relief. His stomach had been in a knot all morning, wondering if he was going to get the deal. With recession in the air, belts would undoubtedly be tightened, and contracts could be lost if companies felt that glossy publications were a luxury they could no longer afford.

It would be very satisfying indeed to go home and tell Aimee he had cut a lucrative new deal for his company. It would be good for his wife to know he was still a player and that she wasn't the only one in town making a success of her career. He sat back in his chair, good humour dissipating as he thought of his wife and the current state of antipathy between them. Since their heated exchange at Debbie's wedding over two weeks ago, the atmosphere between them was still decidedly frosty. This was the worst low in all their years together. Yes, there'd been troughs before, but they'd always been anxious to sort things and get back on an even keel, but this estrangement was different: harsh, biting words had been hurled which couldn't be taken back, and the shards of bitterness were still embedded deep.

He wasn't having much luck with his current and ex-spouses, he reflected gloomily. Connie, his ex-wife, was making it decidedly clear she wasn't interested in progressing their relationship, despite their becoming close again in the run-up to the wedding. More than close, he thought wryly, remembering the ardour she'd shown when they'd had a hot and heavy, unexpectedly lusty encounter in the lead-up to their daughter's big day.

He'd re-imagined it often, and it still made him horny. He wanted more. He certainly wasn't getting hot rides from his wife; all he was getting from Aimee was the cold shoulder. Even before the row at the wedding she'd gone off sex. She was too tired when she got home from work. And she was bringing much more work home with her. His wife's career trajectory was having a major impact on their marriage, and she couldn't even see it, he thought bitterly.

It was because of that he hadn't thought twice about sleeping with his ex-wife. He couldn't understand why Connie was so reluctant to continue their delightful dalliance. She'd enjoyed it as much as he had, and he was fairly sure she'd been celibate for much of the time since their divorce. She was a sensual woman; they could have a no-strings-attached relationship: win-win scenario. Still, at least Connie had agreed to his suggestion to meet up with himself and Melissa. It was important that they all try and bond as a family, even if Aimee wasn't happy about it. He finished his coffee and prepared to go back to the office.

'Barry, how is it going? Haven't seen you for a while. I heard your daughter got married. Have a wedding coming up myself. Have you any tips?' a plummy voice asked from behind him.

Barry turned to see Jeremy Farrell bearing down on him. Suave, dapper in his sharp pin-striped suit, Jeremy was one of Barry's least favourite club members. The older man loved the sound of his own voice, loved boasting about his business exploits and the famous names he'd dealt with during his stockbroking years. He'd recently taken early retirement because of heart problems, but he continued to work on a consultancy basis for his old company, Crookes & Co. He was constantly advising his golfing buddies on their investments, advocating this share or the other.

Eighteen months previously, he'd told Barry that AdCo, a private banking group, was being floated on the stock exchange and suggested he should invest a few bob. Barry had taken his advice, as his own accountant had agreed that it was a good bet. He'd made a fast buck on the tip, selling high a year later, making about five thousand. Buttons to the high flyers in the club, some of whom had raked in a small fortune. Barry had been sorry he'd been so conservative, especially when he saw the gleaming new Series 5 Beemer Glen Harris had bought out of his profits.

'Jeremy! How are things?' Barry put on his best hail-fellow-well-met voice and gave the other man a hearty handshake.

'Good. Things are good, apart from this damn wedding. Three sons went up the aisle with no trouble. Now, my youngest, and only daughter, is on the move, and the difference is unbelievable. Tears, tantrums, traumas. All I'm getting is hassle and a fast-depleting bank account.' Jeremy rolled his eyes.

Barry laughed. 'Tell me about it. Thank God I won't be going through that again for another few years.'

'Listen.' Jeremy leaned in conspiratorially. 'Have you five minutes? I've a good tip for you if you're interested. If you did well with AdCo, you'll hit the jackpot with SecureCo International Plus. Are you interested?'

'I'll listen to what you have to say, Jeremy,' Barry agreed.

'Good man. Sit down there and I'll sort out two coffees.'

Barry sat down. No harm in listening to what Jeremy had to say, and this time he wouldn't be a wuss. If he felt it was worth while, he'd throw more than a few measly thousand at it. This time, he'd make a killing like Glen Harris had. A brand-new Beemer would go down a treat with Aimee and Melissa. His younger daughter liked swanky cars. It was crucial, she'd once told him, to keep up with the girls in her class. Was it possible she'd asked for him to buy them a holiday home abroad as so many girls in her class had one and she'd like to be able to say she was going to France or Portugal, or Spain or wherever? Melissa thought money grew on trees, he thought fondly, thinking he must ring her and check in to see what she was up to. She was on her summer holidays, and it was the first time she'd been allowed to stay at home alone without a child-minder. Aimee had been having second thoughts about it after finding empty alcopop bottles on the balcony the day of Debbie's wedding. His wife was seriously pissed off with their daughter, and Melissa knew that, if there was any more misbehaving, she was in deep trouble. He'd phone her as soon as he got to the car, he decided, clearing a space for Jeremy to place the steaming coffee cups and settling back to hear what the stockbroker had to say.

AIMEE

Please don't let me throw up, please let me get through this OK, Aimee Davenport prayed silently as she took a deep, steadying breath and walked into the Four Seasons, her heels sinking into the luxurious deep-pile carpet as she walked towards the lounge area, where she had arranged to meet one of her biggest clients, Roger O'Leary.

Two weeks ago, she had overseen the arrangements for his daughter's million-euro-plus wedding, her remit to showcase 'The Best of Irish'. She had followed her brief to the letter, right down to the Royal Tara china, the Louise Kennedy crystal, the prime organic Kilkenny beef and lamb, the oysters, lobsters and salmon, the specially grown herbs. Everything had been superlative, the result of months of hard work and minute attention to detail. It had been a huge success. The O'Learys had been more than happy. Competition between the massively wealthy businessmen in the country to outdo each other, or at least keep up with each other, was intense, and *Chez Moi*, the events and catering company she worked for, and other such companies, were reaping the rewards of such rivalry. Aimee had received many compliments during the big day, which had been deeply satisfying.

Her boss, Ian Kelleher, the MD of *Chez Moi*, had sent her a gushing, patronizing email telling her to stand back and take a well-deserved bow. What a prat, she'd thought in disgust. She'd organized many such events for the company, and it was time he put his money where his mouth was and upped her salary.

Today, she was meeting Roger and some of his business associates, at his request, and she had a feeling something was in the air. He had a business proposal to put to her, he'd said on the phone when he'd called to arrange the meeting. She needed to be in tip-top form, not queasy and tired as she was feeling now. She made her way to the ladies' room to touch up her make-up. Aimee had arrived early deliberately. It always made her feel more in control to be the one doing the greeting. She studied her reflection in a mirror, glad she had the luxurious restroom to herself.

Fortunately, she looked fine, showing no outward sign of the discomfort she was feeling. Her green eyes, fringed with a fan of dark lashes, were bright, and clear. Her high cheekbones emphasized her good bone structure, inherited from her mother. Her glossy black hair was coiled up in a classy chignon, giving her a very groomed, business-like air. The sharp grey Donna Karan suit she wore was softened by a pale lilac cami. A single strand of pearls adorned her throat, matched by two pearl earrings. Her make-up was immaculate. Understated, chic – sophistication was the look Aimee had gone for, and she'd succeeded, she thought, studying herself critically as she retouched her lipstick. No one would ever know she was below par, she decided, slipping a small mint into her mouth in an effort to quell the queasiness she was feeling.

It was on the day of the O'Leary wedding when she'd been overcome by a sudden wave of nausea, that she'd had the heart-stopping realization that she might be pregnant. It had been a bolt out of the blue, and she'd almost cried with misery that this could be happening. She hadn't even taken a test yet. She'd bought one, but she didn't need it to tell her what she already knew, and she didn't want to see the ultimate proof of what she considered to be an absolute personal disaster.

Aimee felt despair engulf her as she put her lipstick in her Prada handbag and snapped it shut. She emphatically did *not* want another child, with all the hassle it entailed. Melissa was more than enough to deal with and, now, with her career really going into orbit, bottles and nappies and sleepless nights, not to mention childcare arrangements, were the last thing Aimee needed or wanted.

What brutal timing. Melissa was at an age where she was old enough to look after herself without supervision, freeing Aimee up considerably to concentrate on her work. Children were so time-consuming and, right now, she needed all her time to capitalize on all her hard work over the past couple of years. The rewards were coming, and she wanted to embrace them and forge ahead.

She hadn't told Barry she was pregnant – hell, she was hardly speaking to Barry. After the disaster of Debbie's wedding, when she had embarrassed him in front of Connie and their daughter by bringing up the cost of the bash, there had been little thaw in the Arctic relations that currently existed between them.

She wished things were sorted. She missed their intimacy, their companionship. She was dying to tell him what was going on workwise. Until the lead-up to the O'Leary wedding, Barry had always shown great interest in her career, encouraging her, motivating her. That had all changed now. It was clear that he felt she was overtaking him in the career stakes, and he was finding it hard to handle. Now, he was sullen and withdrawn and moaning about having to do the grocery shopping because she was tied up. Had it all been lip service? It looked like it. Bitterness so sharp she could almost taste it swamped her. She'd never expected that sort of behaviour from Barry. It was his respect for her career that had tipped the balance as to whether or not she would marry him. It looked like she'd made a big mistake. But he had known what she was like when they'd married; he knew her goals. If he'd wanted a dull stay-at-home wife he should have stayed married to Saint Connie. Aimee sighed. As well as their problems over her career, they had the episode on Debbie's wedding day to overcome. True, she hadn't behaved very well, but there was no need to hold it over her head until kingdom come. Barry needed to get down off his high horse. Connie had given as good as she'd got; she was no shrinking violet. It had stung that he'd sat beside his ex-wife in the church and left her to her own devices. *That* was when she'd walked out.

How would her husband feel about having another child? How would Melissa feel? She might be highly miffed to have a new arrival. And they'd have to move. The penthouse was big, but for four of them? Aimee frowned. Her guest room would have to go.

What was she thinking? Making plans as if she was going to keep it. It was very early days yet. She had options. No one would know if she decided to have a termination. Why should she have to have a baby she didn't want? Having a baby now would be a seismic shift in her life, a shift she didn't want. Men were so bloody lucky. They never had to deal with consequences like this; it was always the woman left holding the baby, literally. Aimee was pretty sure Barry would be horrified if he knew what she was thinking. A jagged stab of guilt assailed her. This child was his as well as hers. By rights he should have some say. But by whose rights? What about her rights? She wanted to yell, frustration, rage and despair welling up. So many women wanted to have children and couldn't and, now, here she was, saddled with one she didn't have any desire for. She wasn't maternal. She was the first to admit it. When she'd had Melissa she'd blithely assumed she would cope fine. She'd never forget the terror of those first few months, every time Melissa cried – and cried she had. She'd been a colicky baby, and Aimee had been convinced she was poisoning her. Fear had been her constant companion. Was she feeding her enough or too much? Had she a temperature and was she ailing, or was she just hot? Were yellow poos normal? Was the rash on her scalp normal? It had been totally nerve-wracking and she had been on edge until Melissa was well into toddlerhood. She'd tried not to compare herself to other mothers who seemed to cope so efficiently and without worrying. All Aimee had wanted to do was to get back to work, keep her head down and let the crèche deal with all the problems.

For the first time in her life, Aimee realized how good it would be to have someone she could talk with about her dilemma. Now was the time when a friend would be someone to lean on and confide in. And the one person she knew she could have done that with and not been judged or criticized would have been Gwen Larkin, one of her oldest friends. Unfortunately, they'd had a fairly nasty falling-out the day of Debbie's wedding.

Aimee chewed the inside of her lip. Gwen was right to be annoyed with her, she admitted grudgingly. Aimee had treated her badly, pretending she hardly knew her so she wouldn't have to introduce her to Roger O'Leary, but she had looked a sight, with her hair falling out of the comb at the back of her head and her wearing a wrinkled jacket and shabby jeans. And her two kids squabbling. Aimee had been in full career-woman mode that day, dressed to the nines and in killer heels, for the wedding. Her affluent and well-connected client would have had good cause to wonder what sort of set Aimee mixed with had she introduced him to Gwen. Aimee had said hello, and said she'd ring some time. Gwen wasn't a fool, she must have known Roger was a client and that Aimee was talking business with him.

Her friend really had taken the hump. There was no need for her to have turned on her the way she did, and in front of Connie and Debbie, even if she did feel hard done by. Aimee's cheeks burned at the memory. It had been mortifying. Gwen had been like a little fishwife, practically screeching with temper and accusing her of all kinds of things.

Aimee straightened her shoulders and strode down to the lounge. She didn't need Gwen, or Barry, or anyone. She could deal with her problem herself. And deal with it she would, once this meeting with Roger and his colleagues was over.

MELISSA

'Oh crap! Quick, it's Nerdy Nolan. Go into the book-shop,' Melissa Adams urged her friend Sarah as they dawdled along, taking a short cut through the shopping centre on their way to McDonald's.

They hastened through the entrance of Dubray bookshop, hoping against hope that their classmate hadn't seen them. They couldn't stand Evanna Nolan, one of the class swots, who looked down her pointy, pimply nose at them. She was a gangly bean-pole with straight, greasy black hair who liked to think of herself as an intellectual, and Melissa and Sarah had been the victim of several of her acerbic put-downs in the past but, since she'd had a row with her best friend and fellow swot, Niamh Sampson, in a school debate discussing the literary merit of Jane Austen, she wasn't quite so superior and had, in fact, on the few occasions they'd bumped into her around Dun Laoghaire, been cloyingly saccharine, which was most disconcerting.

'Do you think that she thinks we're nerdy enough to be friends with her now that she and Turdy

Sampson have had a row and she's got no one to hang with?' Sarah agonized as they hastened behind a book stack, hoping against hope that Evanna would keep going.

'Bloody hell, how majorly gross is that? You can't be serious!' Melissa exclaimed, aghast. It would be social suicide to be associated with Nerdy Nolan and her set. Keeping in with the cool crowd in their class was of the utmost importance if their school days were not to become a worse nightmare than they already were.

Melissa sighed deeply. It was so hard having to put on a bright, bubbly, confident façade when all the time she was petrified she and Sarah would be edged out and become social outcasts. They were barely on the periphery as it was. She wished mightily that her school days were over. The only small comfort she had was that she'd survived her first year in secondary school, and her first year as a teenager. When she went back to school in September, she'd be in second year and fourteen to boot. Fourteen seemed a hell of a lot older than thirteen.

It would be a lot different going back to school in the autumn. She wouldn't be a new girl, plus she'd be thinner, because she was already losing weight, having heard herself described as a little fat tart at her half-sister Debbie's wedding. Pink scorched her cheeks at the memory. That had ruined what had been the very best day of her life. Until that moment she'd actually felt completely happy. It was the first time she could ever remember having such an amazing feeling, and then that horrible drunk girl had ruined everything with her vicious remark. *Who is that little fat tart?* It haunted her. It took the good out of her life. It made Melissa painfully aware of every fat flaw.

'Oh no! She's heading our way,' Sarah groaned as Evanna pushed open the door and walked purposefully in their direction.

'Hi, guys. How are things? Melissa, what a seriously cool top.' She beamed at them as though they were her very best friends. Insincerity was Evanna's stock in trade.

What a brown-noser, Melissa thought in disgust, privately vowing never to wear her top again. If Evanna Nolan thought it was cool, it was seriously flawed.

'Hi, Evanna,' she murmured. Sarah ignored Evanna and kept flicking through a book she'd picked up.

'What are you reading, Sarah?' Evanna inquired, keeping her smile pasted to her face.

'A book,' Sarah said coolly. She wasn't willing to forget being called a philistine because she'd got mixed up during a school quiz and lost valuable points because she'd answered Keats instead of Wordsworth when asked who had written 'Ode to Daffodils'.

'I can see that.' The smile was starting to slip, but Evanna persevered. 'What book?'

'It's called *The Power of Now*, by Eckhart Tolle,' Sarah said airily.

'Totally never heard of him,' Evanna declared dismissively.

'*Really?* He's like a world-renowned sage and mystic. He writes about how authentic human power is found by surrendering to the Now.' Sarah eyeballed Evanna, while Melissa tried to hide a smirk.

Evanna was gobsmacked. 'Didn't know you were interested in stuff like that, it sounds totally like gobbledy-gook to me,' she rallied.

'It takes a certain questioning mindset to appreciate it,' Sarah sniffed.

'Oh, I'm sure. I just didn't think that would be your kind of thing.' Evanna smiled sweetly.

'There's more to life than Ross O'Carroll-Kelly, Evanna,' Sarah remarked pointedly, seeing the popular read poking out of her classmate's tote bag.

Evanna blushed to her roots. Ross O'Carroll-Kelly was far from literary, and to be caught reading him was totally mortifying. 'Oh, isn't it a hoot?' she twittered. 'Have you read it?' She turned to Melissa.

'No,' fibbed Melissa. 'Not my type of book.' Evanna blushed again, raging at having been caught reading a tome that was even worse than chick lit.

'So, what are you guys doing for the rest of the day?' asked Evanna brightly, changing the subject.

'Chilling on my balcony after we have lunch,' Melissa retorted.

'Savage, I've never seen the view from your balcony, I'd say it's awesome,' Evanna gushed.

'Yep it is,' Melissa agreed.

'So where are you going for lunch?'

Sarah flashed a warning glance at Melissa.

'Oh . . . umm, haven't quite decided. We might just pick up a take-out and eat al fresco at mine.'

'Sounds perfect for a day like today. Why don't I join you?' Evanna suggested.

Melissa was shocked at how blatantly pushy she was. 'Oh—'

'We're not quite sure *exactly* what we're doing yet,' Sarah interjected. 'I've to buy some bits and pieces for my mum first. See you around, Evanna.' She put Eckhart Tolle back on his shelf, grabbed Melissa by the arm and edged away as though the other girl was suffering from a particularly virulent form of plague. 'Is she for real?' she muttered as they hurried out of the bookshop. 'If she was still friends with Turdy Sampson she wouldn't even bother to say hello to us. Did you hear her inviting herself up to your place?'

'I know.' Melissa shook her head. 'You handled it really well. How did you know all that stuff about that book by that Ekkey fella?'

'I read it on the back of it.' Sarah giggled.

'I loved the "questioning mindset" bit. Did you see the look she gave you? Good buzz, you big spoofer.' Melissa chortled.

'Yeah, it was good, wasn't it?' grinned Sarah. 'Let's go and have a Big Mac and go and flop on the balcony for the afternoon. We've had a lucky escape. If she starts hanging around us in school, we've like totally had it.'

'I know,' Melissa agreed glumly as they made their way out on to the street. 'We'll just have to do our best to ignore her.'

An hour later, Melissa stood in the bathroom of the penthouse she lived in. Sarah was draped on a lounger outside reading *OK*. Melissa's heart pounded. This was her first time, and she knew she was crossing a line that could lead to trouble if she was not very careful.

'I'll only do it when I eat junk,' she promised herself, kneeling down in front of the toilet and opening her mouth. She felt sick just thinking about making herself sick. How could girls do it five and six times a day? She hated getting sick. But she'd just stuffed herself with a large portion of fries, burger, ice cream and Coke, enough to pile on the precious pounds she'd lost since the wedding.

She dithered, and then thought of those horrid words that were seared in her brain: '*Who is that little fat tart?*' The words that had ruined the best day of her life.

It was enough. She shoved her fingers down her throat and puked.

When it was over she stood up and wiped her mouth. She caught sight of herself in the mirror. Her eyes were unnaturally bright, her cheeks were red. Melissa felt strangely exhilarated. She'd done it. She'd taken that first step. She knew two girls who were anorexic. She'd watched them fade to nothing before they were hospitalized. One was even being force fed through a tube up her nose. She wasn't going to end up waxy as a candle, emaciated, hollow-eyed and gaunt. She just wanted to lose a stone and a half, and then she'd stop.

She wouldn't be like the lollipop heads. She'd stay in control. She would be in charge of IT. IT would never control *her*, she vowed as she flushed the toilet and made her way out to join her best friend.

JUDITH

Judith Baxter lay drowsing against her pillows as the sun emerged in a shaft of piercing light from behind a drift of clouds. It shone in through the hospital windows, bathing her in unwelcome brightness. Its intensity woke her, and she sighed deeply.

She was tired and sore, the effect of the painkillers having worn off earlier, and she wasn't due any more medication for another hour. Judith struggled out of the rumpled iron-framed bed and padded over to the window to pull down the blind. She stared out the window, glad that she had a room with a view. She was several floors up, and the panorama across the suburbs to Howth and the sea was remarkable.

She paused for a moment to study the SeaCat gliding across the glassy sea, many miles away. And it seemed, as it glided along the horizon, to sail into the sky. Usually, this optical illusion fascinated her, but today she had a headache and was restless and agitated. She was itchy all over, and she knew, because the nurses had told her, that she was having morphine withdrawal.

She was hot, bothered and irritable. She did not need a scorching sun mocking her. It was bad enough that her body was crocked, her car was a write-off, and she'd had to endure a week of sharing a ward with other patients, half of them elderly, who snored, groaned and rang their bells for nurses throughout the night so that she'd hardly had a wink of sleep.

'Stop giving out,' she muttered as she pulled down the blind with her uninjured hand and grimaced as a pain shot through her neck and shoulders. Her right arm was encased in a plaster cast, her neck in a brace, and her skin itched inside them. But at least she'd finally got a private room, and it was a huge relief to close the door on the madness and noise and controlled chaos of the busy teaching hospital she was in.

It was bliss to be alone and silent. Her previous ward had rarely had moments of silence. Patients came and went. Technicians came to collect blood; there was always some doctor or other trailing a bunch of students, doing rounds. Visitors seemed to come all hours; visiting times were not strictly enforced. Did hospital managements not realize how wearing it was on patients to have people in and out, even during meal times? There were patients who'd been woken at 6 a.m. You could never rest or sleep without some disturbance or other.

Her mother, Lily, had been meticulous about leaving at the designated times, and Judith was very grateful for it. Lily had shown a kindness and thoughtfulness that Judith had never thought her capable of. Her mother's behaviour was a revelation.

She settled back into bed, trying to regain her previous state of lethargy. Sleep was so precious and gave her such relief from her pain and all her worries. She took the sleeping tablets they offered her each night and would fall asleep relatively quickly, only to wake a couple of hours later twisting and turning, trying to find a comfortable position and longing for her next dose of painkillers.

At least when she was in the coma she hadn't been in pain, and she'd had no worries. All she could remember of her days then was a fleeting memory of peacefulness.

Sometimes she wished she hadn't come out of it.

Judith sighed. That was an ungrateful thing to say. Her life had been spared. She could have been killed in the accident that had mangled her car beyond recognition.

Her gaze alighted on the mass bouquet Lily had brought her, and she rummaged under her pillow for the small, round, glass-encased angel that fitted in her palm. Lily had bought it for her and pressed it into her hand, saying earnestly that the angels were minding her. Judith wasn't sure she believed in God or religion any more and, these days, she certainly didn't believe in the mercy of God, but the little angel her mother had given her gave her some small comfort.

It was strange, she reflected: the old saying that every cloud has a silver lining was certainly true for her mother. Who would believe that Lily, the nervy, dependent, fearful woman of yore, was now staying in the house on her own, doing her own shopping,

hopping on buses to visit Judith in hospital and re-discovering what it was like to live a normal life again? Until the accident, Lily would go nowhere without Judith. She wouldn't go to mass, she wouldn't go to the shops, she wouldn't visit her sister unless Judith drove her. She wouldn't dream of spending a night alone in the house, petrified she'd be burgled. It had been so binding for Judith. She'd felt like a carer, despite the fact that her mother was perfectly healthy, apart from her 'nerves'.

If only Lily had found her courage years ago, life would have been so different for her and Judith. Judith tried to swallow the bitterness that engulfed her. It was too late for her now to have a family of her own. And what man would be interested in a fifty-year-old crock? She was stuck on the shelf, still living at home with her elderly mother, with not much to look forward to except trying to take an early retire-ment from work in ten years' time.

What had she done in her life that was so awful that she was now being so horribly punished? Judith pondered, taking a sip of lukewarm 7UP. She'd looked after her sick father and, then, when he died, gone back to live with her mother. Surely she deserved some sort of reward from on high and not another massive kick in the solar plexus.

'Thank God you survived,' her mother had said fervently several times since she'd come out of the coma.

'Thank God nothing,' she'd wanted to retort. 'Why did He let me crash in the first place?'

She rolled the little angel in her palm. Lily had told her she'd discovered an angel shop in Finglas, just across from her optician's, when she'd gone to get a new pair of glasses after accidentally standing on her other pair. 'Oh Judith, it's a lovely little shop. I'd love you to see it some time,' she'd enthused as she'd sat beside Judith's bed, knitting blankets for children in Africa.

Just even listening to her mother it was hard to believe that Lily was the same woman. Imagine her mother getting two buses from Drumcondra, where they lived, to Finglas. Unheard of. Judith studied her mother intently. Her eyes were bright and animated. Her fingers flew over her needles. She was chatting away about her trip to the library, her walk in the park and the queues for the bus going home in the evening. Sometimes Judith wondered if she was in a different universe. And the tenderness of the little kiss on her forehead that Lily now greeted her with was far from anything she'd ever previously experienced in her relationship with her mother. All the years of hostility and sharp exchanges which had been the fabric of their lives seemed to have gently dissolved and wafted into the ether.

Lily never came to visit without some little treat for her. And always the anxious inquiry: 'Are you feeling any better, Judith? Is the pain still bad? Will I ask the nurses to give you something?'

It was as if she was rediscovering lost mothering skills that had been buried deep for years and years. And, in spite of her pain and her torment, Judith was content to let her mother's newfound affection and kindness act as a balm to her own deep unhappiness.

She would never have believed that she would look forward to spending time with her own, once-despised mother. Lily was so joyful that she had come out of her coma that Judith had to try hard to pretend that she was glad to be alive.

She made no such effort with her brother, Tom, and sister, Cecily. Had she not recovered, she would have gone to her maker on bad terms with both of them. She'd rowed with Cecily for being late to collect her mother on the day of the crash and rowed with Tom over their mother's will. He probably wouldn't have minded if she'd died, she thought sourly. More for him, when Lily passed on.

Cecily, to give her her due, had been weepily apologetic for her tardiness on the day of the crash and was constantly phoning, asking Judith if she needed anything. Judith just wished she'd leave her alone. She didn't have the energy to deal with her sister's guilt. They weren't close and, after all her years of bitterness about being left to look after their mother, Judith didn't think they ever would be. Still, it had been a comfort of sorts to know that her younger sister was upset at her near demise. She couldn't say the same about her brother.

Tom had been all brash and hearty, telling her not to be malingering and that some people would do anything to get out of going to work. Lily had flashed him a filthy, needle-sharp look which had amused Judith in spite of her discomfort. 'Judith was *critically* ill, Tom. I don't think you realize how close to death she was,' she had snapped. 'Don't be talking like that.'

'Ah, just joking, Ma,' he said gruffly. 'Get off my back.'

It had been nice, though, having her mother come to her defence. She'd closed her eyes, too tired to pretend to be glad he was there, and it had been a relief when he'd gone. Whatever about having some sort of rapprochement with Cecily, not even a near miss with death would repair her relationship with her only brother, she reflected, with a strange sense of detachment.

She wondered who was running her section at work. She was in charge of a busy wages and salaries department in a big insurance company. It was a demanding job, with no leeway for error. Odd, she felt completely detached about work too. She wondered if Debbie Adams was back from her honeymoon. No doubt she was using her new married name, whatever it was. At least Judith had missed having to view the wedding and honeymoon photos. Photos of the happy couple were the last things she needed to see. What was it about Debbie Adams and her charmed life that made Judith feel an utter failure when she compared it to her own? It was irrational and unreasonable, she knew, but still, she was glad she hadn't been around for all the wedding talk. Maybe she wouldn't be able to go back to work. Perhaps she'd end up on disability, she thought idly, as a fly buzzed her. But what would she do with herself? Oh, she'd think about it some other time. She hadn't the energy for it now. Judith yawned.

The phone by her bed rang. It was Lily.

'Is there anything you'd like when I come in this afternoon, Judith?' her mother inquired.

'No, Ma, not a thing, thanks.'

'And how are you today? Is the pain any easier?'

'Yes, Ma, a little,' she fibbed.

'That's good, Judith, that's very good. I'm praying night and day for you.' Lily sounded so earnest. And Judith could see her, mother-of-pearl rosary in her hands, sitting in her favourite high-backed chair in her sitting room, praying as the beads slipped through her thin, bony fingers, or with her hairnet on, kneeling beside her bed in her floral winceyette night-dress, face furrowed in deep concentration as she prayed earnestly to the Almighty and the plethora of saints whom Lily had great faith in.

'Thanks, Ma, I'll see you later then,' Judith managed before hanging up.

'I'm praying night and day for you,' her mother had said. For some reason, it touched her in some deep, hard, closed-off place in the depths of her.

Two big tears rolled down her cheeks. And then it was a waterfall, as Judith cried her eyes out, wondering what was to become of her.

LILY

Lily Baxter stirred a spoonful of sugar into her cup of tea, took a mini Jaffa cake out of the biscuit tin, placed it on the side of her saucer and carried it into her small front parlour. She turned on the little transistor radio she kept on the table beside her armchair. The sound of Dean Martin singing 'That's Amore' filled the room, and she smiled. She and her beloved husband, Ted, had danced to that tune on their wedding day, many years ago. It was their song. It was strange; since Judith had had her accident and Lily had been living in the house on her own, she had felt her late husband's presence very strongly. Maybe he had got Ronan Collins to play that song on his radio programme today especially, to help her keep her chin up, she thought, firm in the belief that the dead had little ways of sending messages of love just when they were needed.

And she did need to keep her chin up. She was very worried about Judith. Her daughter was in turmoil, not just physical pain but emotional turmoil. It was as though this accident was just one blow too many. Sometimes, Lily felt her daughter was sorry to have survived it.

Don't think like that, she said sternly to herself as the familiar flutters of fear and anxiety began their dreaded waltz. She could not go back to her old ways and give into the panic attacks and heart-stopping, stomach-knotting apprehensions that had dogged her all her life. She was strong now, she told herself, as she sipped her hot, sweet tea slowly and nibbled on the Jaffa cake. A measure of calm returned. She had amazed herself and her family with her behaviour since Judith's accident.

She'd come up trumps, she thought, giving herself a mental pat on the back. She hadn't fallen to pieces as everyone had expected her to do. She hadn't gone to stay with Cecily, her younger daughter, because she was afraid of living on her own. No, she'd stayed in her own home and slept in her own bed and ventured out in the world again. She, who had depended on Judith to do her shopping, take her to mass and drive her thither and yon, was now going into the Spar supermarket in Drumcondra. She'd even taken two buses over to Finglas village to go to her optician's when she'd broken her glasses. That had been a great day for her, even though her heart had been thump-ing at having to make the journey. When she'd got to Finglas, she'd relaxed. Her parents had once lived near the big church, and it was familiar territory. She'd pottered in and out of the shops and couldn't believe she was out by herself on a little jaunt.

By now, she was an old hand at travelling to the hospital and hopped on the bus at the end of the road with increasing confidence every afternoon on her visit to her daughter.

So, there was no need for her to feel fluttery, Lily assured herself as she caught sight of Mr Ryan, one of her elderly neighbours, walking slowly down the street, pain etched on his face as he concentrated on each step, leaning heavily on his stick and stopping to rest every so often. He wasn't that much older than she was, mid-seventies, but he was crucified by breathing difficulties and arthritis.

She was so lucky, she reflected, taking another sip of tea. She could walk sprightly, her breathing was fine and, apart from the cataract, which was now sorted after her little operation, she was hale and hearty. If she were like Mr Ryan she'd have been in a sorry state indeed and would have to have thrown herself on the mercy of Tom, her son, who rarely made an effort to see her, and Cecily, her youngest daughter, to whom she was simply a nuisance.

God had been good to her. She was managing on her own, even if it was this late in her life that she had come to the realization that she was perfectly capable of looking after herself.

Lily gave a sigh that came from the depths of her as guilt cloaked her. She had ruined Judith's life, of that there was no doubt. By her clinging so leechlike to her daughter, Judith had had no chance of forging a life of her own and was now a bitter, discontented, fifty-year-old woman with not much to look forward to.

Lily had to do something about it. She was going to explore the possibilities of raising a loan from the bank using her house as collateral so that Judith could buy a place of her own. Her daughter knew nothing of these plans, nor did her other two children, who wouldn't be at all happy. Lily knew that Tom was expecting a share of the proceeds of the house when she died, but he could expect. The house was left to Judith, and that was that. But she could live for another ten years. Her parents had lived well into their eighties. She could easily do the same, and Judith needed something to live for now.

She watched Mr Ryan, bent like an S hook, pause at her railings. The poor man was in a sorry state; she should offer to do the odd little bit of shopping for him when she was getting her own messages – milk, bread and the like. It wouldn't kill her. All her neighbours had been kindness itself when they'd heard about Judith, had offered her lifts if she needed them, and told her to call them any time, night or day. Even though she and Judith kept to themselves, it had been heartening the way the neighbours on the street had rallied around her in her hour of need.

It was time for her to do a good deed or two herself. Better late than never, Lily thought wryly. A line of St Francis's famous prayer came into her head: 'For it is by self-forgetting that one finds.' It had been sung on *Hymns of Praise* the previous Sunday, and it had really struck a chord with her for some reason. It almost described what was happening in her life.

Lily had never said that particular prayer. It made her feel guilty. Too much was expected from one. And she felt she wouldn't be able to live up to it. *She* had wanted to be the comforted one, not the comforter, the consoled, not the consoler, the under-stood one, not the one doing the understanding. What was so awful about wanting that? It was only human, and she was far, far, from being a saint.

And yet, she reflected, here she was, doing her best to understand Judith, doing her best to comfort and console her, praying for her recovery night and day. Planning ways to help her when she came out of hospital. For the first time in her life, she was putting someone else's needs before her own. And, in doing these things, she was finding a strength she never knew she had in her.

'It is by self-forgetting that one finds . . .'

So, that's what it meant, Lily thought with a sudden sense of illumination. While she was help-ing Judith, she was finding her own courage and strength. She'd never looked at it like that before. Lily's angular face broke into a smile. There was so much to learn from life but, today, she'd discovered a profound truth that would help her put one foot in front of the other in the days to come. And there were going to be stormy days ahead when Tom found out that she was going to assist Judith financially. He would object, she knew that. But he could object all he liked, her mind was not for changing. Judith needed her as once Lily had needed Judith, and she would stand firm for her.

Lily turned off her radio and reached down to the little shelf under the tabletop and found her prayer missal. She knew she had St Francis's prayer on a memorial card for one of her aunts. She found it and took a deep breath. It was not a prayer to be said lightly. Much would be expected, but much help would be given if she said it with the right intention.

'Lord,' Lily said, in a voice that quavered only slightly, 'make me a channel of your peace . . .'

A TIME OF RECKONING

CHAPTER ONE

'Welcome back, Mrs Kinsella.' Sally Ford grinned as Caitriona Slater gave Debbie a hug and Ciara Williams plonked a cup of coffee on her desk and said, 'Photos!'

Debbie glanced over at Judith Baxter's office, half-expecting her boss to emerge and send them scattering back to their various desks. It was such a relief coming into work knowing that she wouldn't be here. It made her first day back from her honeymoon so much easier. She smiled around at her friends and colleagues and was delighted with the warmth of her welcome. If it weren't for Bitchy Baxter always on her case, work would be much more enjoyable.

'Who's in charge while Judith's out? Have we time to look at the photos?' asked Debbie, logging on to her computer, sliding her photo disk in and producing a big box of handmade American chocolates from her tote bag.

'I am,' Caitriona grinned. 'And yes, we most certainly do have time for photos. And, seeing as

I'm the boss, I get first choice of the chocolates.'

'*You're* the boss?' Debbie stared at her friend.

'Yep – you're looking at your new Acting Head of Wages and Salaries.' Caitriona gave a bow. 'I'm the most senior after Judith, and they offered me "acting" which will be good on the old CV whenever a chance for promotion comes along.'

'Congratulations, you deserve it. Can I have a day off and go home?' Debbie teased.

'Absolutely not, and you better give me no back cheek or impudence, or I'll make you stand in the corner with your back to the rest of us. Now, show us the photos, and I better look good in them.'

They all spent ten minutes laughing and reminiscing as they studied the wedding photos, and then Caitriona said briskly, 'I guess we better get to it. Debbie, will you look after any new sick-leave items and, Ciara, will you do the annual-leave requirements. Everyone else, keep an eye out for glitches. IT were on this morning, they're upgrading the system, and you know the way these things can mess up our stuff. I've to go to a meeting in HR at eleven. If the lunch trolley comes around and I'm not here, will someone get me an egg and onion roll and a doughnut? I'll leave the money on my desk.'

'I'll do that for you, hon,' Debbie assured her.

They all went to their individual desks and spent the morning working harmoniously, with none of the tensions usually engendered by stiff and starchy Judith. It was one of the most pleasant mornings she'd ever spent at work, and it took the whole sting out of being back at the grindstone.

From what they had heard, it seemed that Judith was lucky to be alive and would be out of work for the foreseeable future. While she wished her boss a speedy recovery, Debbie couldn't help but be cheered with the news that the biggest thorn in her side would not be troubling her for some time to come.

Or so she thought.

'Right, my little band of merry workers,' Caitriona announced during their mid-afternoon coffee break, 'we have to sort out who's going to visit Judith. I was talking to Janice in HR, and it seems our beloved boss is out of the special care unit and back in a ward, so it behoves us to pay a visit and give her our best wishes and a few flowers. Any volunteers?'

'Aaww, Caitriona, do we have to?' Emily Moran groaned, as no one stepped forward to offer their services.

'Ah, come on, girls, it's the decent thing to do. She nearly died—'

'Well, you go then, seeing as it's your bright idea,' challenged Linda Kelly sourly.

'OK, I will then but, honestly, you're a mean shower,' Caitriona said crossly.

'We could put the names in a hat. That would be the fairest way of doing it,' Orla Ryan suggested.

'I suppose so,' agreed Emily, grimacing. 'Fair is fair. It shouldn't be left up to Caitriona.'

'Oh *nooo*,' groaned Debbie. 'She hates me. What happens if I get chosen?'

'Oh, get over yourself. She doesn't like any of us, so we're all in the same boat. Let's get it over and done with.' Emily reached for a piece of paper, tore it into strips and wrote her name on one of them.

'Look, forget it. I'll go,' Caitriona offered. 'Linda's right – it was my suggestion.'

'You only suggested it because you're a good person, and we're all mean wagons,' Emily retorted, handing out the strips. 'And even though it's my fervent wish that you do get picked and I don't, at least we're all in with the same chance. Is everyone agreed?' She looked around.

Heads nodded in assent, and they all wrote their names on the strips of paper, then Emily folded them up and placed them in an empty brown-paper bag she found in her wastebasket.

'OK, you're the boss, you pick. The first two names out get to visit Ms Baxter,' she ordered, giving the bag a shake and holding it out to Caitriona.

'You go, girl, and don't pick me,' warned Orla, laughing as Caitriona took out the first piece of paper, opened it and called out Ciara's name. Everyone else cheered as their colleague made a face.

'Bitches!' she swore good-humouredly, giving them the finger.

Thank God, thought Debbie. If she was picked, she'd

be horrified, but she had to admit it was the fairest way of doing it.

'You pick the next name then,' Caitriona said magnanimously, offering the bag to Ciara.

'With pleasure.' Ciara selected a folded-up strip and waved it around.

'Open it and put us out of our misery. If I have to visit that cow, my weekend will be ruined,' Linda growled.

Ciara opened it and caught Debbie's anxious gaze. 'Sorry.' She made a face and handed her the strip with her name on it.

'Oh shit,' muttered Debbie, her heart sinking.

'Well, at least there're two of us in the same boat,' Ciara shrugged. 'When do you want to go?'

'The sooner the better. Let's get it over and done with. What do you think?' She eyed her colleague glumly.

'Good thinking, Wonder Girl. How are you fixed for tonight?'

'Well, I was supposed to be meeting Bryan for a bite to eat—'

'Look, seeing as you're representing us, and you'll have to go and get flowers and a card – which will come out of the kitty, of course – why don't the pair of you get changed and head off around four?' Caitriona offered kindly. 'It would give you a chance to get there early enough, and you'd only have to stay for ten minutes or so, and at least she'd have had a visit from her section. If Judith's in for a long time, I'll go on my own for a visit. Janice told me she'll be going in, and I suppose some of the other managers she has her tea break with will visit. So is that OK?'

'Yeah, it's fine, Caitriona. Thanks.' Debbie smiled at her friend, not wanting her to feel bad, knowing that she understood very well how she was dreading having to visit Judith.

'Thanks, Caitriona.' Ciara got up and rinsed her coffee cup in the sink. 'I think we should take a taxi to the hospital. I'm not sure of the bus routes on the Northside,' she suggested as they went back to their desks.

Just as well it was payday, Debbie sighed, thinking of her precarious financial position. Taxis were a luxury for the moment, until she got back on the straight and narrow financially.

'Good idea,' she agreed. 'We can always get a bus back into town, and I can meet Bryan later. We can buy the flowers and the card in the hospital, which will save us some time.'

'Look, if she's in hospital for ages, some of the others will have to go, so at least we've done our duty and we won't have to do it again.' Ciara was doing her utmost to make the best of the situation.

'You're right, and we get off an hour early, which was decent enough of Caitriona,' Debbie agreed with false cheeriness as she bent her head to her keyboard and began to key in some figures for a pension package one of the receptionists was getting on her retirement the following week.

Her enjoyable day back was ruined. The thought

of having to see Judith brought on that tense, stomach-knotting feeling of anxiety she always felt around her boss. None of the others realized just how stressed Judith made Debbie feel. None of them was picked upon as much as she'd been this past year. Judith had it in for her for some reason. That bitch had held back her salary increment, a raise she could have badly done with, and now Debbie was going to have to pretend to be nice to her and offer her sympathy when it was the last thing she felt like doing.

The thought of seeing her boss was actually making her feel nauseous. She supposed she could have refused outright to allow her name to be put in the hat, but all the others felt they had as much of an excuse not to want to visit Judith as she had, and it had been the most democratic way to do it. It was just her tough luck, she thought glumly, sending her husband an email to tell him the score.

No probs, Debbs, he emailed back. *Meet us in Farringtons and then we can have a bite to eat in Eden later. Going to book a table for 8.30. You should be back in town by 7.30. Love ya and miss ya. Wish we were in NY. B XXXXXXXX*

Debbie read his email and shook her head. Bryan needed to realize that they were going to have to economize for the next few months. And while she loved the food and the ambience in Eden, she'd been thinking of somewhere more cheap 'n' cheerful to eat, to suit their current financial circumstances.

Well, they wouldn't be having starters or desserts

if it was Eden he wanted to eat in, she decided. Cutbacks would just have to be made, whether her darling husband liked it or not.

Bryan sat at his desk and stared at the worksheet in front of him. The office-design and fit-out company he worked for had secured a contract for planning and structuring three floors of offices in a big new block just across the river from where he was based in the IFSC. Appointments had been made for him to meet with the clients to discuss their requirements. The first one was at nine thirty on Monday morning, so he had a little leeway to ease himself back into work mode.

He tried to look on the bright side. As long as he was on the project, he could take the Dart into work and walk across the Liffey at Matt Talbot Bridge, so at least he wouldn't have to drive and be stuck in traffic snarl-ups like he'd been that morning. He was being given the task of designing the CEO's office as well as the rest of the management team's, so he'd have a chance to use a bit of flair and imagination, if the budgets allowed. It was better than having to design and fit out the ordinary employees' open-plan space, which didn't offer a huge amount of scope for innovation. Having come up in the ranks, he was now being entrusted with the more expensive and coveted jobs. He could do open plan in his sleep!

Bryan sighed and chewed the top of his pen as he stared out at the sun shining intermittently on the gunmetal-grey waters of the Liffey. An easterly breeze was blowing up the river, and choppy white-capped waves pummelled the quay walls, not with the ferocious intensity of stormy weather but with a relentless, angry slapping which suited his mood. The traffic on the street below had ground to a halt, and he saw a woman in a blue Focus talking on her mobile as she stood beside her car at a junction, the flashers on. Behind her was a stream of traffic waiting to turn left, horns honking in impatience.

Two men got out of their cars to give her a push, and Bryan brushed his fingers through his silky black hair and turned back to his worksheet, glad that it wasn't him stuck at the lights. He stared at the figures in front of him but couldn't concentrate. Work was the last place he wanted to be.

At least it was payday. It had been a great idea of Debbie's to come back to work on a payday and get that horrible first day back over with. They were planning to eat out after work, and even her hospital visit shouldn't interfere with their plans. Eden was his restaurant of choice, with a few drinks in Farringtons first, with any of the gang who were going to a film in the Film Centre.

He picked up the phone on his desk and dialled 11890, got put through to the restaurant and made a reservation for eight thirty. If he and Debbie couldn't enjoy a night out on their first day back at work, it would be a poor life indeed, Bryan felt, starting to text a few of his mates to let them know they should meet up for drinks after work. Slightly cheered up by the prospect of a night on the tiles, he bent his head to his work and tried his best to concentrate.

Any chance you could meet me in Meadows & Byrne tomorrow morning? Was thinking about getting a new table for the kitchen. Would like your opinion. And we could have a cup of coffee.

Connie keyed in a text to Debbie as she sat in the supermarket car park, having done her weekly shopping. The nap she'd had earlier had revived her, and she thought she might take a walk on the beach as soon as she'd put away her groceries.

She'd promised Barry she'd facilitate a meeting between Melissa and Debbie. It wouldn't take up too much of her morning, or Debbie's either. It was so handy that they all lived on the Dart line. Debbie would be in Dun Laoghaire in five minutes, and Barry and Melissa were only a stone's throw from the station.

Her phone rang.

'Hi Mum, it's me,' Debbie said. 'I'm just on my way in to visit Judith Baxter in hospital; my name was picked out of a hat, unfortunately. But I'd love to meet you in the morning. What time?'

Her daughter's cheerful voice crackled on the mobile.

'Will you be having a lie-in, seeing as it's Saturday? How about ten thirty? Would that suit? I'll ramble around the store until you get there.'

'Perfect, I'll look forward to it, Mum, I'll see you then.'

'Bye, love.' Connie smiled as she hung up. It was great to have Debbie home again; she'd really missed her when she was in New York. They had been such a tight little unit for so long, just the two of them, it was hard to believe she was now a married woman with a home of her own.

It had been a real wrench when Debbie had moved out of home the previous year. It had taken Connie a long time to get used to the silence in the house. She still hated eating on her own, especially in the evening after work, or on Sundays at lunchtime.

She loved meeting Debbie for lunch or dinner when it was just the two of them. Bryan was a different kettle of fish. Connie shook her head as she put her phone back in the handset and straightened up her steering wheel. She still couldn't take to her new son-in-law. He was far too laidback for her liking. And he spent money like it was going out of fashion. That ridiculous sportscar, for one thing, and those designer sunglasses he wore. Debbie had told her they cost 280 euro. He spent a fortune on grooming products, she knew that for a fact because, when she'd asked Debbie what to get him for birthday and Christmas presents, Debbie had told her the moisturizers and hair products he used, and they weren't cheap. Where was he getting his money from, with a big mortgage to pay off and their wedding and honeymoon expenses? *I see and I want* seemed to be Bryan's motto.

Debbie had let slip when she'd come back from her honeymoon that their Visa card was maxed out. Bryan would really want to be reining in his spending and getting on with decorating the house, Connie reflected as she switched on the engine and began to manoeuvre the car out of the parking space. Her phone rang, and the Bluetooth kicked in.

'Hi, is this Connie Adams?' a woman's voice asked.

'Yes, that's me. Who's speaking?' inquired Connie as she mentally cursed the owner of the massive SUV parked carelessly beside her, which was causing her great difficulty in seeing approaching traffic.

'I'm Jessie Sheehy, Mrs Mansfield's other part-time day nurse. You and I will be job-sharing, and I was just wondering if I could ask a big favour of you? I know you haven't even started working here yet, but I was wondering if you could cover for me for a wedding in six weeks' time? I know I've an awful cheek asking you when we haven't even met.'

'Not at all.' Connie laughed. 'Who knows – I might even need you to do the same for me some time. Are you working right now?'

'Yes, I'm on duty at the moment. We've just been for a walk, and Mrs Mansfield is having a little rest.'

'Look, how about I pop over for ten minutes and introduce myself. I just need to go home and store my groceries. I have some treats for Mrs Mansfield's cat. I was telling her about them, they're ones you get in Aldi, and my one goes mad for them. I told her I'd get her some. I've had them here for a

76

week, so I could kill two birds with the one stone.'

'That would be lovely,' Jessie agreed. 'I look forward to meeting you.'

'Right, I should be over in about half an hour or so. See you then,' Connie said, as she finally managed to squeeze out of the parking bay and head for home.

It would be good to meet her co-worker. And of course she'd oblige her for her day off. Connie might need the favour returned some time. Hopefully, she and this Jessie woman would have a good working relationship. She'd unpack the shopping, drive over to Mrs Mansfield's and then go for a quick walk on the beach. She was dying for a breath of fresh sea air. She always felt so much better having done a walk.

It didn't take her long to put away the shopping, and she slipped into a pair of jeans and a light pink and grey fleece. Even though it was a peachy evening, there was an easterly breeze blowing in off the sea and it would be nippy enough down on the beach.

She ran a brush through her short, layered auburn hair, noting the odd strand of grey. She was lucky, she reflected: her mother had gone grey in her thirties; she was in her late forties and still had her own colour. She didn't look too bad, Connie decided as she applied some lipstick on to her full lips. She was beginning to get those pucker marks around her mouth, and the spiderweb of lines around her blue eyes was nothing to cheer about, but her skin was good and she looked healthy. The band of her jeans was a bit tight, and, she thought ruefully, her ass was sinking fast, and not all the walking in the world was going to change that. But she was tall and that helped, and walking on the stony beach was challenging to her calves and great for toning thighs. She was so lucky to have the beach ten minutes down the road. Life was good these days, she decided happily. It could only get better.

CHAPTER TWO

Lily Baxter sat on the bus on her way home from the hospital feeling quite perturbed. Judith had been in very bad form today, hardly even making the effort to chat. When Lily had asked her for the third time if she was in pain and did she need a nurse, her daughter had snapped, 'No, Mother, I'm fine. Stop fussing.'

It had been just like she used to be in the bad old days in their relationship, and Lily had felt a spurt of temper and been tempted to retort, 'There's no need to be so rude, madam.' But she'd refrained from making any comment, reminding herself that her daughter wasn't that long from being near death.

'Sorry, Ma. I didn't mean it, just having a bad day,' Judith had muttered when Lily had eventually packed away her knitting and stood up to leave, not wanting to get stuck in the tea-time rush hour.

'That's all right, Judith. I suppose it's to be expected. I'm sure you're fed up in this place anyway.' Lily softened, and gave her daughter's hand a little squeeze.

'Thanks, Ma. And you know you don't have to come in every single afternoon. Hospital visiting is tiring.' Judith squinted against the sunlight, and Lily went over to the big plate-glass window and pulled down the blinds.

'I know that,' she said firmly. 'But you'd do the same for me, so we'll have no more of that talk. Now try and have a little rest for yourself. I know Cecily is coming in tonight before she goes to France for a month, so she told me, and your Aunt Annie and your cousin are coming over from Lucan. So you'll *need* your strength for that.' At least that had got a laugh out of Judith but, on her way out, Lily had gone to the nurses' station and had told the staff nurse she was worried about her daughter. 'She seems very down in the dumps, and I know she's in pain,' she explained.

'It's natural to get a bit depressed after a big trauma like that, and being in pain doesn't help,' the staff nurse said reassuringly. 'We're hoping to start her on physio and get her moving about a bit more, so that will help. Don't worry – we're keeping a good eye on her. These things take time to recover from.'

Lily had thanked her but, nevertheless, she was troubled and, as she sat on the bus heading back towards town, she came to a decision.

It was something that had to be done. She'd shilly-shallied long enough. She glanced at her watch. She just might make the bank in time. She should have made an appointment, she knew.

Getting to see a bank manager was like getting to see a hospital consultant these days, she'd heard. But her manager, Francis Long, always made time to talk to her and never rushed her. He was a gentleman of the old school, not like some of the young whippersnappers who wouldn't give an elderly person the time of day.

The bus whizzed along, leaving the traffic on her right crawling. These bus lanes were a gift, Lily approved, as she sat up ramrod straight, her hands gripping her handbag tightly on her lap, preparing in her mind what she would say to the bank manager.

She needed to have her wits about her, to make everything clear to him and to be clear herself about the consequences of her actions. Tom, her eldest child, would be furious with her if he knew what she was about to do, but bad scran to him, he'd left her in the lurch and never gone out of his way to help her. He'd left it all up to Judith, and now Judith was going to get what she deserved, Lily thought grimly as she stood up to get off at the next stop.

Her heart was beginning to race, and she could feel the familiar nervy flutters in her tummy. 'St Michael give me courage, Holy Spirit guide me in what I'm about to do,' Lily prayed fervently as the bus shuddered to a halt and she stepped out into the warm afternoon sun.

She could cross the busy main road and walk home, or she could take a deep breath and set in

81

train a chain of events that would cause ructions in the family when it came to light.

'*Do it.*' Lily gave a start and looked around. She was sure she'd heard a voice, a voice like Ted's, her beloved husband. But that was only fanciful imagining. Ted and Judith had been very close. A shaft of shame pierced her as a memory of long-forgotten jealousy surfaced. Yes, she admitted, she'd been jealous of their bond, jealous of their mutual interest in those Greek and Roman history books they used to read. Had that played a part in the way she'd treated her daughter when her husband had died? Had she, at some level, taken out her malice on her eldest daughter? Lily bowed her head as her lip trembled. It was hard recognizing your flaws, and she had more than most. She had been a bitter old woman and taken out all her anger and resentments about her failed life on Judith. It really was time to make amends.

Ted would want her to do it. She wanted to do it herself. She was being given another chance, a chance to give rather than take, as she had always done. This was St Francis showing her how, and she would not shirk from it even though she was very apprehensive. The safety net of her home would be gone. She might be at Judith's mercy in the future, but she would have to trust her daughter. She would have to have faith that the good Lord would take care of her, she decided firmly, straightening her shoulders and gripping her handbag even more tightly. Ted was guiding her from the grave, she was sure of it. She wasn't alone.

She made her way into the bank and stood at the information desk. A young bank clerk looked up and smiled at her. 'Can I help you?' She was so young and bright and alert, with all her life ahead of her, Lily thought with a little jolt, remembering how Judith had been like that once. Fresh-faced and bright-eyed and full of enthusiasm.

'I was wondering if it was possible to see Mr Long for a little chat. I know I don't have an appointment, but I'm a long-standing customer of his. Tell him it's Mrs Lily Baxter who's looking for him.' It all came out in a rush, and she was annoyed with herself for her lack of composure and the way her knees felt shaky.

'Certainly,' the girl said, and lifted up the phone. She had a lovely Kerry accent, Lily noted, trying to keep her heart flutters at bay, almost tempted to hurry out of the bank. *Now, stop your nonsense, Lily*, she instructed herself sternly.

The clerk relayed the message and listened for a moment before hanging up. 'He's with a customer now but, if you don't mind waiting a little while, he'll see you when he's finished. If you'd like to take a seat, I'll let you know when he's ready.'

'Grand.' Lily was utterly relieved that Mr Long would see her. Having taken the first step, she would have been terribly disappointed if the manager had been unavailable and she'd had to wait until after the weekend to see him. It would have preyed on her mind, and she might have lost her nerve. Lily sank gratefully on to the chair and took some deep breaths, willing her nerves to calm down. She should have taken one of her tranquillizers, but then she hadn't known that she was going to take this step today. Perhaps it was just as well she hadn't. Tranquillizers dulled your wits, and she needed her wits about her. Tom could get nasty and say that she wasn't in control of her faculties and challenge her actions. Well, she'd be able to take an oath that she had been completely in control of her actions and had taken no medication, which might alter her state of mind. So he could take a running jump for himself. It was a terrible thing to have to admit that she did not like her own son, she thought sadly. It surely had to be a reflection of the way she had reared him. But he was a taker, and always had been. Always the one with an eye to the main chance; the what's-in-it-for-me type.

She remembered Mrs Meadows, the woman she had shared her semi-private room with when she'd been in hospital getting her cataracts done. Mrs Meadows had been a revelation and an inspiration to Lily. Even though she was older than Lily, she lived alone and wouldn't hear of going to live with any of her children. She had been completely and happily independent, enjoying her life and her family. And those boys had been good to her, Lily remembered. She'd listened to their affectionate teasing of their mother and heard the laughter and chat between them and compared their rapport with her own taut, tense relationship with all her children. She'd never had fun with her children, and now it was too late. Tom and Cecily didn't want her in their lives. They had their own family units and were doing well for themselves. But if it was too late to change things with them, it wasn't too late to change things with Judith and she had to take some small comfort from that.

Maybe when her time came, the Lord would look kindly upon her that she had tried in some small way to make amends for being a very poor mother. Her lip trembled. She hadn't meant to be a poor mother; she'd just been frightened and nervy, content to let Ted take care of everything. She had wasted her life giving into her nerves. There was nothing she could do about that now; regrets got you nowhere, and it would be self-indulgent to slip back into miserable self-pity. She might have wasted her life up until now, but she wouldn't waste what was left of it, Lily determined, as Mr Long walked over to where she sat and greeted her with a smile and an outstretched hand.

'Mrs Baxter, how are you? Good, I hope. And what can we do for you today?'

'Well, it's not really what you can do for me, it's about what we can do for my Judith,' explained Lily earnestly as he led her into his office and closed the door behind him.

She'd been a bitch to her mother today, Judith reflected as the nurse took her temperature, pulse and respiration and then handed her a little cup containing her painkillers and anti-inflammatory tablets. She put them in her mouth, took a gulp of water and swallowed them greedily, looking forward to the dreamy lethargy they would bring, taking the edge off the pain and giving her some small relief. It was easy to see how you could become addicted to drugs, she reflected. She lived for her painkillers now, and took everything she was offered, including sleeping tablets at night, in an effort to numb both her pain and her despair.

'We'll be giving you another scan tomorrow, Judith, and a cholesterol test, so you'll be fasting from midnight for that. We might as well check everything out while you're here.' The nurse took the cup from her. 'And we're going to start you on light physio, which will help with the pain. Especially with that trapped nerve in your neck.'

'Busy day so.' Judith felt some response was required. She liked this nurse, a kind Filipino woman called Lourdes, but today she didn't seem to have the energy to talk to anyone.

'You're a bit down, your mum was saying. That's normal after a traumatic event. Emotions seesaw, so don't worry if you're up one day and down the next. Why don't you try and have a little nap before tea comes?'

'Thanks, I will,' Judith agreed. Sleep was precious, and she took it when she could. Lourdes plumped up her pillows and straightened her blankets, and Judith began to relax. It was nice being taken care of for a change. And if it weren't for the pain, she wouldn't mind being in the hospital. For the first time in her adult life she felt no sense of responsibility, no pressure to be in charge, no pressure to take care of anyone. Now, she was the one being taken care of, and all her worldly concerns and worries had floated away beyond the plate-glass window where they couldn't reach her. She knew she would have plenty of problems to deal with when she left hospital. All the insurance stuff with the car, having to buy a new one and all that entailed. Having to sort her sick pay with work. But, for now, she could snuggle up in her bed and drift off into drugged sleep and forget everything.

CHAPTER THREE

'I just don't want to go, Mom. Why do I have to? It's only going to be full of old people and people your age. It's going to be majorly boring, and Sarah and I were going to go to hang out with Clara for a couple of hours, 'cos she's going to her villa in Spain tomorrow and we won't see her for a month.' Melissa was whining, feeling very sorry for herself at having to attend a dreary art exhibition where her grandmother was showing her silk paintings. It was Juliet's first exhibition, and she'd invited the three of them to attend.

'Listen to yourself. How selfish are you, Melissa Adams? Your grandmother is very good to you, and she asks you to do one thing and you whinge and moan like a spoilt brat. Life isn't all about you, you know. You can phone Clara when we get home,' Aimee snapped as she dropped her briefcase on the sofa and kicked off her high heels.

'Bitch,' muttered Melissa under her breath as she stalked off to her bedroom. Her mother was being so mean since the wedding. She was a real crosspatch. OK, she'd found the empty alcopop bottles that she and Sarah had been drinking from on the day of the wedding, and Melissa had pulled a fast one by not wearing the dress Aimee had wanted her to wear, going in her Rock & Republic jeans instead, but she'd been well punished for that. Her mother had given the precious jeans to a charity shop. If anyone had a right to be cranky and unfriendly, it was her, Melissa thought angrily, giving her bedroom door a good slam and flinging herself on the bed. Going to an art exhibition was something Nerdy Nolan and Turdy Sampson would do. How sad was that? She picked up her phone, and her fingers flew over the keys: *Can't come 2 Clara's. Have to go to Gran's thing. Tlk ltr. X*

She sent the text to Sarah and got a sympathetic *Bums. Poor u. XXXXXXXX* in return.

She went to her wardrobe and pulled out a pair of white jeans she hadn't worn since last year. They'd been very tight, she remembered as she slipped out of her combats and stepped into them. Melissa was more than pleasantly surprised that they fastened without a struggle, and she spent five minutes twisting and turning, looking at herself critically in the mirror and noting every bulge and flaw. She wasn't eating anything else today, she decided, even though she was starving and her stomach was rumbling like crazy.

She lay back down on the bed and picked up a magazine she'd bought earlier. She read how a celebrity had lost half a stone in a week to finally get to the prized size zero, and then she turned the page to read how Posh maintained her zero size by drinking a special tea. She'd definitely give that a try, Melissa decided as she read her horoscope and saw that a new romance was coming her way. Perhaps she might meet a hunk at the art exhibition – but, somehow, she seriously doubted it. She lay sprawled on the bed, picking at a spot that had been annoying her all day.

Aimee rubbed her aching feet and yawned. How she would love to collapse on to the sofa and stay put for the rest of the evening. The last place she wanted to go was her mother's art exhibition, but she couldn't let her down. Juliet was so excited about it and, to be fair to her mother, she rarely imposed on her. From what Aimee had seen of her mother's paintings so far, she had a natural talent for art. Juliet had been terribly upset at having to give up playing tennis because of injury and had thrown herself into her new hobby. If *she* had to live with her father, she'd need a hobby that engrossed her too, Aimee thought caustically, wondering what he would have to say to her tonight. Several of Ken's golfing buddies had been at the O'Leary wedding, and she wondered had they made any comment about it.

Well, her autocratic father, the esteemed Professor Davenport, wouldn't be able to look down his aquiline nose at her career for much longer, she thought, strolling out on to the wraparound balcony of their penthouse. Aimee gave a deep sigh which came from the depths of her. Today was the day she had worked towards all her working life, and the prize had finally come to her. She'd been offered the position of managing director of a new company. Roger O'Leary and Myles Murphy, two of the country's leading businessmen, had come to her with a proposal to set up their own events and catering company, which would cater for the very top-end clients – clients who didn't have to ask the price of things, clients who wanted seriously to impress, clients to whom money was no object, clients like themselves, who owned helicopters and private jets, who holidayed in Sandy Lane and the Maldives. The mega-rich. The people thoroughly insulated from recession, who would never have to stint on their entertaining.

It had been an exhilarating meeting. Roger had proudly introduced her to Myles, a tall, distinguished man in his late fifties who said little but took everything in, interjecting a pertinent comment here or there. A far different type to the loquacious Roger, whose enthusiasm for the venture could hardly be contained.

'I've been thinking Celtic Carousing Events and Catering would be a good name,' he declared exuberantly. 'You know – the Celtic tiger and all of that. Let's be a part of it.' His little round face, glowing with excitement, reminded Aimee of one of those big cookies that had two currants for eyes and a red cherry for a nose. Aimee and Myles glanced at each other. 'Tacky,' she could almost hear Myles say.

'Perhaps a bit obvious; a little more subtlety might work better,' Myles murmured. 'Especially now that the tiger's more of a scrawny cat,' he added dryly, referring to the economic downturn.

'Oh!' Roger was disappointed. Subtlety was not his strong point. He liked to be full on.

'How about something like Hibernia, which is the ancient name for Ireland? Or Hibernian Festivities . . . Celebrations . . . Dreams . . .' suggested Aimee.

Myles nodded. 'I like it,' he approved. 'More class.'

'You see, I told you she was the woman for the job, Myles,' Roger said, generously accepting defeat, rubbing his podgy little hands together and winking at her. 'Now, with your contacts and ours, we can't fail. We'll rent some impressive offices, with good views, maybe here in Ballsbridge—'

'A more central location would be better, actually, Roger, and with easy parking,' Aimee pointed out. 'Businesspeople like yourself who are in town a lot might find it less time-consuming than having to make the journey out here. No one knows better than you that time is money.'

'True,' he agreed.

'But then, on the other hand, I would most likely travel to meet clients of the calibre we're looking at, in their own offices or homes, should they prefer,' she suggested.

'Of course, of course. Naturally, there'll be a car to go with the position and a salary commensurate with your skills.' He named a figure that made her eyes widen. It was twice what she was getting at *Chez Moi*.

'It's important that you make a good impression – you know, give an idea what the company is about, so you can choose a top-of-the-range car. We don't want you driving around in a little Yaris,' he chuckled, delighted with himself.

The corner of Myles's mouth lifted, and he smiled at Aimee. 'Appearance is everything indeed,' he murmured, and she laughed and began to relax as they got down to the nitty-gritties of how the company would be financed and what would be expected of her if she took on the challenge. It was the career opportunity of a lifetime, and she'd earned it. She should be dancing for joy.

Now Aimee rubbed her hand across her washboard stomach, achieved through hours in the gym and constant vigilance over what she ate and drank. There was a baby in there, and that baby was going to muck up everything she had worked so hard to achieve. If she was going to get rid of it, she'd want to do it sooner rather than later. She had to make up her mind and stop dithering. What was the point in having a baby when she would only resent it? Surely it would feel the vibes of anger and resentment flowing into it in the womb. Why would it want to be born to a mother who just didn't want it?

Aimee felt tears well up. This should have been the happiest day of her life, and here she was feeling trapped, resentful and deeply troubled. And there was no one she could talk to about it. She'd let all her friends fall by the wayside in her rush up the career ladder. The only one who might have kept the news to herself was Gwen, and she hated Aimee's guts now, after the incident on the day of the wedding. She'd accused Aimee of snubbing her and wouldn't have anything more to do with her. That left Jill and Sally. What was she going to do? Just pick up the phone and say to them, 'Hi, I'm up the duff, and I want to get rid of it, what advice can you give me?' She could just imagine the jungle drums working overtime after that.

'Did you hear, Aimee's knocked up and wants to do something about it . . . what do you think of that then?' Sally, who was pregnant herself and happy about it, would be shocked. Jill might understand. Jill was a successful careerwoman like Aimee. Of the trio, Jill was the one who was most like her in outlook. But no doubt Gwen had gone to her and Sally with her sob story, and Aimee wasn't sure what sort of reception she'd get if she made contact. She made a face. She couldn't *bear* to be the subject of girly gossip. That just left her mother and Barry.

Aimee gazed over the panorama of Dublin Bay and Howth, oblivious to the white racing yachts scudding across the waves and the patchwork of purples and greens and ochres shadowing and lightening as the sun burst through the clouds on the landmass across the bay. She saw none of it as she stood there agonizing on the balcony. Her mother would be horrified to think she was even considering a termination. Juliet's view was, you make your bed, you lie on it. She'd put her own life on hold to rear her children and be the kind of wife Ken wanted her to be. There wouldn't be much sympathy for Aimee's position there, Aimee reckoned. That left Barry. Her husband, the love of her life, the one who knew her inside out, her rock, allegedly. And how could she tell him she wanted to abort their child? She just couldn't. She knew him well enough to know he would be against it. He'd actually always wanted another child, company for Melissa. Aimee felt this desire had something to do with trying to get things right on the second go around after making such a mess of it with Debbie.

But why should she have to facilitate his need to get things right, thought Aimee angrily. She wasn't part of the mess he'd made of his first marriage. How ironic that most of the women she knew in second marriages wanted children, and a lot of the husbands, who had children from their first, didn't want to go down that route again. Barry would welcome another child, and she was the one rebelling against it. If she told him she wanted an abortion, it would probably be the end of them, and things were shaky between them as it was at the moment.

It was bad enough having to tell him that she'd been offered a job that would double her salary and leave him way behind in the earning stakes. Ever since Debbie's damn wedding he'd been touchy about his earnings. Now that she was going to be earning more than him big time, he was going to be even worse. Aimee shook her head. Men's egos were such fragile things. She'd have been better off if she'd stayed single. She was on her own with this one, she thought forlornly, turning to go into the bedroom to get ready to go out.

Right at that moment, she had never felt as lonely in her entire life.

Barry dropped his keys and mobile phone on the hall table and glanced into the lounge. It was empty. He peered into the kitchen, wondering had anything been done about dinner. He was starving. Nothing was bubbling on the hob, the small kitchen table wasn't set, the microwave wasn't on and, he thought crossly, he was clearly going to have to make his own dinner. Aimee *was* home, because her car was parked in her space in the underground garage. He poked his head out into the hall and cocked an ear. He could hear the shower in their ensuite. Had she eaten? Was she interested in eating? Lately, no one in the house apart from himself seemed to be bothering with food. He yanked open the fridge door and perused the contents.

Some Brie, half a melon, a couple of slices of Serrano ham and some wilted asparagus spears. He investigated further. A dish of tapenade. Some olives and tomatoes and a carton of coleslaw.

He wanted *proper* food. Meat and potatoes and veg. Was that too much for a man to ask? He pulled open the freezer drawer and thanked God for the

Butler's Pantry as he pulled out two aluminium containers of Pepperpot Beef and Duchesse Potatoes. He marched out into the hall. 'Melissa, Aimee, have you eaten yet? Do you want Pepperpot Beef and potatoes?' he called loudly.

'No thanks, Dad,' came the mumbled response from his daughter's bedroom.

'Not for me, thanks,' his wife responded.

'Good. More for me,' he muttered, hurrying back into the kitchen, his humour darkening by the minute. He'd been looking forward to coming home and announcing his new deal over dinner and maybe a glass of champers, and neither of the females he lived with were interested enough even to come out of their bedrooms and say hello to him. God be with the days when he'd been married to Connie and he'd come home to a cooked meal and a warm reception, he thought sorrowfully, conveniently forgetting how absolutely stifled he'd felt in his first marriage.

And he had to go to his mother-in-law's blooming art exhibition. How riveting would that be? He emptied the entire contents of the containers on to a plate and shoved it into the microwave before switching on the small kitchen TV to catch the six o'clock news.

Aimee appeared ten minutes later, looking immaculate in a pair of red trousers and a cream silk cami and cream shrug. She looked effortlessly elegant and chic, one of the things he'd always admired about her.

'You look very nice,' he ventured, offering an olive branch.

'Thanks,' she said tonelessly, and he wondered why he'd bothered. 'Is Melissa ready?' She stood with her back to him, looking out the window.

'Don't know, haven't seen her.' He opened the dishwasher and noticed that it needed to be emptied. 'It wouldn't kill her to empty the dishwasher while she's hanging around at home,' he grouched, putting his dishes in the sink instead.

'I'll do it later. Don't start a row, she's in a snit about coming to Mum's exhibition,' Aimee said tiredly as their daughter walked into the kitchen dressed in white jeans and a multicoloured smock top. She looked sullen, ignoring them as she flounced over to the fridge and took out a can of Diet Coke.

'Well, seeing as we're all here, I've a bit of good news to announce.' Barry turned to face them. 'In case anyone's interested,' he added dryly.

Aimee looked a little taken aback as she turned to face him. 'Really?'

'Yep. I hooked a brand-new client today, a biggie. Haven't lost my touch.' He grinned from ear to ear, very pleased with himself.

'That's great news,' she said slowly. 'Well done, Barry.'

'Congratulations, Dad. Does this mean we can buy a place in Spain? Clara's going for a whole month. Could we buy a place near her?' Melissa asked excitedly, sulks forgotten.

'Don't rule it out some time.' He hugged her, thinking about his proposed SecureCo International Plus profits.

'Don't be putting notions in her head,' Aimee said, a little sharply.

'It's not a notion – it might happen yet,' Barry retorted, stung by her attitude. And when it's bought it will be bought with my money, he thought angrily. He'd been going to propose a champagne toast but, if that was her attitude, he wasn't going to bother. 'We should get a move on if you want to be there on time – the traffic was heavy enough when I was coming home,' he said flatly, all the good taken out of his achievement.

Aimee sat beside her husband, stuck in gridlock on the Merrion Road, which was, yet again, undergoing roadworks. She'd been driving on this damn road for more than twenty years and never once had it been cone-free. The money that had been spent digging and re-digging it would have funded half a dozen schools or hospitals, she reflected crossly as Barry cursed a taxi driver who had shot out of the bus lane and cut in ahead of him in an effort to beat the lights further on.

She hadn't handled the news of her husband's new client very well, thought Aimee guiltily. Barry was like a little boy sometimes, expecting a big clap on the back for his achievements. What would his response have been if she'd said, 'And I have a little announcement of my own to make: I'm pregnant, darling, and I'm not going to keep it. What do you think of that?' That would knock the self-satisfied grin off his face. She'd hardly be able to tell him her own news about her job offer and big salary increase; he'd feel emasculated – and *that* had to be avoided at all costs.

Working wives really had it tough, Aimee raged silently. Stay in your box and, for God's sake, don't become more successful than your husband. Never forget his cherished position as hunter/gatherer. Be the perfect mother as well as trying to juggle work and your relationship. Never let your bosses see that you are anything less than in control and on top of things.

Barry had none of those pressures. All he had to worry about was getting new clients. Well, excuse her if she wasn't dancing up and down with excitement at his news. She had her own problems to deal with, problems of a sort that he would never, ever have to face.

CHAPTER FOUR

The rattle of the big tea trolleys woke Judith. She wished she could have slept longer. A tea lady brought in her tray and pulled her trolley up along the bed for her. 'I've cut it up for you, seeing as you have the arm in a sling,' she said kindly as she left, in a hurry to get all the teas served.

Judith picked up the silver cover and studied her tea unenthusiastically; bits of leathery brown omelette lay limply on the plate. She poked it; it was almost cold. She replaced the cover and nibbled at the buttered white bread. Her mother had brought her some scones; she'd have one of those, she decided, flicking on the TV to watch the teatime episode of *Stargate SG1*, her favourite programme. If any of the girls at work knew she was a *Stargate* fanatic, she'd lose all her credibility, she thought with wry amusement, watching the lean, fit and very sexy Jack O'Neill battle with some Washington-bigwig bureaucrats in an effort to save the planet from the Replicators, her favourite aliens. Yes, indeed – if word ever got out about her TV show of choice, Judith would never live it down at work.

Her heart sank when she heard a knock on the door. Surely they couldn't want to take more blood from her at this hour of the evening. Dracula had nothing on the vampires that lived in the bowels of the hospital, she'd told the last technician who'd taken a big syringeful from her. The young girl had managed a weak smile; no doubt she heard that tired old cliché day in, day out. Even as she'd said it, she'd felt foolish, making daft chitchat for the sake of it.

Perhaps it was a visitor, she thought irritably, wiping a smear of jam from her mouth.

There was nothing worse than trying to eat when you had visitors. Tom, her brother, who had visited her twice, had arrived at meal times. If it was him again – although she doubted it – she was going to tell him to go away until she had finished her tea.

'Come in,' she called, in a none-too-welcoming tone, and her eyes widened in delight when she saw her best friend, Jillian, poke her head around the door. It was Jillian she'd been going to spend the weekend with when she'd crashed the car.

'Oh, Jillian,' she managed before bursting into tears.

'Ah, Judith, poor, poor petal,' her friend said sympathetically, enveloping her in a bearhug.

'Sorry, sorry,' sniffled Judith. 'I thought you were Tom.'

'That would make *anyone* cry,' Jillian said

wickedly, and Judith hiccuped and laughed at the same time. Jillian was the only one who really knew her inside out. Jillian understood everything. Judith didn't mind crying in front of her; in fact, it was a relief to cry. She'd wanted to cry all day.

Her friend handed her a tissue. 'Rough, huh?'

Judith nodded. 'The pits,' she gulped.

'God, Judith, I got a terrible shock when Cecily rang me that day. I thought you were a goner.'

'I thought I was a goner myself. And you know, Jillian, and you're the only one I could say it to, part of me was sorry when I woke up out of the coma. Isn't that an awful thing to say?'

'Yes, Judith, it is, hon, but I understand why you might say it. It's been hard for you the last couple of years. But you know life is precious, and maybe this is a wake-up call for you to make changes.'

'Well, I'll tell you one thing.' Judith wiped her eyes. 'It's certainly made a big change in Ma. You wouldn't believe it. She's coming in and out to see me on the bus, she's staying in the house on her own, she's doing the shopping and visiting the library and going for walks in the park. She's a new woman.'

'Are you serious?' Jillian pulled up a chair. 'Mind you, she sounds quite chirpy on the phone when she rings me with the news bulletins about you. I told her I was coming to see you but not to let on.' Jillian grinned. 'She was enjoying the plotting and planning, if you ask me. So that's one good thing that's come out of it all. Sometimes things happen to us, and we think that they're the worst thing that can happen but, when we look back on them, we find that they're really precious gifts, which change our lives in some way or another,' her friend said matter-of-factly.

'Oh, don't do all your spiritual stuff with me,' Judith grimaced. 'This is not a gift, believe me. I ache from head to toe. My car's a write-off, not to mention all the other disasters in my life.'

'Ah, poor you. Poor, poor tormented, afflicted you,' teased Jillian, and Judith grinned.

'Bitch,' she retorted, delighted to see her friend.

'What have you got there?' Jillian picked up the plate cover and made a face. 'Uggh! Just as well I came prepared.' She opened the big tote bag she was carrying and took out a cellophane-covered dish, followed by two small Tupperware containers. 'Your favourite, meat loaf, and pine nut, feta cheese and olive salad, and strawberry roulade for dessert. I was going to bring some wine, but I thought I'd better not with all the tablets you're on. Now, eat up like a good woman,' she urged. 'God that man has a sexy ass,' she added grinning as she caught sight of Colonel O'Neill retreating from an attack by the Replicators. She too was a fan.

'It's great. There're two episodes on every afternoon, and I lie here and watch them and feel like I'm in a little bubble. If it wasn't for the pain I'd be quite enjoying myself,' Judith admitted.

'Yeah, it's nice sometimes just to let go of everything. You see, you're being given time to rest and reflect, that's one of the positives of your situation. But it's awful being in pain, and I don't mean to be dismissive of it,' Jillian said sympathetically, cutting another slice of meat loaf.

'I know you don't. I know you think about things differently. That's what you get for going off to live in bogger land and doing all those healing things and reflexology and stuff.'

'You wait, Ms Baxter. You'll see how well reflexology and acupuncture work by the time I've finished with you. Lily and I have decided that, when you're discharged, you're coming up to me to recuperate, and no ifs, ands or buts about it. A good dose of fresh country air, some nice therapies and healings and a glass or three of whatever you fancy will do you all the good in the world,' her friend said firmly, removing the plate of omelette from the tray and replacing it with a tasty feast.

Judith looked at her open-mouthed and didn't know whether to laugh or cry.

'So you see, I feel I've held poor Judith back, and I want her to have a place of her own, so I was thinking of selling my house to the bank and giving her the money. But I can live in it until I die, can't I, Mr Long?' Lily twisted her wedding ring around her finger and stared anxiously at the bank manager, who had listened in attentive silence as she told him of Judith's accident and her plans for her daughter.

'Well, now, firstly, I hope Judith makes a full and speedy recovery and, secondly, Mrs Baxter, I think there are better options than selling your home to the bank.'

'Oh!' Lily said, deflated.

'What I'm going to suggest would, in the long run, be better for you, I think, and would ensure that Judith gets a mortgage and that you get to keep the house. You see, we don't actually operate that method of finance here. Our operation in the UK did for a while, but it caused so many problems that our banks here decided not to go down that route. The banks in the UK were being sued by families, who got a big shock when the mother or father died and they discovered that the banks owned the property. There were accusations of pressure being put on the client to sell and accusations that the clients hadn't realized the implications of what they were doing, or accusations that the clients weren't compos mentis. It was all very difficult and caused such legal problems that we decided it wasn't an efficient or profitable system to run with. Do you see where I'm coming from, Mrs Baxter?'

'I certainly do, Mr Long. I can understand that very well indeed,' Lily said, relieved that he had explained it so well to her. Tom would be the first to sue the bank if she'd gone down that road, of that she was certain. 'So what do you suggest then?' She leaned forward, anxious to hear what he would advise.

Mr Long sat back in his chair and steepled his fingers. 'I'd suggest that you have a chat with your solicitor and get Judith's name put on the title deeds of the house. Then she could use it as collateral for a loan. Just let me check something a moment.'

His fingers flew over the keyboard, and he studied the screen intently. 'Yes, indeed, Mrs Baxter, I can't of course discuss her account with you – client confidentiality and all of that – but I'd be very happy to have a chat with your daughter about providing a loan. Unless she defaults on her mortgage – and there's no reason to think she would – and if she passes the medical, I can't foresee any problems. And the good thing is that your home can go to her after you pass on, if that's what you wish, and she will certainly be able to clear her mortgage.'

'There'd be a medical? Oh dear.' Lily frowned.

'Nothing to worry about. I'm sure once Judith is discharged, all will be well,' the manager assured her. 'And, of course, we mustn't forget that there's a slowdown in the property market and prices are dropping considerably, so she'll be in a buyers' market. An excellent time for her to be buying. Couldn't be better actually.'

'That's true.' Lily brightened. 'Every cloud has a silver lining, I suppose.'

'Now, of course you *can* go the other route, I can give you some numbers to ring – I wouldn't like you to think I'm pressurizing you to take my advice and follow a certain course of action. I'm sure you've seen the advertising on TV. Judith is certainly free to go wherever she likes for a mortgage or home loan, but I can assure you that our rates are competitive, Mrs Baxter. And do have a chat with your solicitor.'

He smiled benevolently at her, and Lily felt herself relax. She trusted the man in front of her completely. He had no airs or graces, and she understood very well why the elderly people in her area liked their bank manager. He had told her once when she had been investing a bequest left to her in an aunt's will that he would never advise anyone who couldn't afford to take a risk to invest in something he wouldn't let his mother and father put their money into. After that, she trusted him implicitly. He wasn't one of these wide boys in their sharp suits. He was one of their own sort and, whether they realized it or not, one of his bank's greatest assets.

By the time Lily and Mr Long had finished their chat, the bank was closed to the public. The bank manager walked her to the door, shook her hand, and she left with a sense of great accomplishment and a spring in her step. She had set the wheels in motion, and the next time she saw Judith, she'd have great news for her. She must start buying the papers with the property pages in them, to give Judith an idea of what was on the market. Lily tried not to dwell on the idea that, when Judith eventually bought a place, Lily would, like Mrs Meadows, be living on her own.

Tom Baxter sat in his car outside his mother's house, drumming his fingers impatiently against the leather steering wheel.

Where the bloody hell was the woman, and why

wasn't she answering her damn mobile phone? He'd tried to ring Judith's, but that was turned off too, and he vaguely remembered Lily saying the nurses had told her to keep it off so she would get the rest she needed.

He'd been at a business meeting in a hotel at the airport and, seeing as he was on the Northside and not too far away, and rather than endure the M50 rush hour on a Friday evening, he'd decided to call in to see his mother and see if she was still managing all right while Judith was in hospital. She might give him a bite to eat while he was at it. He was starving, and she usually had some tasty scones or a cream sponge on the go. Glenda, his wife, was not one for baking, unfortunately. Spending money was more her forte, he thought caustically, remembering the row they'd had that morning about her spending 200 euro on a pair of ridiculous shoes with heels like pipe cleaners for a charity lunch she was going to. It was all very well keeping up with the Joneses, but surely she could have bought a pair of shoes for half the price.

'If you want me to go to these things, I'm not going looking like a pauper. Those shoes are cheap compared to what some of those flashy ones wear, believe me,' Glenda had snapped. 'You can't be seen in the same outfit twice. You know that as well as I do. That's the game, and that's the way it's played, and it's stressful enough without you giving me grief.'

She was right, he supposed: if you wanted to mix

with movers and shakers, you had to act the part and dress for the part. When he'd first met her, all those years ago, she bought all her clothes in Dunnes Stores, and he'd thought she looked lovely. Now, it was all designer labels and posh boutiques. It was just as well she had that part-time job in the boutique and got a discount off her clothes, because she spent a small fortune on them. It was hard keeping up the lifestyle they'd become accustomed to in the boom years. A big house, huge gas-guzzler of a car, private schooling for the kids, property abroad. It had been a dream come true, but now the economy was slowing down, inflation was rising, his properties in Spain were dead in the water, and the bottom had fallen out of the Spanish market. You couldn't give apartments away there; the rent he was getting was far from covering the mortgages. His investments and pensions were being hammered, the stockmarket was a disaster area, and his own alarm and security installation business was beginning to feel the pinch. Tom felt more than a little oppressed sitting in his BMW, flicking a piece of lint off his Louis Copeland suit.

He eyed his mother's redbrick house with a detached eye. Despite the slump in property, it would still make a good price when it was sold. It was well kept. He had to give it to Judith that she wasn't letting the place go downhill and, not that he was wishing for his mother's imminent demise, he was certainly banking on the guts of a hundred and fifty thousand, minimum, for his share out of the place eventually. And God knew he could do with it. That was, if Judith didn't get her claws into their mother. That was his greatest worry.

OK, he admitted, she'd looked after Lily, but she'd also had a house over her head rent free all these years, allowing her to save a fortune, if she wanted, and that wasn't to be sneezed at. Why should she get the house, lock, stock and barrel? Cecily had to be considered also, he thought self-righteously. There were three children in the Baxter family. It would be patently unfair to single one out, even if Lily felt she owed Judith a debt.

If only he could get a look at the will. Judith had caught him snooping around one day when Lily was in hospital getting her cataract done, and they'd had a vicious row. They'd never made it up and, if Judith had died after her car crash, she'd have gone to her grave estranged from him.

He sighed. He was glad his sister hadn't died, of course, but the truth was they had never got on and it was unlikely they ever would. But, they could be civil to each other, as long as she didn't try and pull a fast one. He glanced in his rear-view mirror and saw Lily marching smartly along the road towards him. She looked extremely well, he noted, not at all like someone who was in danger of kicking the bucket any day soon. It was a bit late for her to be coming home from her afternoon visit to Judith; it was gone six. He wondered where she'd been. She really had come out of her shell since the accident. He opened the door and got out of the car. 'Mother, where on earth were you? I've been trying to ring you,' he exclaimed jovially.

Was it his imagination, or did a flicker of guilt flash across Lily's features? Hadn't she looked at him in dismay before recovering her equanimity?

'I had business to attend to. I didn't know you were coming. You never let me know,' she said tightly.

'What sort of business?' he inquired, trying to keep his tone light.

'Business. *My* business,' said Lily sharply, before inserting her key in the lock of the front door.

Tom followed her into the house. He wasn't at all happy. Lily was up to something and he'd very much like to know *exactly* what it was. He was going to have to spend some time with her and keep a close eye on things.

'Any chance of a cuppa before I go?' he asked, following his mother into the newly done-up kitchen. His sister had painted it before her accident.

'Every chance,' Lily said briskly. 'Fill the kettle there and put one in the pot for me, I want to get out of these shoes. There's a fresh-baked cream sponge in the cake tin,' she instructed as she took off her jacket and went out to the hall to hang it up. Tom stared after her. She'd always been bossy, but there was a new confidence in her which he'd never seen before.

'So where were you?' he tried again as she came into the kitchen wearing her navy and pink slippers and tying an apron around her waist.

'Doing some business. I told you. Now, if you're thinking of going to visit Judith, seeing as you're over this side of the city, I don't know if you should go in tonight. Your aunt and cousin, and Cecily, are going, as well as one of her friends, so that's a lot for one night. She's not up to too many visitors, so I think you should wait until tomorrow.' His mother took the knife off him just as he was about to cut a chunk of cream sponge and gave him a slice far smaller than what he would have cut for himself.

Bloody hell. I'm not traipsing back over here tomorrow, thought Tom crossly as he made the tea. He came to a decision. It was time to act and stop dithering. 'I was thinking, seeing as Judith painted the kitchen, how about if I get a painter in to do your bedroom and hers? It's been a while since they've been done. We could give Judith a surprise,' he offered expansively.

Lily looked at him, astonished. 'Well, that's very good of you,' she said slowly. 'Let me have a think about it.'

'Well, don't think about it too much. They don't keep you in hospital for very long these days. By the way, your mobile phone is off,' he said casually, and she fell into his trap, as he hoped she would.

'I know. I turned it off when I went in to see the bank manager.' Lily sat down and took a welcome sip of tea.

'What were you going to see him for?' Tom was all ears. He knew he'd get it out of her one way or the other, eventually.

113

'Oh, this and that,' Lily said offhandedly, but she had two dull, red spots on her cheeks, and Tom knew his instincts were absolutely right. Something was going on, and the sooner he got to the bottom of it the better. If he had the painters in, he'd get a chance to have a look around. Lily would have to go and visit Judith, and he would make it his business to have a good poke around when she wasn't there. It was terrible that he had to go spying on his mother but, if she wasn't going to be open with him, that was his only option. He had an inheritance to protect, and protect it he would.

Lily watched her son drive down the road in his big flashy car and bit her lip. She'd let it slip about going to see the bank manager; it was out before she knew it. Now he'd know something was going on. He'd been asking her nosy questions about her will when she was in hospital a few months back and, today, he was wondering what business she was doing at the bank. She knew full well he was concerned about who she was going to leave the house to. And he was right to be concerned, she thought grimly, closing the door and going into her sitting room. Her priority was Judith, and Tom could go and take a great big running jump in the lake for himself if he thought he was entitled to as much as his sister.

Lily knew there'd be a show of grief at her funeral, but that would be precisely it: a show. After the burial, he'd hardly give her a thought, and it sickened her to think that he was plotting and planning while she was still alive. It was obvious as far as he was concerned that the sooner she went the better. She couldn't imagine Mrs Meadows's sons behaving in such a fashion. They would truly grieve their mother.

She sat in her high-backed chair staring out through pristine net curtains and saw the shadows of evening encroach as the sun filtered dappled light through the trees. Two small children were playing hopscotch on the pavement across the road, and a young couple who had moved in further along the street strolled by hand in hand, laughing at some private joke.

She and Ted had been a young couple once, and their three young children had played hopscotch on the pavement. It seemed like another lifetime ago, and it was too sad to think back and regret all that she had lost because of her edgy, uptight personality. She had run away from life all her life and had missed out on so much because of it. Regret was such a dreary, energy-sapping emotion, it would get her nowhere; and she shouldn't dwell on the past. She was doing her best to make amends. She could do no more.

Lily yawned. She was very tired. It had been a long and stressful day. But at least she'd achieved something positive by her visit to the bank. That was good, she lauded herself, trying to take the edge off her feelings of failure, remembering all the days when she'd sat, a prisoner in this room, afraid to go anywhere on her own.

If Tom could plot and plan, so could she. She might very well take him up on his offer to have the upstairs rooms painted. She'd make sure that the painter picked the same shades of cream and ochre for Judith's room that were on the walls already. Her daughter liked those colours, and they suited that room, which got the evening sun. It would be a surprise for her. And, even if the time was coming when she would be looking for a home of her own, it would be good for her to know that there was always a room for her with Lily if ever she wanted it.

'You're doing very well, Lily,' she murmured to herself approvingly, striving to keep her spirits up. 'Keep going, and do this one good thing in your life.'

She yawned again. She gave a wry little smile. What did they say about people who ended up talking to themselves? That would be right up Tom's alley. Her son might think he was smarter than she was and that she was only a timid old lady and not to be reckoned with, but he was in for a surprise. Forewarned was forearmed, and he'd soon find that to his cost.

CHAPTER FIVE

Judith's heart sank to her boots as she limped slowly along the crowded hospital corridor and saw Debbie Adams and Ciara Williams walking towards her. She had to do little walks twice a day and had decided to go for one when Jillian was leaving. Her eyes darted right and left, wondering if there was some escape route she could take, but it was too late. They had seen her, and Ciara was giving an embarrassed little wave. Judith knew in her heart and soul that this visit was for form's sake and nothing more. She wondered how the pair had been nominated to come because, certainly, Debbie, she was sure, would not have come voluntarily. Judith knew full well that she was not a popular manager, and it rarely bothered her. She did her job, supervising the busy salaries section she ran in the big insurance company she worked for, and she did it well, by pushing her staff and keeping them on their toes. Mistakes could not be made in her department and, if they were, they landed at her door. She had to keep her distance from her staff; she was not their friend, she was their boss, and it was in everyone's best interest that she and they remembered it.

Judith felt strangely vulnerable knowing that they had seen her, hobbling, leaning on a crutch, her arm in a sling, in her dressing gown and slippers, with no make-up on and the roots of her hair in need of a touch-up. She was never less than perfectly groomed at work and always wore a smart business suit. It was her armour and, now she was without it, she felt unnerved.

She had dreaded the 'visit from work' and had hoped it wouldn't happen until further down the line, when she was more in control of herself. She should have told Janice Harris, the human resources manager, when she'd been talking to her on the phone to give her an update on her situation, that it was family visits only for the moment.

'Hello, Judith,' Debbie said warily. 'How are you feeling?'

'Well, I've been better,' Judith said wryly, wishing she didn't have to bring them into her room but not feeling fit enough to go down to the coffee shop on the ground floor.

'My God, Judith, you took a bashing all right,' Ciara said cheerfully, waving a bouquet of flowers at her. 'From all of us, with our best wishes. Where would you like us to put them?'

Up your arse, Judith would love to have said, and then felt ashamed of her utter ungraciousness. They wanted to be here as little as she wanted them to be here, but façades had to be kept up. 'This is my room. There's a vase on the window, you can fill it at the sink in the bathroom,' she said calmly, leading the way into her small private room.

'Oh, what a fabulous view,' Debbie exclaimed, making her way over to the window. She handed the vase to Ciara. 'There you go.'

'Thanks,' her friend replied and busied herself filling it and then arranging the flowers, glad to have something to do.

'They're very nice,' Judith said politely, easing herself down into the armchair. She was damned if she was going to struggle into bed in front of the two of them, but she ached after her walk and would have liked nothing better than to stretch out and wilt.

'Is there anything we can get you?' Debbie asked, and Judith was taken aback to see a flicker of sympathy in the younger girl's eyes. She and Debbie had never got on, and she was the last one Judith would expect sympathy from.

'A new arm, a new car,' she said dryly.

'We saw your car on the TV the morning after our wedding day,' Debbie remarked, perching uncomfortably on the edge of the bed. 'Of course, we didn't know it was your car at the time. My husband said it was a write-off, and I remembered thinking you had one like it. It was only when I got an email from the girls on our honeymoon in New York that I realized it was yours.'

How proudly she said those words – *my husband* – Judith thought irritably, glancing at the slim

119

white-gold wedding band on Debbie's left hand. *Our honeymoon in New York.* She suddenly remembered why she didn't like Debbie Adams – or Kinsella, as she now was. She had everything Judith had always wanted: husband, home of her own and the prospect of having a family. She was so smug, sitting there looking so youthful and healthy in a pair of turquoise cut-offs and a clinging white top with a sweetheart neckline showing off her pert boobs and glowing tan.

'So how did the wedding go?' She tried to keep the edge out of her voice.

'Best wedding I was ever at,' interjected Ciara, who was arranging the gypsophila artistically between two yellow roses.

'It went fine,' Debbie murmured awkwardly.

Judith hadn't even been invited to the afters, not that she would have gone even if she had, she thought snootily. 'Well, let's hope you've turned over a new leaf at work now that you're a married woman, or are you doing any at all now that I'm not there to keep an eye on you?' Judith said tartly.

Debbie did a double take. Had she heard right, she wondered? 'Excuse me?' She stared at her boss.

'I said I hope you're doing some work now that I'm not there to keep an eye on you.' Judith's eyes had a strange, piercing glitter as she stared at Debbie. The atmosphere in the small room changed, its very ions bristling, charged with hostility as the two women eyeballed each other as though mesmerized, like boxers in a ring waiting for the bell to start the fight – a fight that had been a long time coming.

Debbie flushed. She stood up and picked her bag off the floor. 'Actually, Judith,' she said slowly, 'it's a pleasure to go into work, if we're being honest and speaking our minds. Maybe it's because, as you say, I'm a "married woman", but I'm more inclined to think it's because I'm not getting bullied. Because, you know, you're a bully, that's what you are, accident or no accident. A bully of the highest order. You've made my life a misery, and I'm not going to let you do that any more. And how dare you speak to me like that? How *dare* you try and belittle me in front of my friend. I came to visit you to wish you well, but your ungraciousness says so much about the type of person you are – a mean-spirited, miserable bitch. I'll wait for you in the coffee shop, Ciara.' She glanced at the other girl and walked out with her head held high.

Judith watched her leave, her own cheeks as flushed as Debbie's at the humiliating exchange.

'Um ... well, I'm sure you're tired,' babbled Ciara, picking up her own bag.

'I am a bit,' Judith agreed wearily, stunned at Debbie's onslaught.

'Yes, well, get well soon, and don't rush back to work ... I mean ... er ... take it easy and give your-self time to recover. Umm ... I wasn't saying not to come back to work—'

'It's all right, Ciara, I know what you were saying, and thank you for your good wishes,' said Judith quietly to the flustered young woman in front of her. She swallowed hard. 'And tell Debbie thanks for coming, I didn't mean to offend her. I suppose I shouldn't have said what I said, it was uncalled for.'

'OK. I'll tell her. Bye, Judith.' Ciara took off like a scalded cat, not even bothering to close the door.

Judith hauled herself up out of the chair, shut the door and promptly burst into tears. Now they'd go back to the office and tell the others that Bitchy Baxter was as bitchy as ever. And they were right. Even worse, Debbie had accused her straight to her face of being a bully and been vicious about it. Imagine having the nerve to call Judith a miserable bitch. What insolence. Anger surged through her. The cheeky little cow. Judith climbed on to the bed and grabbed a pillow, rocking back and forth as a torrent of emotions battled for supremacy. Anger, grief, humiliation, regret. What had possessed her to have a go at Debbie outside of the office setting? The girl had been kind enough to come to visit, even, no doubt, if it hadn't been voluntary. Judith was sure some selection process had been gone through in the office. But, in fairness, Debbie had unexpectedly shown some sympathy for Judith's plight and asked her did she need anything. Couldn't she have taken the gesture at face value without having a go? How typical of her to let her dark side get the better of her. Sometimes, she really was her own worst enemy! Tears spilled down her cheeks.

Debbie's accusation had shocked her to her core. To be accused of bullying was a serious matter.

What if the younger woman took it to HR? Would Judith be able to stand over her treatment of Debbie? She sobbed uncontrollably as she lay down on her bed. What a horrible person she was. Not even a near-death encounter had softened her cough. She was still a bitter, twisted, resentful woman with a sharp tongue and a hard heart. She hated her life, and she hated herself because, deep down, she knew Debbie Adams was right. She *had* bullied Debbie the last year or so, and she had withheld her salary increment out of spite. The girl was good enough at her job, and better than some, but Judith had just wanted someone to take her own resentment out on, and Debbie had been the perfect target.

How disappointed her father would be in her; how disappointed she was in herself. She had made another human being's life miserable, because she was disappointed with her own life. She *deserved* her nickname, Bitchy Baxter, and she deserved to be called a bully, because that was what she was. She couldn't run away from that inescapable fact.

Why hadn't she died in that accident, she thought frantically as she tried to compose herself. It would have been a welcome release from her dismal life. She had a flashback to the moment the car had juddered out of control and the tree had loomed ahead of her. She'd had time to wrench the wheel and avoid it but, Judith remembered with a sudden stomach-lurching jolt, she hadn't. She'd driven straight into it. She'd tried to commit suicide because the opportunity had presented itself. Suicide had always been at the back of her mind, all these years. A safety net when life got too unbearable. She had done nothing to try and prevent the car from crashing into the tree. She'd been prepared to die. She'd *wanted* to die.

Attempted suicide. It sounded so dramatic, but it hadn't been really; it had been an inviting option. And that was what truly frightened her. Mentally, emotionally, you couldn't sink lower than that. Judith remembered the depths of her misery that awful day and felt it was nothing to how she felt now. She hadn't succeeded then, but what was to stop her trying again? Fear wrapped itself around her, tight, dark and malevolent. She was becoming like Lily had once been. Weak, mentally fragile and very frightened. She buried her face in her hands and cried bitterly, fearful of what was to become of her.

'She's a bitch, Ciara, a walking bitch,' Debbie fumed as she hurried down the long corridor to the hospital exit. 'How dare she accuse me of doing nothing at work? She's such a minger. I'm glad I said what I said to her. I'm glad I finally stood up to her, because she deserved it, and she's had it coming for a long time. You and the others don't know the way it's been for me this past year. God, I feel sick even thinking of it. And I feel sick after what's happened, because I'm no good at fighting with people. I'm no good at having rows, my stomach gets tied up in knots and I think I'm going to puke, and I'm just crap at arguing, but she had no business talking to me like that – and in front of you as well. You'd think I was twelve, the way she went on.' Debbie was almost in tears as she hurried along the hospital corridor.

'Yeah, well, she did tell me to say she apologized if you were offended,' Ciara said breathlessly, trying to keep up, and dodging between people who were coming in to visit. 'She said she didn't intend to offend you.'

'Yeah, well, she bloody well *did* offend me, and I won't be going near her again,' Debbie raged as they emerged from the foyer into the sunlight. Cigarette smoke wafted over them from the smokers congregated at the door.

'Phew!' Debbie waved her hands in front of her face and grimaced. 'Bad enough having to visit her, without getting lung cancer.' She glowered at a middle-aged woman in a pink dressing gown who was waving her cigarette in the air as she made a point to her companion.

'Keep your voice down; she'll hear you,' muttered Ciara, red-cheeked.

'I meant her to hear me,' retorted Debbie. 'Why should I have to inhale her smoke, and why do they ignore the instructions that people are not supposed to smoke in that area? It's outrageous, and so disrespectful of others,' she ranted.

'Do you want to get a bus or a taxi?' Ciara sighed.

'Might as well get the bus, seeing as there's one

there.' Debbie scowled, heading for the queue. 'Sorry for flying off the handle,' she murmured a few minutes later, as they sat in a seat near the back.

'That's OK. Don't worry about it.' Her friend patted her on the arm. 'Mind you, I think Judith got a major shock when you called her a bully. She certainly wasn't expecting that – she went white,' Ciara remarked as the doors whooshed closed and the bus moved away from the stop.

'Well, she deserved it. Like I said, she's done nothing but pick on me for months, and then she stopped my increment, and I'm just sick of it. I hate coming into work, I'm always petrified I'll be late. I'm always petrified I'll make a mistake and have her coming down on me like a ton of bricks. I hope it gives her something to think about.' Debbie sat, flushed and angry, none the better for the encounter.

'I think it will. She really went pale when you said it,' Ciara reiterated. 'And then she went pink. She looks a bit shattered, doesn't she?'

'Yeah, well, I suppose if you'd been at death's door, you'd look shattered too. I hope she's out for months,' Debbie said viciously.

'Hmm,' murmured Ciara, and prudently refrained from any more discussion of the matter. She took her phone out of her bag and began texting, leaving Debbie to regain her equilibrium.

Debbie gazed out the window when the bus stopped at traffic lights at the junction of Collins Avenue and Grace Park. The pace of the traffic was slow, and the sun beat in on top of her head, making her squint. If it hadn't been for Judith, she could have been enjoying a nice glass of chilled white wine with Bryan, instead of sitting in traffic seething. Her husband wouldn't be interested in listening to her account of the blow-up. Emotional dramas were not his thing. He'd just tell her she was imagining things and to get on with it. Well, she *was* getting on with it. She'd finally made a stand.

Maybe Judith's barb had been a mixed blessing, because it had enabled Debbie actually to confront her boss with the accusation of bullying. There had been no pussyfooting. She'd said it as it was, and it was a victory of sorts that Judith had apologized for offending her, via Ciara.

The bus lurched forward when the lights went green, but some idiot driver was stuck on the yellow box, impeding their progress. A cacophony of honking horns ensued, and she was grateful for the fact that at least she wasn't driving in the Friday-evening mayhem. The rush-hour traffic was heavy and, even with the advantage of the bus lanes, it took them an age to get into town. Ciara was going to meet her boyfriend at the Savoy, to go to a film, so they parted company on O'Connell Street. Debbie made her way towards Temple Bar, determined to forget her encounter with Judith and looking forward to a drink and then a romantic meal with her husband.

'Judith, why are you so upset? I'm going to have to call one of the house doctors to write up some sedation for you. You've got yourself into a terrible

127

state.' The nurse lifted her wrist and took her pulse. Judith sobbed, unable to compose herself. She wanted to be sedated. She wanted to go into oblivion and not have to think about anything.

The door creaked open, and Cecily appeared, looking smart and well groomed in a pair of white linen trousers and a navy jacket. Her jaw dropped when she caught sight of Judith's teary, red-eyed, woebegone face.

'What's wrong?' she asked, dismayed, glancing at the nurse.

'I don't know. She won't tell me.' The nurse wrote a note in her chart. 'Judith, I'm going to get one of the doctors to have a look at you. Stop crying now,' she ordered briskly. 'You have a visitor.'

'Don't you speak to me like that. You know nothing about her, or me,' Judith spat, incensed by the nurse's authoritarian tone. 'Cecily is just visiting because she feels it's her duty, not because she wants to. I have no one in my life who really cares about me except my friend Jillian and my mother, so don't patronize me, Miss, and don't order me about. I'm old enough to be your mother.'

Cecily and the nurse stared at the wild-eyed woman in front of them.

'I was just coming in to say goodbye. I'm off to France with my family for a month, but I don't think this is a good time to visit,' Cecily murmured, taken aback.

'Perhaps not,' agreed the nurse. 'I'll get them to put a No Visitors sign on the door.'

'Yes, do that. That will suit me down to the ground,' Judith hiccuped. 'Go away, the two of you, and leave me alone. That's all I want – to be left alone.' The nurse ushered Cecily out the door and turned back to Judith.

'Now, Judith. You have to tell me what's brought this on. It can't be that bad,' she soothed, as though speaking to a very cantankerous toddler. She was only short of going, 'There, there,' and patting her on the back. It was the last straw for Judith.

'Oh, what would you know?' she screeched, the last remnants of control deserting her. 'I tried to commit suicide and didn't succeed. The girls at work think I'm a bully, and they're right. I'm manless, childless, completely physically crocked, and I don't even have a home of my own. How fucking bad do you want it to be?'

She turned her back on the nurse and curled up on the bed and wailed with grief and despair.

Cecily made her way towards the lifts, shocked by what she'd just witnessed. Judith had really lost it. She looked like a madwoman with her wild, red-rimmed eyes, keening and bawling. It was scary. Her elder sister was always so reserved and controlled. And never less than perfectly groomed. The woman she'd left behind was someone unknown to her.

She bit her lip as she jabbed the button on the wall for the lift. If Judith was having some sort of a nervous breakdown, would she be expected to stay at home and have to cancel her trip abroad? It would be so inconvenient. They'd booked a house in Brittany for a month, and friends were coming to stay for the first week and, later on, her sister-in-law and her children were joining them. Too many people would be discommoded if she cancelled, but could Lily cope on her own? Tom wouldn't want to know. He and Judith were not on speaking terms, and he wouldn't go out of his way to help.

Families, they could be such a nuisance. Cecily sighed as she stepped into the already crowded elevator, hoping she wouldn't catch any germs from a wheezy old man who was hocking and spitting into a dirty grey handkerchief. She'd take her cue from Lily and play it by ear. This time, though, she was the one who had to take some responsibility where their mother was concerned. It had been a long time coming, and she'd got away with a lot, but now she was up against it, and the timing couldn't be worse.

CHAPTER SIX

It had taken longer than Connie had planned to get to Mrs Mansfield's house. Karen, her sister-in-law, had phoned her to discuss their forthcoming holiday, then a neighbour had called by, so she'd had to call Jessie back and say she was running a little late. As she drove up the wide, curving drive, she thought how elegant yet homely the impressive, ivy-clad Georgian mansion was. Dappled in the fading sun, it reposed in the manicured grounds like something from a Jane Austen novel. It was a pity Mr Darcy didn't come riding across the fields to greet her, Connie thought, amused at the notion.

Jessie must have been watching out for her because, as soon as Connie parked the car beside several others at the side of the house, she opened the kitchen door and waved.

Dressed in her nurse's uniform and wearing a short, navy cardigan, she wasn't what Connie imagined from talking to her. She'd half imagined someone, like herself, in her late forties and, from her voice on the phone, someone warm and motherly. Jessie Sheehy was a small, wiry, black-haired woman in her late thirties, with sallow skin and white, uneven teeth which gleamed when she gave a broad smile and held her hand out. 'Connie, nice to meet you, and thanks so much for dropping by. Have you time for a quick cuppa? Mrs Mansfield is entertaining Drew Sullivan, and three's definitely a crowd when he calls on Friday evenings, so I get to have a cuppa in the kitchen.'

'Oh yeah – he's the guy with the stables where Mrs Mansfield keeps her horses. I met him the day I came for my interview, nice man.' She followed the other nurse into the kitchen.

'Well, Mrs M. loves him, and he humours her. He's kind like that. She could pay him directly into his bank account, but she insists on writing a cheque out for him every week, so that she'll get to talk to him for a little while. And she visits the stables once a week to see the horses. If she goes in the morning, you'll bring her; if she goes in the afternoon, I will,' Jessie said, pulling out a chair at the table for Connie. 'I hope you didn't mind me asking you about filling in for me next month. I'll return the compliment if you ever need to swap,' she added, as she poured boiling water into the teapot.

'Not at all,' Connie assured her. 'I'm going to be pretty much a free agent, as regards time. I can tell you I'm certainly looking forward to giving up agency nursing for a while and going part time.'

Connie sat down as Jessie brought the tea and two mugs over to the table, which already held a plate of buttered scones and milk and sugar. They chatted easily over their tea, and Connie discovered that her new colleague had a teacher husband and two teenage daughters.

She told Connie that, apart from a few little foibles, such as not liking her nurses to wear trousers as part of their uniform, making sure they wore their caps and being somewhat fussy about taking her medication precisely as instructed and at the same time each day, Mrs Mansfield was an easy patient to look after.

'She was in hospital for months as a child with TB, and I think that's why she likes the cap and dress. I suppose we're lucky not to have to wear the starched headdress we wore when we started out years ago. Remember them? The weight of them!' Jessie grinned.

'I know.' Connie laughed. 'I could never keep mine from going limp; they were the bane of my life.' They were laughing when a deep male voice said, 'Excuse me interrupting, ladies. Jessie, Mrs Mansfield wants to take her tablets. She told me to ask you to go up to her.'

'Right, I better get going.' Jessie stood up.

Connie reached into her voluminous bag and took out two dozen long sachets. 'The cat treats, as promised.'

'She'll love you for that,' Jessie said, putting them in a press under the sink. 'Connie, have a great holiday. I'll see you when you get back. See ya, Drew.' She filled a carafe with water, added a slice of lemon and hurried out of the kitchen.

'So hello again. Is there tea in the pot? Those little china cups that your new boss drinks from wouldn't quench a thirst.' Drew Sullivan hooked a long leg around a chair and straddled it.

'Hi.' Connie smiled at the tanned, healthy-looking man facing her. 'This is porter, it's been standing so long. Will I make you a fresh cup?' she offered.

'Not at all, it will be fine, I like a strong cup of tea,' Drew said easily, loping over to take a mug off a hook under one of the kitchen presses.

'Me too,' Connie said, pouring the dark-brown liquid into his mug and handing him the milk jug.

'So when are you starting?' He studied her quizzically, and reached over, took one of the buttered scones and bit into it.

'I'm off to Spain at the end of next week, to recover from my daughter's wedding, and I'll be starting the Monday after I come back.' Connie eyed him back over the rim of her mug and wondered how was it that, as men got older, their lines added to their looks, but on women they looked so ageing. He was one of those men who were sexy and didn't even know it, wouldn't even be aware it was an issue with him. Men like that were lethal, Connie mused. He reminded her of an older version of that gorgeous TV presenter on TG4, the one with the laughing eyes and the voice like treacle. Debbie was a fan, too, so she might like Drew. What was she like? she thought in amusement, at the notions that were flitting through her mind. She took another sip of tea and lowered her eyes.

'My daughter got married in Boston last autumn,' he was saying, 'so I recovered from that in New England for a few days. It was glorious. I never saw anything like the foliage,' he added, demolishing the scone in the second bite.

'Oh, you've a daughter?' She remembered Rita, Mrs Mansfield's housekeeper, telling her he was divorced. She hadn't realized he had children.

'Two, but I don't see them that much. They live in the States. My ex-wife moved there years ago, taking them with her.'

'Oh! That must have been hard,' Connie murmured.

'It was. Very,' he said succinctly, and his eyes darkened momentarily.

'My ex-husband went to the States after he left our daughter and me. I could never understand how he could leave her and go so far away. He came home a few years later and married again and had another child. My daughter couldn't forgive him for it. But the wedding brought a reconciliation of sorts.' Connie sighed.

'Oh! Well, that must have been tough too,' he said quietly, his blue eyes meeting hers for a moment, before he drained his tea and pushed his mug away.

'Yeah, it hasn't been easy but, you know what, Drew, this is my time now. It's going to be all about me, and they can all get on with things. I've done my bit,' said Connie firmly as she took the mugs over to the sink and rinsed them.

'That's a good attitude you have, make sure you hang on to it,' he grinned, walking over to her, picking up the tea towel and beginning to dry the mugs. 'And were you ever tempted to get married again? It must have been hard raising your daughter alone,' he inquired as he hung the mugs back on their hooks.

'It was, but I got on with it, I had no other choice and, no, I was never really tempted to remarry, although maybe it would have made sense when I was younger. I would have liked another child, but I never met the right man. One marriage break-up makes you wary. Well, in my case it did,' she amended, just in case he'd got married again or was in a second relationship. 'Now, I'm very glad to be a free agent. You?' She arched an eyebrow at him, curious as to what his answer would be.

'Nope. As you say, a break-up makes you *very* wary . . . been there, done that and won't be wearing *that* T-shirt again,' he said emphatically, and she laughed.

'I guess I better go, I want to get a walk in, and if I dawdle much longer I won't bother.'

'I'm off too. I have a mare in foal I want to keep an eye on; her time is near.' Drew hung the tea towel neatly on the Aga rail, and she noticed his hands – tanned, long-fingered, with short, clean nails. They would be gentle hands, she imagined, picturing him with a newly born foal.

'Poor horse,' she smiled, 'even to this day I can still remember *my* labour pains.'

Drew chuckled as he put the milk and sugar away before holding open the back door for her. 'I got a saucepan thrown at me the second time round. Things went downhill from there.' They walked across the crunchy gravel to the cars. His was a black jeep covered in muck and dust.

'Good luck with your foal.' Connie smiled up at him, shading her eyes from the glare of the setting sun.

'Enjoy your holiday.'

'I intend to.'

Drew raised his hand in farewell, climbed into the jeep and started the engine, and she got into her own car, threw her bag on the seat and revved up. He waved her to go ahead of him, and she reversed out of her space, hoping she wouldn't do anything foolish, like grating the gears or stalling. She could see him behind her in her rear-view mirror, the evening sun shining on him. He really was a handsome man, and a real countryman, she observed, the kind that aged well. Even his tightly cut grey hair suited him. He was obviously well used to looking after himself, and he hadn't expected her to wait on him and dry his mug. She'd been impressed when he'd casually picked up the tea towel and stood beside her drying up and then put everything neatly away.

What had happened in his marriage, she wondered as she drove towards the big iron gates.

And how hard it must have been for him to be so far away from his daughters, and not of his choice. She indicated left and slowed down for a moment to check that the road was clear. Drew indicated right and gave a toot on his horn. As she emerged on to the narrow country road, she tooted back, and drove away smiling, feeling quite perked up.

CHAPTER SEVEN

Drew Sullivan watched in his rear-view mirror as Connie's car disappeared around a bend. He'd enjoyed chatting to her. He hadn't intended to reveal so much about himself, but it had just seemed natural when he was talking to her. They were birds of a feather to a degree, he thought ruefully, wondering why her marriage had broken up and why an attractive woman like herself was footloose and fancy free. He'd got the distinct impression she was on her own when she'd said she was glad to be a free agent. She had a good sense of humour, too, he noted, a most important attribute in a woman. Marianna, his ex-wife, had had precious little sense of humour, he reflected wryly as he slowed down and pulled in to let a tractor drive out of a field.

She certainly hadn't been amused to be left alone much of the time to bring up two young children, but he'd been a dairy farmer when they married, as well as having fields under tillage, and it had been tough going, especially trying to find money for the affluent lifestyle she expected him to provide for her.

'You never spend time with me. Don't you want to be with me? You prefer those bloody cows and that damn tractor to me and the kids' was her constant refrain, especially around harvest time, when he was out on the land morning, noon and night and would come home, bone weary, to arguments and tantrums. He understood her frustration. It wasn't easy being on her own so much, with young toddlers, and she spent a lot of her time driving over to Wicklow with them to spend time with her family and friends.

She'd never really wanted to settle in the country. She was from Wicklow town, her father was a successful solicitor who entertained a lot. She'd told Drew once that she far preferred the townie lifestyle to *vegetating* in the country.

'Well, why did you marry me then? You knew what I was and the way I worked,' he'd demanded angrily, fed up to the back teeth of her constant whingeing and moaning.

'Don't ask me,' she'd retorted. 'It was the biggest mistake of my life.'

That had hurt him to the core. He, like a fool, had thought he was doing his best for her and the children. In the end, she'd left the farmhouse and gone to live in a house in Brittas, where she could meet her hoity-toity friends and drink in McDaniel's and have barbecues on the decks of their expensive mobile homes.

He'd missed his daughters so much. Missed standing beside their beds looking at the moonlight

140

slanting down on their sweet, flushed little faces. He'd be so tempted to pick them up and kiss them and say, 'Daddy's home, my little darlings.' He missed them trotting into the bedroom at the crack of dawn for their morning cuddles and tickles, until Marianna would moan long and loudly enough about getting some sleep. He'd take them down to the kitchen and give them their breakfast before saying goodbye to them and rousing her to mind them, then head out to help his farmhand feed the cattle.

He'd hoped very much, when they were older, to give them each a horse and teach them to ride. Drew loved riding, loved the feel of the majestic animal beneath him and the breeze enveloping them both as they galloped across the fields, completely at one with each other and nature. He'd wanted his daughters to feel that same sort of buzz and exhilaration.

The plans he'd had for them, he thought bitterly. Plans that came to nothing. Marianna had gone to visit relatives in America for six weeks and taken the children with her, and he'd been crucified with loneliness he'd missed them so much. She'd come home and gone back within three months, and he knew she'd met someone. She'd been very straight about it. She'd met an investment broker who was divorced with a young daughter. He had wooed her attentively, spent money on her and wanted her to come and live with him while she waited for a divorce from Drew.

'But what about me, what about my time with the girls?' Drew had been horrified.

'What time?' she'd snorted sarcastically. 'An hour in the morning, an hour in the evening, if they're lucky. Don't be so selfish, Drew. Don't put your needs before theirs and hold them back from the great life Edward and I could give them in America.'

The girls had been full of excitement about America and Disneyworld and having a swimming pool in the back garden.

'Would you like to go and live there?' he'd asked his three-year-old, Katy, and his five-year-old, Erin.

'Oh yes,' they'd chorused.

'But I can't come,' he pointed out.

'Pleassee, Daddy, couldn't you get holidays?' Erin had nestled into him and kissed his neck, while Katy had pulled his hair, sure in the knowledge that she'd get a tickle.

'And who'd feed the cows and their calves? Would you not prefer to stay here and get a horse when you're bigger?' he'd pleaded.

'A horse! Mom, Dad said we're getting a horse.' Erin went racing in to her mother with the news.

Marianna had been spitting with fury when she heard this. 'Go up to your rooms, girls. I want to talk to Daddy,' she had ordered, and when they'd scampered up the stairs, not daring to argue, such was her tone, she'd turned on him in rage and said, 'How low is that, Drew Sullivan? Trying to bribe them to stay with talks of a horse. How selfish are you? I might as well have been a deserted wife for all the time you spent at home, and you have the nerve to talk about your time with them—'

'I wasn't out enjoying myself, Marianna, I was working damn hard to give you and the girls a decent lifestyle,' he'd hissed, wanting to shake her for her selfishness.

'Yes, and coming home and falling asleep in the chair after you'd had your dinner. I never knew it was going to be like that, Drew. I nearly went out of my head with boredom when I lived on the farm, that was why I moved back near town, and that's why I want to go to America. I've met a man who wants to spend time with me and the girls—'

'It wasn't that I didn't want to spend time with you,' Drew had retorted hotly. 'Farming is 24/7, and there's nothing you can do about that.'

'Yes there was, and I did it, Drew. And if you want to stand in the way of our girls having a chance of a good family life and plenty of opportunities, then you go ahead, but, for once, you think of someone other than yourself and your precious farm. I'll bring them home in the summer and every second Christmas, as long as you pay for their fares.'

Marianna had stood with hands clenched by her sides, her eyes flashing with antagonism, and he'd wondered, not for the first time, how he'd been so deluded to marry her. What had possessed him to think that he and she, who were so different in personality and outlook, would ever stay the course?

He – quiet, shy, awkward around women – had

been drawn to her bubbly, bright, chatty personality and hardly able to believe that this little blond bombshell would be at all interested in him. But interested she had been, and he had eventually invited her to go for a drink. She had done most of the talking, and he had been content to let her, but he'd enjoyed the night and asked her out again. Gradually, she'd taken him in hand, buying clothes he, happy enough to live in jeans, would never have dreamt of buying. He'd liked her proprietorial air and the fact that she seemed proud to have him at her side when other girls flirted with him. Their sex life had been adventurous and satisfying. She had few or no inhibitions, and the early years of their marriage had been relatively happy. Marianna had been a young woman who was used to getting her own way, and he'd resisted that. They'd fought, but they'd made up, usually with hot, hungry sex. He'd loved coming home from work knowing that she was waiting for him and wanting him but, as routine set in and their two children had been born, she had grown dissatisfied at the amount of time he spent working, and the rows became more frequent, and coming home was no longer something he looked forward to.

It was a sad irony that he'd lost his wife and children to the hard work he'd put in trying to give them the lifestyle Marianna aspired to.

'Even if you don't agree to me bringing the girls to America, I want a divorce,' she'd told him viciously.

'You can have that with pleasure,' he'd barked and had been glad to see her flinch. Glad that for once he'd hurt her as much as she was crucifying him.

'So, are you going to stand in their way or not? You won't have the time to spend with them, even if we do stay here. Why would you be such a dog in the manger and deny us all our chance?' Her eyes raked over him, cold and unloving, and he knew their marriage was well and truly over, and that he wanted to be free of her as much as she wanted to be free of him. They had gone past the point of rescue. To stay together would be toxic and of no use to their daughters.

She stood there before him, full of anger and dislike. Her features had lost their girlish softness over the years, and she'd become pinched and dissatisfied, hard-faced even. Had he done that to her, he wondered, or was it her true nature asserting itself? He had begun to realize a few years into their marriage that whatever he did would never be enough for her. Marianna had always been a daddy's girl, spoilt within an inch of her life. Drew reckoned that part of his initial charm for her had been the fact that he wouldn't give her everything she wanted and was quite capable of saying no to her. She was right about him not having a huge amount of time to spend with his daughters. He wasn't yet wealthy enough to employ a farm manager, although it was something he wanted to do eventually. His assets were his land and property but, if he sold his land, he reduced the size of his farm, and it wasn't feasible. Could he give up farming altogether? But, even if he did that, their marriage was finished. All these thoughts raced through his mind, but he kept coming back to her assertion that his daughters could have a very good life in America with this new man of hers.

Could he stand in their way? Was he being a dog in the manger, as she put it, wanting it all his way? What was the best for their girls? He was in turmoil trying to find the answers. He couldn't let them go, just like that. They might think, in years to come, that he hadn't cared enough to fight for them.

He stared at his wife and said, very quietly, 'You go if you want to, Marianna, but the girls stay here in their home with me. Over my dead body will you take them to America.'

'You're a selfish bastard, that's what you are – a prick, Drew Sullivan,' she swore, furious that her emotional blackmail hadn't worked and that she wasn't going to get her own way.

She'd gone to America on her own for six weeks, and his heart had almost broken when the girls would come crying to him, 'When is Mommy coming back?' 'Why can't we go on holidays with Mommy?' 'Daddy, I miss Mommy, can I go and stay with her?'

His own mother had helped out as much as she could but, in the long term, Drew knew he'd have to make other arrangements if he was insisting on the girls staying in Ireland. He had to face the fact that they would soon be starting school, with all the running around that entailed, and how traumatic that would be for them without their mother around to ease them into it. He'd been fraught, trying to juggle everything, but he would have done it with a heart and a half if he'd thought the girls were happy to stay with him. It wasn't that they didn't love him. They adored him, but Marianna was their mother, when all was said and done, and he couldn't take her place, no matter how much he wanted to.

Marianna had come home laden with presents one dark November evening, and Erin and Katy had run into her arms, ecstatic at her return, and Drew had known, with gut-wrenching despair, that he couldn't part them from her again.

'I want to meet this bloke. If you're going to bring my daughters to live in America, I want to see who they're going to be living with,' he growled a week after her return, when she'd told him she was going for good the next time. He turned on his heel and walked out, leaving her standing with her mouth open.

A week later, Edward Delahunt had come to visit. A well-built, black-haired, jovial man in his early thirties, he'd held out his hand to Drew and said, 'Buddy, I appreciate your meeting me like this, and I completely understand where you're coming from. I'll give Marianna and your girls the best life I can. And you can visit any time you wish. I've a thriving investment and taxation practice in Boston; I own several properties and a big share portfolio. I have no financial problems. They'll have a good lifestyle.'

'Is that so?' Drew said. He wanted to say, Don't call me 'buddy', but he felt it would be childish. 'If it's all the same to you, Mr Delahunt, I'll support my own daughters.'

'But, of course, buddy, you and Marianna can work out your divorce settlement between yourselves. I just want you to know I'd have their best interests at heart. They are sweet little things, and they get on big time with my own young daughter. She's seven, and she lives with her Momma, not too far from us. We share custody.'

There was nothing actually to dislike about him, Drew had to admit, and he could see why Marianna was drawn to his larger-than-life personality. He could see, also, how she was drawn to his wealth, he thought sourly, studying photos of the big house and swimming pool and the gleaming Mercedes in the driveway.

Drew's father-in-law had advised Marianna on their divorce settlement, and she had fleeced him. Had it not been for the girls, he would have fought her claims tooth and nail, but he'd given her what she wanted, even though he'd had to sell the dairy farm and farmhouse. He'd put money in a trust fund for his daughters, happy that Marianna wouldn't be able to get her greedy mitts on it.

Saying goodbye to them had been the most devastating experience of his life. They'd run into his arms, all excited that they were going on a big plane on holidays again, to the house with the swimming pool, not realizing that it would be six months before they saw him again.

He had cried solidly for two days when they left, shutting himself away from his concerned parents and sister, who were also devastated that their granddaughters and nieces were leaving Ireland. He tormented himself, asking himself whether he had let them go too easily. But they needed their mother. They'd pined for her in a way they wouldn't pine for him, and they might have held it against him in years to come that he'd been so intransigent.

'They need you too, Drew, she's only a selfish shrew,' his mother exclaimed bitterly when he told her what was happening. 'You can't let them go. We'll muddle through somehow.'

'I have to, Mam, I tried it and it didn't work. It's too hard on them being parted from her. Children need their mother.'

'Even though she's a selfish, irresponsible woman, and now you have to sell the farm as well as losing your daughters? May she never have a moment's peace of mind,' Margaret Sullivan had raged, wishing she could get her daughter-in-law on her own for ten minutes at the slurry pit.

It had been the darkest, loneliest period of his life. Losing his girls, his farm, his reason for living. The kindness of friends and family had brought him through the deep, black depression he'd sunk into and, gradually, he'd hauled himself out of the mire and got his life back on track.

He'd started up a riding stables and livery on

land an uncle had left him in Greystones and thrown himself into his work. He'd built a house with a room each for his girls for their holidays – and what joy it had been when they'd come racing into his arms at Dublin airport, that precious first visit, which he'd lived for. He'd marvelled at how tall they'd become and hated the faint twang of their newly acquired Boston accents. But by the time their holiday was over and he had to kiss them goodbye, they were Wicklow women again, he told them. That was the pattern of his life: waiting for their visits; despair when they went back to America, until his routine would set in again and keep him focused on work.

He hadn't been a monk. For some reason that he couldn't even fathom, women were attracted to him. He'd had a couple of relationships, but he'd never let himself get deeply involved, and the women had become tired of trying to get him to commit. The barriers were up. He'd been hurt unspeakably once, and he'd never let a woman do that to him again. He had regained his equilibrium, but buried deep in his heart was the sense of loss he carried. It had never left him from the moment he kissed his daughters goodbye when they left for Dublin and a life without him in America.

Although Marianna tried to be friendly once she'd got her own way, Drew, though civil and polite, never gave his ex-wife an inch when they were together. She wanted to be pally-wally and to 'forgive and forget', as she'd said herself, and she'd urge him to stay at her and Edward's house when he was visiting the girls and, years later, when he'd gone over for Katy's wedding.

'You're fine, I'll look after my own accommodation, thank you,' he assured her every time. And though he made an effort when the girls were around or they were out for meals together, when he and Marianna were on their own, he didn't indulge in idle chitchat, no matter how hard she tried to engage him. He'd never been a hypocrite, and he had no intention of starting because of Marianna's desire to bury the past. No woman should ever put a man through what his ex-wife had put him through. No woman should ever separate a father from his children. Some things were beyond the pale.

It had been a long, long time since he'd allowed himself to remember those painful memories which his conversation with Connie had brought up, Drew reflected as he drove into the stable yard. He had a great relationship with his daughters. They spoke on the phone and emailed each other constantly, Erin had been over for a visit just six weeks ago, and Katy and her new husband had spent a week of their honeymoon staying with him after their trip to Venice. He loved them dearly, and it gave him great satisfaction to know that, when he died, both of them would inherit a considerable amount of money when the stable, house and lands were sold. He'd provided for them well, and paid for Katy's wedding, despite Marianna's protestations that Edward would be very pleased to.

'Katy is *my* daughter, Marianna. I've never forgotten that, even if *you* have,' he'd replied calmly but very, very firmly. That had shut her up quick enough.

He shook his head. What the hell was he doing, raking up the old coals of his past? He had plenty to concentrate on in the present. He cut the engine and got out of the car, hurrying into the stall, where the pregnant mare whinnied when she saw him. He ran his hand over her swollen belly. 'It won't be long now, my beauty,' he said soothingly, and smiled as she nuzzled him affectionately.

Women – you could keep them. He was happy with his horses.

CHAPTER EIGHT

'Hello, Mum, you look fabulous. Where's Dad?' Aimee looked around the crowded art exhibition, expecting to see her father's handsome, leonine head or hear his booming tones discoursing on some topic or other.

Juliet's eyes narrowed, and her lips thinned. 'He couldn't come. He had to go to Larry Wright's retirement dinner. It was essential that he be there, he informed me. He forgot about it when he agreed to come.'

'Larry Wright? But he can't stand him!' Aimee tried to frown, but couldn't because of her Botox.

'Exactly,' declared her mother tartly. 'But he'd prefer to be at dinner with a man he can't stand than come and see my "little art shindig", as he called it himself. Never mind,' she declared brightly, turning to embrace her son-in-law. 'Thank you for coming, Barry. I hope you didn't have to forego a golf game or anything.'

'Wouldn't miss your exhibition, Juliet. Good luck with it,' Barry said cordially, privately thinking that his father-in-law was an even bigger plank than he'd previously thought. It was clear the older woman was very hurt by her husband's non-appearance. He liked his mother-in-law. She was a 'lady', as his own mother called her. Pleasant, unassuming, easy to talk to and very much in her husband's shadow. Juliet had never made any demands on Aimee during their marriage, and she was a far different kettle of fish to his ex-mother-in-law, Stella. She'd been an interfering old biddy, and he hadn't been in the slightest bit sorry to lose contact with her when his marriage to Connie had broken up. And she hadn't changed either, he reflected, remembering their frosty encounter at Debbie's wedding.

'Melissa! Hello, darling, thank you so much for coming – I'm sure you had much better things to do than come and see your old grandma's paintings.' Juliet turned to her granddaughter with a smile, noting her sulky, bored demeanour.

'Don't say that, Gran,' Melissa protested weakly, hoping she wasn't blushing. 'I think they're gorgeous. I really like the tiger in the jungle.'

'Do you?' Juliet couldn't hide her pleasure. 'Well, if it doesn't sell, I'll give it to you and, if it does sell, I'll do you another. How about that?' she offered.

'Cool,' Melissa exclaimed. 'Thanks, Gran.'

'Your cousins are here. Steven and Gemma and the girls came up from Kildare. Wasn't that good of them?' Juliet remarked, peering through the throng. 'They're down at the far end. See them?' She pointed out her son's gangly figure between a gap in the crowds. Melissa looked over. 'Deadly – I'll just go and say hello,' she said, cheering up. She liked her cousins. Even though they were culchies and totally uncool and she had little in common with them, she secretly envied them their lifestyle. Her Uncle Steven was an equine vet, and her two cousins, Mandy, fourteen, and Anna, sixteen, both had horses. They had part-time jobs in one of the big racing stables near their home and had little interest in fashion and make-up or in hanging out in shopping malls or Starbucks. They weren't even on Facebook or Bebo; their lives revolved entirely around horses. They liked school – unheard of! – and they had a lot of friends who liked the same things they did. They didn't seem to have groups and cliques, which was so much the norm in her school. There was no edgy rivalry among *their* schoolmates.

Melissa was fascinated by them. She'd always felt a touch superior when she was with them, feeling sorry for them that they lived in Hicksville, as she mentally termed it. Imagine having no Miss Selfridges, Topshop, Mango, McDonald's or Starbucks. How seriously deprived was that? she'd said to Sarah when they'd been talking about them one day.

Her cousins slagged Melissa good-humouredly and told her she was posh, with her D4 accent, and yet they were great fun. And she loved being with them. She felt she could be relaxed and giddy and not have to worry about making an impression. She called them Boggers, which they took with great good humour, and she wished she could have their self-confidence and joie de vivre.

One of the best weekends of her life had been last year, when they'd gone to her Auntie Gemma's fortieth birthday. Her cousins had brought her to the stables where they worked, and she'd helped muck out the stalls and fallen head over heels in love with a chestnut gelding called White Star. He had a beautiful white star on his forehead and melting, chocolate-brown eyes. He'd nuzzled his nose into her neck and eaten the apple she'd produced from her pocket, and she'd spent ages stroking his face, talking to him. She'd felt he understood every word she'd said.

Then – treat of treats – her cousins had got permission for Melissa to ride him around the yard, her first time ever on a horse. She'd been so nervous she'd almost chickened out. But White Star had been patient and very gentle, walking sedately along, giving an encouraging whinny every so often, and she'd been exhilarated beyond belief.

That evening, there'd been a big family barbecue and, as the sky turned fiery orange with the sunset and then the stars had come twinkling into the black velvet sky, there'd been singing and dancing, and then more food to warm them up as the night grew cool. Everyone had drawn up close to the glowing barbecue embers and watched shooting stars flame across the sky. They were meteor showers, Anna had explained, as one bright star left a dazzling burst of light as it streaked southwards. Every time Melissa saw one she made a wish that she could save enough money to buy White Star, and she'd fallen asleep against her dad's shoulder, filled with optimism that the beautiful horse she'd fallen in love with would be hers one day.

Mandy saw her and waved. 'Hey, Posh,' she called teasingly.

'Hey, Bogger,' Melissa called back, making her way towards her cousin, glad now that she'd come to the exhibition and dying to hear news of her beloved White Star.

'Just as well the girls are here; she might have been bored.' Juliet smiled as she watched her grand-daughters embrace. 'It's good for them to spend time together, isn't it?' she said with satisfaction, beginning to relax and enjoy herself in spite of Ken's absence. 'Now, darlings, can I get you a drink? The nibbles are nice too,' she advised.

'Um . . .' Aimee paused. She shouldn't really drink, she supposed, but if she wasn't keeping the baby, what difference did it make? She needed something to relax her; she was as stressed as hell. Why not? 'A glass of white for me,' she decided, defiantly.

'And I'll have a glass of red, please,' Barry added. One glass wouldn't put him over the limit and he had enough food in him after his big dinner to soak it up.

'I'll be right back,' said Juliet, gliding away,

saying hello here and there to people she knew.

'He's such a bastard,' Aimee muttered, watching her mother weave her way through the crowd.

'Who?' Barry asked, not following her train of thought.

'Dad. The least he could have done was be here for her. It would have meant a lot to Mum. She supports him in everything *he* does.'

'Indeed she does,' he agreed dryly, but the sarcasm was lost on his wife as she began a rant about what a selfish, self-centred human being her father was.

'Like father like daughter' popped into his head; the apple doesn't fall far from the tree, as the old saying went, but he kept silent, and was glad when his mother-in-law returned with the wine, followed by Steven and Gemma, who greeted them warmly. It was a relief to talk to his brother-in-law, with whom he had a good relationship, although they didn't see each other that often. He was relieved not to have to make small talk with Aimee, who was chatting to Gemma about the cost of keeping horses.

A thought struck him. Seeing as they were at the exhibition, they should support Juliet by buying a painting. It would be expected, he would imagine. He'd buy the tiger painting for Melissa. If Aimee wanted to buy one, she could buy her own. But, knowing his wife, he doubted it would even cross her mind. Philanthropy was not a trait she was noted for, he thought sourly, watching her schmooze Bill Kerrwin, a wealthy film director.

Barry knew she was chatting to him in the hope that he might potentially be a client. She never took her eye off the ball. She was always working. He'd been like that once too, he remembered, and wondered was it age that had blunted his business edge and made him less competitive.

'Just going to buy one of your mother's paintings for Melissa,' he murmured to Steven, wishing he could stop comparing himself with Aimee. Ever since the wedding it had become an issue with him.

'Oh, right. Good thinking.' Steven nodded. 'I should buy one too, I suppose. The girls liked the tiger—'

'Sorry,' grinned Barry. 'That's mine. In fact, I'm going to pay for it right now in case anyone else snaffles it. Excuse me.' He made his way over to the wall where the tiger painting was hanging and noted that there was no little red dot on it, but two women were studying it intently, and he overheard one say to the other. 'I think I'll buy this one, it would look good in my dining room. The colours are perfect.' *That's what you think, Missus.* Barry made haste to the desk where the buying and selling was taking place and staked his claim.

'The exhibition runs until after the weekend, so you won't be able to take it tonight. I hope you don't mind,' the organizer told him.

'No problem,' he assured her. He wouldn't tell Melissa he'd bought it. He'd just hang it in her bedroom for her as a surprise. He was walking back to join the others when he noticed a small watercolour

159

of Greystones Harbour. It was a delightful little painting, and he immediately thought of Connie. On impulse, he went back to the desk and bought it. She surely couldn't object to him buying her a little gift, and it might soften her attitude to him. He could do with someone to chat to and confide in these days, and Connie was very good at listening. A woman who listened was a prize beyond jewels. Aimee might listen to her clients, but she certainly wasn't listening to him these days.

CHAPTER NINE

'Just once in all our married life I asked you to come somewhere with me, and you couldn't—'

'Oh, for goodness' sake, Juliet!' Ken Davenport interrupted exasperatedly, unhooking his braces and letting them fall on the floor. 'How many times do I have to tell you? I *had* to go to that dinner. Larry Wright was retiring. He's been a colleague for more years than I care to remember. It was expected of me,' he blustered.

'And I've been your wife for more years than *I* care to remember, and *I* expected you to be by my side after all the times I've been by yours.' Juliet was so angry her voice was shaking. 'Larry Wright is a pompous little toad. You don't even like him.' She stood in front of her husband, eyes bright with anger, her two hands clenched tight by her sides.

'That's neither here nor there, and it's precisely *why* I had to go. I didn't want any of that shower saying I wouldn't go to his retirement dinner because I didn't like the little bastard. Now, for God's sake, give it a rest.' Ken had had enough. He wasn't used to angry tirades from his wife. And, by gum, he wasn't in the humour for it now.

Juliet was whiter than the Jo Malone candles reposing on her armoire. 'How dare you talk to me like that? Just who do you think you are, Ken Davenport? That's all you damn well care about, isn't it? Your image. How you're seen. The great consultant striding through the hospital corridors making life and death decisions—'

'I bloody well do save lives, and don't you forget it,' thundered her husband, purple-faced with indignation.

'You *fool*,' she snapped back, disgusted at his arrogance. 'Don't you know, haven't you realized after all this time that your gifts are God-given? He's the one who decides who lives and dies. Why He chose two pompous asses like you and Larry Wright to be His assistants is beyond me.'

'That's it. You've gone too far. I'm sleeping in the guest room. I won't put up with this nonsense a minute longer. What's got into you? Were you drinking?' He was mottled with rage. He grabbed his maroon silk pyjamas from under his pillow and strode out the door, his shirt-tails hanging over his trousers.

'No, I was *not* drinking. I'm saying what I should have said years ago. And don't bother coming back, stay there and do me a favour,' Juliet hissed, outraged at his drinking slur.

'And let me tell you something before I go . . .' Ken turned and came back and stood in the doorway. 'You're acting like you're bloody Picasso. Get a grip on yourself, woman. It was just an amateur art exhibition. I'm sure young Melissa could do just as well,' he said cuttingly, before turning on his heel.

Juliet sat down on the side of the bed, shocked. That last biting insult had been meant to hurt her. Her outburst was one of temper, a natural reaction to her disappointment. He'd had a few moments to think of something deliberately wounding and demeaning. He'd wanted to put her down because she'd had the temerity to lose her temper and be herself for once.

Juliet took some deep breaths in an effort to calm her racing heart. She wasn't used to confrontation. She couldn't remember the last time she'd raised her voice to her husband. She was such a wimp really, she thought in self-disgust. Aimee was always telling her to stand up for herself and do what *she* wanted for a change. This night that she'd been looking forward to for so long had turned into a disaster. Ken had ruined it for her.

And what was even worse, she thought with a sickening feeling as she took her gold earrings out, she'd let him dictate the way she lived her life for forty years, and that was unforgivable. She'd wasted her life on him. God, how fed up she was of being the dutiful little wife. How fed up she was of cooking and shopping for things he liked. How wearing it was, going to his functions and listening to him pontificate. Ken had an opinion on everything, and to hell with anyone else's. He was such a *bore*.

She slipped out of her silk blouse and black palazzo pants, folded them neatly and placed them on an antique chair beside the window. She'd have her housekeeping assistant, Gina, handwash them in the morning. Gina came in three mornings a week to clean and wash and do various other chores. 'Our housekeeper gives me a hard time for smoking Havanas in the house. It's my one little indulgence,' Ken liked to boast at parties, letting people know he could afford both a housekeeper (he never mentioned that she was part-time) and expensive cigars. He was such a pompous prat. How could she have ended up married to the likes of him?

Juliet wrapped a light robe around her and sat at her dressing table smoothing cleansing cream on to her face. She didn't look sixty-four. She'd kept herself well, but that didn't negate the fact that she was in the last third of her life, and what had she to show for it? Three children, and a husband who took her totally for granted. She was merely an appendage to her larger-than-life spouse. His docile little woman who stood dutifully by his side, saying the right things, entertaining his friends when required in their elegant, detached Dublin 4 redbrick home. The perfect wife, who had no life of her own.

Her one escape had been tennis and the social scene at the club. Ken had never played, his passion was golf, so it was the one place she was assured of not having to listen to him or take a back seat. She'd had to give up playing because of a knee injury, which had persisted despite intensive and expensive physio. Her friend Chloe had invited her to come to a silk painting class just a few months ago, and she'd taken to it like a duck to water. It had sustained her and given her pleasure and helped fill the big gap the loss of her tennis had left.

The group exhibition tonight, that included four of her paintings, was her first. It had been *her* chance to shine. Assuming that Ken was coming, she'd told her classmates that her husband and family would be there to support her. Several of them knew Ken. Some of their husbands had been his patients at one time or another. Several of them moved in his golfing circles. And a few had used Aimee's company to cater for their parties and weddings. But tonight wasn't to have been about Ken and Aimee and their achievements. Tonight was about her, she'd thought with a hint of pride.

Her husband's non-appearance had been a real slap in the face. He was going to Larry Wright's retirement dinner and it was her problem that the two events were on the same night, he'd said tetchily when she'd shown her disappointment. He was sorry for double booking, but there was nothing he could do. By his subsequent hurtful jeers, her husband had yet again put her down and exposed his disrespect for her.

Juliet bit her lip as she acknowledged this undeniable fact. Mostly, in their marriage, it had been subtle: 'Oh what would your mother know about that?' to the children, or 'My wife's biggest problem nowadays is whether to go to the beauty parlour or the hair salon . . .' This at a dinner party when the subject had been the problems of working mothers trying to get to crèches in time to pick up their children. This had caused a ripple of laughter, and she'd sat there with a fixed smile on her face, wondering what he would have done if she'd stood up, poured a jug of water over his head and said, 'Don't be such a Neanderthal, you idiot.'

Tonight, though, he hadn't been subtle, he'd been vicious, because she'd had it out with him. She knew why he'd been so obnoxious. She hadn't lived with him for forty years without getting to know him very well. Ken was feeling guilty, and he didn't like it, and attack was the best form of defence. Juliet rubbed her eyes wearily. Suddenly, it didn't seem to matter. She was tired and fed up and she'd just lived through a life-defining moment. It was hard admitting that she felt a complete and utter failure. She'd always known that Ken was a selfish, self-centred egotist, and she'd accepted it for the big house, the clothes, the jewellery, the affluent lifestyle and the kudos of being Mrs Ken Davenport, wife of the eminent consultant heart specialist.

She had never felt so disappointed in herself as she did at that moment. She walked over to the big queen-sized bed they shared. She was looking forward to sleeping in it on her own. Juliet stepped over Ken's scarlet braces. Typical of him to choose scarlet. He was such an attention-seeker. Well, they could stay there until he picked them up; Juliet was done picking up after him. The worm had taken a long time to turn, but it had turned well and truly. From now on, he was on his own. Life, what was left of it, was going to be all about her. She got into bed and stretched her four limbs to the corners. It felt good. Very good. Maybe her husband's non-appearance at her little art exhibition was the best thing that ever happened to her. The straw that broke the camel's back might be the key to her liberation after all these years.

Mind racing, heart palpitating, Juliet Davenport lay wide-eyed in her big marital bed and began to make plans.

Ken Davenport lay in the unfamiliar double bed in their elegantly appointed guest room, seething.

How dare his wife rear up on him in the manner she just had. How dare she belittle his undeniable gift as a surgeon by trying to make him feel he was God's lackey? He had worked bloody hard to get where he was, and his skills had been honed over many years of time and effort. What had got into the woman? She knew better than anyone the politics that went with his position in the medical world. Other surgeons and doctors referred patients to him; it was all about keeping up professional façades, no matter how you felt privately about an individual. It was imperative to show professional courtesy, and that was what going to Larry Wright's retirement dinner had been all about and Juliet damn well knew that.

She was right, of course, that the other surgeon was a self-important, unctuous little toad but, notwithstanding, he had a list of patients who needed a new cardiac surgeon, and Ken wanted a slice of that list. Some of Wright's patients were well-known talking heads, authors, playwrights and TV personalities whom he wouldn't mind having on his client list. Ken had several such patients himself, but a few more wouldn't do him any harm. He'd have to think about retiring in the next few years; the more dosh he made now the better. And his wife should know that. How did she expect him to keep up their expensive lifestyle? The two big cars? The villa in Spain, which cost a bloody mint. He'd paid out a fortune in Spanish taxes the previous week. And what about Gina? She didn't come cheap either. Did his wife not know how lucky she was? Did she not stop to think that *he* might like to retire? And then he wouldn't have to lick the arses of the likes of Larry Wright and the rest of them.

Sometimes he envied the deservedly well thought of and renowned retired heart surgeon Maurice Neligan, whose column he never missed in the *Irish Times*. How liberating it must be to write what he truly felt about the medical world and the health services, without constraint, now that he was no longer practising. Ken certainly agreed with him about the current health minister and the disaster that was the HSE. Far too many chiefs and not enough Indians. It was a disgrace.

Ken frowned in the dark, turning and twisting. That particular minister should have resigned long ago. She kept insisting that she wanted to sort out the health services, but it was clear she wasn't capable of it, and it wasn't about what *she* wanted but about what the department needed. But if you put your head up too high above the parapet you suffered for it. He had to play the game, incompetent minister or no.

Women – they were the bane of his life. Wanting . . . needing . . . making demands. Juliet's silly little art exhibition was not high on his list of priorities, but he knew well why she was mad with him. He hadn't supported her when she'd asked him. In fairness, she was always at his side when he needed her, attending numerous functions and dinner parties and always immaculately groomed and elegant. She could carry herself anywhere.

He wasn't used to feeling guilty, and he didn't like it one little bit. What a damn shame she had had to give up playing tennis. That had kept her more than occupied and tired her out after her matches, so he hadn't had to give her too much attention, which had suited him down to the ground. He could snooze in his chair in peace with a brandy by his side after a hard day at work, while she was off whacking a ball around the tennis court and yip-yapping with the other privileged wives who played with her. Juliet had a very comfortable lifestyle, thanks to *his* hard work. But, in her behaviour tonight, there wasn't any recognition of this fact, or any gratitude, he thought, working him-self up into a fine state of self-pity.

He wasn't used to the shrew who had verbally attacked him, and he hoped mightily that she'd get over her strop sooner rather than later so that things could go back to normal and he could sleep in his own bloody bed.

Aimee sat at her laptop writing her letter of resig-nation to Ian, her boss. But she didn't want to hand it in until after she'd had the termination. She really needed to make the arrangements, and she was dreading it. But it had to be done before she took up her new position. Roger and Myles would hardly want to employ a pregnant woman. Most employers dreaded the words 'pregnancy' and 'maternity leave', and she could perfectly understand their position. She'd hired a PA once who hadn't told her she was pregnant, and Aimee had wanted to slap her when she'd finally spilt the beans and applied for her paid maternity leave. Aimee had then had to endure a temp, who was hopeless, until the other girl came back and, after that, things went rapidly downhill, as she took off at the drop of a hat when the crèche rang or when the child had a temperature or whatever. It had been totally unsatisfactory, and Aimee had been more than relieved when the girl had left.

If she kept this child, she'd have the same sort of problems that her ex-PA had had to contend with, and she just couldn't face it. Aimee closed her laptop and switched off the two big lamps in the dining room where she'd been working. She felt sick to her stomach, and she didn't know if this was a symptom of her pregnancy, or stress and tension. She caught a glance of her reflection in the big bevelled mirror as she walked past it on her way to her bedroom. She looked haunted, she decided gloomily, seeing the reflection of two shadowed eyes, deepened by the dark circles under them, staring back at her. And she *felt* haunted. Haunted by the speck of a child inside her who lay secure in her womb unaware of what was about to befall it.

She supposed it was a guilt she would carry all her life, knowing that she'd terminated her own child's life, but she could live with it, she'd have to. Whatever route she went, there would be consequences she didn't want. This was no win-win situation; this was a complete and utter catastrophe in her life. Decisions had to be made, unpalatable as they were. If guilt was to be a new companion, so be it, she decided grimly, switching off the hall light and walking down to her bedroom.

Barry was asleep, snoring his head off, arm flung across her pillow. Haven't you the life, Aimee thought bitterly, went into the bathroom and was quietly sick.

CHAPTER TEN

'Come on. Forget about that old bat, do a line,' Bryan urged, rolling a fifty-euro note and sniffing the snow-white powder on the kitchen counter in front of him.

'No, I don't want to, I want to go home,' Debbie hissed.

'Babe, it's the weekend, there's a good crowd here, the night's only starting. Chill, will you?' Bryan bent to snort the second line up his other nostril.

'Look, you know what's going to happen. Kev's going to ring "his man" with his order, and you'll be expected to buy some stuff, and we've spent enough tonight already. We don't have the money, Bryan, we've got to pay our bills,' she protested.

'Aw, for crissakes, stop being such a wet blanket. It's our first night out since we got home. Just because we're married, it doesn't mean we have to live in seclusion on bread and water. Come on, babe, this is good stuff.' Her husband's eyes were bright and glazed, and she knew she was wasting her time.

They'd met Kev Devlin and some of his crowd in Eden, and, instead of their having a meal together as she'd hoped, when she could tell Bryan the big step she'd taken in confronting Judith, Bryan had been delighted to accept Kev's invitation to join them, and the meal had turned into a raucous drink fest, including several bottles of champers, which had cost an arm and a leg. The bill had been divided among them and had cost them far more than Debbie had budgeted for this evening. Kev had invited them all back to his loft apartment on the quays, and the party was getting into full swing, with most of the crowd being fairly pissed, and high on the Es, coke and hash that were on offer.

'And how's married life suiting you, Debbie?' Jake Walls gave her a kiss on the cheek and slipped an arm around her. He was a friend of Bryan's, and his eyes gleamed as the coke hit.

'Great,' she said flatly. 'Couldn't be better.'

'You'll have to throw a party – you've never done a house-warmer. I know a great caterer, must give you the name.' He sniffed and rubbed his nose. 'Think I'll go get a beer. Ya want one?'

'No thanks, Jake.'

'A beer did you say?' Bryan slung his arm around his friend's shoulder. 'Sounds good to me. Nice and chilled, straight from the cooler.'

'Was just saying to your wife,' Jake grinned. 'You must throw a house-warmer.'

'Fantastic idea, Jake, old son, fantastic idea. What

do you think, Debbie?' Bryan ran his fingers through his hair and smirked at her.

'Yeah, fantastic idea. I'll arrange it, no problem,' Debbie said dryly.

'Terrif!' Her husband planted a smacker on her lips. 'Just gonna get a beer with Jake. Back in a mo.'

And I'm going home, Debbie decided as, edging through the throng of guests, she caught sight of a couple having sex in a bedroom off the hall. They didn't even care that the door was ajar.

She let herself out and took the lift to the foyer. Bryan was as high as a kite, and she hated it when he was like that. It was a relief to get outside and feel the breeze blowing up the Liffey. There was a time when she was in her early twenties when she would have enjoyed a night like tonight, but getting wasted held no allure for her these days. She didn't need the hassle of a horrible hangover to add to her financial woes. What was it going to take for Bryan to sit down and discuss their financial situation? It wasn't dire yet, but it was heading that way.

She walked along towards the Matt Talbot Bridge, saw a taxi with its light on and flagged it down. She gave her address and slumped into the seat, hoping the taxi driver wasn't a chatty one. She wasn't in the humour. Fortunately, she was in luck and he was as disinclined to talk as she was, so she settled back for the journey, tired and disheartened. What a day it had been. It had started out so well, until her name had been picked to visit Judith. Then it had all gone downhill.

Bryan had been well on the way to being pissed by the time she got to Farringtons and hadn't wanted to hear about her trials with her boss, or to discuss their lack of finance. Even though she'd had a few drinks, it hadn't taken the edge off her, as it usually did. It was one of those nights when alcohol had no effect, so there was no point in sticking with it. She didn't want to do drugs. She didn't like the effect they had on her. Bryan would be annoyed with her for leaving the party early, but let him. She was just as annoyed with him for the amount of money he'd spent tonight.

It was after one thirty and she was knackered. She'd worry about everything tomorrow, she decided as the taxi pulled up outside her door a short while later. She was meeting her mother in Meadows & Byrne – that would be something to look forward to. She paid the taxi driver, let herself in and left a light on in the hall for Bryan, if he came home. Knowing him, he'd kip on Kev's sofa.

Debbie didn't even switch on the bedroom light, just undressed and let her clothes fall to the floor. Her bed welcomed her, and she snuggled under the soft, Egyptian-cotton sheets, one of their wedding presents, and stretched luxuriously, yawning her head off. She was asleep in minutes.

'Kev, trust me – it's the way to go, mate. Rent a loft space, have it all brilliant white and sharp angles – and orchids, definitely orchids.' Bryan stabbed his finger in the air for emphasis. 'High-class lighting, I could sort that. It would be the perfect space to hang cutting-edge art . . . our own gallery, mate, just think of it. We could do photographic exhibitions in one section. We saw some terrific exhibitions in NY. I got great ideas while I was there. I just need a backer, y'know. I could remortgage the house for collateral, but I'd need someone else on board. Someone who appreciated art, just like you do.'

'Yaw, sounds cool. Let's keep it in mind, dude.' Kev passed the spliff they were sharing back to him. Bryan took it, inhaled deeply and held. This was the life: friends who appreciated what he was about. Friends who were enthusiastic about his plans. He'd never felt so laidback in his life. All his dreams were about to take shape. Kevin Devlin was loaded. He was a whizzkid in financial services, working in the same building as Bryan and earning huge bonuses. He drove a Jag and always had a beautiful blonde on his arm. His family was in the drinks business. They owned pubs and wine bars all over the city, including one in Temple Bar. Bryan envied him his wealth and affluent lifestyle. He actually owned this penthouse outright. There was no mortgage on it. That would be him and Debbs some time in the future, Bryan thought woozily. Living in a riverfront penthouse with no mortgage, throwing hip and happening parties. He hadn't even noticed that Debbie had left the party hours ago. His eyes drooped, and his head flopped down to his chest.

'You go for a little sleep there, dude, but give me back my spliff.' Kev grabbed the joint from him.

'It's mine, actually – I paid for it, and the last lot of coke,' Bryan muttered, before passing out on his friend's soft Italian-leather sofa.

CHAPTER ELEVEN

On way 2 Meadows & Byrne 2 meet D around ten. C

Barry read Connie's text as he sat in his dressing gown on the wraparound balcony drinking a mug of tea. The wind had died down from the previous day, and the early morning sun shone over a pearly, flat, calm sea. Faint wisps of fog hugged the hill of Howth, and only the cawing of the seagulls disturbed the peace around him.

Barry inhaled deeply, drawing the tangy salt-flavoured air into his lungs. This was his favourite time at the weekend. Winding down, enjoying the vista from the balcony, having two whole days away from the office, with time to read the paper from cover to cover or get in a game of golf or a walk on the pier with Melissa. Then dinner and drinks with friends in a good restaurant, or as guests at the various dinner parties they were invited to.

Years ago, Aimee would join him in his recreational activities but, nowadays, after a lie-in, she spent much of her time catching up on emails or working out in the gym, and they'd only get together if they were going out socializing. Certainly, in the past year, as she had become immersed in work, their time together had waned. It would be nice having coffee with Connie and Debbie. Enjoyable and companionable . . . like a real family at last.

He finished his tea and went inside and put his mug in the dishwasher. The cleaner had been the previous day, and the kitchen gleamed. The sunlight glinted on the stainless-steel taps and drainer. It could have been a kitchen in the pages of an interior-design magazine. They'd spent a fortune getting a new state-of-the-art kitchen installed, but the irony was that Aimee was rarely in it, even though she was the one who'd pushed to get it. Barry had been perfectly happy with the kitchen they'd had previously. It was a showhouse kitchen and more than adequate for their needs. But Aimee had been to a dinner party too many and seen too many upgraded kitchens and had to have one herself, despite the fact that, these days, she rarely did more than pour herself a glass of wine or make herself a cup of coffee in it. Whatever cooking was done, he did it. Otherwise, they lived out of the Butler's Pantry and Donnybrook Fair. Just as well they were both earning hefty salaries; it was an expensive way to eat, he thought wryly, as he ambled down the hall to wake Melissa.

His younger daughter was already propped up against her pillows, busy texting. He shook his head when he saw her, tousled head bent, fingers flying across the keys. Kids these days were superglued to their phones. He'd heard a psychologist on the radio talking about how youngsters were texting late at night and, as well as suffering sleep deprivation, were often being bullied by phone. He should take that damn phone away from her at night. But that wouldn't go down too well.

'You know, you shouldn't be recharging that phone in your room at night. I read somewhere it's not good for you. All those electromagnetic rays and things, they fry your brain,' he said mildly, sitting at the side of her bed and ruffling her hair.

'Oh, Dad.' She threw her eyes up to heaven.

'I mean it. It's really not good for you. I hope you don't sleep with it under your pillow like Madonna does.'

'She's like *sooo* your generation, Dad. Trying to be cool,' his daughter scoffed.

'So who's cool?' he teased, a tad miffed at her superior dismissal of his Madonna fandom. 'Amy Winehouse with a bird's nest on her head? Now her brains *are* fried.'

'Yeah, but she's legend. She can really sing. *No, no, no.*' Melissa hummed 'Rehab', the song so familiar that even he knew it.

'Are you coming for our Saturday cup of coffee with your old, uncool dad?' he asked lightly, hoping she'd say yes. Lately, she hadn't been so eager to accompany him on his Saturday-morning jaunt to get the paper and coffee and doughnuts.

'You're not old,' she said stoutly, and that made

him feel even worse, that she felt she had to reassure him about his age. Barry sighed. Middle age was the pits. Fifty plus. Invisible to women. As high as he was going to go on the career ladder. A Madonna fan. That about summed him up right now.

'Well, come on. It's a lovely day, let's have our coffee al fresco opposite the yacht club.'

'OK.' She grinned at him, the sprinkling of freckles across her nose so similar to Debbie's, and so endearing.

'That's my girl,' he said heartily, leaning over to kiss the top of her head. He wanted to tell her how much he loved her. How much he feared losing her, as she grew older, when coffee with her dad would be a chore and not a pleasure. He wanted to tell her how lonely he would be when she flew the nest. Hell, he was lonely already, he thought with dismay, wondering would relations with Aimee ever thaw, or would she keep up the brittle façade a lot longer.

Aimee never told him she loved him these days. She never showed much interest either in what went on in his business, when once she'd been full of enthusiasm and suggestions. She was so completely consumed with her own career now; she might as well be on another planet. Even their sex life, which had always been pretty satisfying, had dwindled over the past few months.

Was this how Connie had felt all those years ago when he'd withdrawn from her and their marriage? He'd treated her pretty shabbily, when he looked back on it. She was a very forgiving woman and one he'd taken for granted. She was going out of her way for him this morning so that he could bring Melissa to 'bump into' Debbie. He was glad he'd bought the little painting of Greystones Harbour for her. It was a pity he couldn't give it to her today but they were supposed to be meeting by chance and, besides, he could hardly present Connie with a gift in front of Melissa, just in case it got back to Aimee, who would be less than pleased to hear that he was giving his ex-wife presents, particularly with the frostiness between them since the wedding. It would take a miracle to dissolve that. He'd give it to her when she came back from her holidays, and he'd tell her how very grateful he was to her.

'Right, Muffin, I'm just going to have a quick shower. Be ready in ten.'

'OK, Dad,' Melissa agreed distractedly, head bent to read a reply to the text she'd just sent. At that age, friends were far, far more important than parents, he acknowledged, leaving her to her phone and heading for the shower.

Aimee was still fast asleep, her face, flushed pink, half hidden by her hair. Even in sleep she looked worried and stressed, as if her dreams were fraught. She was going to have to step back and chill a bit, or she'd burn out, but how did you tell a driven, ambitious, successful woman that? She'd only accuse him of sour grapes or of being sexist, or something in that vein.

How the world had changed, and how the roles

had been reversed, he reflected, stepping under the powerful jets of water. Or was this what came of marrying a woman a good deal younger than himself? Was this second-marriage syndrome just about him, or did other men in similar circumstances feel the same way? He should set up a club, the Second Husbands' Club. Now, wouldn't that be interesting, he grinned, as he soaped himself and let the steaming water sluice over him and wished that he had a hot, horny woman to share the shower with.

Meet u in the People's Park l8r just have 2 go 4 coffee with Dad, Melissa texted Sarah.

Can't meet u until afternoon, have 2 clean bedroom, have visitors coming. Mam on rampage like a volcano. All hell going 2 break loose if my sis doesn't get out of bed soon. U'll probably hear her yelling in yrs, came the dejected response.

Ok. Stay calm. c u when I c u, Melissa texted back and put away her phone and hurried into the shower. She stank, she thought, sniffing under her arms. She needed to shave. She ran the razor over her skin and winced when she cut too close. Her mom got her underarms waxed, but Melissa had tried it once and howled with pain and never went back to have it done again.

She wasn't really in the humour to go and have coffee with her dad. She was beginning to find their Saturday morning ritual a little boring, especially now that she wasn't eating junk food as much, but she knew her father looked forward to this time with her, and he was a very kind father, she had to admit. Much kinder than her mother. She scowled, remembering her Rock & Republic jeans. Her mother was far stricter than her father and always had been.

Melissa showered quickly and dressed in a pair of jeans and a black T-shirt. The jeans were pleasingly loose around her waist, and the T-shirt didn't make her arms look chubby any more. She slipped into a pair of new, red, chunky wedges which she'd bought a few days ago but hadn't worn yet, and stood in front of the mirror twirling around as best she could on them, admiring her new, improved shape. She'd lost nine pounds since the wedding, and it was deeply, deeply satisfying. Her stomach was rumbling, and she was starving, but she'd only have a regular coffee with no sugar or milk and definitely no doughnut. The coffee would keep her going until she met Sarah later, and she could have a smoothie and coffee for lunch. A thought struck her. She'd need her purse out of her bumbag. She'd given the bag to her mother to mind at her gran's art exhibition the previous night after the strap had broken.

Melissa clumped down the hall, not yet used to her new footwear, and slipped into her parents' bedroom. Her dad was still in the ensuite, and she stared around, looking for Aimee's handbag. She was just edging past the end of the big bed when she tripped over one of her father's shoes and staggered, jolting the bed.

'For God's sake, Melissa, would you watch where you're going? I'm trying to have a lie-in,' her mother snapped irritably, gazing at Melissa through heavy-lidded eyes. 'What are you looking for?'

'Sorry, Mom,' apologized Melissa hastily. 'I just wanted to get my purse out of my bumbag.' She grabbed Aimee's handbag, opened it and looked puzzled, as she saw no sign of her little red bag.

'It's in the Prada, not the Louis Vuitton,' Aimee said blearily.

'Oh, right, thanks,' Melissa murmured. She turned to see where the other bag was and caught her heel in the valance, tottering like a marionette as she fought to regain her balance.

'Will you take those shoes *off*? You can't walk in them!' Aimee exclaimed, exasperated, as Melissa landed in a heap on the floor and the contents of the bag went flying.

'What's going on?' Barry emerged from the ensuite, rubbing aftershave into his jaw.

'I tripped,' Melissa said plaintively.

'She can't walk in those ridiculous shoes,' Aimee retorted, yawning as she brushed her hair away from her face. 'It's the first Saturday I've had a chance for a lie-in for ages, but it's impossible to have one in this madhouse.' She couldn't hide her irritability. 'Pick that stuff up, and go away and leave me in peace, the pair of you.'

'Go back asleep,' Barry said calmly, hauling his daughter up off the floor and bending back down to pick up the scattered contents of his wife's bag.

He did a double take when he saw the long, narrow, rectangular box. 'What's this?' He looked at his wife in astonishment, holding it up.

'Pregnancy test kit,' Melissa read out helpfully. And her jaw dropped. 'Oh my God, Mom! Are you *pregnant*?' she exclaimed, in absolute horror.

CHAPTER TWELVE

Jesus, Mary and Joseph, this can't be happening. Aimee gazed at her husband aghast as her heart began to hammer against her ribcage. She knew by the heat that suffused her cheeks that she was puce with guilt.

'Are you pregnant? Well, that explains a lot,' Barry said slowly, staring intently at her. 'Is that why you've been in such bad . . . er . . . ?' He'd been going to say, 'in such bad form,' but he stopped himself. 'Um . . . Looking peaky before you put your make-up on? I heard you being sick one morning, but you said it was a bug. Why didn't you tell me, or when were you going to mention it?'

'I . . . I . . .' she stuttered uncharacteristically, completely thrown.

'Oh, Mom, you and Dad . . . uugg! How majorly uncool.' Melissa wrinkled her nose at the thought of her parents having sex.

'Look, I thought I was, but I don't think I am. OK?' Aimee struggled to regain control of the situation.

187

'Well, do the test then . . . duh!' her daughter said with exaggerated condescension. Aimee felt like slapping her.

'There's no need. Just go away and leave me alone. I'm tired,' she ordered.

Barry shot her a look, and his eyes narrowed as comprehension began to dawn. She could see it in his eyes, the realization that she hadn't been going to tell him, the realization that perhaps she'd been going to do something untoward.

'Yeah, why not do it now? Either you are or you're not,' he said, quietly challenging, and eye-balled her.

'Come on, Mom. I want to see how it works,' Melissa urged, whipping the packet from her father and giving it to Aimee, who nearly had a heart attack. She was really trapped now, she thought in panic. How *could* she refuse to do the test? Barry would cop what she was planning, if he hadn't copped already.

'Come on, share the news with us, seeing as we're all here,' Barry persisted.

'Are you going to watch me pee?' she snapped, unable to bite back the sharp retort.

'Do I need to?'

There it was: the unspoken accusation. He knew what she'd been planning. They stared at each other. *Stop bullying me*, she wanted to shout. *I will do this when I want to. When I choose to.*

'Aw, come on, Mom,' Melissa begged, oblivious to the tension between her parents. 'Can I watch the lines turning blue? If it's a boy, I'll go mental. '

'It doesn't matter what *our* child is, as long as it's healthy.' Barry stared at her. 'Isn't that right, Aimee?'

'Yeah,' she said, defeated. She got out of bed and went into the bathroom with the package, closing the door firmly behind her. If Melissa hadn't been there, Barry would probably have insisted on going in. Aimee sank on to the toilet seat and put her head in her hands. Would ordinary water work on it, she wondered in panic. But wasn't it the hormone in the urine that caused the line to go blue? Could she let it fall down the loo? She was desperate for options. She knew she was grasping at straws. Knowing her husband, he'd probably go out and buy half a dozen kits until she did it properly. Barry would know if she fudged it. He was clearly suspicious already. He knew her so well, she thought in despair.

She could argue with him about her right to go for a termination. And she would. She could tell Melissa that she'd miscarried. Her daughter's reaction to her mother's possible pregnancy had been far from encouraging. Maybe it was better this way, she reflected, staring at the kit in her hand. At least she wouldn't have to carry the burden of her decision alone. Barry could stand by her or not. That would be *his* decision to make.

Resigned, she tore the wrapping off the wand, lifted up the toilet seat and sat down ready to pee. Her stomach was churning and her throat was dry. Seeing her pregnancy confirmed would be a jolt.

Even though in her heart and soul she knew she *was* pregnant, without the test to confirm it she'd had some small comfort that maybe she wasn't, that perhaps it was only her imagination.

Melissa was knocking on the door. 'Bring it out. Can I see the line changing colour?'

'Hold on,' exclaimed Aimee tetchily as she positioned the scarifying instrument which brought untold joy to hundreds of thousands and untold misery to just as many more.

It seemed as though time slowed and all she could hear was the steady flow of her urine, as loud in her ears as Niagara Falls. Tears smarted her eyes. She was a grown adult. What right had her husband and daughter to be standing outside, like the police waiting on a criminal? She should have refused point blank to take the test and told them she'd do it in her own time. How *dare* Barry treat her in such an authoritative manner? He was as bad as her father, she thought in fury, and she knew she'd never forgive him for making her feel like an impotent little girl again. She laid the damp wand on the sink and wiped her eyes with some loo roll. She wouldn't let them see her crying.

She flushed the loo, washed her hands and wiped the wand dry and, head up, shoulders back, she walked back into the bedroom. Barry was staring out the window, and Melissa was sitting on the end of the bed. She handed her daughter the wand. 'Look for two blue lines if it's positive. One if it's negative,' she instructed flatly, and got into bed

190

again. She was staying there for the day, she decided.

'Oooohhh!' squealed Melissa. 'It's starting to turn. Ohmigod, ohmigod, Mom, this is nerve-wracking.'

Aimee almost puked she was so tense. What if, by some miracle, it was negative, she thought wildly. Would the gods be that kind to her? Barry would be going for the snip whatever happened, she decided viciously. That was, if he wanted a sex life. Right now, the way she felt, if she never saw a dick again it wouldn't bother her in the slightest. And that was saying something for a woman who, until the last year or so, had always thoroughly enjoyed sex.

'Oh yikes! It's very faint, but it's getting stronger.' Melissa gave a running commentary, completely engrossed in the process, eyes glued to the slender white rod.

Stop. Please, please stop, Aimee pleaded silently. This was torture. She slanted a glance at Barry. He was granite-faced. He knew she was pregnant. He didn't need to wait for the results.

'Mom, there's two – look, look.' Melissa thrust the tester under Aimee's nose. The two blue lines were unmistakable.

'I can see it,' she murmured.

'Look, Dad, look.' Melissa got off the bed and teetered over to him, waving the stick triumphantly.

Barry studied it in silence. 'When do you think you're due?' he said finally.

'Mid-January.' She shrugged.

'Oh, Mom, does this mean we can't go skiing?

Bad buzz, Mom. Everyone in the class is going skiing. God, it's going to be so weird having a brother or sister fourteen years younger than me. Don't forget – I'm fourteen next month.'

'How could I forget that?' Aimee arched an eyebrow at her.

'You're not that far gone yet, then?' Barry said.

'No, only a few weeks.' She lay back against her pillows, white-faced with stress. 'I think I'll try and go back asleep. Are you going for coffee?'

'Yes. Can we bring you back anything?' he asked politely, as if he were talking to a stranger.

She shook her head, turned over and pulled up the sheet around her shoulders.

'Are you feeling sick, Mom? Have you got morning sickness?' Melissa asked kindly, tucking her in.

A lump the size of a golfball lodged in Aimee's throat at her daughter's unexpected sympathy. 'Yes, I feel very sick,' she said forlornly, and then she was crying, great big, heaving sobs that shook her slender body.

Barry stopped in his tracks and turned back as Melissa put her arms around her mother. 'Don't cry, Mom,' she said helplessly. 'Please don't cry. I'll help you. I didn't mean to moan about skiing, honest.' It was so rare for Aimee to cry. Unheard of almost. She didn't like to see her mother showing any sign of fragility.

'Go back asleep, Aimee. We'll talk about everything later.' Barry's tone was softer, and he patted her shoulder awkwardly. 'Stop crying. Everything will be fine.'

No, it won't be. It's a disaster for me and nobody cares, she wanted to yell, but she was very conscious of her daughter staring anxiously down at her.

'It's just hormones.' Aimee managed to compose herself. 'Go and have your coffee, and enjoy it, darling.' She squeezed Melissa's hand but couldn't bring herself to look at her husband. He had laid claim to the child within her, and Aimee knew her needs were of secondary importance to him now. She was back to being a second-class citizen, just as she had been all the years under her father's roof. Even Barry, the man she had trusted most in her life to be her champion, had let her down.

'See you later, Mom. Don't worry about anything.' Melissa leaned down and kissed Aimee's cheek, her blue eyes dark and round with anxiety.

'Thanks, darling. Don't forget your purse,' she reminded.

'Oh yeah, thanks, Mom.' Melissa picked up her purse, the cause of the whole episode in the first place. Aimee sighed with relief when they left the room and she was blessedly alone. She heard Melissa *clop-clop* down the wooden-floored hall, and then sweet silence descended on the penthouse when she heard the front door close behind them.

She and Barry would have to talk big time. Maybe if she told him about her job offer, he might be more understanding of how much an unwanted pregnancy and an unwanted child would be a calamity for her. It might help him understand why she wanted a termination. If he didn't, and he insisted on her going through with the pregnancy, their marriage was over, she vowed.

And, if she did stick to her guns and go and have a termination, it would be the end of them from his point of view. Whatever they decided, one of them was going to be the loser. Aimee lay wide-eyed and tense, shocked beyond belief that her hitherto almost perfect life had turned into a complete and absolute disaster.

CHAPTER THIRTEEN

Connie strolled out of the Dart station at Dun Laoghaire and walked up to the traffic lights at the junction. She glanced across the road towards Meadows & Byrne to the block of apartments where Barry lived. It was a great location, everything on his doorstep, and it suited him down to the ground. He particularly hated gardening, she remembered. She'd miss her garden too much to live in an apartment. Her garden was her private little heaven.

She was early and there weren't many people about, so she ambled around Meadows & Byrne in comfort, admiring the china and kitchenware, wishing she could win the lottery. It was eight million tonight, she reminded herself, she must buy a ticket on the way home. Cutting back her working hours would mean less money, but she had paid off her mortgage two years ago, and Debbie's wedding was over, so she'd be fine, she assured herself, as she watched a woman place a half-dozen expensive scented candles into her basket. How wonderful it must be to be able to spend without regard to cost.

She'd never had that luxury and, unless she won the Lotto, it was unlikely that she ever would. She decided to splurge on a cappuccino while waiting for Debbie. She headed outside and sat in the morning sunlight with it, loving the warm rays on her face. She couldn't wait for her holiday in Spain with Karen. She badly needed it. This was the first Saturday in ages that she hadn't had to work, and Connie felt a delicious sense of lazy wellbeing infuse her as she opened her paper and perused the clues in the crossword.

Debbie stretched and yawned and glanced at the clock on her bedside locker. She sat up in shock. 'Bloody hell,' she exclaimed, realizing that it was quarter to ten and she was supposed to be meeting her mother in Dun Laoghaire around ten.

She shook her head to try and clear it and then noticed that Bryan was not in the bed beside her. Her face darkened. He mustn't have come home – or was he downstairs asleep on the sofa?

She scrambled out of bed and hurried down, but she could see through the half-open door into their small lounge that Bryan wasn't there. He must have stayed in Kevin's apartment. Their first weekend home, and her husband couldn't even be bothered to spend it with her. It was typical of Bryan to go spending wildly whenever he felt his responsibilities were crowding in on him. The more he owed, the less he was inclined to cut his costs. It was all right for Kevin Devlin to spend a fortune on champagne and drugs, he was on mega bucks; she and Bryan were earning a pittance in comparison.

She raced back upstairs and hurried into the shower. At least she didn't have a hangover, she comforted herself. Bryan would be wasted. She didn't expect to see him until much later in the afternoon. There was no point in losing her cool with him; he'd feel she was trying to clip his wings, and he never reacted well to that sort of pressure, as she well knew, remembering with a shudder how he'd called off the wedding with just weeks to go, until she'd calmed him down by taking him to Amsterdam for a weekend break. Bryan hated being restrained, but a reality check was going to have to set in sooner rather than later. She didn't want to be a nag, she wasn't his mother, but the facts had to be faced – and so did the mess that was their bedroom, she thought ruefully, wrapping a towel around her and rooting in her wardrobe for something to wear.

She was going to breakfast with Connie, and then come home and attack the washing. If she didn't get on top of it this weekend, they were in trouble. It was a pity she hadn't put a wash in last night; she could have hung it out. It was a fine day. Debbie frowned as she parted clothes-laden hangers crammed together. Was Bryan right? Was she turning into a housewife? Was she becoming dull and boring? His view was that they should get out and about and live life and not worry about housework, but if she didn't do any washing, neither of them would have clean clothes to wear the following week, and if she didn't sort out their bedroom, they soon wouldn't be able to get into it.

She dried herself quickly and pulled on a pair of black cut-offs, a white sleeveless vest top and a pink hoodie. Ten minutes to wash and dress – not bad, she congratulated herself – twisting her hair into a scrunchie and running a trace of lipstick across her mouth. She sprayed some Burberry on to her wrists and neck, grabbed her bag and left her tip of a bedroom without even making her bed. She didn't have time anyway, she didn't want to keep her mother waiting too long, she assuaged her guilt as she locked the front door and hurried towards the Dart. She was dying for a cup of coffee and looking forward to seeing Connie.

She was in luck when she got to the station; there was a train due in three minutes and it was only a couple of stops to Dun Laoghaire. She climbed the bridge to cross to the opposite platform and checked her phone to see was there any message from Bryan. She wasn't really expecting one. He'd probably taken something to bring him down from his coke high, because he'd been in flying form when she left, his eyes glittering, mannerisms more exaggerated as he worked the room. She hated it when he did drugs. She was always petrified that he'd get bad stuff and end up in A&E. He'd taken a bad hit once and puked for hours after it. It had put her off taking drugs again, but not Bryan. If Connie knew they dabbled, she'd go mad. Connie had no time for drugs; she'd nursed enough patients whose lives had been destroyed by them. If her mother asked where he was, she'd say he'd gone into work to collect the car, which wouldn't be a fib, she decided, stepping into the train and taking a seat on the side where she would be able to see the sea once they passed the Merrion Gates.

It would be wonderful to have a sea view, she thought wistfully a few minutes later as the train emerged on to the shoreline and she admired the spectacular sweep of the sun-drenched coast, with Dun Laoghaire in the distance. She remembered the magnificent view from Judith Baxter's hospital window and wondered had her words had any effect on her boss, or was it water off a duck's back? Once Judith came back to work, her life would be a misery, Debbie thought despondently. Even though she'd sent a half-hearted apology via Ciara, Judith was the type who held grudges, and she'd never forgive Debbie's impertinence for calling her a bully.

Don't think about it now. Worry about it when she comes back, Debbie told herself sternly. She had enough worries on her plate about Bryan and their debts without worrying about Judith Baxter.

Judith drifted in and out of drowsy, drugged sleep. Something had happened; she couldn't quite remember what. It seemed a long time ago. She'd been shouting and crying, and then she'd had an injection and gone into dark oblivion. She'd vaguely realized it was morning when the sunlight slanted into the room. She'd been given tea and toast. Was it breakfast? Or lunch? She didn't know. She was so tired, so utterly, utterly tired. Her mouth was dry, and her tongue felt thick and furry. A nurse came quietly into the room and took her pulse and temperature. Judith watched her through lead-lidded eyes, trying to remember where she was and what was wrong with her.

'How are you feeling now, Judith?' the nurse asked kindly.

'Not so good,' Judith said heavily. 'Strange.' It was an effort to talk. She wanted to close her eyes and go back asleep, but she was troubled. Something had definitely happened, but she couldn't focus on her thoughts, couldn't penetrate the fog that smothered her brain.

'That's all right, that's just the effect of the sedation we've given you. Why don't you go back asleep until the registrar does his rounds? He's running late this morning.'

'Yes, yes I will,' murmured Judith, and closed her eyes. The nurse wrote something in the chart and glided out as silently as she'd entered, checking to see that the No Visitors sign was in place on the door. Judith had been doing quite well until yesterday; whatever had upset her had had a big impact. Until she'd had some psychological assessment, she'd be sedated. If the poor woman was talking about a failed suicide attempt, there was no point in curing her physically without sorting her out mentally. The nurse felt sorry for Judith's mother.

Lily Baxter had been very upset on the phone the previous evening, wondering what was wrong with her daughter. The nurse had suggested that perhaps she should give visiting a miss for a day or two, but the elderly woman had been adamant. She was coming in to see her daughter, and that was that. No Visitors sign notwithstanding.

'I've had enough of this carry-on, Saint Francis. If you're going to make life hard for me and Judith, I won't be saying that prayer of yours,' Lily grumbled as she washed up her cup and saucer. 'She was doing fine until I started saying it, and I'm very vexed.

'Oh, what are you wasting your time talking to him for, he's not going to answer you,' she said crossly, shaking her fist at the marmalade tabby who stared insolently in at her from his favourite perch on the dividing wall between her neighbour's house and her own. That cat thought he owned her garden, and the stink of him as he marched around spraying was an added insult. Of course, Saint Francis liked the horrible creatures. That said a lot about *him*. Lily was not in good form and had to vent her spleen on someone.

What on earth had happened between her leaving Judith the previous afternoon, and 7 p.m. that evening, when Lily had had a phone call from Cecily to say that Judith was crying and in hysterics and she had been asked to leave? It was very strange and unsettling, and Lily was feeling disheartened and fearful. It wasn't like Judith to be hysterical. The last time Lily had seen her daughter cry had been at Ted's funeral, and that was a long time ago. With furrowed brow, Lily finished tidying up the kitchen before going to get ready to visit her daughter. It was early, and she didn't generally visit until the afternoon, but Lily didn't care. She wanted to see her daughter. Besides, Judith was a private patient, and they weren't at all strict about visiting times in the hospital. She would just slip in as unobtrusively as possible.

The traffic was light, as it was the weekend, and she caught a bus within ten minutes. She felt tense and apprehensive as the almost empty bus raced along the bus lanes. Her heart was palpitating agitatedly as she finally made her way along the now-familiar corridor to Judith's small room. No one took any notice of her. Nurses, doctors, white-coated lab technicians, none gave her a second glance. The No Visitors sign on the door brought her up short. *I'm not a visitor, I'm her mother*, she thought, with a spark of defiance. She opened the door and saw the huddle of her daughter's form under the bedclothes, curled foetus-like and turned towards the window.

Lily felt her old tormentors, fear and apprehension, assail her. This was not the time for her to be weak. 'Saint Francis, help me to comfort and console my poor Judith,' she prayed solemnly as she stole around the bed and pulled the chair up close to her daughter. Judith was as pale as candle wax. She opened her eyes, and Lily could see they were dull and drugged. 'I'm here,' Lily said. 'Don't worry about anything. Everything is going to be sorted. I've been to the bank to see Mr Long. He's made a very good suggestion, but not a word now to anybody, mind. He wants me to get your name put on the deeds of the house, and then he's going to give you a loan for a mortgage. As soon as you're well you can start looking for a place of your own. Won't that be wonderful? Something to look forward to. You'd like a place of your own, wouldn't you? And it's right you should have one.' Lily peered worriedly at her daughter, wondering had anything she'd said penetrated through the drugged haze.

Wordlessly, Judith reached out and took her mother's hand and gave it a weak squeeze before her eyes closed again and she drifted back to sleep.

It was enough for Lily. Courage renewed, she placed her daughter's hand back under the sheet and took out her knitting.

'Maybe we should go back and see is Mom OK?' Melissa suggested as Barry paid for his *Irish Times* and tucked it under his arm.

'I think she's probably better off on her own for a while. She's tired and she needs to catch up on her sleep. She's been very busy lately.' Barry gave her a quizzical look. 'So! What do you think of this baby business then?'

'It's a real shock,' admitted Melissa. 'I bet it's a

mega shock to Mom. I wouldn't think she wanted a new baby after all this time, would you?'

'Well, these things happen. We just have to adapt.' He sidestepped the question.

'That's probably why she's so cranky lately. She takes the nose off me for no reason at all,' Melissa said mournfully.

'Me, too. We'll just have to make allowances,' Barry advised.

'I wonder will it be a boy or a girl? Where's it going to sleep? Not in my room, I hope. It'll have to go into the guest room.' Melissa tucked her arm into her father's as they headed for the seafront. She suddenly remembered that it was seriously uncool even to let on you liked your father and hastily removed her arm, pretending to close the zip on her purse. She'd just seen two girls from her class on the other side of the street and was mightily relieved that they hadn't seen her.

'Don't worry. Your room is safe,' Barry assured his daughter, hardly able to believe that they were having this conversation. It was ages since he and Aimee had had sex. It must have been that sleepy quickie in the middle of the night a few weeks before the wedding. Or – was it his child? The thought flashed across his mind, and his jaw dropped. *Oh, don't be a bastard*, he thought, disgusted with himself.

'Well, by the time it's my age, I'll probably be married or living in my own place, so it won't matter,' Melissa declared, airily bringing him back to earth.

'Good God! You'll be twenty-eight, and I'll be in my mid-sixties.' Barry was utterly shocked. It was only just beginning to dawn on him what a seismic shift this was going to make to their lives. No wonder Aimee was distraught. He felt a frisson of sympathy for his wife, which tempered the anger that was bubbling inside. He was certain by now that his wife hadn't been going to tell him that she was pregnant. She was planning on getting rid of it. He'd seen the guilt in her eyes when he'd held up the test kit and asked her if she was pregnant. She'd blushed puce, something he'd never, in all the years he'd been with her, seen her do. She hadn't been able to hold his gaze. It had been like a kick in the solar plexus, that realization that his child, his son or daughter, was to be got rid of and he would never have known anything about it.

How could she do that to him? Hadn't she even considered the fact that he was entitled to know and have a say in deciding if his child lived or died? Was her damn career so important that it was all that mattered in this?

Yes, having a child would be a huge upheaval in their lives, but that was no reason to shirk their moral responsibilities. What an irony, he thought ruefully. When Connie had miscarried their second child, he couldn't have been more relieved and she'd been the one who was devastated. Now it was Aimee who would welcome a miscarriage, and he would be the one who was upset. So much for his lip service to a mother's right to choose. It was a

205

different kettle of fish when the father had no choice, he admitted. The truth was, he had always wanted another child with Aimee. He'd loved parenting Melissa and realized he was good at it. He wanted her to have a sibling. But, as the years had passed and Aimee had refused outright to consider it, he'd let go of the notion. But, now, even though the timing was not favourable, he wasn't as thrown by it as Aimee was. He had made such a mess of things with Debbie. Now, it was as if the universe had forgiven him and was giving him another chance.

He suddenly remembered the meeting he'd planned for his daughters this morning. In the whole drama of the pregnancy test he'd completely forgotten the arrangement he'd made with Connie.

A hasty glance at his watch showed him that it was ten twenty, just a little later than planned, he thought in relief. They rounded the corner of Meadows & Byrne, and he saw Connie at a table outside, head bent, engrossed in her paper. Barry's heart lifted at the sight of her. Connie would never have gone behind his back in something as important as this. To think he'd been foolish enough and immature enough, years ago, to think that Aimee, with her hungry ambition and strong independent streak, was someone his ex-wife could have done with emulating. What a fool he'd been, he thought bitterly, remembering the look in his current wife's eyes when he'd challenged her to take the pregnancy test there and then. They'd been having a real low in their marriage these past few months, but nothing had prepared him for this scenario. What would happen if things went even further downhill? This time, he wouldn't be able to run away to America, the way he had on Connie. This time, there was nowhere to run.

Connie was engrossed in her crossword, her cappuccino almost finished, when she heard a familiar voice say, 'Look, Melissa, there's Connie.' She looked up to see her ex-husband and his daughter walking in her direction.

'Well, hello,' she smiled, pretending it was a big surprise.

'Hi, Connie,' Melissa smiled back at her. 'How's Miss Hope?'

Connie laughed. 'You say that every time we meet. She's fine and lazy, sunning herself in the garden when I was leaving. Hi, Barry.' She looked up at her ex, noting that he looked stressed and tired. To her surprise, he leaned down and kissed her cheek. 'Hi, Connie, what a nice surprise. What are you doing here?' He played his part perfectly.

'Well, I'm supposed to be meeting Debbie to look at some furniture, but she's running a little late so I decided to treat myself to a cappuccino,' Connie explained.

'We were just going to have a coffee ourselves – would you mind if we joined you?'

'Not at all,' she said warmly. 'Is that OK with you,

Melissa, or did you want to go somewhere else?' Connie asked the teenager.

'No, this is cool. Will Debbie be long?'

'Shouldn't be. I got a text to say she was on a Dart, so she should be here in the next five minutes.'

'Random. Just a regular coffee for me, Dad, please.'

'What? No mocha?' He looked at her in surprise.

'No, just coffee please.'

'And a doughnut of course?'

'No thanks. Just coffee. I'm on a diet,' she murmured.

'You look very well, Melissa, you've dropped a few pounds. Well done for staying off the junk. I wish I could.' Connie sighed.

'You look great,' Barry assured her. 'Will you have another cappuccino?'

'Ah, what the hell. Why not?' laughed Connie, thinking how nice it was to spend a Saturday morning sipping cappuccinos with extended family. It was a good thing that Melissa had gone into the church on the day of the wedding, before the confrontation with Aimee had occurred, or she might not have been so friendly, and it would have made things very awkward. Connie felt a little sorry for Barry. It must be a bit like walking on eggshells for him at times, having two families to contend with.

'Here's Debbie,' Melissa pointed out, waving shyly at her half-sister, who was hurrying along the footpath.

A look of surprise crossed Debbie's face as she caught sight of the three of them. 'Well, hi, what's all this? A family gathering?' she said a little breathlessly, coming to a halt beside the table. 'Sorry I was a bit late, Mum,' she apologized to Connie, leaning down to give her a kiss.

'I was having a cappuccino while I was waiting for you, and who came along but Barry and Melissa, bound for an early coffee too, so I said I'd have another one with them. But if you're in a hurry we can head off,' she said easily, not wanting it to look too staged.

'Aw, don't do that,' Barry exclaimed, shooting her a glance of dismay.

'No, no, it's fine.' Debbie sat down. 'I'm gasping for a cup of coffee.'

'Latte, cappuccino, mocha, regular? Let me get it,' Barry said, smiling at Connie, noting how well her strategy had worked.

'Latte, please.'

'And a doughnut?' he urged.

'Oh, yes please.' She grinned at Melissa, who was smiling back, delighted to see her big sister. 'Hi Melissa, how's life?'

'Cool. Have you any photos of the wedding?' she asked eagerly.

'Aw, heck, I have some on a disk, but it's in my other bag, and I have a present for you too,' she added.

'Have you? Savage.' Melissa was chuffed.

'Yeah – if I'd known I was going to bump into

you, I'd have brought it with me. I've one for Dad too.'

'Thanks, Debbie. I appreciate that.' Barry smiled at his daughter, and Connie was glad she'd done as he'd asked. It was very enjoyable sitting having coffee with him and Melissa and, best of all, Debbie was completely relaxed about it.

'So, Mum, you're thinking of buying a new table?' Debbie leaned back in her chair and squinted in the sun as they waited for their order to be delivered.

'Actually, the table I was looking at is gone, and it was an end-of-the-line model,' Connie fibbed. 'So I won't be buying it, unfortunately. It was too late to tell you when I found out. You were already on the Dart. So I've brought yourself and myself on a wild goose chase.'

'Oh, that's a shame.' Debbie made a face. 'Anyway, it's nice to see you for coffee on a Saturday morning. And I'm glad I'm up reasonably early, the house is a shambles and I've a load of washing to do and I haven't even unpacked from America, so I won't stay too long, if you don't mind.'

'No problem, love,' Connie assured her. 'How's Bryan?'

'Oh, fine,' she said nonchalantly. She turned to look at Melissa. 'Hey, how about, if you don't have anything on, coming back with me to the house, and I could give you your present. You can pop back to Dun Laoghaire on the Dart after I show you the photos if you'd like?' she invited.

'Deadly.' Melissa beamed. 'My friend Sarah can't

meet me until later 'cos she's got visitors coming and has to tidy her room, and I've nothing on. Mom's, like, not feeling well, so I guess we won't be doing anything today, so thanks, that would be savage.'

'What's wrong with Aimee?' Connie asked politely.

'You'll never guess.' Melissa rolled her eyes dramatically, unaware of the look of dismay on her father's face as he tried to flash a warning glance at her. 'She's got morning sickness; she, like, just did a pregnancy test. Half an hour ago. It was totally amazing. I watched the lines turning blue. Debbie, you're going to have another half-brother or sister and you're going to be twenty-five years older than it and, by the time it's my age, Dad will be in his mid-sixties, and if you have a baby, our baby will be its aunt or uncle, and it will only be a bit older than it. How random is that?' She rattled on artlessly, completely unaware of the shocked expressions on Debbie and Connie's faces, and the consternation on her father's.

'Melissa, it's a bit early to be telling people, in case anything goes wrong,' he interjected quickly.

'Oh!' his younger daughter said, putting her hand to her mouth. 'Sorry, I wasn't thinking. But Connie and Debbie are family anyway,' she pointed out.

'Don't worry, we won't say anything to anyone,' Connie said, kindly patting her hand. She was astonished by the news. Knowing what she did of Aimee, she suspected a baby would be the last thing the younger woman would want. No wonder Barry looked stressed and distracted. Having a baby around in your mid-fifties was no joke. Aimee would probably go mad if she knew Melissa had spilled the beans to her and Debbie.

'Wow, Dad!' Debbie stared at her father.

'Wow indeed,' he said sheepishly. 'A big surprise all round, you might say.'

'Well, I hope the morning sickness passes soon. Oh, look, here's the coffees,' Connie said diplomatically, bringing an end to the discussion.

'Are you enjoying your hollies?' Debbie took her cue from her mother and changed the subject.

'It's, like, a bit boring sometimes,' Melissa confessed as she took a gulp of coffee. 'My friend Clara has gone to their place in Spain for a month, and Sarah's going to the country next week for a fortnight, so that's a bummer.' She gave a deep sigh.

'Umm . . . well, maybe some evening I could meet you after work, and we could go to the pictures, if you like,' Debbie suggested, licking the doughnut sugar off her fingers.

Connie could have kissed her daughter when she saw the look of pure happiness light up the younger girl's eyes.

'Do you mean it? I'll give you my mobile number, and we can arrange it whenever it suits you,' she said enthusiastically.

'Maybe the two of you might go out to the house when I'm away and just check up on Hope for me. My neighbour is going to feed her, but I'd say she'd love the company,' Connie said casually, not wanting to railroad the half-sisters. They had, after all, only met half a dozen times or so. It was much better for their relationship to evolve at its own pace, and not because she and Barry were pushing them into it.

'Sure,' Debbie agreed easily. 'I'll bring you for a spin in the soft-top. We'll be like Thelma and Louise,' she grinned.

Melissa guffawed at the notion. Riding around in a convertible with her half-sister was a seriously cool scene, and she'd make sure to get Debbie to drive down past the People's Park, where lots of her schoolmates hung out, so that they'd see her. She'd wear her Moschino sunglasses and look ever so sophisticated.

'*That* I must get a photo of,' Barry chuckled, smiling at Connie. This meeting was working out far better than he could ever have hoped for, and it was all thanks to his ex-wife. He felt like kissing her. He'd seen the shock in her face when she'd heard about Aimee's pregnancy. He should have warned Melissa to say nothing, but he'd been in such a heap he hadn't thought of it. Connie had been extremely tactful, changing the subject so easily that Melissa hadn't even noticed. Aimee would go ballistic if she knew that Connie and Debbie knew about the pregnancy. If Melissa was going to go to Debbie's now, it would give him a chance to have a talk with Aimee in private. They were going to have to discuss the matter at some stage. Why not get it over and done with? He was not relishing the prospect.

Connie saw his distracted expression and felt a pang of sympathy for him. Here she was as free as a bird more or less, with only herself to worry about, and he was staring fatherhood in the face. She might be alone and lonely sometimes but, right now, she was glad she wasn't in Aimee's shoes.

'See, they had flash flooding in the south of Spain and torrential rain,' Debbie said wickedly as she finished the last of her doughnut, unaware of the longing glances Melissa was giving it.

'Don't be such a horrible child,' Connie remonstrated.

'Seriously, the weather's pretty appalling. One of the girls at work went a week ago and only got one fine day.'

'It will be gorgeous when Karen and I go,' Connie said firmly.

'My gran and granddad have a villa near Marbella, but we haven't been there in ages,' Melissa sighed. 'I wish we had a place there. Dad said he'd think about it.'

'Really?' Connie arched an eyebrow at him. This was news to her.

Barry shook his head. 'Melissa, don't be saying things like that,' he rebuked. 'It depends on how an investment I'm considering goes. With the downturn in the property market over there, it's a good time to buy.'

'Well, the best of luck with it,' Connie murmured, wondering whether, if they'd stayed married, would she have ended up with a pad in Spain.

'How about we head off?' Debbie glanced at her watch and then at Melissa.

'Yep.' Melissa stood up readily. 'See you guys.' She smiled at her father and Connie. 'And don't worry, Connie, we'll go visit Miss Hope for you. Enjoy your holiday.'

'Thanks for the coffee, Dad. Are you going to come to the Dart with us, Mum?' Debbie asked Connie.

'No, I think I'll hop over to Marks, seeing as I'm in Dun Laoghaire. I could do with a new swimsuit and sarong for scorchers on the beach,' she teased.

'OK, I'll ring you later, then.' She dusted the crumbs off her trousers and stood up. 'Bye.'

'Bye, girls, have fun.' Connie smiled as she watched the pair head off towards the Dart station, both laughing as Melissa stumbled briefly in her impossible-to-walk-in wedges and Debbie held out a steadying hand to straighten her teenage half-sister up.

CHAPTER FOURTEEN

'Well, that's a sight I never thought I'd live to see.' Barry couldn't hide his delight. 'It's great, isn't it? Thank you so much, Connie. You've been a real tower of strength. I very much appreciate what you've done over the years to try and bring Debbie and I and Melissa together. And I really, really am grateful for what you did today, and the fact that you don't hold grudges.'

'Why would I hold a grudge?' asked Connie in surprise.

'Well, I walked out on you and Debbie, so there's that . . . and then the business with Aimee outside the church.' He grimaced.

'What went on between you and me is our stuff, the same as what was said between me and Aimee is between us. It's nothing to do with Melissa. Why would I try and sabotage her relationship with Debbie? I'm not *that* petty, Barry,' she retorted, a touch caustically.

'That's what I'm saying, Connie,' he said hastily. 'You haven't an ounce of pettiness in you, and it's thanks to that that our daughters will become close, real sisters. That's what I'm trying to say, however ham-fistedly I'm doing it.'

'It wouldn't have happened if you hadn't persisted, so there's a pair of us in it then,' she said crisply.

'You've a generous nature, Connie,' he said earnestly.

'Ah, will you give over.' She leaned down to pick up her bag.

'Don't go.' He placed his hand on her arm.

'I've chores to do, Barry.'

'I think Aimee wants to get rid of the baby. I didn't know she was pregnant, and I don't think she was going to tell me. Only that I discovered the pregnancy test I don't think I'd ever have known. Can you believe it? I don't know what to do or how to deal with it. I'm in shock, at my wits' end. She's completely betrayed my trust. She wants to abort our baby.' It burst out of him, an eruption of words and emotions that left her open-mouthed.

'You don't know that for sure. Have you spoken to her about it?' she asked quietly, dropping her bag back to the ground.

'No, not yet. I literally only found out an hour ago. I suppose now's the perfect time, with Melissa out of the way but, to tell you the truth, I'm dreading it.'

'That's understandable,' she murmured.

'What will I do if she wants a termination? I'm convinced she was going to have one without telling me. How can I make her keep the baby?' Barry looked at her beseechingly.

'Barry, that's for you and Aimee to decide. It would be totally inappropriate for me to tell you what to do or say,' she demurred.

'Ah, Connie, don't be like that. I need your advice more than I've ever needed it.' Under his golfing tan, he looked pale, tired, defeated even. Gone was the brash, boyish, confident man she'd married.

'Look, I can understand very well why Aimee wouldn't want a child at this stage in her life. If I found myself pregnant, I wouldn't be very happy—'

'Yeah, well, you're that bit older,' he interrupted.

'Thanks for reminding me,' she said dryly.

'Ah, you know what I mean. But just because she made a mistake getting pregnant—'

'*She* made a mistake! *She!*' Connie arched an eyebrow at him.

'Well *we* then,' he amended irritably, and she glared at him.

'If you want one piece of advice, Barry, don't lay all the blame at Aimee's door when you're having your conversation,' said Connie acidly.

'OK. Point taken. But what am I going to do? I don't want her to get rid of our child. I feel I've been given another chance to be a good parent, to make up for the mistakes I made with Debbie. Does that sound daft?' he said, embarrassed.

'No, not at all. I would have *loved* another child. My miscarriage was one of the hardest things I ever had to deal with. But maybe it was a blessing in disguise. You would have felt completely trapped, even more than you felt with just one child, and God knows how we would have ended up. I don't think we'd be sitting here talking today,' she said quietly. 'And I'm not sure if that's the tack you should take with Aimee. After all, she could come back and say that *she* didn't make any mistakes, and *she* doesn't feel the need of another child to have a second chance at good parenting.'

'Oh right, I see what you're saying. Thanks for that.'

'Look, it's your business. I shouldn't have said that. I'm not getting involved, Barry,' Connie said crossly.

'Look, please don't apologize. I honestly and sincerely value your opinion. You're so easy to talk to.'

'Well, you didn't feel like that when we were married,' she said tartly, fed up of being the understanding ex. Did he ever think that she might have problems of her own, without him offloading on her? Typical Barry. Me. Me. Me.

'I'm sorry, Connie. I really mucked up your life,' he said contritely.

'*What?*'

'I mucked up your life,' he repeated.

Connie laughed. He had such a sense of his own importance still. *That* certainly hadn't changed. 'Don't be ridiculous, Barry. OK, you walked out on us, and it was hard, I'm not denying that. It was very, *very* hard going. But I got over it. Trust me. You needn't go around feeling guilty on my behalf. I'm fine.'

'But you're on your own.'

'There's worse things, believe me,' she said emphatically.

'But isn't there anyone you felt you could have got involved with?' he probed.

'Not when Debbie was growing up, no,' she said matter-of-factly. 'But that could change now. I'm footloose and fancy free, and a very sexy and interesting man has appeared on my horizon,' she exaggerated, thinking of a man with a lean and rangy body, the bluest of blue eyes and a very handsome face.

'Oh! Who?' Barry asked peevishly.

'You don't know him. Now, I really must be off. Go home and sort things with Aimee while you have the chance is my advice to you, and good luck,' she added, softening when she saw his woebegone face.

'Thanks, Connie. I'll let you know how it goes.'

'Barry, you don't have to tell me what goes on in your marriage. That's your business,' she said firmly.

'I know, but it's nice to have a friend to talk to.'

'Go and talk to your wife,' she advised, giving him a quick peck on the cheek.

'OK, I will. Have a great holiday with Karen. You deserve it.'

'Will do. Bye, Barry, I hope you get things sorted.'

She left him sitting dejectedly and headed off to take a short cut through the grounds of the Royal Marine. Barry was something else, expecting her to advise him on his marital problems. And having the arrogance to think he'd mucked up her life and that she was a sad and lonely woman. She wasn't going to let him get away with that, even if he *had* mucked it up for a few years. She wouldn't give him that satisfaction. A woman had her pride, after all! And he needn't be so smug, she thought indignantly. Right now, it seemed, she was in a much better place than he was, although she wouldn't have said that several months ago, remembering the acute pangs of envy she'd had when she'd seen him, Aimee and Melissa strolling into a nearby restaurant for lunch earlier in the year, looking affluent and elegantly turned out. But appearances were deceptive and, as she'd discovered in the run-up to the wedding, Barry's second marriage was far from perfect.

Typical, though, of her ex to think he could dump all his woes on her and expect her to get involved. Aimee would have a fit if she knew he'd been discussing their very personal problems with her. Connie wasn't having anything to do with it, and that was why she'd thrown in the red herring of the attractive man on her horizon. And Drew *was* an attractive man, she grinned, so she hadn't been dishonest, so to speak. It was just that the distance of the horizon was a lot further than she'd implied.

Still, it had been a joy to watch Debbie and Melissa walking off together, and the fact that

Debbie had issued the invitation off her own bat was the icing on the cake. There'd been nothing forced about their encounter. It had gone so smoothly, and the two sisters had no inkling that she and Barry had been in cahoots. For that alone, the get-together was a complete success.

An interesting morning all in all, she thought, dying to get on the phone to Karen, her best friend and Barry's sister. Karen had no time for Aimee, so perhaps she wouldn't go so far as to say that Barry's wife wanted to have a termination. She'd hate to be in Aimee's position herself, and she certainly wasn't going to make any judgement on the woman. What was it the Native Americans said? Walk a mile in my moccasins before you judge me. Aimee had enough on her plate to deal with, without a bitchy sister-in-law and ex-wife ... even if she was a stuck-up, snooty cow.

He supposed he should go home and have it out with Aimee. Barry almost groaned out loud at the thought. He just couldn't face it. How he wished he hadn't discovered she was pregnant this morning. It was true: ignorance was bliss! If she'd gone and had her abortion, he would be none the wiser and far happier for it.

It would have been a perfect morning. Sitting sipping coffees with his daughters – and Connie had been lovely. The soothing balm of forgiveness had worked its magic, even though he'd never thought it would happen. He'd felt shriven, if that wasn't too fanciful to imagine, and now he had this to deal with. Just when life seemed to have settled on a relatively even keel, he'd been dealt a body blow that was going to have a colossal impact on his life whatever route he and Aimee took.

Life had suddenly become complicated again, he thought dejectedly. And even Connie had deserted him. She'd been quite firm about not getting involved or offering advice. He needed her as a friend right now; she didn't seem to understand that. He certainly needed her much more than she needed him. How the tables had turned. And what was it with this guy – no, this *sexy* guy – she'd been going on about? When had he appeared on the scene, and who was he, Barry wondered petulantly.

She definitely had a sparkle in her eyes. She looked terrific. Hardly any make-up. Her skin tanned, her hair windswept, she looked so ... he searched for an adjective ... wholesome, he decided. Wholesome and healthy and natural. Unlike Aimee, who would never set foot outside the door without her full armour of make-up and her immaculately coiffed hair. How disloyal was that, he thought, thoroughly disgruntled. What was he doing, comparing his wife and his ex-wife? Well, Aimee had certainly shown him no loyalty, either at the wedding, or by not telling him she was pregnant. She'd behaved as if she were a separate entity and not part of a marriage. She'd definitely not behaved like a loyal and loving wife – or even as someone who respected him. That was the worst thing of all.

And where was that train of thought going to get him? Precisely nowhere. Barry stood up and shoved a five-euro note under a mug, tucked his paper under his arm and made his reluctant way home.

Aimee froze when she heard the key in the lock. Mantled in tension since they'd left, twisting and turning restlessly in bed had left her headachy and exhausted. She needed to be sharp and on the ball. She needed to be able to argue her case to Barry. She needed to be herself and not this weepy, weak, wimpy person she didn't recognize. Where was her confidence, her certainty and her focus? She hurried out of bed and raced for the shower. Bed was not the place to make her stand.

The sharp, cold needles of water made her gasp before the heat came into it, but it was just what she needed to get her adrenalin flowing, and she rubbed herself vigorously with a shower mitt and body scrub until her flesh turned red from the friction.

She held her face up to the water, letting its steaming fountain buffet her. By the time she was finished, she felt in control again. Ready to get her confrontation with Barry over and done with – because that was what it would be, she reckoned. She'd seen the look in his eyes and knew that they were in trouble.

She dried herself, twisted a towel in a turban around her hair and slathered moisturizer over her limbs before wrapping a soft terry-towelling robe around her. She was tying the belt as she walked into their bedroom when she saw him standing, arms folded, by the French doors.

'When were you going to tell me? Or were you going to tell me?' His eyes were like flints, and hostility oozed from him like poison, taking her aback. She hadn't expected him to be so full on in his attack.

'Where's Melissa?' she asked sharply, not wanting their daughter to overhear them arguing.

'She's not here. She'll be back later.' Barry wasn't going to get into explanations about meeting Debbie and Connie. 'When were you going to tell me, Aimee, or have I any rights at all in this?' he persisted angrily.

Aimee took a deep breath. 'I wasn't going to tell you, Barry. I was going to deal with it myself,' she said coldly, 'if it's the truth you want.'

'The truth would be good, Aimee. At least let's have that between us, if there's no loyalty, no respect, no consideration,' he snarled.

Aimee flinched. She'd never seen Barry so incensed.

'I'll give you the truth so, if that's what you want, so listen carefully,' she enunciated resolutely. 'I don't want another child. I don't want my body out of control. I don't want to be feeling sick and tired and in a few months' time waddling around like an elephant—'

'You wouldn't be an elephant, you were very neat with Melissa,' he cut in.

225

'Whatever. *I* felt like an elephant. And here's some more truth for you, Barry. I've just been offered a position as MD of my own events and catering company, with double the salary and a top-of-the-range car, and I'm not putting that in jeopardy for a pregnancy that I've absolutely no desire for.' She glared at her husband defiantly.

'You mean you'd put your career before our child?' He was shocked, and bitterly disappointed in her.

'Oh, for God's sake, Barry, don't be so emotive. It's only a tiny speck, no bigger than my thumb—'

'It's a *baby*, Aimee. Our baby! A little boy or a little girl, a brother or sister for Melissa, and we created it and, if you call that emotive, fine. But I want to keep the child. Be very clear about this. I do not want you to abort our baby, Aimee.' He was ashen, his hands curled tightly by his side as he stared at his wife.

'Stop, Barry, stop bullying me,' she shouted. 'Have I no say at all about what happens to my body, to my life? I can't tell these people I'm pregnant – they might withdraw the job offer, and I've striven for this all my working life. I'm not good with children, I'm not maternal, you know that, and I'm not making any apologies for it. It's what and who I am. It's me. I had Melissa. I do my best with her, but she's more than enough for me. Nothing's going to change with this one. I just can't do it.'

'Aaww, Aimee,' he groaned. 'We'll get a nanny. If you're taking on this job with a whacking big salary, we'll be well able to afford one.'

'I don't want a nanny,' she wailed. 'I don't want to be spending half my salary on childcare. With this money we could buy a lovely house in Dalkey or Killiney. We could consider a place in Spain or Portugal. Buy on a golf course, so you could play golf,' she pleaded, feeling everything slipping from her control.

'And what will you tell Melissa?' Barry demanded.

'I'll tell her I had a miscarriage. They happen all the time. You told me Connie had one,' she reminded him.

'Yes. She had a miscarriage, and don't dare even put yourself in the same sort of position as Connie was in. She grieved that child. She knew what she'd lost. A baby, not a speck the size of whatever you want to compare it to. So you're a hypocrite as well as everything else,' he spat.

'Why, what do you want me to tell her? That I went for an abortion? Is that what you want?' She was red-faced with frustration.

'I want you to keep the baby, that's what I want, Aimee,' he shouted.

'And if I don't?' she challenged.

'I don't want to stay married to you!' he muttered.

'So you're blackmailing me,' she said in disgust.

'No. It's up to you, Aimee. You decide.'

'But if I feel I have to keep it, I'll hate you, Barry. Our relationship will change completely.'

'It's changed anyway. You know that as well as I do and, as regards you hating me, that's a risk I'm

227

prepared to take. I want this child not only for us, I want it for Melissa. I want her to have family to turn to in times of trouble. It's not all about you and me and our needs.'

'If you make me have this baby, *I'll* be the one who won't want to stay married to *you*,' she threatened.

'Well, we'll cross that bridge when we come to it,' he said implacably. 'It's my baby, too, Aimee.'

'I hate you already,' she exploded. 'I hate you for not understanding, I hate you for putting everyone else before me, and I hate you for bullying me with threats of leaving. I'll have this baby if it's so important to you, but we're finished, Barry. I'll never forgive you for turning your back on me in my hour of need. Once it's born, I'm going to get a place of my own, and you can do what you like with it.' She turned away from him and walked back into the ensuite, leaving him shaken to his core.

Barry watched his wife walk away from him and knew things would never be the same between them again. If he hadn't found out she was pregnant, she would have gone behind his back and got rid of their child, and he would have been none the wiser. She'd admitted it, and hadn't been the slightest bit apologetic. His feelings or emotions or rights to be a father again would not have entered the equation. He would have been a passive bystander in his own marriage, and she would have walked all over him. God, she was as hard as nails.

She'd more or less admitted her career was more important than her child's life, and then she'd tried to bribe him with offers of a pad on a golf course abroad.

There was still nothing to stop her going ahead and having the abortion. He couldn't stop her or police her movements. She travelled abroad a lot for work; there was nothing to stop her booking into a clinic in the UK and pretending she was off at a trade fair. Little short of accompanying her every second, he had no guarantees that their child would be kept.

Tears sprang to his eyes. What a horrible, horrible mess to be in. He understood a little of how she was feeling, particularly with this big new career opportunity, but a child's life was much more important than a mere job. Life was such a cruel lottery sometimes, he thought dejectedly, brushing the tears from his face. Connie would have loved another baby. She'd been devastated when she'd lost their second child. He knew women in their social circle who were going through the crucifixion of IVF. And here was his wife, loathing the idea of pregnancy and having another child. Not only did she loathe the idea of a new baby, she loathed him. There'd been no mistaking her antipathy when she'd told him she hated him.

He'd have to do his best to protect Melissa from the fallout of what was to come. What a contrast his life was compared to his ex-wife's. She was looking forward to a relaxing holiday and a life of relative freedom, and here he was feeling every second of his middle age, with burdens so heavy to bear he didn't know if he could carry them. A headache pounded his temples. He walked out of the bedroom, picked his car keys up from the hall table and left the apartment. He didn't want to be in the same space as Aimee right now. He wanted to go to Connie and tell her all that had unfolded, but she'd made it clear she wasn't getting involved. It looked like he was completely on his own.

Aimee was shaking. She sat on the side of the bath and took a few deep breaths, trying to quell the nausea that engulfed her. Her heart was racing, her palms were sweaty, and she felt faint.

The die was cast now, she thought forlornly. There was no going back. Her marriage was over, she was going to have to endure a loathsome pregnancy and her job offer would probably go down the tubes. She couldn't have the termination now. She just couldn't go through with it knowing the level of his opposition. Even she wasn't that hard. Barry would hold it over her for the rest of her life, and that would be unendurable. She couldn't be sure he wouldn't tell Melissa when she was older. Or even Saint Connie, she thought bitterly. Well, Saint Connie could take him back with open arms, and the baby too, because if he was insisting she go through with it, he was going to have to take the consequences of his decision. Barry Adams was not going to make a fool out of her and leave her minding the baby while he swanned off playing golf. He wasn't going to get off scot free when the child was sick and time had to be taken off work. And he could do the crèche and, later, the school run. She'd done all that, and she wasn't going to do it again. If he wanted this baby so badly, he could have it and all that it entailed, she thought fiercely. Because there was one thing she was definitely sure of: when this baby was born, Barry was on his own with it. And no man would ever, ever have control over her life again.

CHAPTER FIFTEEN

Ken Davenport hurried to his parking space in the Blackrock Clinic. His rounds in three private hospitals had taken longer than he'd anticipated, and he had a game of golf booked for eleven. He was hungry, and he was looking forward to his breakfast. He allowed himself a cooked breakfast once a week, bacon and sausages grilled rather than fried. He was, after all, a heart surgeon; he knew the dangers of clogged arteries.

He sat back into the soft black leather seat of his Merc and dialled home. It was his custom to phone Juliet when he was leaving Blackrock to tell her he was on his way, so she could start cooking. To his surprise, the phone rang out and went to the answering machine.

'I'm on my way,' he said loudly. 'And I've a game of golf booked for eleven. Could you put out a polo shirt, a pullover and my cream trousers? Thank you.' He hated talking to bloody machines. Why hadn't Juliet answered? How long was she going to keep up this bloody nonsense and stay in a huff with him? She hadn't even put out his cup and saucer and a plate for his croissant the night before. He always ate something light before rounds on Saturday, knowing he was going to have a substantial breakfast when he got home. The traffic lights were against him, and he tapped his fingers impatiently against the wheel. His stomach rumbled. He hoped his wife had heard the message, he was absolutely starving. The lights turned green and he scorched out of the Blackrock Clinic and headed for Ballsbridge.

'So you're on your way and you've a game of golf booked, bully for you.' Juliet Davenport's nostrils flared as she listened to her husband's message.

She'd recognized his number on the caller ID and had let the answering machine take it. Ken had some nerve, expecting that she would cook him breakfast after the way he'd behaved the night before. And, even worse, expecting that she'd put his clothes out for him. She sighed as she turned over and pulled the duvet up to her shoulders. He expected it because she'd done it for him for more years than she cared to remember. The little wifely doormat. It was her own fault that he treated her like a servant sometimes. But the day of reckoning had come. Worms turned. He was going to find that out sooner than he thought.

What a rare treat it was to have a lie-in on a Saturday, she reflected, snuggling down with the latest Cathy Kelly novel, which she was thoroughly enjoying. Her book-club reading list was heavy going this month, and Juliet wasn't in the humour for any of the worthy titles suggested. She wanted a good, meaty book she could get her teeth into, not something she had to plough through, and *Past Secrets* fitted the bill perfectly. She was deeply engrossed when she heard her husband's car crunch over the gravelled drive.

The lord and master was home. She heard his key in the door, and heard him stride briskly to the kitchen. She could imagine him sniffing the air, wondering why he wasn't smelling the enticing aroma of sizzling bacon and sausage.

Ha ha! she thought nastily as she heard him thunder up the stairs.

'What's wrong with you? Why are you still in bed? Are you sick?' he demanded as he barged into their bedroom.

'No,' she said snootily, putting her book down momentarily.

'Where's my breakfast then?' He stared at her flabbergasted.

'Get it yourself. I'm not your servant. I'm having a day off,' Juliet said coldly, and picked up her book.

'Well . . . well . . . what am I going to have to eat? I've a game of golf at eleven. I need something substantial.' He was aghast.

'Do I look like someone who gives a toss?' Juliet retorted, and turned her back on him and resumed reading her page-turner. She knew he was apoplectic with fury and it gave her immense satisfaction.

'I'm disgusted with your behaviour,' he said icily.

And she couldn't help herself. Juliet started to laugh. She saw the look of outrage on his face.

'Oh, listen to yourself, Ken. Don't be so pompous. I'm not one of your poor unfortunate underlings. I've seen the skidmarks on your underpants, remember?' She turned to face him.

'What's got into you? That's *appalling*, Juliet, you should be ashamed of yourself.' He was slack-jawed with shock.

You'll be a hell of a lot more appalled when you find out I've booked myself on a flight to Spain on Wednesday and you're going to have to cook for yourself, she thought, feeling hugely liberated as he turned on his heel and marched downstairs.

She could hear press doors slamming and the clatter of a frying pan. Why didn't I do this years ago, she wondered, tuning him out, and carried on reading.

Ken cursed viciously as spits of oil spattered his expensive grey suit after he'd cracked two eggs into the pan. This was *indefensible*. Juliet was behaving totally out of character and in a most spiteful and disgusting way. What had got into her? Her menopause was over. She couldn't blame that. She looked healthy; he didn't think she was sickening for anything. Was this all because he hadn't come to her silly art exhibition? If that was all she had to worry about in life, wasn't she damn lucky, he thought angrily, as he buttered a couple of slices of bread. How did he deal with this . . . this defiance . . . he wondered? It was something new to him. He wasn't used to being defied and dismissed. No one had ever treated him with such disrespect before. Juliet was the last person he would have expected to behave so unspeakably. He was at a loss.

Ken cursed again as he broke the yoke of the first egg when he flipped it over. The sooner his wife came back to her senses the better. And he would have to make it abundantly clear that, in future, throwing tantrums was just not acceptable.

God, he felt dog rough, and he smelt pretty iffy too. Bryan shifted on the sofa and winced as a beam of light sliced through the blinds, causing him serious difficulties. He should have just stuck to the coke – he'd been up, ready for anything, the life and soul of the party; coming down with pot had been a mistake, big time. He glanced at his watch and groaned when he saw the time. Twelve fifteen, Debbie would have a fit. It was a wonder she hadn't been calling him on his mobile. Maybe she had and he hadn't heard it.

He slid it out of his jacket pocket and was surprised to see that he hadn't had any missed calls, and neither were there any messages. She must really be in a snit and rightly so, he thought guiltily. He'd behaved like a total prat. Spent a fortune on drugs, crashed out on a mate's sofa, like he was some idiot twenty-year-old.

He strained to see the keys on his BlackBerry and

236

tapped out a text message to her. He needed to cop on to himself. He wasn't being very fair to Debbs. They were married now, and this wasn't the way to treat her, he chastised himself silently. That was it; he wasn't going on a bender again for the next six months at least. He must have spent at least 500 euro last night, trying to keep up with Kev and the others, he remembered, utterly dismayed. Five hundred smackers out of his salary, and a maxed-out Visa card and a multitude of bills unpaid. Debbie probably wouldn't talk to him for a week.

Bleary-eyed, he gazed around the lounge. There were bottles everywhere, and the remnants of an Indian takeaway lay strewn on the low glass coffee table. The stale smell of pot hung stagnant, wreathed around him in a taunting reminder of his folly.

There was no sound other than the muted clamour of the traffic on the quays below and a rumbling snore from somewhere across the room. Bryan peered around and saw that some guy was asleep in one of the recliner chairs by the window.

He moved his tongue around his mouth. He was parched. He heaved himself off the sofa and made his way out to the kitchen, which was in an even worse state than the lounge. Half-empty takeaway cartons littered the island and countertops. Beer bottles, champagne bottles, cans, soggy green garlic bread and dried-up olives. He opened the massive double-door fridge, took out a litre of Tropicana and drank it straight from the carton. The chilled liquid revived him somewhat, and he took a couple of slices of smoked salmon from a plate and ate them hungrily. He took another slug of orange juice, wiped his hands on some kitchen roll and walked out into the hall.

The door to the master bedroom was ajar, and he could see Kev and a naked blonde sprawled across the massive bed, asleep. His house would fit in the shagger's bedroom, he thought enviously, as he walked further down the hall to the bathroom. It was only after he'd had a slash and was washing his hands that he realized that a pale-faced redhead was asleep in the bath, wrapped in a duvet. She opened her eyes and tried to focus. 'No worries,' he said hastily, closing the door behind him. He heard her begin to puke noisily and was mightily relieved she hadn't done it while he was there. He let himself out and took the lift to the foyer, feeling grubby and grotty. Maybe the smoked salmon hadn't been a great idea, he thought, as the air hit him and nausea swept over him. He swallowed hard. But it was no use. He knew he was going to barf. He managed to make his way down a small lane and was wretchedly sick. Definitely the last time, he swore as he straightened up. It wasn't worth it. A rat scarpered out from behind a pile of rubbish sacks, and he shuddered. He took a few deep breaths and emerged back on to the quays, feeling decidedly ropey. He needed to cross the river and go and collect his car from the car park at work. Then he'd better get home and face the music. Debbie hadn't answered his text. He was in the doghouse for sure.

'I used to think you were real stuck up,' Melissa confided as she and Debbie walked from Sandymount Dart station to the small cul-de-sac of townhouses where Debbie and Bryan lived.

'I used to think you were a spoilt brat.' Debbie grinned. 'And now look at us, getting on like a house on fire. Much to the relief of our dad and my mum. I'm sorry it took so long, but better late than never.'

'It's nice having a sister,' Melissa remarked, following Debbie down the small path to her front door. 'Although my friend Sarah is like a sister to me too.'

'Yeah. My cousin Jenna is like my sister, that's why I asked her to be my bridesmaid—'

'Jenna's my cousin too,' Melissa reminded her.

'Oh yeah, she's Dad's niece. I forgot. It's a bit weird, all these relationships.' Debbie led the way in, just as her phone buzzed.

'Got a text, it's probably from Bryan. Let's have a cup of coffee while we're looking at the photos,' she suggested. 'I'll switch on the computer and bring them up and I'll put the kettle on while you're looking at them.'

'Cool,' agreed Melissa. 'Nice house, Debbie.'

'It will be nice when we do it up. It needs re-decorating.' Debbie grimaced as she brought the younger girl into the dining room cum study. She switched on the computer and clicked on to the photos icon. 'There you go. I'll be back in a sec.'

She went back into the kitchen and took her phone out of her bag. The message was from her mother to say how much she'd enjoyed their coffee earlier and to say how happy she was that she'd invited Melissa home. Debbie smiled. Connie was great. A really loving and supportive mother. She saw that there was another message in her inbox from earlier. She mustn't have heard it come through while she was on the Dart. It was from Bryan and had been sent in the last twenty minutes.

Sorry Debbs. I'm a prat. Going 2 collect the car and will b home then. B x

'I won't argue with that,' she muttered, but she was glad to know he was up and about. She always worried when he was taking drugs. She'd seen friends end up in A&E, and she always had a fear that it would happen to Bryan some time, although he pooh-poohed her fears.

And at least he knew he was a prat, so maybe, now, having got it out of his system, he might knuckle down and start getting their finances back on track. She'd just play it cool when he came home, no recriminations, no nagging, but if he pulled a stunt like this again, he was in for the ear-bashing of his life.

She filled the kettle and spilled some chocolate biscuits on to a plate. She hadn't had a proper breakfast; she was peckish. 'Like a ham and tomato sandwich?' she called in to Melissa.

'Yes, please, I'm starving,' her half-sister called back.

'That makes two of us,' Debbie said light-heartedly and began to butter the bread. She made their sandwiches and carried them out to the small mosaic table on the deck. 'Just going up to get your prezzie.' She poked her head in through the door.

'These are great. Will you send them to me?' Melissa asked. 'I'll write down my email address for you.'

'Sure. Why don't you go and sit outside when you're ready? It's a nice day. But don't mind the state of the garden. We haven't cut the grass in three weeks – it's like a jungle,' Debbie apologized.

'Where's Bryan?' Melissa asked.

'He had to collect the car from work. We went out to dinner last night and had a few drinks, so we didn't drive.'

'That's very responsible. Dad doesn't drink and drive any more since the points thing came in.'

'Pour out two mugs of coffee, and I'll be out in a minute. I might as well stick in a wash while I'm at it.' Debbie ran upstairs, took anything white of her own she could see in her case and the linen basket, bundled them up in a flowing white skirt, grabbed Melissa's T-shirts and hurried back down. She shoved the whites into the machine, added two tabs of washing powder and some Comfort and set the dial. At least she'd made a start.

'Hey, these are gorgeous. Thanks so much, Debbie,' Melissa exclaimed when Debbie handed her half-sister the T-shirts she'd bought her. The younger girl jumped up and threw her arms around her. And as Debbie hugged her back tightly, she knew that all the old bitterness and hurts of the past had finally drifted away, and that she and Melissa and Barry and Connie were a real family at last.

MOVING ON

Moving On

CHAPTER SIXTEEN

Juliet checked that she had her passport, e ticket, keys to the villa, sunglasses, reading glasses and her mobile phone. It was 4.15 a.m. and she was getting the 7 a.m. flight from Dublin to Malaga. Her check-in was 5 a.m. She'd tried to book a seat on the afternoon flight, but she hadn't a hope. She'd been lucky to get a seat at all. It was the height of the season, and both Ryanair and Aer Lingus were almost fully booked. It didn't matter what time of year you flew to Malaga, she reflected, as she sprayed Chanel No. 5 on her wrists and neck, the flights were always full, and they rarely came up as special offers.

Juliet caught sight of herself in the mirror. Her hazel eyes were bright, and a faint flush of excite-ment shone through her sprayed-on tan. Her navy cotton jacket, white sleeveless top and white trousers looked smart and summery. Her ash-blond hair hung in a soft bob, and her make-up, subtly applied, emphasized her high cheekbones. She looked what she was, an affluent, well-groomed, classy wife whom no one would give a second glance. They were ten a penny on Malaga flights. It was a flight she had taken many times, but today was different. Today, she was going away without telling her husband.

It was *so* liberating, she thought gleefully, switching off the light. The house was still, with just the odd familiar creak and groan of tired timbers and ageing water pipes, the moonlight fashioning a painting of willowy silhouettes of leaves and branches on the wall opposite the landing window. In the guest room across the landing, Ken's snores rumbled thunderously and, slingbacks in hand, Juliet padded silently past his room and downstairs. Her husband's snores didn't cease, and she turned off the alarm and let herself out of the house, confident that he wouldn't wake. She hadn't bothered with breakfast; she'd have coffee and croissants at the airport.

Her taxi was waiting at the wrought-iron gates. She'd instructed the firm they had an account with to flash the lights when the driver got to the house. She opened the boot of her Volvo and hoisted out her Samsonite. To make her departure as secret as possible, she'd packed her case the day before and stowed it in her car so that Ken wouldn't see it. The first he'd know that she'd gone was when he got up at 6 a.m. and saw her bedroom door wide open and the bed made. For the first time ever, there was no freezer well stocked with home-cooked dinners, no extra shopping done for all the basics. His dirty

246

linen basket was full. This time, Ken was well and truly on his own – well, apart from Gina's assistance.

That would give him a good shock. Juliet smiled at the taxi driver as he took her case, and settled into the back seat for the journey to the airport. The pearly light to the east, dawn's kiss, lifted her spirits even more. The start of a new day and a new life.

From now on, it would be all about her. Ken's rude awakening was just beginning.

Karen nearly gave herself lockjaw, sitting in the crowded airport restaurant sawing at a pale, un-appetizing slice of rubbery, curled-up bacon accompanied by leathery, overcooked scrambled eggs. 'They have some nerve charging those prices for this rubbish,' she complained bitterly, 'and it's always cold by the time you get to the table.'

'Sausages aren't bad,' Connie said cheerfully, starving after the rush to get up in the middle of the night and the long drive to the airport.

'They call this toast? It's as white as my legs were before I fake-tanned,' Karen snorted, holding up a piece of grey-white bread, which had seen a toaster for about eight seconds. 'They get away with it because people don't complain. The French would never stand for this.'

'There there, you'll be fine,' soothed Connie. Karen was not a morning person. This middle-of-the-night stuff was a complete trauma to her.

Her sister-in-law grinned. 'Sorry. The older I get,

the grumpier I get. Honestly, I could grump for Ireland.'

'I'd noticed. I think it's called the menopause. I wouldn't know yet, of course. I'm younger than you. I'm only peri!' Connie buttered a croissant and slathered it with jam.

'Ha ha, smug bitch!' Karen made a face at her. 'Now, madam, we're officially on holidays – what's the piece of news you've been holding on to since last Saturday? You promised you'd tell me on holidays.'

'We're not in Spain yet,' Connie teased.

'And you won't be getting there in one piece if you don't enlighten me. Now come on . . . spill!'

'OK,' Connie relented. 'You'll never guess.'

'*What!*' Karen couldn't hide her exasperation.

'Aimee's up the duff!'

'I don't believe it.' Karen's eyes widened. '*Oh! My! God!*'

'So don't tell me I never give you any good gossip,' Connie said smugly, sitting back sipping her coffee and enjoying Karen's reaction to the news.

'Who told you?'

'Melissa let it slip . . .' Connie regaled Karen with a rundown of the previous Saturday morning's events.

'I wouldn't be in her shoes for anything.' Karen found it in her heart to be sympathetic to her detested sister-in-law. As a woman who juggled career and family life, she understood all the difficulties Aimee's pregnancy and a new baby would entail. 'I wouldn't wish that on my worst enemy, not at her age, with a career and a teenage daughter.'

'I know. Even I found it easy to be sorry for the woman, despite our history. Barry's totally stressed, but, interestingly though, happy enough to have another child.'

'How things have changed,' Karen murmured, remembering her brother's dismay when Connie had become pregnant with Debbie.

'I know,' Connie agreed ruefully.

'When's it due?'

'Early next year, I think.'

'I better save up for an outfit for the christening,' Karen drawled. 'Designer labels only. The Holdens' daughter is getting married in September. And it's black tie. John will have to get a monkey suit. What a pain in the ass.'

'You might get something nice in Marbella,' Connie suggested.

'You mean in one of those boutiques where they don't even have price tags? Ha! I don't think so,' scoffed Karen. 'Come on, let's go treat ourselves in the duty free.'

Connie finished her coffee and picked up her bag. 'This is my favourite bit of travelling,' she remarked ten minutes later, as she selected several glossy magazines and then meandered over to the books.

'You buy two, and I'll buy two, and I have a couple of good thrillers in my bag, so we'll have plenty to read,' Karen advised. As she browsed the bookshelves, Connie could feel herself beginning to relax. The prospect of ten days doing nothing other than reading, sleeping and eating was *so* appealing, and Karen was the perfect holiday companion. How lucky was she? Connie thought gratefully as she picked up a book called *Party Animal*, a collection of stories about pets by all her favourite authors, the royalties of which went to animal charities.

Oh, lovely, she thought, dipping into it, and feeling a pang of loneliness for Miss Hope. Her little cat had rubbed against her leg when she was leaving, and Connie had lifted her up and burrowed her nose in her silky black fur, wishing she could take her with her.

That loving little pet had got her through the loneliness of Debbie's leaving, and yet so many people just didn't like cats. She'd be lost without hers, she thought, as she added *Party Animal* to her selection of purchases.

'Oh, this is the life I was born for, Karen,' she said happily, three-quarters of an hour later, as they made their way along the jetway to the massive green and white Aer Lingus airbus.

'Wish we were turning left – *that's* what *I* was born for,' Karen murmured, as she stepped through the doorway of the plane and turned right for economy.

'Dream on,' grinned Connie, following her down the aisle to a side row with just two seats. As she reached up to put her duty-free bags into the overhead cabin, a woman passing to the seat behind jolted her.

'I beg your pardon,' the woman said, and did a double take. 'Oh . . . Connie, isn't it? Karen, hello. Are you off to the Costa too?'

Good Lord, it's Aimee's mother, Connie thought, dismayed. She'd met her at a few of her ex's family gatherings over the years, when she and Aimee had been on speaking terms.

'Juliet! Isn't it a small world!' Karen exclaimed. 'Is Ken with you or are you travelling on your own?'

'I certainly am,' Juliet said briskly, settling herself into the seat behind. 'All I have to worry about is me, thankfully.'

'Well, enjoy your flight,' Connie said politely. She wasn't sure if the older woman knew about the dust-up between her and Aimee on the steps of the church at Debbie's wedding.

'I will indeed.' Juliet smiled, and there was no animosity apparent, Connie noted with a sigh of relief. It would be horrible to have an 'atmosphere' to ruin the start of her much-needed holiday.

'Did you know your mother was going to the villa?' Ken boomed down the phone to Aimee.

'*What?* Dad, it's seven a.m.'

'Well, I'm sure you're up planning tea parties, or whatever it is you do,' Ken said tetchily. 'The point is, I've had a text from your mother to say she is on the plane to Malaga, and she never said a word to me that she was going. There's nothing in the fridge,

251

there are no dinners in the freezer and there's a load of dirty washing in the linen basket, so you better get over here and give me a hand to get organized. It's not the housekeeper's day today, and I'm already late for my rounds and will be late for my clinic as a result.' Her father was clearly up to ninety.

'I didn't know Mum was going to Spain,' Aimee said icily, stung by his 'tea-party' barb and his arrogant assumption that she could just drop everything and go over to his house to cook his dinners and do his laundry. 'And I'm afraid I'm up to my eyes. I'm just arriving at my office, so I suggest you eat out or buy ready-prepared meals and get your housekeeper to bring your laundry to a launderette.'

Aimee reversed into her designated parking space, noting that Ian, her boss and owner of the company, had already arrived at work.

'Well, that's not very helpful,' blustered her father. 'I don't know what's got into you women. Your mother hasn't spoken to me since that bloody art thing – in fact, she's been extremely rude and vulgar,' he raged, remembering the 'skidmarks' taunt.

'She was hurt you didn't support her. She's always supported you, so I'm not surprised she's gone away,' Aimee said tartly.

'I beg your pardon, Missy. Who pays for her lovely lifestyle, with all the perks, including a villa in Spain and all that entails? Who pays her credit-card bills? Don't give me nonsense about not

252

"supporting" her.' Ken almost spat the word down the phone.

'Fine, whatever you say. I have to go, bye.' Aimee hung up, determined not to get into an argument with her father, which would end up reducing her to the level of a seven-year-old. She was in her late thirties, married with a teenager, and he still thought he could call her 'Missy' and talk down to her like a child. It was just as well he had clinics and wasn't operating. God help any patient under his care today, she thought nastily, as she hurried into the offices of *Chez Moi* and took the lift to her floor. So her mother had gone to Spain without telling him. 'Well done, Juliet,' she applauded, delighted that her mother was showing some flicker of independence. It was time she stood up for herself and stepped out from under Ken's shadow after all these years. She stopped for a moment and scrolled through the messages on her phone. She hadn't bothered to look earlier. Yes, there it was, one from her errant parent.

Hello, Dear. Am on plane. Going 2 villa, don't know how long I'm going to stay. Didn't tell your father. Expect fireworks ha ha! Love Mum xx

Aimee grinned. Fireworks wasn't the word for it. Ken was outraged. This was a real challenge to his authority, and he never reacted well to that, as she knew through bitter experience. Her face darkened, as childhood memories flooded back. One in particular had never gone away. She'd back-cheeked Ken on the way into the children's library when she was about seven, and he'd chastised her as loudly as he could, so that everyone in the library could hear. The customary silence of the premises had been broken only by his strident tones as he'd told her she was an impertinent child, and did she think she was being smart by giving him cheek? He was in his element, the centre of attention. She remembered the nettle stings of mortification as she'd stood, head bowed, listening to his tirade, before he'd allowed her to join the queue at the desk, where everyone was looking at her. She was bright pink with humiliation, and on the brink of tears, but she wouldn't let her father see her cry. She wouldn't give him that satisfaction. The girl at the desk had taken her books and given her a little wink, and she'd taken some small comfort in knowing that she had an ally.

'Oh, for God's sake!' Aimee muttered irritably to herself. What was she doing thinking about something that had happened all those years ago when she had an important meeting which could decide her whole future coming up. She slid her phone into her bag and headed for her office.

Ian motioned to her to come into his office as she strode along, and she groaned silently. He was like a great big spider in there, watching everything through the glass panels.

'So how's La Davenport this fine morning? We're getting tremendous feedback from the O'Leary wedding. Gallagher, Simpson want us to organize their twenty-five years in business celebration, and you, I suspect, are just the woman for the job. Edward Gallagher was at the wedding, and he was mega-impressed. He specifically requested that you take charge. Take another bow.'

Unctuous little toad, Aimee derided silently, unimpressed with his smarmy sweet talk. 'Ian, I can't stop to talk now, I've a breakfast meeting with Roger O'Leary in the Shelbourne, and I need to collect some files for another meeting at nine thirty. I'll catch you later,' she said crisply from the doorway.

'Oh! OK!' He was a tad miffed. Today, her boss was wearing his pink shirt, blue jeans and a big Gucci belt. Mutton dressed as lamb wasn't in it, or even mutton dressed as mutton! Although in his late forties, he dressed much younger, and had his hair dyed blacker than black. Aimee was convinced he was gay but in denial. Unmarried, Ian always had a blonde on his arm at functions. He lived in a tastefully decorated but sterile apartment in Blackrock that was all glass and chrome and John Rocha. He was such a self-important little diva, with his bumptious emails telling her to take a *well-earned bow* after the success of the O'Leary wedding. She could just visualize herself standing in front of the mirror, bowing to herself indeed, she thought crossly as she logged on to her computer. Would he yet rue the success of that particular wedding if she set up a business in opposition to him?

Aimee suddenly felt sick to her stomach. She hadn't lied to Ian when she'd said she was having a breakfast meeting with Roger O'Leary. She'd set it up after the revelation of her pregnancy the previous Saturday. She had to know one way or another what his reaction would be to her news. Would he pull out of the proposal, or would he still be keen to go ahead? She couldn't bring herself just to take the position and say nothing. It would lead to a lack of trust, and bad feeling further down the line, and she was realistic enough to acknowledge that if the new company was to work, she needed Roger onside.

At least she hadn't handed in her letter of resignation to Ian. If the new job offer went belly up, she still had the option of negotiating a substantial pay rise commensurate with her new, elevated status. She'd show him what La Davenport was made of, she thought with grim humour, glancing at her new emails.

She thought of her mother on her flight to Spain and suddenly wished she were going too. How nice it would be to lie in the sun for a few days and forget all the stresses and strains of her life in Dublin. Melissa had arrived home on Saturday afternoon with a request to spend Saturday night and Sunday with a friend who had just come back from three weeks in the south of France and was dying to tell Sarah and Melissa all about it. Seemingly, there was a big romance with 'a real tasty guy', as her daughter had put it enviously. Melissa had been so anxious to go it seemed unkind to refuse and, besides, Aimee was fed up being the baddie all the time. Barry was the one who let their daughter do what she wanted, and she was the one constantly saying no, and it just wasn't fair. 'Go on,' she'd said. 'But no drinking, or you'll be grounded for the rest of the summer.'

'Thanks, Mom, you're the best,' her daughter had exclaimed, racing off to her bedroom to pack, having first removed her wedges with a sigh of relief. Silence had descended yet again upon the penthouse after she'd left with fifty euro in her purse to tide her over. Barry hadn't come home until late that evening, and he'd gone out on the balcony with a book and stayed reading until long after the sun had set.

She'd been working at an event at the races on Sunday and hadn't arrived home until after ten that night, much to their mutual relief. He'd tried to engage her in conversation, but she'd just said savagely, 'Don't talk to me, Barry. I've nothing to say to you, you selfish bastard. You're every bit as bad as my father.' He'd walked away, taken aback at the ferocity of her onslaught.

Now that the cards were on the table between them, hostility and resentment were the order of the day. She was consumed with impotent fury. She hadn't felt so out of control of her own destiny since her school days, when her father had insisted that she choose science subjects over art and home economics, and then made her do another year at school and repeat her science exams when she failed them.

In her eyes, Barry and her father had become one.

Ken's phone call this morning, his total lack of respect for her career and his presumptions that she would do his bidding, infuriated her. Barry's authoritative demands that she keep her unwanted child, with no discussion of her needs or feelings, had stirred a hornets' nest of emotions. Did men not realize that the era of the patriarchy was over? Or was it? she questioned dejectedly. Not if *her* life was anything to go by.

Aimee sighed deeply. Barry couldn't physically restrain her from going for a termination, she knew that, but she would feel his censure like a straitjacket around her for the rest of her life if she did, *and* she would live with the fear that Melissa would find out. That, more than anything, was what kept her from booking her flight to London and doing what she felt was right for *her*.

Heavy-hearted, she finished her emails, left a page of instructions for her PA and set off to meet Roger and see what *he* would decide about her future. Would the day ever come when no man would have power over her? When she would be her own boss? What a wonderful notion that was, she thought wistfully, stepping out on to the traffic-jammed street. Aimee hailed a taxi and instructed the driver to bring her to the Shelbourne.

'You really should take up that offer before the share prices jump even higher.' Jeremy Farrell's ingratiating tones filled the Merc as Barry drove to work along the Stillorgan dual carriageway, inching towards his right-hand turn at RTE.

'Yes, I've got it all under control, will sort a bank draft for you and stick it in the post, Jeremy,' Barry said firmly, wishing the other man would stop annoying him. He'd had numerous phone calls since their initial conversation in the clubhouse.

'Just ring me when you have the draft, and I'll send a courier over with all the paperwork,' the older man said suavely.

'Fine, Jeremy. I'll be in touch. Cheers.' Barry hit the off button, and the sound of Roy Orbison singing 'She's a Mystery to Me' echoed from the speakers. Barry could identify with Bono's emotive words. Aimee's words had torn *him* apart. She'd called him a selfish bastard with such intensity he'd been shocked. She'd glared at him with a naked hatred that wounded him. Her rider, that he was as bad as her father, had hit home. Of course, she would think that, he had thought in dismay as he sat on the balcony afterwards, necking a cold beer. Ken was an authoritarian bully, from whom she'd struggled to obtain a modicum of respect. He had told her what to do, and laid down the law until she'd left college and started to work.

Barry had taken the wrong approach to the whole issue of Aimee's pregnancy. He'd got her back up. He'd been too heavy-handed, he thought ruefully. He'd come on too strong at the start. He should have known better, knowing her history and what pushed her buttons. But his going at it like a bull in a china shop had stemmed from his fear that she would ignore *his* wishes about their baby. As it was, he might never have known she was pregnant, only that fate had intervened. He was *meant* to know, he comforted himself. Nevertheless, it was a black-and-white choice, and only one of them was going to be happy with the result, and, consequently, their marriage was in tatters.

He pushed all thoughts of his wife into the compartment labelled 'Aimee', and began to ponder his options about the share prospect. He had savings and investments, but the investments were long term and nothing he could get his hands on quickly. His best strategy was to borrow, he decided. Normally, he wouldn't dream of borrowing for an investment, but this was such a hot prospect. He'd read up about SecureCo International Plus, and the financial pedigree of the backers couldn't be argued with. Even with his limited knowledge of the financial world, he recognized the names, and their financial achievements were impressive.

There was no point in discussing it with Aimee, with the mood she was in; and she certainly wouldn't sign any papers to use their assets as collateral. She'd probably use the situation as a bargaining chip to secure his agreement to a termination. In her eyes, he had rendered her powerless; she would do the same to him if she got the chance. He remembered a quote that had stuck with him, from an article by the journalist Mary Kenny: 'Much of wedlock consists of two persons in mortal emotional combat for dominance and power.' 'Welcome to my marriage, Ms Kenny,' he muttered, slowing to a halt at the traffic lights at Vincent's.

He'd just go ahead under his own steam with the share thing. He had a small cottage his grandmother had left him which he rented out; that would do fine as collateral, and he wouldn't need his wife's signature. He might need the extra finance this deal would make him if she went for a divorce. Barry swallowed hard, and tears pricked his eyelids. He would *hate* to go through another divorce. One was more than enough for any man in his lifetime, and he'd been lucky with his and Connie's. Barry blinked rapidly, trying hard not to lose his composure. Maybe after a while Aimee would get used to the idea of a new baby and accept her pregnancy, and things would calm down. He could only hope.

CHAPTER SEVENTEEN

'Bryan, the car tax has arrived,' Debbie yelled up the stairs. 'And so has the NTL.'

'OK, leave it with me,' he called down to her, and she placed them back on the hall table. 'And the Holdens' wedding invitation has arrived, it's friggin' black tie, and it's in Wexford – that's going to cost an arm and a leg.'

'We'll talk about it later,' he shouted back.

'See you tonight, then,' she called and hurried off to get the Dart. Her mother would be on the plane to Spain, she thought enviously, glancing at her watch. If they were on time she'd be flying over the Pyrenees about now, experiencing the bumpy air pockets over the mountains that indicated they were only an hour away from their destination. Debbie and Jenna had spent a couple of mad holidays in her relative's apartment, and Debbie wished she was with her aunt and mother, enjoying the anticipatory laughter and chat on the flight. She was back to work less than a full week and she was feeling overwhelmed already.

How had they accumulated so much debt that the arrival of two household bills and a wedding invite caused her stomach to get tied up in knots? Bryan was going to have to get rid of the convertible, which, because it had depreciated so much from when he'd bought it, was now a loss maker. She noticed, as she did every morning, the For Sale sign on a house several doors down from theirs. It had been on the market for several months now without moving, and rumour had it that the young couple who owned it had dropped fifty thousand in the asking price and were desperate to sell because they couldn't afford their mortgage due to the rise in interest rates and the cost of living. It scared the hell out of Debbie listening to tales like that, and she tried not to think about it. There was definitely a marked slowdown in the property market, and people in their circle were beginning to talk about negative equity a lot more.

And now they had Sandra Holden's wedding invitation to contend with. Debbie felt prickles of sweat at her hairline just thinking about it. Sandra was a friend of Jenna's, but Debbie had hung around with her a lot and had invited her and her fiancé to her own wedding. Now the invite was being reciprocated, and it couldn't have come at a more awkward time, financially.

Jenna had told Debbie that Sandra was going all out to impress. She'd spent a fortune on the dress, a lavish, feathery, frilled creation, and had been considering hiring a full orchestra rather than a band.

That certainly *was* raising the bar, Debbie reflected, thinking how crazy it was to be getting into horrific debt just to impress their peers. If only Sandra realized what it was going to be like post-wedding, she'd run away and get hitched in Gretna Green!

Going to the wedding would cost herself and Bryan a packet. The guts of a hundred for the black-tie palaver, a minimum of a hundred and fifty for a prezzie on the BT wedding list. No one wanted to be seen picking the cheapest present, so you really couldn't spend less than a hundred. A hundred and fifty at least for overnight accommodation, and another couple of hundred for petrol, drinks, meals, etc. And that was without her buying anything new. She'd probably have to hire a hat, though, if it was black tie; she was damned if she was going to pay through the nose for something she wouldn't wear again.

Had she caused disquiet to any of her guests when they'd received their wedding invites, she wondered. It was hard to know. Everyone in their circle seemed to be doing fine, with plenty of money to socialize and entertain. Were she and Bryan the only couple up to their eyes in debt, or were their friends and acquaintances in hock just like they were? Could they get away with buying a present and not going to the wedding, she worried as she quickened her pace. Sandra wouldn't be impressed, but so what? Sandra didn't have mega financial woes yet! Another thought struck her – Sandra had invited her on her hen weekend. She'd forgotten all about that. Sandra was dithering between a trip to Latvia or a spa weekend in Galway. There was no way Debbie could go on either. She simply didn't have the money. It had to stop somewhere. Today she was going to do what she'd been putting off for a long time, she was going to total the full amount of their outstanding loans. It was time to take action, and Bryan was going to have to take his head out of the sand and face up to the fact that they were pretty broke.

She had made no reference to his extravagant purchase of several bottles of champagne the night of the party, nor had she asked him how much he'd spent on coke and whatever else he'd taken that night. She hadn't even made any reference to his overnighter at Kev's or the fact that he'd looked very much the worse for wear when he'd finally got home the Saturday afternoon. She'd been relieved that Melissa had already left. He smelt of drink and stale pot and cigarettes, his eyes were bloodshot, and his face was rough with stubble. Not a pretty sight.

No, she'd said not a word; she'd been a perfectly behaved wife and pretended nothing was amiss. But enough was enough, she decided grimly as she made her way into the Dart station and fumbled for her weekly ticket. No more Mrs Nice Girl. Their problems had to be addressed.

If Connie knew how skint they were she'd go mad. She'd been so annoyed the time they'd gone to Amsterdam before their wedding. That had been

265

Debbie's solution to de-stressing Bryan when he'd got uptight about the wedding and had been tempted to call it off. Debbie sighed. That had cost them almost 1,500 euro. That would have paid off a few household bills, she conceded reluctantly, realizing she had to accept her part in their fiscal impoverishment.

Debbie was freaking him out, Bryan had to admit as he tied a knot in his tie and pulled on the jacket of his suit. Not a word about Saturday night, no angst about the bills. It just wasn't like her. Usually, the arrival of a couple of unexpected bills would send her into spasms of anxiety, and she'd fret and worry until they were paid off.

Today, not a word. It was seriously weird. Bryan sighed. They had a month to pay the car tax, and then they could just pay it for three months. If he was the only named driver, he'd risk not paying at all; loads of his mates drove their cars untaxed for months at a time. But Debbie'd go loopers if he suggested it. She wouldn't risk driving in an untaxed or uninsured car. She was just like his mother-in-law in that regard. Dull, boring and playing it safe, being law-abiding citizens. It was only a tax, after all, not a matter of life or death.

Connie was always on at Debbie, too, about over-borrowing, when really it was none of her business. Maybe she might meet a gigolo in Spain, who'd ride the arse off her and give her something else to think about other than interfering in their business, he thought spitefully, smoothing moisturizer on to his face.

Debbie hadn't sounded too enthusiastic about the invite to Sandra Holden's wedding. Black tie was a complete pain in the ass. He hated hiring a suit that had been worn by someone else. He was particular about his clothes. He had some perfectly fine Armani suits of his own that looked the biz. What was wrong with wearing one of them? At least *they* hadn't dictated a dress code for their guests. Theirs had been a classy but informal wedding, and had been all the more fun because of it. No speeches, no seating plans, no formality. It had been a great wedding, small but perfectly formed, Bryan decided, smiling at the memory. It would be interesting to see how Sexy Sandra's compared.

He grabbed his car keys off his bedside locker. He had to drive out to Lucan to inspect a fit-out because the clients were unhappy about the space allocated to a filing system, even though they'd signed off on the plans. He wouldn't mind doing a line of good coke – that would dispel his bad humour, he thought longingly, and then realized what he was thinking.

'Slippery slope, mate, slippery slope,' he muttered as he ran down the stairs. Taking coke was OK socially every now and then, but he'd seen people start taking it at work and, before they knew it, they were depending on it. One guy had even ended up owing thousands and had been beaten up by his dealer. He'd ended up in rehab and out of a job.

That would never be him, he vowed as he got behind the wheel of the convertible, slid his shades down over his eyes, let the roof slide back and drove out of their little cul-de-sac looking like a Hollywood star.

Melissa stood on the weighing scales and frowned. She'd put on a pound, and she was disgusted with herself. She and Sarah had spent Saturday night and all day Sunday at Briony Caulfield's house and had eaten Chinese takeaways and drunk copious amounts of Bacardi Breezers and Smirnoff Ices, which were loaded with calories. There was only one thing for it. She knelt in front of the loo and, with practised ease, made herself sick. She would starve herself for the rest of the day to get back on track.

Briony had shown them photos of a really hot boy she'd dated on holidays. She'd confided in the girls that she'd gone all the way, including bj's. Although they'd pretended to be impressed, she and Sarah were secretly horrified.

'Is it just us? Are we freaky nerds?' Sarah fretted on the way home the following evening.

'I don't know. Everyone seems to be doing it. Briony is only six months older than us.'

'I'd be *sooo* scared that it would hurt.'

'Me, too – remember I told you about that time that horrible boy put his fingers up me? *That* hurt,' Melissa responded glumly, remembering the horrific experience at a New Year's party at friends of her parents when their son had grabbed her, pressed himself against her and thrust his fingers up her privates.

'Eewwwww! Poor you.' Sarah draped an arm around her shoulder and gave her a comforting hug.

'Oh shit, look, there's Rosanna Troy looking over at us. Crap, she'll tell the rest of the class we're lezzers,' Melissa wailed. They separated quickly and gave an embarrassed wave to their schoolmate.

'Don't say that! We're in enough trouble as it is, with Nerdy Nolan trying to latch on to us,' Sarah moaned.

'I wish we were finished school. I hate it. At least we have our first year over. I was totally scared going in my first day last year.'

'Me too,' sighed Sarah. 'I bet Briony can't wait to get back to tell everyone she's done it with a real hot boy. Everyone will think she's dead cool.'

'Well, she'd want to be careful,' Melissa said darkly. 'Look at my mom, preggers, and she's been having sex for years. Just one of those horrible little spermy things is all it takes.'

'Yeah, look at Kelly Wright, having to be pregnant all of sixth year and giving birth during her mocks. I saw her wheeling her baby in the People's Park. And if her mother doesn't agree to babysit, she can't get out at all! How horrible is that?

'You'll probably be babysitting your brother or sister,' Sarah added.

'No way, no way ever!' Melissa declared emphatically.

'Don't forget we have our wedding photos to show off. Remember our gorgeous waiter?' Sarah reminded her.

'Yeah, we can at least let on we scored him, so we're not, like, totally uncool.' Melissa cheered up at the prospect as they said their goodbyes, without their customary hug, as they were conscious of Rosanna paralleling them across the street, and went their separate ways.

At least she and Sarah thought about things the same way, Melissa comforted herself as she sat on the edge of the bath, taking a few moments after making herself sick, enjoying the rush the feeling of being in control gave her. It was such a comfort having a best friend. She hoped fervently that nothing would spoil their friendship. She'd seen girls who'd been the closest ever end up bitter enemies, in rival camps, with not a good word to say about each other, writing horrible things on Bebo.

It was best to keep a low profile at school so as not to become a target. Briony would want to be careful. She could end up being called a slapper and worse, if some of the others turned on her through jealousy. Briony had assured herself and Sarah that sex had been deadly. But Melissa was not convinced. How could it be deadly, all that gross stuff? She hated when boys stuck their tongues down her neck at discos, and when they pressed their hard thing against her, thrusting and grinding and trying to get her to touch them or, even worse . . . give them bj's.

That had to be the most gross thing *ever*! She'd puke if she had to do it, she was sure of it.

Maybe she was frigid, she thought dolefully as she went downstairs to make herself a cup of coffee. She definitely didn't think she was gay; she really and truly wouldn't fancy snogging Sarah. She *must* be frigid, she decided. Everyone else seemed to like sex. Those fab girls in *Sex and the City* were always having mind-blowing orgasms . . . and with loads of different men. Melissa would be mortified to appear nude in front of a man the way Samantha did. She'd even allowed a man to shave her bush on film!! Had her dad ever done that to her mom?

'*Eeewwwwwwwwwwwww!*' She banished the thought as quickly as it had come. It had to be her; they couldn't all be wrong. Definitely frigid, Melissa decided. One more thing to have to worry about.

CHAPTER EIGHTEEN

'Roger, I won't waste your time or mine,' Aimee said crisply as she buttered a slice of toast and lightly covered it with marmalade. 'Something's come up that could affect your job offer.'

'Oh! What's that?' Roger paused from shovelling Clonakilty pudding and sausage, doused in ketchup, into his mouth. 'Do you want more money? Gave in too easily, did ya? Ian's made you a better offer, has he?'

'I'm pregnant,' she said baldly.

'Hell's bells,' he said, taken aback, his little beady blue eyes registering dismay.

'Exactly,' she said coolly. 'I felt it was only fair to tell you. I just confirmed it at the weekend.'

'Well, that's decent of you, Aimee. A lot of women wouldn't say,' he said, putting his knife and fork down. 'Er, was it planned?' he queried delicately.

'No. Not at all.' She sighed. 'It couldn't have come at a worse time, to be honest.'

'I see.'

'I wouldn't be taking a long maternity leave or

anything like it. And I can work from home. I'll also employ a nanny, but I do understand if you wish to withdraw the job offer, Roger. Having a pregnant MD at the start-up of a new company is far from ideal.'

'No, it's not, Aimee, I have to agree with you there. But if anyone can pull it off, I feel you could,' he said slowly, as he resumed eating, this time dipping his forkful of food into a runny egg, which then proceeded to dribble down the side of his mouth.

Aimee felt her stomach heave and swallowed frantically as perspiration beaded her upper lip.

'Excuse me, Roger, back in a sec,' she murmured, before walking swiftly out of the crowded dining room. She made it to the ladies and retched miserably. *I hate you, for making me endure this, Barry Adams*, she thought viciously. *If you had to go through it, we'd see how keen you were to keep a baby.*

She took some deep breaths, flushed the loo and went out to wash her hands. Her eyes were bright, her cheeks flushed. She felt completely rattled. She retouched her lipstick and smoothed down her hair.

'Come on, you can do it,' she said to herself, trying to get herself back on form as she walked back along the carpeted corridor.

'Sorry about that. Morning sickness,' she said calmly, sitting back on her chair and spreading her napkin on her knees. He might as well see her at her worst, Aimee decided.

'Bugger of a thing,' Roger said cheerfully. 'My

wife was murdered with it. Upchucked everywhere at the drop of a hat. I don't think she ever forgave me, even though it was over twenty-eight years ago with our youngest.'

'I'm sure she's long forgotten it,' Aimee said diplomatically.

'Who knows? We've drifted apart over the years. We stay together because it suits us, but we do our own thing, if you know what I mean.'

'If it works for you both, why not?' Aimee did not really wish to hear the intimate details of Roger's marriage.

'I suppose I lost the run of myself when I was younger and began to get a taste of the good life – and it was a very good life – but I lost my wife in the process because I neglected her.'

'That's a shame.' She risked a piece of croissant.

'It's very interesting to see how women treat you when you're wealthy,' Roger expounded, taking a slug of coffee. 'I know I'm no oil painting. If I was my age now and still on the farm I grew up on, women wouldn't give me a second look. A little fat man trying to hide his bald patch – no, indeed, Aimee, I wouldn't even rate a first look, let alone a second, but having money changes all that. And you know something?' He put his knife and fork back down and looked at her earnestly, 'I'd love to meet a woman who likes me for *who* I am and not for my wallet. Because now I never know.' He shook his head. 'When you have money, people think you have it all, but money doesn't put its arms around you, and the older you get, the less you want to be out socializing with all that crowd who secretly look down their nose at you but wish they had your lolly. And what's worse . . . lick up to you because you have it.'

'You're highly respected out there, Roger,' Aimee assured him.

'Maybe I am, maybe I'm not, but my point to you, Aimee, is, on your climb up the ladder, and you are climbing fast, don't lose sight of what's important.' He pointed towards her stomach. 'Family is all that matters, Aimee, and take that from one who knows. Now, what I propose is to have a chat with Myles and let him know the score, and then we'll take it from there. Obviously, he may have his own views on the matter. But, from my point of view, your pregnancy is not an insurmountable problem, and you have my respect for being upfront about it. As I say, a lot of women wouldn't have said anything until after the contract was signed. And, as someone who climbed a hard ladder once, I understand that too.'

'Thanks, Roger,' Aimee said sincerely, seeing a whole new side to the stocky, red-faced man opposite her. She had been one who had looked down her nose at him, although happy to grasp the opportunity he'd given her. His brash, hail-fellow-well-met façade hid a surprisingly sensitive and self-aware man who was also, it seemed, rather lonely, despite constant appearances in the social diaries.

'Now, Aimee, I'll let Ian treat us to breakfast. He made enough out of me, God knows, and I bet I'm right in thinking you haven't even been given a bonus yet.'

Aimee laughed. 'How did you know that?'

'If he was treating you properly, as an asset to his company deserves to be treated, you wouldn't have said yes straight away to our proposal, because he would have made sure to keep you sweet. We would have had to woo you. That's how I know. I've been in business a long time. Don't forget that. I'll be in touch.' He stood up and shook her hand firmly. 'Peppermint tea and plain biscuits.' He winked and barrelled out of the dining room like a mini tornado, greeting various other diners with a handshake, a wave or a quick word.

Aimee exhaled a deep breath and felt much of the tension seep out of her body. That had gone much better than she'd expected. Yes, she'd seen the dismay on her prospective employer's face when she'd told him her news, but he hadn't felt it was an insuperable barrier. Maybe she should start thinking like that too, she reflected, as she sipped the last of her tea. A more positive attitude might help her get through the months ahead and, at least, if Roger was able to persuade Myles to stay on board, she'd have her new career move to keep her occupied.

More satisfying than anything else that had occurred, though, was the fact that a hugely successful, multi-millionaire businessman felt she was an 'asset', whom he would have 'wooed' if she'd played hard to get.

Roger O'Leary certainly respected her, that was more than obvious, and that, after her row with Barry and her father's presumptions, was balm to Aimee's weary soul.

'It was bumpy coming down, wasn't it?' Juliet remarked as she walked briskly alongside Karen and Connie, down the pink-speckled, marbled floor of Arrivals, to Passport Control.

'I hate that steep descent over the mountains, it always makes my ears pop.' Karen wriggled her jaw, not the better for the rough approach, when crosswinds from the sierras had buffeted the plane. 'I suppose we were lucky we weren't flying Ryanair; you know the way they throw the plane on to the runway. I've never once had a smooth landing with that lot.'

'Still, we're here, and I for one am looking forward to a stiff gin and tonic with lunch,' Connie remarked, holding her passport up for inspection.

'That sounds lovely,' Juliet sighed. 'I think I'll do the same.'

'Do you rent a car when you're here?' Karen asked as they clattered down the stairs to the baggage hall.

'Actually, we bought one here; it's cheaper in the long run. Manolo, who takes care of our villa, was supposed to be meeting me off the flight, but he ended up in hospital yesterday with a broken wrist, so I'll take a taxi. Would you like to share, or are you renting a car yourselves?'

'I'm going downstairs to car rentals now to queue up to get the keys while Connie collects the luggage. Sure, we could drop you off, if you like. It's in Cabopino, isn't it? And we're between Riviera and Calahonda. It's only a few miles, five minutes in the car.'

'Oh, I wouldn't dream of putting you out,' Juliet exclaimed.

'You're not putting us out at all, we're practically neighbours,' Karen said hospitably as they reached their luggage carousel.

'Well, thank you so much, it's very kind of you,' the older woman said appreciatively.

'Let me go get a trolley before you go down to the car place,' Connie suggested. She weaved her way through swarms of passengers, to two lines of trolleys, which were disappearing rapidly. The queues at the car-rental agencies would probably be long, and they could be here for a while, and she'd have to make small talk with Juliet Davenport, she supposed. She extracted a trolley and tried to steer it through the throngs without inflicting damage on anyone's ankles. Her heart sank at the prospect of prolonged polite chitchat. While the woman seemed pleasant enough, Connie was very conscious that she was Aimee's mother and wondered had the other woman ever discussed her with Juliet.

'God, it's mad trying to get a trolley,' she remarked a few minutes later as she joined the other two women at the carousel, which had started to move creakily, indicating that the luggage wouldn't be long coming.

'I'm going to leg it, see you down there. Don't forget, mine's got a red ribbon on it,' Karen declared, taking off at speed along the crowded concourse.

'It's almost impossible to see,' Juliet complained, trying to edge in between two six-foot golfers who wouldn't budge. 'Bloody men,' she muttered to Connie. 'They're all the same. Thank God I came by myself.'

Connie laughed. She'd met Ken Davenport, and not been impressed with his loud, overbearing manner. 'Sometimes it is nice to get away on your own, but I love going on holidays with Karen because I live on my own.'

'Of course. Company is lovely, but living on your own ... how peaceful that must be sometimes,' Juliet remarked. 'Do you know what I did, Connie?' she confided impulsively. 'I came away and never told Ken I was going, because we had a row. I didn't fill the freezer, I didn't do any shopping, I didn't even do his laundry.'

'Ummm ... I'd say there's a fairly disgruntled husband at home then.' Connie elbowed her way between the golfers, to the edge of the carousel.

'Yes, well, I was a fairly disgruntled wife coming to Spain. What's sauce for the goose is sauce for the gander. It might teach him not to take me for granted,' Juliet declared. 'I've been too

279

accommodating all along, but he pushed his luck once too often. And there comes a time when you just aren't willing to put up with bad behaviour any more. Better late than never,' she said dryly, having edged in beside Connie, as luggage careered along past them on the belt.

'Oh! Well, you certainly made your point in no uncertain terms, I'd say. Good for you.'

'I did, didn't I?' Juliet grinned. 'As I say, it's never too late, Connie. And if my husband doesn't like it, he can lump it.'

'Get me *Derek* O'Mahony's file, not Dermot O'Mahony's,' Ken barked into the phone at his secretary before slamming down the receiver. He was in a foul humour. He had three patients in his waiting room. He was running late, and he had to make two important phone calls before he started seeing the people outside, and that stupid woman had brought him in the wrong file. Incompetent carelessness was not what she was paid a very good salary for.

He picked up his mobile phone again and scrolled through his messages. No report to indicate that Juliet had received his text message. The damn woman hadn't even turned on her phone.

He played back her message to him. 'Ken, I'm sitting on the plane for Malaga. We're taking off in a few minutes. I've booked myself an open ticket. I don't know when I'm coming back. I've had enough. I need a break to decide my future. Bye.'

What the hell did she mean by that? *I need a break*

to decide my future. Juliet looked at far too many rubbishy soap operas, that was her problem. Ungrateful woman. He was surrounded by them. Aimee had been most unhelpful this morning. She was his daughter; the least he could expect from her was some sympathy for his predicament and a cooked dinner or two. Not too much of a require- ment, considering the business she was in, he thought sourly. Hadn't he paid for her to go to catering college, for heaven's sake, seeing as she hadn't the brains to do medicine? If it wasn't for him paying for her college course, she'd never have got a job in the first place. But, of course, did she ever stop to think of that? Did any of them ever stop to think of how hard he had worked to give them life's luxuries? It clearly meant nothing to his wife. He sat, shrouded in self-pity.

His secretary sidled in with the correct file, and he snatched it rudely from her. 'File that other one properly and see that I have no interruptions until I've made my phone calls,' he decreed imperiously.

'Yes, Professor Davenport,' she murmured respectfully, and scuttled out of the office with the offending file.

He picked up his mobile and rang Juliet's number. Infuriatingly, it went straight to her mail- box. The daft woman hadn't even turned her mobile phone back on; she was surely well ensconced in the villa by now. He didn't have the landline number handy. He knew he had to put in a 34 code, but that was all he remembered.

'Would you kindly ring me,' he clipped, leaving his second voice message in her mailbox. It was most disconcerting not knowing how long she was staying. They usually went to the villa six times a year, and sometimes she would go with some of her friends for a week or two, but to have bought an open ticket was completely out of character for Juliet, and he was beginning to wonder was she psychologically unbalanced. Could there be some physical cause for this uncharacteristic behaviour? He began to think of probable causes and stopped himself when he got to a possible brain tumour. This was not helpful. He needed to speak to his wife to try and evaluate for himself what her state of mind was. But she was uncontactable, and he was beginning to get worried.

'Ring my villa and put me through,' he ordered his secretary, and he beat a tattoo on his desk until she said down the line, 'Ringing for you,' and he heard the unmistakable long dial tone that signified a foreign number was being called.

'Hola.' At last, Ken thought with relief, as he recognized the voice at the other end of the phone. It was their Spanish maid.

'Incarna, is my wife there please? I wish to speak to her.'

'No, Señor, she not here. Ze señora she has gone out to ze lunch, and I will be gone when she come back. I leave ze message and get her to ring you, si?'

'Si, thank you, Incarna,' Ken sighed, defeated, and hung up.

Gone out to lunch, had she? And not a thought for him. What had got into her at all? Inconsiderate and unacceptable, that's what her behaviour was, and he'd be letting her know what he thought of it in no uncertain terms, as soon as an opportunity presented itself.

'Bottoms up, girls. This was completely unexpected.' Juliet giggled, a little tipsy, as she drank her second glass of chilled Chablis. They'd already had a G&T as they perused their menus.

'To the perfect holiday,' grinned Connie, clinking her glass with Juliet's.

'To no cooking, for ten days.' Karen patted her stomach, replete after a meal of tapas starters and a pepper steak with roasted vegetables.

They were sitting under an awning at a beachside restaurant listening to the swish of the sea as it lapped the golden curve of beach in front of them. It was one of those exquisitely clear, bright days which allowed you to see right across the glistening waters of the Mediterranean to the peaks of the High Atlas mountains in Africa. A massive white cruise liner glided serenely along the horizon towards the Straits of Gibraltar, and a sleek motor yacht sailed closer to shore on its way to Puerto Banus. A cooling breeze took the intense heat out of the day, ruffling the red-paper tablecloths, and a buzz of chat and laughter added to the holiday atmosphere as diners, in various stages of undress, enjoyed their meals.

The ladies were totally relaxed, the hassle of airports and queues at car rentals already a dim and distant memory. Juliet was surprisingly witty and entertaining out of her husband's shadow, and Connie found herself thoroughly warming to the older woman. She had invited Karen and Connie to lunch at the beach restaurant close to her villa and insisted that they all take a taxi from Karen's apartment so that they could enjoy a few drinks with their meal. It was a most enjoyable start to their holiday.

Connie's phone tinkled, and she opened a text from Debbie reminding her not to forget to buy a couple of sarongs at the market. 'I've to buy sarongs in the market in La Cala,' she informed her companions. 'Don't let me forget them, Karen, my mind's like a sieve these days.'

'Do you think Ken would look good in a sarong *à la* Beckham?' tittered Juliet, and Karen choked on her wine at the image that presented itself.

'I bet he's sizzling at this stage, turning a nice shade of purple.' She'd given her two companions the gory details of events that had led to her early morning flit to Spain. 'The flight into Egypt had nothing on me,' she'd chortled as she'd sipped her G&T. She fished her phone out of her bag and turned it on. A half-dozen messages flashed up on the screen. 'See' – she waved it around – 'he's as mad as hell.' She dialled 171 and put the phone on loudspeaker.

'What do you *mean* you've booked an open ticket

and are taking a break? You're behaving extremely childishly, Juliet. It does not become you! Ring me as soon as you get this message!' Ken's exasperated tones resounded around their table.

Connie and Karen looked at Juliet, awaiting her response. Ken sounded absolutely livid. 'Listen to that! "It does not become you," indeed,' she jeered. 'Here's the next one.'

'Would you *kindly* ring me?'

'He's just barely holding it in,' she confided giddily. 'The next one's going to be good.'

'JULIET. TURN ON YOUR DAMN PHONE AND RING ME,' Ken bellowed, and the three of them guffawed loudly.

Juliet dialled straight into his mailbox. 'Ken, I'm having lunch with friends, mostly liquid, if you must know. I'll turn my phone on when I'm good and ready and may or may not call you, depending on the state of my hangover. Have a good day and don't forget to put the green bin out.' She turned her phone off and put it back in her bag. 'That will give him something to think about. Who knows, he might get so mad he'll have a coronary and make me a happy widow. Let's have another bottle of wine . . . on Ken,' she suggested wickedly, signalling to the waiter.

'Oh God, I'll be asleep if I drink any more,' groaned Connie.

'Weren't you up before dawn? It's not drink that will make you sleep, it's tiredness,' Karen soothed, taking another slug of hers. 'What have we to do except go home and plonk ourselves on our loungers? We're fed and watered.' She waved her glass around. 'We can unpack tomorrow.'

'True,' agreed Connie. 'When you put it like that, what can you do only have another glass?'

Juliet sniggered. 'I'm having such fun. Eat your heart out, Ken. Aimee would be delighted if she saw this, she's been telling me for years to do my own thing. And she was right. Just as well I came to my senses before it's too late, Kenneth Bartholomew Davenport!'

'Mum, have you been drinking?' Aimee demanded as her mother answered the phone in a faintly slurred, dopey voice.

'Yes I have. I was asleep, I'll have you know. I had a long and very liquid lunch with Connie and Karen. I was up before dawn and I was having a siesta. I'm in Spain, remember? That's what they do here.' There was a faint edge to her voice.

'You had lunch with Connie Adams and Karen?' Was she hearing things, Aimee wondered.

'Yes, I met them on the flight over. You know the way you can never fly to Malaga without seeing someone you know?'

'Oh! How were they?' Aimee asked, taken aback. She'd never told Juliet that she'd had words with Connie; her mother wouldn't like that sort of thing. Barry's ex must have been friendly enough with Juliet if they'd all had lunch. Aimee felt an uncharacteristic stab of envy. How jolly for them, being able to have a long, liquid lunch. She hadn't even been able to keep down her breakfast, and it would be a hell of a long time before she could indulge in a liquid lunch again. And who would she have lunch with anyway, she thought morosely. She'd no real friends left, thanks to her race up the career ladder; she'd let them fall by the wayside because she hadn't had time to have long girly lunches and go to films and the like with the crowd she'd socialized with.

'They're both in terrific form and looking forward to their holiday. You should take one yourself, Aimee. Come over for a few days with Melissa and Barry. I'm going to stay for a while,' her mother urged expansively.

'We'll see,' Aimee demurred, knowing that a holiday in her parents' villa was not going to happen with Barry, not with the way things were at the moment. 'Are you going to see them again?' She was curious.

'Oh yes. We're going to have dinner in Orange Square some night, or maybe over at Da Bruno here at the marina, and we're going shopping in La Cañada. Connie's never been there.'

'Oh! Right! And you enjoyed lunch with them?'

'Immensely. We had a great time and, though I may be suffering a bit now, it was well worth it, I haven't had such fun in ages.' She yawned loudly. 'I'm going to take this phone off the hook. Just as well you rang. I don't want your father roaring at me – you should have heard the messages he left on my mobile.'

287

'He's fairly mad, all right. I had three phone calls from him before lunch to see had I heard from you.'

'Don't worry, darling, I left him one back telling him in no uncertain terms that I'd ring him when I felt like it, and that won't be tonight, I can assure you. Don't take any nonsense from him.'

'I won't,' Aimee said slowly. 'Mum, are you OK? Is everything OK? This isn't like you.'

Juliet laughed at the touch of uncertainty in her daughter's tone. 'Hark at you. Have you not been telling me to do my own thing, for years? Aimee, I'm sixty-four and still have a bit of go in me, so I'm going to take your advice and do my own thing, and your father better get used to it. He pushed it one step too far, this time. He said some very obnoxious things to me, which showed a complete and utter lack of respect, and now he can take the consequences. I should have stood up for myself and done what *I* wanted to do years ago. But at least I've taken the first step. Now let me go back asleep, and I'll talk to you during the week.'

'Enjoy yourself.'

'I have every intention of doing so. Bye, dear.'

'Bye, Mum. Well done,' Aimee approved, replacing the receiver. What a very strange day today had been, she mused, clicking open an email from an Italian glassware firm she did business with.

First her father's phone call, then Roger's candid confessions, and now her mother telling her about a liquid lunch with her sister-in-law and Barry's ex, who Aimee detested. It was almost surreal. She

288

yawned. A deep weariness assaulted her. How she longed to put her head down on her forearms and sleep for twenty minutes. She glanced at her watch. It was just gone four.

She remembered Roger allowing her to buy him breakfast on expenses because he felt Ian had made a lot of money out of him. There were no flies on Roger, she thought admiringly. That money had been made for Master Ian because *she* had worked her tush off, so sod her boss, she decided, logging off her computer and picking up her bag and brief-case. 'I'm heading off, something's come up. I may not have my mobile switched on, so deal with any-thing that arises and I'll sort any problems out tomorrow,' she instructed her PA. 'And,' she added as an afterthought, 'see what's the availability on any Aer Lingus flights to Malaga the week after next. Check for two. I might take a few days' leave; I haven't had any since last year. I could do with taking Melissa away. Lindsay can fill in for me, at the Jennings Callely event.'

'Sure, Aimee,' her PA said, taking notes. Aimee struggled not to yawn in front of her. She was going home, and she was going to get into bed, and she was going to sleep her brains out. If her mother could make a stand, so could she. *Chez Moi* would manage without her for a couple of hours. And, she was going to go to Spain, she decided. If Roger gave her the go ahead, she'd hand in her notice im-mediately. If Myles nixed the venture due to her pregnancy, she still had a lot of leave to take anyway so, whether Ian liked it or not, she was going to take it. Melissa would be thrilled; she could hook up with Clara when she was out there and that would keep her happy. And it would be nice for her to spend some time with her mother. Aimee hadn't made much time for her over the past few years, she thought a little guiltily. Besides, she was exhausted; the last two years of almost non-stop work was starting to take its toll. She badly needed to recharge her batteries for what was to come.

'You had lunch with Juliet Davenport, and you all got pissed! Way to go, Mum.' Debbie laughed as she chatted with her mother on the Dart on her way home from work. The line was excellent, and Connie's voice was as clear as a bell. 'Did she know about the row with Aimee at the church?'

'She didn't seem to,' Connie said. 'She was very friendly and entertaining. We had great fun.'

'Well, that's what it's all about. What are you doing now?'

'Sitting on the balcony watching the sun start to set and listening to the waves, and sipping yet another glass of wine. It's a spritzer actually. We took pity on our heads. As soon as it gets dark we'll be in our beds. It's been a very long day, but most enjoyable. I feel thoroughly relaxed already.'

'That's terrific, Mum. Give Karen my love, and have a great holiday. You both deserve it.'

'Thanks, love. I'll be in touch, and I'll get the sarongs at the market on Saturday.'

'Great, love ya.'

'Love you too. Bye.'

Debbie glanced at her watch as the phone went dead. It was almost 7.15. She'd been stuck on a Dart for half an hour because a train had broken down further along the line and they were between stations.

She wished mightily that she was sitting on Karen's balcony watching the sun set. Her stomach was in knots. She'd sat at her desk earlier and worked out her and Bryan's debts, not including their mortgage, and had been deeply horrified to realize that, between their credit card, a credit-union loan and the repayments for the car they were in debt to the tune of 55,000 euros. She felt sick with dread just even thinking about it. They were barely managing to pay off the interest. When were they ever going to start on the principals involved? What a way to begin married life, she thought dejectedly, and how was Bryan going to react when she told him they were really and truly on their uppers?

CHAPTER NINETEEN

'I think we'll put you on Prozac for a little while, Judith. Just to get you over the hump. All your resources are depleted, you've had a rough time. The Prozac will help to get you on an even keel again. Don't worry about taking it. I don't envisage you on it long term but, between your accident and what you've told me about your background, plus the fact that you're at that difficult age when your hormones are awry and your oestrogens are declining, a little help is called for. Have you ever discussed HRT with your doctor?' the psychiatrist inquired as he wrote some notes on her chart.

'He didn't think I was a suitable candidate,' Judith said stiffly. She wished the tall, thin, balding man in front of her would go away. She was mortified at having to discuss all her intimate personal history with a complete and utter stranger. She felt strangely disloyal to Lily, remembering how, two days previously, in a session with him all her pent-up resentments had come pouring out as she'd revealed how she'd ended up living with her mother and how angry she had been with Lily and her sister the day she'd had the car crash.

She'd been off guard and unprepared when he'd come and sat down beside her bed. Although much less sedated than she had been for the previous twenty-four hours after her hysterical outburst, she was still woozy from drugs and had responded to his gentle probing with unsuspecting candour, which she now bitterly regretted.

What had she been thinking of, losing control and ranting about wanting to commit suicide? How had she let herself become so overwhelmed by her emotions, when she usually kept such a tight rein on them? She'd lost it completely and made an exhibition of herself. That had only given them licence to drug her and make her see a shrink. Now everyone knew her personal business; it was on her chart that she was having a psychiatric evaluation. Her neurosurgeon knew it, as did her orthopaedic guy, and she was more embarrassed than she'd ever been in her entire life to think that they all now thought of her as a looper. How she wished she could leave the hospital and never have to see any of them again. Today, the psychiatrist had brought up the subject of work, but she'd clammed up and refused to talk about it, remembering how Debbie Adams had called her a bully and she'd shouted something about it to the nurse when she freaked out.

He could frig off; she'd told him enough about herself, she was not going to embarrass herself further.

Poor Lily had been pinched with worry these past few days, wondering was there anything she could do to help. It wasn't fair on her elderly mother, having to trot in and out to the hospital every afternoon. Judith was going to have to get a grip on herself and get the hell out of the place.

'Dr Fitzgerald.' She stared at him through heavy-lidded eyes. He had, Judith observed, the look of a druid, one of those composed, wise elders that dispensed wisdom and radiated calm reassurance.

'Yes, Judith?' he responded, sitting on the side of her bed, head cocked sideways, looking over at her as she lay against a bank of white pillows.

'I'll take those drugs for a while, as you say to . . .' *What was it he'd said to her? She could barely remember, it reminded her of a boat. Oh yes, keel, that was it.* '. . . get me on an even keel again, but I don't feel the need for any more of these sessions. I had a momentary . . . er . . .' *How would she describe shrieking like a fishwife, she pondered.* '. . . er . . . upset.' *Yes, that was a good word, she congratulated herself.* 'Everything probably got to me. Thank you for your . . . um . . .' *What would she say, she wondered, trying to catch the words that seemed to be floating away from her.* 'Er . . . kind attention, but I don't wish to . . . take up any more of your time.'

There! She'd managed it, even though her tongue felt thick in her mouth and her voice had seemed quite far away. She was rather proud of the note of authority she'd managed to inject into her tone, but she hoped he'd hurry on and go. She was exhausted and wanted to close her eyes and go back asleep.

'It's no trouble, Judith,' the doctor said mildly, patting her hand as he stood up. 'But it's good to see that you're feeling a little better. We'll talk tomorrow.'

That's what you think, Judith sniffed as he put his pen in his top pocket and walked to the door.

'And, by the way, Judith, you're very hard on yourself; you sacrificed a lot for your mother. That was difficult to endure all these years. Carers have a very hard path in life. They need all the support they can get. You got none. You're entitled to fall to pieces now and again. There's no shame in being vulnerable.' He smiled at her in a benevolent fashion before closing the door behind him.

Judith felt a lump rise to her throat. That was the kindest thing anyone had ever said to her, apart from her father and Jillian. It was the first time someone had actually *acknowledged* her sacrifice. Judith felt the tears begin to fall, but she did nothing to try and stop them. She *was* entitled to cry, she thought sorrowfully. Life *had* been hard to endure and a stranger had just affirmed how very difficult it had been for her, something neither of her siblings or extended family had ever admitted. Well, she didn't need them to state it now. Someone with more compassion than they'd ever have had applauded her endeavour. That man would never know how much his kind words had helped. 'There's no shame in being vulnerable,' he'd said. 'You're entitled to fall to pieces now and again.'

Even in her drugged state those two sentences stood out clearly. Well, she *had* gone to pieces, she'd hit rock bottom. Now she could begin to pick herself up and move on as best she could.

'Yes, Mr Martin, I'll be wanting to put my daughter Judith's name on the deeds of the house as soon as she's out of hospital. If you can have it all prepared, I'll make an appointment to sign any papers necessary.' Lily gave her instructions over the phone, twirling the cord nervously between her bony, gnarled fingers.

'Are you sure about this, Mrs Baxter? It's your own idea? No . . . ah . . . pressure is being applied?' her solicitor inquired tactfully.

'None whatsoever. As I say, poor Judith is in hospital recovering from a terrible accident. I don't know if she even remembers that I told her I was going to do this. But thank you so much, Mr Martin, for being concerned on my behalf,' Lily assured him, very pleased that he had her best interests at heart.

'We always like to be vigilant where our elderly clients are concerned,' the solicitor explained.

'And rightly so, Mr Martin. I know one or two who would be quite devious about such matters.' Lily nodded as Tom came to mind. 'Needless to say, this is a matter for Judith and myself and should there ever be any, em . . . dispute or queries about the matter when I die, you will be able to state *unequivocally* that I was of sound mind when making this decision.'

'Indeed I shall, there is no doubt about that what-soever, Mrs Baxter, no doubt at all,' the solicitor responded, and Lily felt he was smiling.

'That's that sorted then,' Lily declared decisively. 'I'll be in touch. Thank you for your kind assistance.'

'You're most welcome,' replied the solicitor before hanging up.

Lily stared out the window as she replaced the receiver in its cradle. It was raining today, torrential downpours that detonated out of a black leaden sky with a ferocity that made her worry if the roof would stand up to the onslaught. Rivulets of water ran down the windowpanes, distorting the view as the rain bounced off a parked car after hammering down on to the roof and bonnet.

She'd have to wear her rain mac and bring a brolly today going to visit Judith. They'd offer poor protection from this sort of weather, she reflected, as a flash of lightning and then a clatter of thunder rent the sky. Lily almost jumped with fright. She didn't like thunder and lightning. It scared her. Another flash and rattle had her scrabbling for her rosary beads.

'Our Lady and St Michael protect me,' she prayed fervently as another roar of thunder rattled the windowpanes.

She closed her eyes, but then opened them quickly, deciding she wouldn't like to be caught unawares. Her heart was thumping against her ribcage. Another flash of lightning, but slightly fainter this time as the thunder rolled to the east. She wondered would there be floods. The Tolka river at the other side of the park had burst its banks several times, but it hadn't affected Lily's street, for which she was truly grateful. Houses had been ruined because of the floods. She must remind Judith to be careful where she bought her property. She wouldn't need complications like flooding. She had enough difficulties in her life. Just as she was thinking about her daughter, the phone rang. 'Hello,' she quavered, hoping a flash of lightning wouldn't explode the phone on her.

'Hello, Ma, just checking if you're OK.' Judith's voice came down the line.

'Oh, hello, Judith. Yes, yes, don't you worry.' Lily pretended bravery.

'It's just I know you don't like thunder and lightning. Ma, don't come in this afternoon,' Judith said firmly, even though her voice still sounded slurred from the drugs they were giving her.

'I'll be in,' Lily declared stoutly.

'Ma, please. I'll only be worrying about you in this weather. You'll be drenched. I'm much better today, honestly.'

'Are you?' Lily said doubtfully.

'Yes I am. I had a very good chat with a doctor. Everything's going to be all right. So please, why don't you sit in your chair for the afternoon and rest.'

'Are you certain? I'll come in if you want.'

'I'm positive. And Ma . . .'

'Yes, Judith?'

'Ma, thanks for everything. You've been very, very kind to me.'

Lily swallowed hard and blinked rapidly as tears welled up in her eyes.

'Did you hear what I said?' Judith asked when there was no response.

'I did ... dear. And I'm only trying to repay in some small way all your kindness to me down the years,' she managed.

'I wasn't that kind, Ma. I'm sorry I was so cranky. I didn't treat you very nicely.' Judith sounded close to tears herself.

'I was fairly cranky myself, so we won't be like that with each other any more, sure we won't?' Lily dabbed her eyes with her lace handkerchief.

'No we won't, Ma, we'll make a fresh start.'

'Yes we will. And I've taken the first steps this very day,' Lily exclaimed, remembering her conversation with the solicitor. 'I was on to Mr Martin just a little while ago, would you believe. And I've instructed him to put your name on the deeds of the house so you can use it as collateral to get your loan for a mortgage. And the house will still be yours when I'm gone, so you'll be a woman of property. Does that make you feel better?' she asked anxiously, desperate to make amends for what she'd put her daughter through.

'Oh Ma, you don't have to do that. You really don't. I—'

'Oh yes I do, Judith. It's something I should have done long ago, so we won't argue about it or I'll get vexed, and you don't want that,' Lily declared humorously.

'No, I don't want you vexed, Ma. But you know I don't expect you—'

'I know you don't, Judith, but it would make me pleased and contented to know you have a place of your own.'

'Thanks, Ma, we'll talk about it tomorrow. Go and have a rest for yourself, now,' Judith urged and gave a yawn.

'And you do too,' Lily said kindly. For the second time that day she replaced the receiver in the cradle. A feeling of peace washed over her. In their own peculiar way, she and Judith loved each other, she realized. Even from her sickbed, her daughter had been thinking about her and had phoned to make sure she was OK during a thunderstorm. If she hadn't given a hoot about her, she wouldn't have bothered. Neither Tom nor Cecily had ever taken the trouble to get in touch with her during a thunderstorm. Cecily, in fairness, *had* offered to cancel her trip to France because of her sister's setback. Lily had told her to go ahead. What was the point in her staying, it wasn't as if Judith was in any danger. She was having trouble with her nerves, and Lily, not Cecily, was the expert in that department, she'd told her younger daughter.

Sometimes good things came from bad. She and Judith were starting afresh, and all because her daughter had almost been killed in an accident. Now, though, Lily was being given a chance to repay Judith in some small way for all the years her daughter had been at her beck and call, especially when there had been no need for it, she thought guiltily. When the chips were down and she'd had no choice, she'd had to fend for herself. She'd managed very well. If Judith had not had her accident, Lily would never have known the freedom of independence. God certainly worked in strange ways, she mused, as another roll of thunder, much further away this time, growled over the city.

Lily gave a gusty sigh. There was one other reason she was in Judith's debt. And it had troubled her for a long, long time. Lily bowed her head, trying not to cry as she remembered how she had left Judith alone at Ted's deathbed. She had abandoned her dearly loved husband when he needed her most because she had been terrified. Terrified of watching him die, terrified by the drunks and druggies falling around the A&E where her husband lay on a trolley for his last hours. Even the immense kindness of the nurses when they'd wheeled Ted into a smaller section off the main area hadn't calmed her. She'd wanted to get out of there as quickly as she could, and so had Tom. Thinking back, she knew Judith must have been just as scared and lonely and heartbroken as she was. Father and daughter had been so close. But Lily had thought only of herself. Tears slid down her cheeks. She was a selfish woman and a failure as a wife and mother, she scourged herself, as all the old memories came flooding back: Judith, white as a ghost, Tom fidgeting, unable to look at his father, and Ted lying shrivelled and waxen with tubes everywhere and machines beeping, frightening the life out of them all.

When Judith had suggested that Tom take her home she had needed no second urging, even though she knew she would never see Ted alive again. Ted would never have left her, never have *deserted* her the way she had deserted him. She'd squeezed his hand but said nothing, her throat was so tight with terror and emotion. She hadn't even told him she loved him or thanked him for being a wonderful husband. She'd hurried out of the A&E without a backward glance, desperate to get to the sanctuary of her bed, where she could burrow under the bedclothes and set the world aside, leaving Judith alone with her dying father.

Lily had been so angry with Ted for such a long time after he died. How could he have left her to face the world she was so afraid of without him at her side? Looking back, she wondered how Judith had been so patient with her. Never by so much as a word had she ever made Lily feel guilty for abandoning her. Until now, Lily had never even acknowledged that. Shame flooded her. She had been so hard on her elder daughter, so demanding. It was more than time to repay her. Ted would want her to make sure Judith was well looked after.

'I'm sorry, Ted, so very sorry, I love you very much, and I let you down,' she wept, knuckles rubbing her eyes as great waves of sadness and loss and regret surged through her. Eventually, her crying stopped and the tumult ceased, the emotions ebbing away leaving her drained but strangely purged. It was as though the release of the guilt that had been deeply buried for all these years had changed something in her. She wiped her eyes with her handkerchief and went upstairs and sat on the side of her bed with her framed photo of her husband clutched against her chest, and sat in silent prayer. After a while, comforted, she went back downstairs and took out her dusters and polish and worked her way through the rooms, glad to be occupied. She worked diligently, dusting her precious ornaments in her sitting room, all of which held special, happy memories of her marriage to Ted. Judith called them clutter, but she didn't really understand, Lily mused, as she polished a set of brass candlesticks that Ted had bought her for their first Christmas together.

The room grew darker and the rain began again, great spills of water assaulting the windows. Lily shivered. It had grown cold. The weather was very intemperate. One day it was warm and close, the next cold and raining, and not just ordinary rain, deluges that drenched you after only a few seconds. She was very relieved that Judith had insisted that she not visit today. She was going to light her fire and make herself a cup of tea and hot buttery toast and then she was going to snooze in her chair beside the fire for a while before watching *Countdown* and Paul O'Grady, her favourite afternoon shows. It seemed like a lifetime ago since she'd seen them. Lily loved Paul O'Grady; even in her darkest moments when she was anxious and fluttery and tense, he'd make her laugh. He had a kind face. And he loved that little dog, Buster. He was a real character that dog, turning his behind to the camera when he wasn't in the humour to entertain the audience. It always made Lily laugh. It was the programme she most looked forward to, and today she could do with some cheering up.

The fire was blazing up the chimney, casting flickering shadows on the walls, and she was nice and full after a cup of hot sweet tea and two slices of toast with melting butter. She turned her chair to the fireside and settled herself comfortably. She was just beginning to drop off when a car pulled up outside and the banging of the car door startled her awake. She twisted around and peered out behind her lace curtains, and her heart sank as she recognized Tom's BMW.

What was he doing here, she thought in dismay. Just when she had a free afternoon to enjoy. He hardly knew about her phone call this morning, she worried. Surely Mr Martin wouldn't have betrayed her confidence and contacted him.

Don't be silly, she scolded herself as the doorbell rang. She flattened herself against the wall beside the window. She wasn't going to answer it. He could go and hump. He'd be wanting tea and cake, and she'd have to listen to him waffling on. The doorbell rang again, longer this time, and her lips tightened in anger as the phone started to ring, its tone louder and shriller than the bell. She peeped out again and saw him with his back to her, mobile up to his ear. Ha! He was ringing her. She wasn't going to answer.

She saw him thrust his phone impatiently back into his pocket, and then he hurried back to the car.

Well done, Lily. She gave herself a mental pat on the back. But why wasn't he starting up the engine? He was hardly going to sit there and wait for her? She wouldn't be able to relax if that was the case. 'Oh!' she exclaimed in dismay. Tom was out of the car again and coming back to the door.

'Go away and leave me in peace,' she muttered – and heard the letter box open. He was leaving her a note, no doubt to tell her he'd called.

Her strategy had worked. Two minutes later, Tom was driving away in a spray of water and crashing gears. Lily sat back in her chair and settled herself for her nap. It wasn't to inquire about the good of her health that Tom had called, she knew fine well, so she didn't feel one bit guilty about not answering the door to him. It would be a relief to her when Judith's name was on the deeds and she'd got her loan because, then, he'd be able to do nothing about it. And if that didn't suit him he could go and take a good long running jump.

His ma must have left early to visit the hospital because of the atrocious weather. It was amazing what she could do when she had to, Tom reflected as he slowed down to drive past an awkwardly parked car. Judith had pandered to her far too much. She should have got on with her own life and not ended up feeling bitter and sorry for herself, he thought unsympathetically. He'd arranged for the painter to have a look at the place tomorrow. He'd ask Lily for a key, and then get a duplicate cut for himself. He didn't like it that he couldn't access his mother's house.

Having the painters in would give him the perfect opportunity to root around and have a look for the will, and his mother's bank statements and post-office book. He wanted to know exactly what was what financially, so that Judith wouldn't be pulling the wool over his eyes when Lily went to her rest. Knowledge was power, Tom reflected, swerving to avoid a mini-lake.

Cecily was not so keen to pursue his lines of inquiry these days, Judith's accident had given her a shock and her conscience was at her. Well, his wasn't bothering him, he thought grimly, remembering the abuse his elder sister had hurled at him a few months back when Lily had been in hospital having her cataract done and he and Judith had rowed fiercely. Judith had played a very cute game as far as he was concerned, and she wasn't going to get away with it. Accident or no accident, he was entitled to his share of Lily's estate and he would make damn sure he got what was his due.

* * *

Judith lay in bed, drowsily aware of the rain battering the window. She felt almost serene in her snug cocoon. The telephone call to her mother had been strangely cathartic. They really were at a new phase in their relationship. It was like the past and all its traumas and tensions had drifted away and they'd sailed over the rapids into calm and peaceful waters.

Lily had called her 'dear', and that more than anything had almost caused Judith to break down in a flood of tears that would rival the torrents outside, she thought with a rare flash of humour.

Her mother was insisting on Judith getting a place of her own. How she'd always longed for her own roof over her head, and now it was within her reach. Would she go for a cottage, or a semi-detached, or an apartment? All the options she had. A whole new vista was opening up for her; it was time to grasp her opportunities. Having a place of her own wouldn't mean she was deserting Lily. She'd still be a big part of her mother's life, but she'd be independent and free to do as she pleased. That was a rare gift and one taken for granted by many. But not her. Judith would cherish every minute of this second chance that life had unexpectedly bestowed upon her. She had finally made her peace with Lily. She just had one more person she felt the need to make amends to. As soon as she was able she'd make a phone call that would set something she felt bad about to rights. Her eyelids drooped. It had been a momentous day in several ways, and now she could let sleep continue its healing process.

For the first time in many, many years, Judith felt a flicker of optimism. Her father would be very pleased for her; she owed it to him and to Lily, too, to let go of the past and make a fresh start. She fell asleep with a smile on her thin face, and dreamt of a room with floor-to-ceiling windows through which the sun shone brightly on shelves laden with books, all brand new and waiting to be read.

CHAPTER TWENTY

Debbie stared out at the downpour and watched the lightning streak across the rooftops of the city, zigzagging from a black sky to chimney pots and phone masts with gay abandon. She'd just had a text from her mother to say that she and Karen were shopping in Marbella with Juliet Davenport. The previous day she'd got a text to say that Karen and herself were lazing on the beach at La Cala enjoying massages from two Thai girls.

She could do with a massage to iron the knots of tension out of her neck and shoulders. She'd hardly had a wink of sleep last night. When she'd got home all ready to confront Bryan with the amount of their debt, his sister and cousin were there, sipping wine, while he cooked a stir-fry for them. They were in the area and had dropped in, and he'd invited them to stay for dinner. She'd tried to join in the banter and chat, but her heart wasn't in it and, eventually, around ten, she'd pleaded a headache and gone to bed. It had been impossible to sleep. The trio were in the lounge under her bedroom listening to music and making no effort to tone it down, and she lay in bed, furious at being kept awake in her own house.

They hadn't gone home until well after midnight, and Bryan was half tipsy and in no humour to talk about finances when he came to bed. He'd wanted a shag instead. She'd said she was too tired, but he'd persisted, stroking her and kissing her, trying to get her in the mood. It was easier to say yes than end up arguing, and she'd half-heartedly given in, but their coupling had given her no pleasure – not that he'd noticed – and as he lay snoring beside her, she'd felt tense and resentful, wondering why was she always the one in their relationship to have to do all the worrying about their unaffordable lifestyle.

It was ridiculous: she was only a newly married woman, this should be one of the happiest phases of their life together, not fraught with anxiety over money issues. She remembered how carefree and happy they'd been when they'd first started living together. Maybe Bryan had been right about not buying a house or getting married. It was when they'd bought their house that their problems had started. Then the wedding had added to their expenses. If they'd even waited until now to buy a house, they'd have got one much cheaper. They'd bought at the height of the boom and paid crazy money for what they'd got. In one way, Bryan could say that *she* was the architect of their indebtedness, and she wouldn't be able to argue with him. It was she who had pushed for them to get married; she was as much to blame for their sorry state as her husband.

She'd slept fitfully after that moment of self-realization and now, as she sat looking at the storm raging outside, she was finding it hard to keep her eyes open and her concentration focused on her computer screen. It was just as well that Judith Baxter wasn't in her office, Debbie thought wryly, otherwise she would have been down on her like a ton of bricks, to add to her woes.

'I was very specific in my requirements, Mr Kinsella. Kindly rectify your error immediately and have me and my staff in our new headquarters by the beginning of next week. Do I make myself clear?'

'Perfectly, Mr Devoy. That will be sorted by Friday,' Bryan said reassuringly, running his fingers agitatedly through his glossy locks. He didn't want that little wart going over his head to complain to his boss. Pat Devoy had been a briar from the moment Bryan had had his first consultation with him, and had caused him nothing but grief.

'See to it,' retorted the wart at the other end of the line before hanging up.

'Little bald-headed bastard,' muttered Bryan, remembering how the sun had shone on Devoy's bald pate, giving him the appearance of a just-cooked shiny egg about to be topped.

His phone rang again. 'Hey, Kinsella, are you on for a night on the tiles Friday night? A couple of mates are coming over from London, and they want to go clubbin'. Strictly stag, leave the trouble and strife at home,' Kevin Devlin said breezily.

'Ah . . . sounds good, mate. Leave it with me, I'll get back to you.'

'No probs, just wanted to flag it up,' Kevin said and hung up.

He wouldn't mind a night clubbing after the week he was having, Bryan thought longingly. But with their joint credit card at its limit, and his own card close, he'd have to eat into his salary, and so far he hadn't paid the car tax or the NTL bill and, only that morning, their gas bill had floated through the letter box, so that was another couple of hundred down the Swanee. Where could he lay his hands on a few bob, he wondered. His phone rang again. What an instrument of torture it was, he sighed. 'Hello!' he said, frazzled, waiting to hear Pat Devoy with some new 'requirement'.

'Ah, son, how are you? I've hardly set eyes on you since your wedding. Your sister said she'd had dinner with you last night. I miss you terrible, love. We haven't seen you in ages. When are you going to drop by?' His mother's honeyed tones came as a welcome surprise.

'Mam, it's been mad busy here since I got back,' he lied.

'And I suppose you're having dinner and so on with Connie – that's what always happens after a wedding. It's always the bride's mother who gets involved; the groom's ma never gets a look in,' said Brona mournfully.

'Not at all, Mam. It's not like that,' he assured her.

'I only saw Connie once. She's away in Spain – for the next few weeks,' he exaggerated slightly. 'Honest, it's been crazy here catching up with work since I've come back.'

'Oh, is that so?' she said, somewhat mollified.

'If there was any chance of one of your speciality rack-of-lamb dinners, I could call over after work,' he suggested lightly.

'Go on with you – what time will you be here at? Are you bringing Debbie?'

'No, she has something on,' he fibbed. 'It will just be me. We can have a good natter. I should be there around sixish.'

'Lovely. I'll be looking forward to it immensely, son.'

'Me too, Mam, me too,' Bryan said as he put the phone down. It would be nice to be made a fuss of and have one of her scrumptious roasts. She did his rack of lamb perfectly pink on the inside, just the way he liked it. Debbie always tended to overcook it when she made it. And, if he confided to Brona that he was a bit skint, she'd give him a few bob, like she always did. She was a great mother, he thought fondly. And he was her pet.

She knew he had the extra credit card, because the bills came to her house. He'd been living there when he'd applied for it a few years ago. When he'd asked her not to mention the bills in front of Debbie, she'd understood perfectly. She'd encouraged him to have a little extra money on the side, said it was good for a chap. Brona understood him better than anyone, and wouldn't like to see him broke. Maybe he might get a night out, after all, on Friday, Bryan thought, cheering up as he sent a brief email to Debbie before trying to get a team together to sort out Baldy Devoy's 'specific requirements'.

Having dinner at Ma's tonight as will be in that neck of the woods for a fit-out. Should be home around nine. Love ya, babes. B xxxxxx

Great, thought Debbie as she read her husband's email, she wouldn't have to cook. She'd get something ready-made on the way home. Maybe it was just as well Bryan wouldn't be home until nine, because he'd be well fed and in good humour. He always was after a visit to his doting mother.

She'd have all their figures on the table, ready for him. She'd done an Excel spreadsheet with everything clearly displayed. Tonight, whether he liked it or not, Bryan was going to have to finally face facts because, at the rate they were going, they'd be lucky to have a roof over their heads with another ECB interest hike on top of the one their building society had imposed ratcheting up their repayments.

'So there's your draft for a hundred thousand, Barry. Just sign here, if you will.' Malachy Ormond passed a form over his desk for Barry to sign, which he did with a flourish, as the banker slid the draft into a slim white envelope and handed it over to him.

'Appreciate it, Malachy,' Barry said, standing up and shaking hands with the portly, grey-haired man sitting across the mahogany desk from him.

'Pleasure, as always, doing business with you, Barry,' Malachy said expansively as he walked with him to the door. 'Must have a round of golf some day.'

'Yes, we'll set one up,' Barry agreed, pocketing the envelope.

As soon as he was sitting in his car, he dialled Jeremy's number.

'I have that draft for you, Jeremy. If you want to pop those papers in the post, I'll sign them and send them back with it.'

'Not at all, my boy, I'll send a courier over,' Jeremy declared. 'You'll be getting them at three fifteen; they've slipped from three twenty – rocky day on the market.'

'Yes, I saw that, checked it up on your index. All shares are getting a walloping, my investments are getting a battering, particularly my bank shares,' Barry moaned.

'Indeed. We're all in the same boat there, unfortunately, but it's only temporary, Barry, nothing to worry about. They'll come back up.'

'So you're sure about investing with SecureCo International Plus?'

'Absolutely certain. These are rock solid. I had one investor spend three million on them last week,' Jeremy said suavely, implying that a measly one hundred grand was a pittance in comparison.

'Right so,' said Barry, reassured despite all the

gloom-and-doom talk about the economy and looming recession.

'Trust me, Barry – when SecureCo International Plus is floated next year, shares are expected to go as high as five hundred. These guys wouldn't be putting big money into a company that wasn't going to do the business, believe me. These are all astute financial heads who know their stuff, and they get sound advice. We, at Crookes and Co., feel SecureCo International Plus is good to go, despite the downturn in the markets. We are advising all our clients that it's one to buy into. You'll be laughing all the way to the bank, my friend.'

'That's something to look forward to for sure. Cheers, Jeremy.' Barry hung up, feeling more optimistic than he had in a while. It was good to feel he was still a player ... a minnow perhaps, compared to some, but a player nevertheless. Imagine being able to whack out three million smackers on shares, he thought enviously. These were the kind of people Aimee was working for now, the super-wealthy, and they were in a different league entirely.

He wondered would her humour have improved any. He'd had the shock of his life when he'd come home from work the previous evening to find her in bed with the curtains drawn, fast asleep. Melissa had told him that she'd come home and gone straight to bed, saying she was exhausted.

It was just so unlike Aimee, and he was worried. He hadn't wanted to disturb her, so he'd let her sleep, and had left some poached salmon and salad in the fridge for her when she woke up.

She'd come down to the kitchen around nine thirty and eaten a small amount of the meal. Melissa had gone to the pictures with Sarah, so his wife hadn't felt the need to be particularly civil to him, and had answered his queries as to how she was feeling with a sarcastic 'What would you care?' before going back to bed. She was asleep when he went to bed around eleven thirty. As he lay in the dark listening to her deep, even breathing, he remembered how exhausted Connie had been in the early months of her pregnancy, with a tiredness that just overwhelmed her. Was he being thoroughly selfish insisting that Aimee go through with the pregnancy, he asked himself miserably as he twisted and turned beside her. She was so bitter towards him now, so antagonistic. Would they ever surmount this obstacle in their relationship? Their child would always be a reminder that he hadn't respected Aimee's wishes. Her taunt that he was just like Ken had hurt. He was far from being an authoritative, dictatorial bully. They would never have lasted all these years together if he had been but, clearly, in Aimee's mind, he was now cut from the same cloth as her father, and there was no going back.

He wished he could ask Connie's advice, but she was away in Spain and, besides, she'd made it quite clear she didn't want to be involved. Aimee would hit the roof if he ever thought he discussed her with his ex-wife. He wondered had she discussed her pregnancy with the businessman who'd offered her the job. He couldn't really ask what was going on because she'd just tell him to mind his own business, but he hoped mightily that the venture would go ahead. If she lost her chance at being the MD of her own company because of her pregnancy, she'd never forgive him for that either. Eventually, he'd fallen asleep, gaining some respite from his racing thoughts.

Aimee had left for work before he'd finished shaving, and they hadn't spoken that morning so he had no idea if she was feeling better or not. Impulsively, he decided to ring her.

'Yes?' Her tone was pure frost.

'I just wanted to see if you were OK,' he said evenly. 'I was worried about you.'

'I'm fine, thank you,' she clipped.

'Aimee, we're going to have to talk some time,' he retorted.

'I've nothing to say to you,' she snapped back, and hung up.

Stung, he placed the phone into the hands-free kit and drove back to the office, sorry he'd even bothered to call to see how she was. If that was her attitude, she could get lost, he fumed. He wouldn't bother his ass to make the effort again. And she could get her own bloody dinner tonight, because he was going to eat in town and then go and have a round of golf and a couple of drinks at the golf club. He'd had enough of martyrdom.

* * *

'That was a great day's shopping,' Juliet exclaimed, kicking off her shoes and wriggling her toes. She was surrounded by bags. 'I know my luggage allowance is going to be well over the limit.'

Connie grinned as she leaned back on one of the cane loungers at the side of Juliet's pool, and stretched luxuriously. 'I'm baked.' She blew her hair away from her face.

'How about we change into our swimsuits, have a swim, then an ice-cold Pimm's and a snooze, and then have a light supper? Incarna's left a selection of tapas and a lovely tuna salad for us in the fridge,' Juliet suggested.

'That sounds heavenly.' Karen smiled over at the older woman.

'Or if you prefer we can meander over to the marina and eat in Da Bruno,' said Juliet.

'Incarna's supper sounds lovely,' Connie interjected. 'Honestly, I couldn't eat a big dinner. That lunch in Marbella was gorgeous. And, besides, my feet are killing me, I could just about meander into the pool. Thank you, Juliet, for such a lovely day.'

'Oh no, girls! Thank *you!*' Juliet exclaimed. 'I haven't had as much fun in such a long time. I feel *soooo* relaxed. Now let's go and swim,' she urged, 'because it's a hot, hot afternoon.'

Half an hour later, the trio lay on plump cushions, sipping the cold refreshing Pimm's that Juliet had made for them. Their swim had cooled them down, and they were in a state of contented lethargy. The sun glistened silver on the pool, and the

319

honeysuckle, mimosa and bougainvillea wafted their perfumed scents through the lush gardens that surrounded Juliet's low, sprawling, whitewashed villa. High walls and gates ensured total privacy. They could hear the soothing, shushy sound of the sea lapping the shore at the end of the winding narrow road where the villa was built.

They had spent the morning in the big shopping centre, La Cañada, just on the edge of Marbella, and had then gone to lunch in Orange Square before taking a stroll along the Paseo. They'd indulged in more shopping and window-shopping in the chic designer stores that lined the sun-drenched streets in the once-exclusive and fashionable resort. No longer the domain of the elite, Marbella still exuded an air of flashy affluence and style. But, as they circled the roundabout to exit the town on their way home, the tackiness of the other side of the coin was there to see. An open-topped car in front of them stopped, in it two middle-aged, olive-skinned, seedy-looking men with their hair slicked back. The driver beckoned to a voluptuous young blonde posing on the side of the road. After a quick word, she'd quickly got into the back of the car.

'God, it's so blatant, isn't it?' observed Juliet.

'I'd be petrified. Isn't she worried going with those two men, two complete and utter strangers?' Connie remarked, feeling utterly sorry for any girl who made her living from prostitution.

'I wonder is that her pimp? He was talking to her before she got into the car.' Karen pointed out a skinny, curly-haired man with designer shades who was speaking to an exotic-looking dark girl with fantastically braided hair. She handed him some money and palmed a small packet he exchanged with her. He was obviously dealing drugs, in broad daylight at the side of a busy roundabout, and didn't seem at all concerned that he might be caught.

'We don't know the half of what goes on, we're so cocooned in our own smug little worlds,' Juliet said as she swung off the roundabout on to the motorway. 'It's a far different world our children and grandchildren are living in to what we were used to. I was just looking at my grandchildren on the night of my art exhibition, and they are so advanced for their age. I look at Melissa, and she's dressed like an eighteen-year-old, and with all the jargon, and she's only a child still. They have to grow up so quickly, don't they? Their childhood is so short now. Those magazines have so much to answer for. And clothes designers. They sexualize kids.'

'I know, it's an awful shame,' Connie agreed. 'Because behind that totally with-it, cool façade, Melissa's still a child at heart. There's an innocence about her that hasn't been compromised yet. Some of those teenagers are living the lives of twenty-five-year-olds. Kids having sex at twelve and thirteen is scary. I would have had a fit if I thought Debbie was having sex when she was in her teens.'

'I mean, look at us. I was in my early twenties before I lost my virginity, and it was a big deal. Now, it's nothing special,' Karen remarked.

'I was a virgin when I married Ken and, girls, I have to say, I've never had an orgasm with him – how sad is that?' Juliet confessed.

'That's awful. That's a bad buzz, as Melissa would say,' Connie sympathized.

'But, God, I should have got an Oscar for faking. He thinks he's a stud. If only he knew. I'm lying there thinking, *Oh, get it over with, for heaven's sake*, and he thinks he's George Clooney.' She chortled, and they all started to laugh, having all faked it at some stage in their lives.

'Wouldn't fancy George Clooney,' Connie grinned. 'He believes his own publicity. He seems completely shallow. All his girlfriends probably have to fake too, to protect his ego.'

'Bet I wouldn't have to fake with Harrison Ford,' Karen said wistfully, as they whizzed past the high towerblock of the Don Carlos.

'Me neither.'

'Or me.'

Juliet smiled, remembering their conversation. They'd had a great laugh on the short journey back to the villa, and Juliet couldn't remember a time when she'd felt so free.

The early evening sun was much less intense now, and she could hear Karen snoring on her lounger. She felt utterly peaceful. She had clicked so well with the two other women. She felt very comfortable in their company. They'd had a thoroughly enjoyable day, and she very much hoped that when she went back to Dublin they could continue to meet occasionally for a meal or an evening out.

Although he had phoned the landline several times, she had not spoken to Ken since she'd left Dublin. She felt insulated from him in Spain, and it was a very restful feeling. She wondered lazily how he was managing, but then he drifted from her thoughts and she fell into a doze, imagining Harrison Ford rescuing her from danger and her falling into his arms, kissing him with wanton abandon.

For the umpteenth time that day, Ken Davenport glanced at his watch on his way to the taxi rank at Malaga airport. It was just coming up to eight, Spanish time. They had been sitting on the tarmac for almost the guts of an hour before the plane had been given clearance to take off, and he was in a very bad mood indeed, despite the fact that the pilot had assured them, as they flew out over the sparkling Mediterranean to line up for landing, that they had made up some of the lost time with the help of tailwinds. His bad humour had not abated one bit when he was hit by a scorching blast of heat as he left the confines of the air-conditioned terminal building and saw the queue in front of him waiting for taxis. By God, he swore to himself as he waited impatiently in line, Juliet Davenport would feel the rough edge of his tongue before this day was out.

CHAPTER TWENTY-ONE

'That was delicious, Juliet. Thank Incarna for us.' Connie popped a last, luscious strawberry into her mouth and savoured its sweet, juicy taste.

'The tuna was melt-in-the-mouth,' Karen declared. 'And that gorgeous salad with the pine nuts . . . they're so flavoursome. Make the most of this, Connie. Got a text from Jenna – they're having thunder and lightning at home.'

'The poor suckers.' Connie grinned. 'Here, let me bring these in, Juliet.' She gathered up the plates and went to carry them in.

'Leave them, Connie. It won't take me a minute to do them. Have another glass of wine.' Juliet topped her up. 'Karen, more Amé? Pity you're driving.'

'Just as well I'm driving – I'm turning into a lush. I haven't drunk so much in years,' Karen retorted.

'Me, too, but I'll go on the dry when I go home. Will you stay for the rest of the summer, Juliet?' Connie took a sip of her wine and sat back, totally relaxed.

'I haven't decided. But it's an enticing prospect. I'm only beginning to realize just how restricting and stressful it's been living with Ken. I mean, I do *everything* on the home front. My life has been spent accommodating him. Here, I'm doing what I want, when I want, with no irate phone calls looking for this, that and the other.'

'Would you ever consider living here?' Connie inquired.

'I'd certainly consider spending a lot more time here. It's lovely in the autumn.' Juliet nibbled on a piece of Turkish delight. 'Wait until I tell Ken I'm going to be out here a lot more. He'll go round nuts. I might wind him up and tell him I've been sunbathing on the nudist beach across the dunes. Cabopino has a noted nudist beach – you know?' Juliet smirked, eyes bright from a combination of alcohol and good humour. The air of guarded reserve and tension that she often carried had dissipated completely, the stress lines in her face had softened and her natural joie de vivre, which had been buried for so long, was beginning to re-emerge.

'We should go there one of the days and give them an eyeful,' Connie suggested giddily. 'We could get an all-over tan. No strap-marks!'

'*Get* an eyeful, more like it.' Karen made a face. 'Aren't men afraid their wobbly bits will get sunburnt?'

'Ken wouldn't have much to worry about in that area – you'd need a microscope to find them,' Juliet said tipsily. 'It's so liberating releasing the inner bitch, I should have done it years ago.'

The others guffawed heartily, and Juliet joined in, feeling happy and carefree.

'And what's the joke? It's nice to see you ladies enjoying yourselves.' The subject of their hilarity strode on to the terrace, grim-faced as he stared at his wife.

'Ken! Ah *no*, Ken! It's not fair; I came away to get some peace and quiet. To think. Could you not have respected me that much and let me have what I needed for once in my life?' Juliet stood up. 'What the hell are you doing here?' she demanded angrily. The colour had faded from her face. She gripped the wrought-iron back of her chair tightly for support.

'Don't take that tone with me, Juliet. It's rude in front of your guests. We'll discuss it inside,' he said dismissively. 'Hello, Karen and er . . . um . . . Carrie, isn't it?' He barely acknowledged them as he stood eyeballing Juliet.

'It's Connie,' Connie responded coldly. He ignored her. She remembered the first time they'd been introduced. Barry had told his father-in-law that Connie was a nurse. Ken had looked her up and down, asked her a few perfunctory questions about where she worked, and couldn't get away quick enough. A mere nurse was not worth more than a few minutes of his precious time. For the short while he'd been talking to her, his eyes had been scanning the room to find someone more worthy of his attention. On the few other occasions she'd

326

encountered him, he'd merely nodded self-importantly at her, and she had made no effort to initiate conversation.

'Would you ladies mind excusing my wife for a while? I need to talk to her. Juliet, I'll be inside.' Ken turned on his heel and marched back into the villa.

'I'm so sorry about this.' Juliet was crimson with humiliation. 'I can't believe he's flown over here. He's so disrespectful of me; he just keeps right on ignoring my wishes. He's getting worse as he gets older. This is intolerable.' She was shaking, dazed with disbelief.

'We'd better go,' Karen murmured.

'Will you be all right? Can you deal with him?' Connie asked sympathetically, noting Juliet's distress. 'Would you like us to wait in the car up the road, in case you need us? Just so you have an option? You can't drive after the wine we've drunk.'

'Would you?' Juliet said eagerly. 'That's extremely kind. I don't think I could bear to stay in the same house as him tonight. Would it be very pushy of me to ask could I sleep on your sofa? Or you could drop me at the Don Carlos and I could get a room. I'm disgusted that he'd fly over here and treat me like a naughty schoolgirl. I'm sixty-four years of age, the mother of his children. I deserve respect.' Her face crumpled.

'You will not get a room in a hotel, Juliet. Of course you can sleep at our place. Open the gates for us, and we'll drive out, and we'll be waiting for you across the road. Don't let him see you crying if

327

you can manage it,' Karen urged, handing the other woman a tissue.

'He's afraid, Juliet. Afraid and seriously rattled. That's what's wrong with him, and he's covering it up with bluster. He needs you much more than you need him, don't forget that,' Connie pointed out astutely. 'Think of wobbly bits and microscopes when he's ranting and raving,' she advised.

Juliet gave a watery smile and straightened up. 'Right. Thanks very much, girls. I'm glad you're here. God must have been looking after me the day I got on the plane to Spain.'

'You go, girl, make mincemeat of him.' Karen patted her arm. 'Remember we're outside waiting for you.'

They collected their bits and pieces and walked over to Karen's rented Focus. 'We'll be waiting, take no crap.' Connie gave Juliet a hug.

'Tell him to bugger off home, we've been invited to a party at the nudist beach.' Karen winked as she got into the car, and Juliet laughed.

Taking a deep breath, by now thoroughly sober, she squared her shoulders and walked back towards the villa, trying hard to compose herself. She was stunned at her husband's arrival. She hadn't even been gone more than a few days. Did he think he *owned* her, she wondered agitatedly as she poured some water into a glass from a carafe. She looked at the half-full wine glasses and the detritus of their meal as she took a sip of water to take the dryness out of her mouth. In the blink of an eye, her relaxed, fun-filled break had turned into a disaster, thanks to Ken. Juliet felt a deep, burning anger. This was a turning point for her, she knew. If she let her husband get away with his obnoxious behaviour, she was finished. Her brief rebellion would be crushed as thoroughly as her spirit.

Ken was pacing the kitchen when she walked in. 'I want to talk—'

'Excuse me, I want to let my friends out,' she snapped icily, pressing the buzzer on the intercom to open the gates. She turned and stared at him. 'How dare you embarrass me in front of them? How dare you march in here and order me about? How dare you follow me over from Ireland when I specifically told you I wanted time to think about—'

'*Enough!*' roared Ken. 'It's how dare *you* treat *me* like this. Do you realize that I've had to cancel two clinics and get Lorcan Carleton to look after my post-op patients for two days so that I could stand in queues and sit on a plane for an hour on the tarmac to get here to find out what the *hell* is wrong with you?' His pale-blue eyes were glittering, his face ruddy with barely suppressed rage. He stood towering over her, his hands clenched by his sides, fury and exasperation emanating from every pore.

'Might I remind you who pays for you to sit entertaining your girlfriends beside your swimming pool, drinking wine? Might I remind you who pays for your air fares, your expensive clothes and shoes, your hair-dos, your car, your big house, your house-keeper here and in Dublin? And all I want in return

329

is some respect, and consideration. And that means a wife who will look after my needs—'

'I want a divorce,' Juliet said coldly. 'I don't care what you want or do not want, Ken. *I* want a divorce. *I'm* the one who's had enough.'

'*What!* Are you on some sort of drugs? What the blazes has got into you? Are you crazy?' Ken couldn't believe his ears. He had removed his jacket before she came in, and she could see two big perspiration patches staining the material under the arms of his shirt. She wouldn't be washing that shirt, she thought in a surreal moment as she listened to him seethe.

'You're giving up everything you've got, at close enough to seventy years of age, because you're in some sort of strop with me. Are you insane, Juliet?' he demanded.

'I've never been more sane in my life. And I'm in my early sixties, not my seventies, you fool. And it wouldn't matter *what* age I was. I've had enough of your arrogance, your bad manners, your temper tantrums, your bullying. You know, Ken, when I married you, I married my father. He was *exactly* the same as you. It's taken me a long time to see that. Too long. And what you did to me, you did to Aimee, too. She was always telling me to stand up for myself, but I was always making allowances for you, because of the work you do – complicated heart surgery, saving people's lives. The pressure had to get out somewhere. So I gave you a safe place to let off steam. What a foolish woman I was to let you get away with such appalling behaviour. I enabled ... isn't that what they call it? ... Enabling ...? Well, I enabled you to be a ... a ... boor! But thank God I've found some small sliver of backbone, even if it's this late in life. It's a dreadful thing to be spineless, Ken. Even worse than being married to a Neanderthal.' She could see her husband staring at her in bewildered perplexity. Even she was impressed with what had come pouring out of her.

'What's wrong with you? Why are you behaving like this? You're not yourself.' Ken couldn't hide his disbelief.

'For the first time in a long, long time, I'm very much myself, Ken. That's the tragedy of it, that it's taken me so long to come to my senses. That it's taken so long for me to have some self-respect. I want a divorce,' Juliet reiterated. 'I'll be on to a solicitor first thing in the morning,' she added, in a precise, clipped tone which momentarily left him speechless, and she turned and walked away from him.

'And where,' he asked nastily, 'will you be getting the money to pay for this divorce?'

'You'll be paying for it through the nose,' she retorted over her shoulder, and marched out of the kitchen, feeling in control of her destiny for the first time in years. She hurried up to her bedroom, slipped a dress over her swimsuit, grabbed some fresh underwear and a nightie, got her toothbrush from the ensuite and packed everything into her tote bag, along with her hair brush and make-up.

She heard Ken thunder up the stairs a minute later, and then he barged into the room. 'Now listen here, Juliet,' he began, and saw the bag on the bed. 'Where do you think you're—'

'I'm going to a party on the nudist beach, if you must know,' she interrupted curtly. 'I'm having fun in my life, Ken. FUN! FUN! FUN!' She stepped into a pair of espadrilles, sprayed some perfume on to her wrists and took the bag off the bed. 'Excuse me,' she said as he stood blocking the doorway.

'You are not going anywhere until we've discussed—'

'Excuse me *now*!' She gave him a withering look.

Ken stared at her dumbfounded, astonished at the authority in her voice. He stepped aside.

'Thank you,' she said coolly. 'My solicitor will be in touch.'

She walked down the tiled stairs, half expecting him to come after her, but he didn't. She heaved a sigh of relief. Her knees were trembling, and she felt sick, but she held her head high as she walked down the drive to the open gates. She knew he'd be looking out from their bedroom balcony, but she resolutely kept her eyes fixed ahead. She saw Karen's car parked across the street, up a little to the right, and increased her speed. Connie got out and opened the back door. 'You OK?' she asked anxiously.

Juliet nodded, unable to speak.

'Get in,' Connie said kindly, sliding in alongside her. Karen started the engine.

'I told him I wanted a divorce.' Juliet gripped Connie's hand tightly.

'Good woman yourself. Well done. Sometimes it's the only route to go,' Connie comforted.

'How did he take it?' Karen asked.

'Badly.' Juliet gave a shaky grin. 'I know he doesn't think I'll go through with it but, if I don't, I might as well give up now and go back to the villa.'

'What do you *want* to do?' Connie squeezed her hand.

'As I told my soon-to-be-ex-husband, to go to the nudist beach and have Fun! Fun! Fun!'

Karen laughed. 'Juliet, if that's what your little heart desires, we're with you all the way. So will we go back to my place?' She caught the other woman's eye in her rear-view mirror.

'Yes, please,' Juliet said firmly. 'Who says you need a man to live happy ever after? It's my time now, and better late than never.'

Ken walked slowly into the bedroom and loosened his tie. Juliet had not looked back as she walked out through the gates of the villa. He'd watched her, her shoulders straight and her head held high, stride purposefully away from him, and willed her to turn around, willed her to show some hesitation or uncertainty. She hadn't. Not an ounce. Juliet seemed uncharacteristically sure of herself. He felt a shiver of apprehension. She wasn't serious about wanting a divorce surely? Ken shook his head, and sat down on the bed, tie dangling from his hand.

She'd said dreadful things to him. Called him a boor. Accused him of being arrogant, a bully. He looked around their tastefully furnished bedroom, all cool creams and pale blues. He'd provided all of this for her. Where was her gratitude? Her acknowledgement of his hard work? She knew better than anyone how stressful it was. Ken sighed and rubbed his hand across his stubbly jaw. Stress didn't begin to describe it, these last few years. He was getting older; it was harder keeping up with new procedures, new technology. When he started off it was eyes and hands only. Now there were computers, lasers, keyhole this, pinhole that. The young bucks coming along in his wake were full of confidence, drive and ambition, just like he'd been thirty years ago.

Once, he'd been a god on the wards, sweeping in to visit patients with a respectful entourage scurrying behind him. When the nuns ran the hospitals, the consultant had been elevated to lofty heights never again attained since the arrival of managers, and health ministers who had no respect, and the damn HSE, which was trying to turn them into lackeys.

When the nuns ran hospitals there was no MRSA, there were no dirty wards or crowded, filthy A&Es, or cardiac patients being given cholesterol-laden, fat-dripping fry-ups for tea. He was a dinosaur now, living in the past, wishing for the past to return. He had had his day. Did Juliet not realize how difficult it was to keep up his air of invincibility? Patients needed the reassurance that they were in a safe pair of hands. His air of command and confidence reassured them. He needed it himself to keep going. It wasn't about being a boor, he thought indignantly, it was about self-protection.

He shouldn't have launched off at her in front of those two women, he reflected guiltily. He'd embarrassed her. He should have held his fire, but patience had never been a strong point with him. She knew that.

He got up and went downstairs, and poked in the fridge looking for a cool drink. He opened a can of tonic water and drank it thirstily. His wife had looked at him with scorn and derision in her eyes. That was hard to endure. Ken mooched out on to the terrace and sat at the table where they had been eating, the remnants of their meal still there.

Where was Juliet getting all this psychobabble? *Enabling* . . . where had she heard that? He grimaced. Too much bloody *Dr Phil*. That's what was wrong with her and half the women in the country. They had too much time to sit and watch silly so-called self-help rubbish. He stretched out and raised his face to the sky. Dusk had tamed the blistering sun, and the shadows were lengthening over the lawn as the cicadas chirruped and the sea sang its lullaby to the shore. It was peaceful, and he was tired – tired and worried. He'd never seen Juliet like this. She seemed adamant about wanting a divorce. She was mad. It couldn't be a worse time to divorce, with a recession threatening and all.

Would she want the house sold? They could lose up to three hundred thousand, or more, if they put it on the market now. They wouldn't be able to give away the villa. All he'd seen on his journey from the airport were '*Se Vende*' signs. She'd want half his pensions, his investments. A colleague of his had recently been divorced and was now living, alone, in a two-bedroom apartment in Glasnevin, when he'd once lived in a detached five-bedroomed house in Howth. The ex-wife was living in an apartment in Clontarf and playing golf every day, with not a worry in the world.

Was that where he'd end up – alone in some glasshouse apartment, having to suffer the indignity of communal living and management-committee meetings? Ken shuddered. It couldn't come to that. Someone would have to talk sense to her.

Ken sat for a long time in the cool of the Mediterranean evening, pondering his life, weary to his bones. There was one thing he was certain of: if Juliet left him, he didn't know what he'd do. For the first time in all their married life, he was beginning to realize just what a sterling wife she'd been. He might have been the provider, but she'd been his bedrock. He'd ring Aimee in the morning. Juliet had a high regard for their daughter. Perhaps she'd listen to her. It was *imperative* that Aimee talk sense to her mother, he decided, as he made his lonely way to bed, full of self-pity, wondering could anyone be quite as miserable as he was this moonlit, star-filled night.

'It couldn't be that much!' Bryan stared at Debbie aghast. 'It just couldn't be.'

'It is, Bryan. Fifty-five thousand euro more or less, and that's not counting our mortgage. If you go there, we're three hundred and fifty thousand in debt. We've got to cut back and start making inroads on the payments, or we're in serious trouble,' she insisted. 'We've got to get rid of the car and get something less expensive—'

'Oh come on, Debbs, it's our only little luxury. What do you expect me to drive around in – a Mini?' he protested sulkily.

'There you go, you see – you won't even face up to our problems. So what if we have to drive around in a smaller car? At least we'll be reducing our debt,' Debbie said heatedly. They were sitting at their small dining table, and each of them had a spread-sheet detailing the amount they owed.

'This is crazy,' Bryan muttered. 'I can't believe it.'

'Believe it,' Debbie said grimly. 'For starters, the car's going. I'm not going on that hen weekend, and we're not staying overnight if we go to that wedding. You can hire a monkey suit; I'll wear something I've worn before. No more meals out or drink and drug binges with Kevin Devlin—'

'You see? You were the one who wanted to buy a house and get married – we could have waited, Debbie. Could have rented an apartment and lived together without all this hassle,' Bryan exploded. 'This isn't what *I* wanted, it's what *you* wanted. We should never have got married. We haven't had a minute's peace since we bought this house and started planning for the wedding. And now I'm the one suffering. It's just not on. I'm going to bed.' He stalked out of the room and pounded up the stairs, leaving Debbie staring after him in frustration.

There was no answer to his accusations. It was just as she had feared: Bryan was putting all the blame on her. Her lip wobbled, and she buried her head in her hands and burst into tears.

Bryan yanked the tie from around his neck, rolled it in a ball and flung it across the bedroom. He was furious with Debbie. He'd come back from his mother's in great form. Brona had cooked him a scrumptious dinner, made a huge fuss over him and, when he'd confided that he was skint, she'd told him that she'd give him 3,000 euro towards paying off his credit card – the credit card that Debbie knew nothing about, and which she'd not included in their outstanding debt calculations.

He'd come home and felt he'd been ambushed when she'd insisted that they sit down at their dining table and given him that damn spreadsheet. Looking at the figures in black and white had been a sobering moment. They might as well be paupers. Their house was no longer an asset. They were in negative equity with it as it was, so selling wasn't an option. There was nothing they could do except cut down on expenses and start paying off their loans.

The good life was over. And, if this was marriage, he knew he wasn't going to stick it out. Bryan got undressed and threw himself under the duvet. He'd fallen for Debbie because he thought she understood him; she'd always given him a lot of leeway, just like his mother. That was until he'd married her, he thought bitterly. Now he might as well be married to Connie, for all the bossing around he was getting:

'We can't do this.'

'You can't do that.'

'Sell the car!'

It wasn't his fault there was a bloody recession. Why should *he* have to suffer? Bryan had never felt so trapped in his life. And, this time, not even his mother could get him out of the mess he was in.

'When I married Ken, I married a replica of my father. He was authoritative, controlling, self-obsessed, just like my husband. And my mother behaved just as I did, putting all his needs first and fading into the background. Isn't it amazing, when you actually stop to think about it, how we constantly repeat old patterns?' Juliet remarked to Connie and Karen as they sat chatting in the balmy moonlight. It was well after midnight.

'I understand that very well. Bryan is somewhat similar to what Barry was like when he was young – restless and not eager for responsibility. I did try to warn Debbie and suggest they postpone their

339

wedding, but she didn't want to hear what I was saying, and I think that she pushed him to get married,' Connie confessed. 'And that's just what I did, so she's repeating my pattern, if you look at it like that,' she agreed ruefully. 'I worry about them, to be honest. Their generation has had it so easy financially that I think there're going to be a lot of troubled marriages now that the boom times are over and belts have to be tightened.'

'Oh dear, I hope not,' Juliet murmured.

'Everyone has to learn from their own mistakes, unfortunately, and you're right, scrimping and saving won't come easy to the Celtic-tiger babes.' Karen shrugged. 'But at least the days of staying in a bad marriage are gone, even though it's also true that a lot of young people give up at the first hurdle nowadays, and I suppose women are much more financially independent – they can get mortgages on their own, so that's why it's easier for them to walk away.'

'I don't think I'd get a mortgage at my age. I'll have to pay cash for anything I buy and, although the mortgages are paid on our house and the villa here, we'll lose out because of the slump in prices.' Juliet looked troubled. Worry and anxiety had crept back into her face, folding back into the lines around her eyes and mouth. The carefree woman of a few hours previously had vanished.

'I know it's a bad time to be selling property, but the balance to it is that it's a good time if you're buying,' Karen pointed out as she filled three glasses with wine and handed Connie and Juliet one each. They were sitting on her wide terracotta fifth-floor balcony overlooking the sea. An almost-full moon shone silver streamers of light on to the rippling pewter water that surged softly against the shore. A cruise ship on the horizon sailed along the coast of Africa, lights strung from its mast, like a floating Christmas tree.

'It's a great time to buy,' Juliet agreed. 'Ideally, I'd go for a small apartment or townhouse in Sandycove or Glasthule. I'd like to be on the Dart and near the sea. This is so peaceful, Karen,' she remarked, sipping the chilled golden chardonnay gratefully.

'That would be handy for you as well for visiting Aimee and the children,' Karen observed, handing around a dish of mixed nuts. 'I suppose you'll want to be back home in Ireland when she has the baby.'

'Children . . . the baby?' Juliet looked puzzled.

Karen's jaw dropped, and she flashed a look of consternation at Connie. 'Sorry, Juliet, I assumed you knew – um . . . Aimee's expecting, but . . . but she probably didn't want to say anything until the three months are up,' she said sheepishly.

'And how did you know?' Juliet asked, bewildered. 'You'd think she would have told her own mother.' She couldn't disguise the hurt that flickered in her eyes.

'Melissa let it slip, and I told Karen,' Connie explained hastily. 'She only found out on Saturday, because that was the day I met Melissa in Dun

Laoghaire, and Aimee had just taken the test, apparently; otherwise I'd never have known. Don't feel bad about it, Juliet,' she urged, conscious of the other woman's injured feelings. 'It really was due to a slip of the tongue that I found out. I'm sure Aimee will tell you in her own good time.'

'I wouldn't think she'd be too happy about being pregnant after all this time.' Juliet frowned. 'She told me she didn't want any more children after Melissa was born. She's going to be most put out, I'd say.'

'It's tough if that's the case,' Connie said diplomatically.

'The Davenport women are having a hard time of it, it seems,' Juliet said glumly. 'But at least Aimee is happy in her marriage. Barry is a very supportive husband.'

Connie refrained from comment. 'Happy' was not the adjective she would use to describe her ex's marriage, or his state of mind. Karen offered around the nuts again.

'Oh ... that was a bit thoughtless. I'm sorry, Connie,' Juliet said contritely, realizing to whom she was talking.

'Nothing to be sorry about at all,' Connie assured her kindly. 'Barry and I are water under the bridge for a long time now.'

'But it must have been hard on you, all the same,' Juliet murmured, mortified at her faux pas.

'It was at the time but, honestly, Juliet, it all worked out very well, and it's wonderful that

Melissa and Debbie are becoming close. That's the best thing to come out of it all.'

'You're a good person, Connie.' Juliet smiled at her.

'Right back at ya!' Connie raised her glass.

'I suppose no one knows better than you what a big step divorce is. Am I mad, I wonder?'

'One thing I will say, Juliet, is that divorce is easier on the person who initiates it, especially if it's against the other person's wishes. But, having said that, and it was Barry who left me, looking back, he was the one who had the courage to recognize that we weren't working. I would have endured the misery for a lot longer, I think. There's always light at the end of every tunnel, and being on your own is far preferable to being stuck in a miserable marriage – that's what I've learned from it all. It also brought out strengths I didn't know I possessed. I'm the woman I am now because of my divorce. And I'm happy with myself.'

'Well, Connie, you should be *proud* of yourself. I stayed because it was easier, and I lost my self-respect, and that's an awful place to be.'

'Might he change his ways now that you've given him something to think about?' Karen asked.

'That might take a miracle.' Juliet gave a wry smile. 'And I'm not sure I believe in them.' She yawned discreetly behind her hand. 'I think I'll go to bed, if you don't mind. It's been a long day.'

'Sleep well, Juliet,' Connie said warmly.

'Thanks for everything. I'm sure neither of you

came on holidays to get sucked into my marital woes.'

'Don't give it a second thought. Glad to be of help,' Karen said as she led the way into the apartment and down to the cool air-conditioned bedroom where Juliet had already left her bag and nightdress. 'Make yourself at home, Juliet, and sleep well.' Karen pulled the pale lilac curtains across the French doors and turned down the matching bedspread. 'If you want to make tea at any time, go right ahead.'

'I will. Goodnight, Karen, and thanks again for your hospitality.'

Juliet sank wearily on to the side of the bed as the other woman shut the door quietly behind her. Her head was beginning to ache, and she searched her handbag for a packet of Nurofen.

What a day, she reflected as she undressed and pulled her cotton nightdress over her head. One thing was sure, she decided as she slid between the cool, crisp sheets, she was leaving Ken. If he didn't want a divorce, she'd agree to a legal separation. She wouldn't be marrying again and, she felt pretty sure, neither would he. Women wouldn't put up with his type any more.

Her children would be surprised, she thought with a wry smile as she switched out the light and lay in the blessed comfort of darkness, Aimee more than any of them. Her thoughts turned to her daughter. It had been a shock to learn that she was pregnant. Knowing her as well as she did, Juliet knew that Aimee must be utterly dismayed at the prospect of having to look after a new baby. It would tie her down enormously. How ironic that, while she was looking forward to a future of liberation and becoming her own woman, her daughter would be tightly bound by motherhood and all it entailed. Juliet drifted off to sleep, comforted by the fact that she had reclaimed her self-respect and her dignity, and made two good friends in the process.

'That was a day and a half,' Karen murmured as she came back out on to the balcony and sat down on the lounger beside Connie. 'Trust me to open my big mouth about the baby. I wasn't thinking. Sorry about that,' she apologized.

'Can't be helped. You always were a blabbermouth,' Connie said affectionately.

'Bitch,' grinned her sister-in-law. 'Imagine being married to that pain in the ass. I don't know how she lasted so long. Juliet's totally different to Aimee, isn't she? Much softer. Too soft to be married to that big tyrant.'

'I think he's possibly the rudest man I ever met. Imagine having him for a father. Not easy either. Maybe that's why Aimee's so driven. You never know what goes on in other people's lives sure you don't,' Connie mused. 'You're lucky to have a happy marriage, Karen. John's one in a million. When I look at Juliet and Ken, and Aimee and Barry, I have to say, I'm very contented in my single state. I won't be going down that road, for sure.'

'And what about that sexy man you were telling me about?' Karen topped up her glass.

'Mmm ... I don't think he's too anxious to go down that road again either,' Connie said firmly.

'Well, I live in hopes of being your matron of honour, madam, so I'm not giving up on it,' Karen giggled as she slugged her wine.

'You have two chances of that, Karen – slim and none,' Connie retorted tartly but, as she gazed out at the moonlit sea, she thought how nice it would be to sit sipping wine and talking all night with Drew Sullivan. Full moons always made her lonely. Full moons should be shared, she thought wistfully, recognizing that all the wine she'd drunk had made her maudlin. Juliet had said you didn't need a man to live happy ever after, and Connie wouldn't argue with that, but with the *right* man, if there was such a creature, happiness was possible and, although she was contented with her life, she wouldn't shut the door on new opportunities that came her way. She didn't have to *marry* the new opportunity, she smiled to herself, looking forward to her new job and to meeting Drew again.

CHAPTER TWENTY-TWO

'Mum's looking for a divorce?! When did she tell you that?' Aimee couldn't believe her ears at the news her father had just imparted.

'Last night. I flew out to the villa to discuss things in a reasonable ma—'

'You're in Spain!' Aimee exclaimed.

'Yes, yes,' her father said impatiently. 'I came over to—'

'What did you do *that* for, Dad?' Aimee couldn't hide her irritation. 'Could you not have just left her alone for a while without going over to Spain and hounding her?'

'I beg your pardon, Missy, I did no such thing. Watch the way you speak to me please,' Ken bristled.

'Oh, get over yourself, Dad. I'm not surprised that Mum asked for a divorce the way you go on,' Aimee said rudely.

'What's that supposed to mean? I'm ringing you to ask you to have a word with her. To try and get you to knock some sense into her. Do you realize how costly a divorce would be? There won't be too much left for you and your brothers if she insists on going down that road,' Ken warned.

'I don't want your money, Dad, I've plenty of money of my own, thank you, so it's no skin off my nose if you and Mum divorce,' Aimee said airily, letting him know in no uncertain terms that his nasty little threat didn't bother her.

'*You* might have plenty of money, but I'm not an ATM, and it's time Juliet realized it,' Ken retorted. 'I found her slugging back wine with that Connie woman who was once married to your husband,' he said, slyly getting his little dig in. 'And his sister was there as well, all of them laughing and tittering and having a great time at my expense. Your mother was having the time of her life, and does she even stop to think who's paying for her life of luxury? Does she ever consider how hard I've worked to provide her with a lifestyle that's the envy of many—'

'And you never stop going on about it. You're always rubbing her nose in it, Dad. Did you ever stop to think how difficult it is for her having to put up with *you*! She's earned every bit of "luxury", as you call it. If I were married to you I'd have been gone long ago.'

'Ah yes, I should have known better than to come to you for a bit of sympathy and understanding. You're the liberated woman, aren't you?' he jeered. 'The feminist. The emasculator of men. It's your sort that have the world the way it is.' He couldn't have been more contemptuous.

'Listen to yourself, Dad. You're out of the ark. I'm not one of your poor little minions who has to take your crap. I've got work to do, so if you're ringing me to ask me to try and get Mum to change her mind, you can think again. I applaud her decision. I'm delighted she's finally stood up to you and your bully—'

'There's no use talking to you. All I'm getting is impertinence,' Ken bellowed down the line.

'And I don't have to listen to you roaring and shouting. Mum should have left you long ago,' Aimee retaliated, and hung up. She felt queasy. Confrontations with her father had never been easy, but at least she could hang up on him now and not have to endure his domineering attitude, which had certainly not diminished with age. It was getting worse, if anything. Typical of him to ring and take his bad temper out on her. That's what a daughter was for if the wife wasn't there to be the butt of it.

He was a fool, Aimee thought bitterly. If he wasn't careful, he'd end up an angry, bitter old man with no one to talk to. And if anything happened to him in his old age, she certainly wouldn't be looking after him. It was the nursing home for him, and it might bring him down a peg or two to have to be looked after by nurses who wouldn't take any of his nonsense. That would be something else, and she'd take pleasure in it, she thought venomously, and looked up to find Barry standing in the doorway of the kitchen staring at her.

'That sounded pretty nasty,' he remarked.

'It was, but it's none of your business, and I'll thank you not to earwig on my phone calls,' she snapped.

'I couldn't help it, you weren't exactly keeping it down,' he shot back, filling the kettle and turning it on.

'That was my father, as I'm sure you guessed. My mother's divorcing him. And about time too. It will be a happy day for her, to get her freedom, and it will be a happy day for me when I divorce you, Barry,' said Aimee coldly.

'Do you know something, Aimee, right now, that's something I look forward to myself, because living with you is like living with a she devil,' he said nastily.

'What did you ever marry me for in the first place?' she sneered, a derisory look in her eyes.

'That's something I've been asking myself a lot these days. And there's something else you might like to think about while you're at it, Aimee: you're much more like your father than you think – intransigent, confrontational, self-centred, dictatorial, arrogant, pretentious. You have it all in spades, my dear. So why would I want to stay married to you?'

'Bastard,' she swore, flushing at his jibes.

Barry bowed and walked out on to the balcony, knowing that she'd be gone by the time he came back in.

Aimee flung her half-drunk tea into the sink and grabbed her briefcase. Men! She hated the species, she raged, fishing her car keys out of her bag and hurrying down the hall.

Melissa's heart pounded as she heard the front door close. Her parents were going to get a divorce! It couldn't be true. Had she been hearing things? Was she having a dream? She gave herself a hard pinch, and flinched. She wasn't dreaming. She closed her bedroom door softly. The sound of the phone ringing had woken her, and she'd lain drowsily in her bed squinting at her clock, wondering who would be ringing so early in the morning. It must have been an emergency in her mother's work, she'd figured, glad she didn't have to get up. She'd heard the rain batter against the window and tried to go back to sleep, but she was hungry. She'd eaten very little the previous day. A glass of water would help take the gnawing hunger pangs away. She'd eventually dragged herself out of bed and padded barefoot down to the kitchen, in time to hear her parents row viciously.

Tears slid down Melissa's cheeks. She didn't want her mother and father to divorce. She knew they hadn't been getting on well lately. In fact, they were hardly talking these days, but she presumed that was because her mother's hormones were all over the place because of expecting the baby. She knew Aimee didn't want to have a baby. All she was interested in was her job. Had she felt like that when she'd found out she was pregnant with her, Melissa wondered unhappily as she sobbed into her pillow, trying to smother the noise so her father wouldn't hear. Was this how Debbie had felt when she found out that Barry and Connie were going to divorce all those years ago?

Had Barry met someone else? Was that why he was no longer in love with her mother? If they divorced, what would happen? Where would they live? Would Barry have to move out? That would be awful. Melissa wept. She loved her father, but she wouldn't like to see him living with another woman. Poor Debbie, she thought wildly. No wonder her half-sister didn't really like Aimee. *Now*, she understood why. She'd hate this new woman that Barry was involved with. She'd HATE her for taking him away from her and Aimee. She'd have to do something to stop the divorce. But what?

'Bye, Melissa,' she heard her father call softly. She froze. She didn't want him to know that she was awake. He always called out goodbye to her when he was leaving. Sometimes she heard him; sometimes she didn't if she was asleep.

She heard the heavy tread of his footsteps down the hall and then the front door closed and she was mercifully alone. She sat up and wrapped her arms around her pillow, and cried her heart out, knowing that life would never be carefree and happy again.

Aimee had just arrived at the cream and gold marquee which was housing an event she was overseeing. The heavens had opened, and she sat in the car waiting for the deluge to ease, not wanting to look like a drowned rat when she went in. Her mobile rang, and Roger O'Leary's name came up on her screen. Her stomach flip-flopped. He'd told her he'd get back to her as soon as possible about whether he and Myles were willing to proceed with the new venture. Was the swiftness of his response an indication of good news or bad, she wondered, staring at the phone. She took a deep breath. This was it. Make or break time. Would she be moving on, or staying with a company which didn't appreciate just how much she had to offer?

'Hello.' Her voice was remarkably calm. She silently congratulated herself on her acting abilities.

'Aimee, Roger here. How are you today?' the businessman inquired genially.

Oh just tell me, she begged silently. 'I've managed to keep my breakfast down.' She injected a cheery note into her tone, trying to gauge from his whether or not he had good news for her.

'Excellent,' he replied. 'Did you try the peppermint tea?'

'I did, it was very helpful,' she lied, curling her fingers into her palms so tightly they left marks.

'Good, you'll need to drink a lot of it then. We're all systems go. Myles and I had a long discussion, and he's keen to progress with the project so, as soon as you've worked your notice, we'll get up and running. In the meantime, we should have another meeting to target our office space, and I'll be putting the word out and about that Hibernian Dreams is the company to do business with. I think Edward

353

Gallagher is looking for someone to organize their twenty-fifth year in business.'

'I'd heard that,' Aimee replied matter-of-factly, although she felt like yelling and dancing with delight.

'I might have a chat with him and give him your number. He'd be as good a client as any of them to start off our new enterprise with. I'm off to Moscow this afternoon; I have some business interests in Russia. I'll be in touch when I get back. I think we'll make a good team, Aimee.'

'I have no doubt of it, Roger. And thank you. I appreciate your trust and confidence in me. I'll do my utmost to live up to it.'

'It pays to take a chance now and again, I've always found. And if you put in the effort that you did for the wedding, that's good enough for me. Keep drinking the peppermint tea,' Roger said enthusiastically, before hanging up.

Aimee sat in her car, savouring the moment. Who would have thought she would end up the MD of her own company, despite being pregnant? It was the crowning moment of her career. She couldn't wait to get back to the office and hand in her notice. And who would have thought that Roger O'Leary, of all people, would be the one giving her the chance to become a big success? And to think she'd looked down her nose at him. She wouldn't make that mistake again. He might be a touch unsophisticated, to say the least, but he was a big player in business, and he was now her boss and he'd get one hundred per cent of her loyalty.

Exhilarated, she went to dial Barry's number to tell him her news and, then, with a sinking heart, remembered that they were at war. After the things he'd said to her this morning, he'd be lucky if she ever spoke to him again, she thought grimly. Before the wedding she would have phoned her friend Gwen, but Gwen wasn't talking to her either.

Maybe she would have calmed down after all these weeks. Surely she wouldn't hold a grudge. It was a misunderstanding. She'd probably be pleased that Aimee had taken the first step by ringing. She'd read an article in a magazine at the hairdresser's which maintained that you had to *invest* in friendships, work at them. She'd been rather lax in that regard, she thought guiltily, remembering how she'd rarely phoned any of the girls, always leaving it up to them to get in touch. She'd make more of an effort once she and Gwen were on speaking terms again. On impulse, she scrolled down her directory and found the other woman's number. A familiar voice answered. It was nice to hear it again. Aimee smiled.

'Hi Gwen, it's me, I just wanted to—'

The phone went dead. Aimee stared at it, taken aback. Gwen had hung up on her without even giving her a chance. 'You don't get another chance with me, lady. Grow up,' she muttered, disgusted. It was one thing to have a row with someone, but to behave in such a manner, at her age, was utterly childish.

She scrolled through her directory again and found her mother's number.

'Morning, Mum, I believe you're looking for a divorce. Congratulations!' she said cheerfully.

'And, I believe, congratulations are in order for you too,' Juliet said crisply.

Aimee's jaw dropped. 'How did you know? I've just got the job,' she said, puzzled.

'You got a new job. Oh, well done!' her mother exclaimed. 'A new job and a new baby – double congratulations so.'

Aimee's eyes widened in shock. 'How did you know I was pregnant? Was Barry talking to you?' she demanded angrily.

'No, he wasn't.' Juliet sounded surprised at the notion. 'Karen mentioned it. Seemingly, Melissa let it slip to Connie last weekend, and Connie told Karen. It would have been nice to know that I was going to have another grandchild.'

'Oh, for God's sake, Mum, I was going to tell you. Does the whole bloody world know?' Aimee fumed, hugely irritated to think that Connie and Karen had been gossiping about her, and probably having a good laugh at her expense too. How mortifying! She could just imagine the smug bitches sniggering about her having a bun in the oven.

'I don't think so. How do you feel about it?' Juliet asked.

'How would you think?' Aimee said glumly. 'It couldn't have happened at a worse time. I'm starting up a new company. I'm the MD. I can't really afford to be taking time off for maternity leave. And looking after a new baby is not what I want to be doing at this stage of my life.'

'Oh dear, that's tough luck. I didn't think you'd be too pleased,' Juliet admitted.

'Well, you're right there, Mother,' Aimee said dryly. 'I'm not at all pleased. And what woman in my position would be? I wanted to go for a termination, but Barry won't hear of it. He's being a real pig about it, if you want to know. You might not be the only Davenport to be getting a divorce.'

'Oh Aimee, don't do anything rash!' her mother exclaimed. 'You have Melissa to think about. And this new child, too.'

'And what about me? What about my needs? I thought you, of all people, would understand,' Aimee said heatedly.

'I do, I really do, Aimee, but unfortunately, when you're a wife and mother, you have to put other people's needs before your own.'

'*You're* getting a divorce,' Aimee retorted.

'Yes, now that all of my children are reared and able to fend for themselves. I would never have gone looking for a divorce with a young family,' Juliet said soberly.

'Well, times are different now. I can afford to get a divorce—'

'I'm not talking about the financial aspect, dear. I was thinking of the effect it would have on Melissa.'

'Saint Connie raised Debbie on her own,' Aimee

pointed out sarcastically. 'She seems to have done OK.'

'Yes, but don't forget Connie worked her hours to be at home when Debbie was finished school; you won't be able to do that with a demanding new job. And, from what you told me, with the events leading up to the wedding, there was a lot of bitterness and resentment on Debbie's part. So, remember that when you're thinking of getting divorced. And another thing – Connie is a good person, Aimee; you shouldn't mock her and look down your nose at her. She and Karen have been incredibly kind to me these past few days. In fact, I stayed with them last night rather than have to stay under the same roof as Ken. I've just had breakfast with them, and they've left me here to relax while they went up to El Zoco to get some groceries. They've told me to stay as long as I like. Connie Adams could teach you a thing or two,' Juliet said crossly.

'Look, I have to go. I'll talk to you soon, and please don't discuss what I've told you with those two,' Aimee said coolly, unwilling to have to listen to any more laudatory words about Barry's ex. It was bad enough being lectured by her mother about her responsibilities as a wife and mother, without having to listen to Connie being praised to the skies. She wouldn't be jaunting off to Spain with Melissa to listen to that sort of rubbish, she decided, hastily revising her plan.

'I've no intentions of talking to anyone about you.

I've enough to worry about myself,' Juliet said stiffly, and hung up.

Thoroughly disgruntled by her mother's attitude, and the fact that she had no one to share her good news with, Aimee got out of the car and marched into the marquee, ready to pick a fight with anyone, if everything wasn't as she'd requested. How had Connie Adams found out that she was pregnant? When had Melissa said it? Where had she said it? Why hadn't her daughter mentioned that she'd spoken to Connie? She'd give her a good telling-off when she got home later. Melissa had no business discussing their personal matters with strangers. Because, as far as Aimee was concerned, Barry's treasured ex-wife *was* a stranger, and one she wanted little or nothing to do with.

CHAPTER TWENTY-THREE

Lily neatly placed the copy of her will, her post-office-savings book and her sheaf of bank statements in her handbag. They would stay there until she felt it was safe to put them back in the drawer that she usually kept them in. She looked around her bedroom. It was neat and tidy, smelling fresh and clean with beeswax polish. Her bed, with its gleaming brass bedstead, was covered in a cream, lavender and green patchwork quilt that picked up the sage-green and lavender paintwork of her room. It was a soothing room, bright in the morning but airy and cool in the afternoon and evening, the sun having moved around the back, to Judith's side of the house.

She'd got a start when she'd read Tom's note to say that he and the painter were arriving this morning. She couldn't decide whether to tell him that she didn't want the painting job done. It seemed the least stressful way to go, but the two bedrooms could do with a lick of paint, she reasoned. And why should Judith have to go to the trouble of getting it done? The Lord only knew how long it would take her to recover fully, mentally as well as physically. Lily knew fine well that getting the bedrooms painted would give Tom a perfect opportunity to snoop, especially if she was out visiting Judith, hence the new lodging place for her papers.

Why had he zeroed in on the bedrooms and not the hall stairs or landing, or her sitting room? She was right to be suspicious, she told herself as she gathered together the items she knew he would be particularly interested in. Her son had made it clear over the years that he expected an equal share in her estate. He had done his best to ascertain had she made a will, going so far as to offer to bring her to his own solicitor. As if she'd be stupid enough to use his solicitor, she thought crossly. The pair of them could be in cahoots. All those rogue solicitors she kept hearing about on the news made her thankful for the stalwart support of Mr Martin.

She had her own solicitor, she'd informed Tom, and her private business was exactly that – 'private', she'd reiterated firmly. She remembered how he'd come to visit her in hospital when she was getting her cataract done and bluntly asked her had she made a will, putting the fear of God in her that she might die under the knife. He was avaricious and untrustworthy, and the last person she would turn to if she was in trouble. Wasn't that a sad state of affairs between a mother and her only son, Lily thought sadly, wondering was it her fault that he had turned out to be such a disappointment. Was it because she had been so self-obsessed, always worried about herself, always nervy and agitated? Had Cecily and Tom learned to think only of themselves because that was what they had learned from her? Lily felt an unwelcome pang of guilt.

Judith had turned out to be a good and unselfish human being, and she'd had the same rearing as her siblings, Lily argued with herself as she stood at her bedroom window, staring out unseeingly. She shouldn't and wouldn't take all the blame for his faults. If he had any sense of decency, he'd see that Judith was more than entitled to a roof over her head. If he was the one who had stayed, she would have done her duty by him too. Tom had no idea of what she was worth financially, and he certainly wasn't going to find out in the next few days if she could help it.

She straightened the folds of her lace curtains and walked out of her bedroom. Houses, land and savings caused such family rows at funerals. Her own grandmother had signed over a house to Lily's uncle, not realizing what she was doing. When she discovered that she wouldn't be able to leave the house to all of her children to be sold and the proceeds divided out when she died, solicitors had been called in on both sides, and a legal battle that had cost a fortune had followed. Her grandmother lost the court case, and the rift that ensued had never been healed. Well, *her* wishes would be followed, Lily vowed, and her wishes were that Judith got the house. She'd lived in it for most of her fifty years, she'd taken care of Lily, and Ted when he was alive, and she was entitled. Tom felt he was *owed* his portion, by merely being her son. He was owed nothing except what she wanted to give him, and that wouldn't be much.

She was going to play a smart game with him. If he tried to get the better of her, he'd come to realize that he'd picked on the wrong person to try to trick. She would let the painting of the bedrooms go ahead, but she would be vigilant at all times. This painter fellow might be in Tom's pay, with orders to find out as much as he could. She wouldn't put anything past her son, from what she knew of him. If she was happy the way the bedrooms turned out and happy with the painter, she'd suggest getting the rest of the house painted. It would be done before Judith moved out to her own place, because Lily knew, as sure as grass grew green, that once Tom realized his elder sister had been favoured financially, Lily might never see sight nor sign of him again, and there'd be no more offers of house painting – or any other house renovations or maintenance, for that matter. She might as well play him at his own game and get as much out of him as she could. If he could be devious, so could she.

'Morning, Ma. I missed you yesterday – did you get my note?' Tom asked, picking his nose with his thumb as he sat at his desk with his feet up.

'I got your note. Yes.' Lily was always rather formal on the phone.

'So if we head over in the next hour you'll be there?' he queried.

'Yes. I will.'

'Grand, I'll see you then.' Tom replaced the receiver of the landline, picked up his mobile and dialled a number. 'Right, Jimmy,' he said to the man at the other end of the line, 'I'll meet you at the address I gave you at –' he glanced at his watch – 'ten thirty, and bring your colour cards and brochures. You'll understand if the ma is a bit pernickety, that's just the way she is. Take no notice. Cheers.

'Brenda, I'll be gone for the morning. Direct any calls you can't deal with to my mobile, and make an appointment for me to see my investment advisor asap,' he directed his secretary as he headed at speed out of the office.

Three-quarters of an hour later he stood at his mother's door in Drumcondra, noting that a house at the end of the road had been sold. He'd check out how much the owners had got for it. Property slump or not, it hadn't stayed too long on the market. A good sign. Drumcondra was a prime location, recession or not, he observed, feeling more cheerful. By the end of this week he was hoping to have a good idea of his mother's finances and see how the wind lay in relation to the will. It would be reassuring to know just how much of a safety net he had coming to him. If he found that he wasn't getting what he expected, he'd take legal advice on the matter and keep badgering his mother until she saw sense. He had his opportunity to ingratiate himself with Lily now that Judith was in hospital.

'Morning, Tom.' Lily was uncommonly cheerful when she opened the door to him. It was amazing, he reflected as he took in her smart appearance and her bright eyes; Judith's accident had been the makings of her. Even her demeanour was different. Her shoulders were straighter. That pinched, worried expression that she habitually wore was less evident. She had colour in her cheeks from being out and about. She didn't look like a woman in her early seventies. She could easily live for another fifteen years and, knowing her, she would, just to keep him waiting. He brushed the thought away impatiently.

'Jimmy, the painter, is on his way. He's bringing colour cards so you can choose what paint you want,' he said, following her into the kitchen. Two china cups on saucers, a bowl of sugar cubes, a milk jug and a plate of biscuits were laid out on the small square table with its floral oilcloth. No cream sponge, he noted, disappointed.

'I think I'll go for the same colours that we have, in both our rooms – ochre and cream in Judith's, and sage green and lavender in mine,' Lily said as the doorbell rang and she hurried out to answer it. A gangly man with a mop of white hair stood in paint-spattered overalls at her door. Tom heard Jimmy greet his mother with a friendly, 'Howya, Missus Baxter. I see Tom's here already.'

'Hello, Jimmy, good timing.' Tom went out to

the hall. 'Ma, this is Jimmy, the best painter in the country.'

'Hello, Jimmy, will you have a cup of tea?' Lily said politely, putting her hand in his outstretched one. He shook it gently, and his blue eyes twinkled at her as he followed her into the kitchen. 'I see you have your china out, just like my granny. She only drinks tea from china cups. She's a lady too.' He smiled down at her.

'Is that so? Tea tastes much nicer from china, I find,' Lily said as she went to switch on the kettle.

'Er . . . Can we just have a look at the rooms first so we can get ourselves sorted?' Tom interjected hastily. Jimmy was a good painter but a real gasbag when he got going.

'Certainly, certainly,' Jimmy agreed, standing back to allow Lily to precede them up the stairs. To Tom's surprise, his mother made her decisions quickly and decisively. No dithering like the old days.

'Umm, I was thinking that I should get a key cut . . . you know, in case you weren't here to let Jimmy in. Or if there were any problems and you were in the hospital,' he said casually, not wanting to seem too eager.

'Oh, there's no need for that, Tom,' Lily said firmly. 'I'll be here to let Jimmy in if he comes in the morning. And if he comes in the afternoon, I can arrange my visiting times to suit him. Judith's a private patient, don't forget. I can come and go as I please,' she reminded him.

'All the same, it would be handy for me to have a key.' Tom tried to keep his tone light.

'I don't see any need for you to be bothering about getting keys cut. You've enough to be doing. Now, Jimmy, when can you start?' Lily turned her back on Tom and faced the painter.

'I can start this afternoon, Missus Baxter. I just have to buy the paint, and that won't take me long now that I know what you want. Is that all right with you, Tom?' Jimmy turned to him, bushy eyebrow raised.

'Fine,' Tom muttered, thoroughly wrongfooted.

'Come and have the tea,' Lily invited, waving imperiously, as if she were the chatelaine of a grand mansion rather than a pensioner living in a redbrick in the suburbs. She gave herself such airs and graces sometimes, Tom thought irritably, annoyed that she'd rebuffed him when he'd tried to offer advice on the colour she'd chosen for her bedroom. 'Hush, Tom, I know what I want,' she'd said sharply, as if he were ten years old rather than the successful, property-owning businessman that he was. Well, she might know what she wanted, but he knew *exactly* what he wanted too. But, the way things were going, he might never get a chance to have a good poke around, and it was going to cost him. Painters didn't come cheap these days, and he couldn't very well turn around and say, *'You can pay for this yourself, I've changed my mind.'*

'Let me go in front of you, Missus Baxter, a gentleman always walks down the stairs first, in case the lady trips,' Jimmy said gallantly.

'What lovely manners.' Lily flushed with pleasure. 'You remind me of my late husband, Ted. He always walked ahead of me down the stairs. A man with manners is hard to find these days,' she said, pointedly glancing in Tom's direction.

'My granny insisted on good manners. We were reared to it,' Jimmy said cheerfully, as he loped down the stairs.

Lickarse brown-noser, Tom thought, wondering how he was going to achieve his goal. He didn't want to be too pushy about the key. He wouldn't like to raise the painter's suspicions either, especially if he did get the chance for a snoop. Jimmy was a real salt-of-the-earth Dubliner type, the sort that respected the elderly. He might not be too impressed if he caught Tom poking around his mother's bedroom and riffling through drawers.

The way they were chatting to each other, Lily was clearly taken with Jimmy. She might trust him enough to leave him on his own in the house, and Tom could call on the pretext of checking to see how everything was going and get his chance then. Things weren't going to plan. It was all very stressful. He didn't have time to sit drinking tea out of china cups, rabbiting on about the 'good old days'.

'So are you going in to visit Judith this afternoon?' he inquired as he sat at the kitchen table chomping on chocolate biscuits, waiting for his mother to make the tea.

'We'll play it by ear – isn't that what they say

these days?' Lily declared airily, and he could have cheerfully murdered her.

'So, Janice, if you could sort that for me I'd be very grateful.' Judith spoke to her colleague in human resources with a much stronger, clearer voice than of late. 'As I say, I think I was a little hard on Debbie about her increment. She's not a bad worker. She was just somewhat . . . er . . . distracted, with her wedding coming up, I suppose. If I was at work myself I'd deal with it.'

'No problem, Judith. How are you feeling?' Janice inquired kindly.

'Do you know, I think I've turned a corner. I won't be back at work for a few months, they've told me, but I could be out in ten days or so, once my orthopaedic surgeon and the physio are happy.'

'That's great news, Judith. I'll be in to see you later in the week, and I'll bring you up to date on all the news, gossip and scandal,' Janice assured her.

'And you'll make sure Debbie gets her increment in her next pay cheque?'

'Am on it as we speak,' her colleague assured her. 'God bless, Judith, keep well.'

Judith exhaled a long, deep sigh and leaned back in the chair beside the bed. It didn't sound to her as if Debbie had made a complaint to HR saying that she'd been bullied. Janice had been friendly and cooperative. There had been no hint of anything untoward. Ever since the altercation with her young colleague, Judith had had it at the back of her mind that Debbie might take a case against her. But that wasn't the only reason she had asked for the other girl's increment to be paid. Judith knew deep down that she'd behaved badly by withholding it and, while redressing the matter didn't remove her guilt, it might assuage it a little.

Being called a bully had shocked Judith deeply. She'd attended a course at work about bullying only three months ago. Every employee in the company had had to do it, under their company regulations. She could still remember the good-looking, articulate psychologist who was running the course listing off a set of criteria which, at the time, hadn't impacted on her as much as it had in the past few days. When she'd allowed herself to face up to Debbie's accusation, she'd recalled that some of the methods a bully used included implied threats and persistent criticism, verbal abuse, and negative comments made in front of other staff. These were commonplace, it seemed. If they constituted bullying, she *had* to hold her hands up and say that was the way she'd treated Debbie Adams. Judith felt riddled with shame.

The psychologist had told his audience that most bullies envied their victims. Judith particularly remembered *that* phrase because she remembered thinking that *she* envied *everybody*. It was a course that held no relevance to the way she conducted her professional life, she'd felt. As far as she was concerned, it was a waste of time. It was only after Debbie's shocking accusation that it all fell into place because, if there was one person in the last two years that Judith had truly envied, it was Debbie Adams, with her sparkling engagement ring and her wedding plans, and her attentive boyfriend, now husband. Yes, envy had been the reason she had halted her young colleague's increment, nothing more and nothing less. She'd done it out of malice, just because she was able to. She had that power. If the truth were told, Debbie was no better or no worse at her job than any of the other girls under Judith's command.

Her own psychiatrist had hit the nail on the head in a follow-up session with her the previous day, when he'd pointed out, in the nicest possible way, that behaviour at work was often subtly and not so subtly influenced by what went on at home. That was when she'd really started to face up to the truly unpalatable fact that she was guilty as charged. Judith blushed, thinking that, if the psychiatrist knew how horrible she'd been to a work colleague, he might not have been so kind and friendly to her. Maybe, some time, she might actually be able to bring herself to apologize to Debbie in person but, for the moment, restoring her incremental pay rise would have to suffice.

Judith sat quietly in her chair, glad that her sedation had been reduced to a minimum. It was a relief to be able to think clearly again. It was necessary to face all these issues, she supposed, because, by confronting them and dealing with them as best she could, she could move on with her life and not stay as she had been, full of simmering resentment, anger and bitterness. It was hard facing up to the fact that she wasn't a very nice person, that she'd taken her bad feelings out on a younger, more vulnerable co-worker. Ever since her last session with her psychiatrist she'd excoriated herself, sparing herself nothing as she'd gone over all the times she'd been thoroughly nasty to Debbie. It made for painful recall.

Facing her dark side was pretty grim, the hardest thing she had ever done, Judith reflected, watching the sullen, black rainclouds roll in over Howth. But hadn't Plato said something about the unexamined life not being worth living? She was certainly getting an opportunity to do plenty of self-examination these days, she thought ruefully. Still, despite the harsh and unpleasant truths she was being forced to deal with, it was a relief to stop running away from things, and to take responsibility for her own behaviour and stop blaming her mother for everything. For the past twenty years or more, Judith had blamed Lily for all that was wrong with her life, because she was the most obvious candidate. That was most unfair, the new, more self-aware Judith admitted. Lily was not to blame. That acknowledgement had to be a step in the right direction. Once, a thought like that would have been given short shrift. Feeling sorry for herself had kept her going all these years. What was she going to do now that she no longer had Lily to blame for her life choices?

We live in interesting times. Was that a Chinese saying? It had just popped into her head. Her whole life was changing and, with that, came a change in attitude. That had to be a positive development, she supposed. The best thing to come out of her accident was her new, respectful, even tentatively affectionate relationship with Lily. Judith smiled, thinking of the phone call she'd got from her mother a little while ago.

'I'll be in later than I usually get in,' Lily had said. 'I have things to tell you.' She'd been quite mysterious, but there was a lilt to her voice that had never been there in all their years together. It was good to hear it.

Jillian had phoned her earlier in the day also, telling her that the guest room awaited her and not to be malingering. For the first time since she'd come out of her coma, Judith found herself looking forward to getting out of hospital.

'Time for your exercise, Judith.' Her physio poked her head around the door, startling her from her reverie.

'I'm ready,' Judith said firmly, getting to her feet with more alacrity than she'd shown since she'd started the exercise regime the previous week.

'You're doing great, Judith,' the other woman praised.

'I'm not doing too bad at all,' Judith agreed, as she positioned her crutches and began her walk down the long and by now very familiar corridor.

* * *

'You're looking a lot better, Judith, and it's great to see you out of the bed.' Lily studied her daughter critically, noting the faint smudge of colour in her cheeks and the more alert expression in her eyes.

'I went for a short walk outside today with my physio. It was wonderful to get a breath of fresh air. I just stood breathing lungfuls of it in,' Judith explained, raising her face for Lily's now daily kiss.

'I'm sorry I'm late today,' Lily apologized, pulling up a chair beside Judith and sitting down. 'I had a painter in.'

'You got a painter in?' Judith looked at her in surprise.

'Not me, Judith. Tom organized it.'

'You're kidding! What's he getting a painter in for?' Judith's brows drew down in a frown.

'Well, he came up with this notion that he would get your bedroom and my bedroom painted to give you a surprise when you got out of hospital—'

'Don't let that fella into my room, Ma. I don't trust him,' Judith warned agitatedly, remembering their last fraught encounter.

Lily held up a calming hand. 'Don't worry, Judith. I have everything under control.' She patted her bag. 'I know he wants to have a good root around. He was trying to get me to give him a key to get one cut, but I wasn't having that. Does he think I came down in the last shower? The painter – a very nice chap indeed by the way – made a start on my bedroom this afternoon. Now, I can stay there all day when he's there, or I can lock your bedroom when

374

he's working on mine. I have all my financial information and post-office book and the will in my bag, so even if Tom does get the chance to pry, he won't find anything,' Lily said triumphantly. 'And the thing is, Judith, we'll have the bedrooms painted, courtesy of your brother. I picked the exact colours to go on yours that're there already. I thought you'd want that. And then, when Jimmy – that's the painter's name – has finished the bedrooms, I'm going to get him to do the rest of the house. Because, once you get your own place, Tom will guess something's afoot, financially, and I'm very sure I won't be getting any more offers of help from him. What do you think of that then?' Lily sat up tombstone straight and looked eagerly at her daughter.

Judith started to laugh. 'Oh, Ma, you're something else. He'll be going mad. That's brilliant. The house was long overdue a painting anyway. Now, listen, there's a beige envelope folder in the second drawer of my chest of drawers, and in it is a brown envelope that all my bank statements and savings accounts are in, and another one with my insurance policies. I don't want him to get his maulers on it. Where could I put it?'

'Well, he won't really have a chance to look around your room, because I'll make it my business to be there when it's being painted but, just to put our minds at ease, I could put them in my bag if you liked,' she offered tentatively. Judith was very private about her personal business, and she wouldn't wish to step out of line in that regard.

'If you wouldn't mind, Ma.' Judith patted Lily's knee. 'I'd be grateful.'

'Thank you, Judith, for trusting me. You know I respect your privacy, and you need have no fears that I'd be nosy about your money or your private business,' Lily said hastily, extremely pleased that her daughter would allow her such latitude.

'Ma, at this stage in our lives, we know each other well enough to be clear that we wouldn't go snooping. You could have done it long ago, and so could I, but we wouldn't sink so low. Anyway, I'd like, when I get out of here, to go through my savings with you so that, when I take you up on your kind offer of putting me on the deeds, you'll know how much I can put towards a mortgage. It's only right for you to know, if your house is going to be collateral.'

'Our house,' Lily said, beaming with pride that Judith would confide her private and confidential business to her.

'And, you know, I should make a will too,' Judith said slowly. 'If I had died, I would have wanted my money to go to you. I've nearly a hundred thousand in savings, after all my years' working, plus an insurance policy. I certainly don't want Tom getting his hands on any of it.'

'Sure, that's a grand amount to put towards a house or an apartment.' Lily was delighted at the news. 'Judith, you'll be living like a queen yet,' she exclaimed. 'But then, you always did live frugally enough. You were never a spendthrift. And now, when you need it, it's there for you.'

'Do you know, Ma, I'm starting to get excited about it,' Judith confessed. 'Are you sure about it, now? I'll stay living with you if you want.' She had to make the offer for her own peace of mind. Would Lily revert to old ways and take her up on it? Judith almost held her breath. Had she scuppered her chances of a life of her own?

'You will not, and ruin my chances of finding a toy boy,' Lily joked. 'Judith, nothing would make me happier than for you to be settled in a place of your own. I just hope you don't move too far away. Especially not to the Southside. I'd miss seeing you.' Lily's cheeks were pink from her little speech.

'Don't worry, Ma, you'll be seeing plenty of me, and I certainly won't be crossing the river. The air is better over here.' Judith felt a wave of relief, amazed that, after all the years of tension and antagonism, this lovely new gentle kindness had emerged between them. It brought a balm to her she hadn't thought possible. For the first time in her life, she actually *liked* her mother. What a wonderful moment was that, Judith reflected gratefully, noticing how Lily was so obviously chuffed to be involved in making plans for her future. *Thank you, God*, she thought humbly, grateful for this second chance to get to know and love her mother. It was as if a huge burden had lifted from her shoulders, a dark and smothering energy had dissipated and she could breathe again, be optimistic about her life. To think she had passively considered allowing herself to commit suicide by not avoiding the tree as the car had careered into it. She would have died a bitter woman, estranged from her mother, and not known any of the unfamiliar but comforting new emotions she was feeling. She would have forgone this ... this new friendship with Lily. Always at the back of her mind, since her father had died, she had toyed with the idea that, if life got too much for her, she would take enough tablets to end it all. Now Judith knew that, no matter what life threw at her in the future, she would never go down that road. In a strange way, it was a liberation to have made that decision. For the first time in her adult years, she finally felt she was in control emotionally, if not yet physically, of her own life.

She smiled across at Lily and felt a surge of affection for the elderly woman sitting beside her. 'Now, what do you think? Should I go for a house or apartment?' she asked, feeling that some generosity of spirit was called for on her part.

'Well, now, let me see.' Lily was all businesslike, and took a small notebook out of her handbag which she used to write her grocery list in. 'Let's do a list of pros and cons and take it from there.'

'Good idea,' agreed Judith happily. 'First pro: apartment ... no gardening.'

'Con: neighbours on either side and above and below, depending what floor you buy on,' Lily batted back triumphantly, pen flying over the pad, as they bent their heads companionably to the task at hand.

CHAPTER TWENTY-FOUR

I need the car tonight and I won't be having dinner. D

Debbie stared at the screen, dithering whether to add a couple of kisses after her initial, as she usually did before pressing send. Bryan had hardly spoken to her that morning, and she'd had no cheery texts or emails from him, as she frequently did during the day.

She saved the draft and picked up her mobile, looking furtively around, before remembering that Judith Baxter was not sitting in the corner office with her eagle eye on her. Judith had been very strict about the use of mobiles during work time. Debbie's fingers flew over the keys.

Hi Melissa are you free 2 drive down 2 Greystones with me after work and will we have supper together? D xx

She pressed send and got the delivery report note. Melissa responded promptly.

Gr8. I'd like that. M xxxx

Debbie chewed the top of her pen. She didn't particularly want to meet Aimee, so she decided against collecting her half-sister from her apartment block.

Pick you up at George's yacht club at 6.30. xx

That would be easier all round, she decided, as a confirmatory text flashed back on to her screen. She studied her email to Bryan and sent it, without the kisses. Why should she send Bryan kisses and pretend that all was well between them? He'd behaved like the lowest of the low, laying all the blame for their financial straits on her and, for once in their relationship, she wasn't going to be the appeaser. As long as she'd been with Bryan, she'd always been the one to give in and make up. She'd given him his chance to back out of the wedding when she'd brought him on a surprise trip to Amsterdam just weeks before they'd got married. She'd asked him did he want to postpone it, and he'd said no, so he could take it back for blaming her for pushing them to marry. She should have thought of that when he'd been flinging his accusations at her, but she'd been so dismayed at his reaction, it had slipped her mind.

She hated fighting with Bryan. It had always unsettled her when they were engaged, and she'd worried that he would call it off, but things were different now. They were man and wife and, short of divorcing her, he needed to work with her to sort out their differences *and* their finances. And the sooner Bryan realized that, the better for their marriage. Her husband needed to grow up, she observed dejectedly as she brought up her section's overtime records and began working on the necessary calculations.

Bryan read his wife's email and scowled. She could have the bloody car. The petrol gauge was nearly empty, so she could fill it up herself, because he wasn't going to pay for her jaunting around.

'Hey, bud, how's it going? Are you all ready for the Galway Races? Some of the guys are thinking of hiring a chopper to get down there. Have you sorted any accommodation? The prices are an arm and a leg this year.' Ed Murray sat on the corner of his desk, tanned and affluent in his bespoke grey suit. Ed was one of the marketing managers and would have his expenses at Galway paid, as he'd be hosting several corporate events on behalf of the company.

'Yo, Ed.' Bryan pretended cheeriness. 'Hope to be going, but I'm a married man now, I have other commitments. I can't be acting like a carefree bachelor,' he joked feebly.

'I'm married, too, but that never stops me going to Galway or chatting up the birds on Ladies' Day,' Ed scoffed. 'Don't let Debbie turn you into a wimp. If you give in the first year, you're going to be pussy-whipped for the rest of your life. Start as you mean to go on, mate, that's my advice to ya. See ya around.'

'Sure thing, Ed. Cheers,' Bryan said flatly, watching the other man swagger down the office. It was well known that Ed did more than 'chat up' the

381

ladies and, if the rumours were to be believed, his marriage of ten years was shaky, and his attractive blond wife had started drinking way more than was good for her. Debbie wouldn't be able to afford to turn to drink if he went off with other women, he thought dryly, sending off an email to her with a curt, *Fine*.

If he told her he was considering a trip to the Galway Races, World War Three would break out, so he'd say nothing and try and scrounge the money together somehow. But where was he going to get a couple of thousand smackers? There was no point in going to Galway with pennies in your pockets. And if he didn't go, the others would agree with Ed and say he was pussy-whipped. So much for happy ever after, he grimaced, staring down at his wedding band and heartily wishing he were single again.

'Hey, Bryan, you wouldn't be interested in buying a Bang & Olufsen stereo system and an almost new flatscreen TV, would you?' Alison Reed, the MD's PA, stopped at his desk, cutting short his dour thoughts.

'No, why?' He looked at her in surprise.

Alison sighed, flicking her chestnut hair back off her face. 'My boyfriend's lost his job, and he's moving back home to his parents', and I live with my parents, so neither of us has any room for them.'

Bryan ran his fingers through his hair as he studied the slender brunette standing beside him. He liked Alison, but he didn't fancy her; she was too skinny for his tastes, all angular, jutting, bony bits and no curves. From the back, she could almost pass for a boy. 'That's rough, who was he working for?'

'He worked in the corporate services of FB Sweeney auctioneers. They let fourteen people go the same day as Gerry.' She shrugged helplessly. 'It had been on the cards for ages. They were cutting down on entertaining and days away and wining and dining prospective clients, so he was half expecting it, but it was a shock just the same. Ed would want to watch out – our corporate entertaining budgets are going to be cut in half. There's a raft of cost-cutting measures coming down the line. We've lost two big contracts this week because the companies involved have pulled out of the office-letting sector. It's going to get rocky here too,' she said sombrely, getting off the desk. 'So are you interested?'

'Sorry, Ali, we have a TV and stereo, but I'll ask around. Why don't you put it up on the newsletter?'

Alison made a face. 'I don't really want the world and his mother to know – it's a bit embarrassing, if you know what I mean. People would start asking questions. I mean, it's the pits not having a place of your own to go back to. We can't even have a decent shag any more. You're so lucky being married and having a house of your own.'

'I suppose I am,' Bryan said slowly. 'Sorry to hear of your troubles, Ali,' he added. 'What's Gerry going to do?'

'He might have to emigrate, the way things are going. We didn't save much, we were too busy having fun, so there's not much to fall back on, and we couldn't manage on just my salary, so it's all up in the air. We never thought the good times were going to end. Anyway, thanks for listening to my moans – I better go, there's a big meeting in twenty minutes to discuss the recession and its potential implications for the company. I wouldn't be surprised if there're a few job losses here too, and he' – she pointed at Ed, who was flirting with one of the secretaries – 'might not be so cocky this time next week. See ya.'

'Bye, Ali,' murmured Bryan, dismayed at what he'd heard. If Ali knew the state of his finances, she might not be so envious of him. This recession thing was getting serious. Ali's boyfriend, Gerry, had rented a cool, duplex apartment in Grand Canal Dock and had often thrown lavish parties to which Debbie and he had been invited. Now he was back living with his parents. That had to be the pits.

And all this talk about job losses was unsettling. It was true the market for offices had contracted. If it got worse, *he* could be in trouble, and then they'd have to let the bank repossess the house, because Debbie wouldn't be able to pay the mortgage out of her salary. Gerry and Ali might not be the only ones living with their parents, he thought gloomily.

Debbie was right, although it pained him to say it. They did need to get their finances sorted, or they were going to be in deep trouble. Going to live with either of their parents, Connie in particular, was an option to put the fear of God in him. His conversation with Alison had been a wake-up call Bryan didn't particularly want. The Galway Races would be the first casualty in his belt-tightening exercise, and life would be all the more lacklustre because of it. If this was what it was going to be like for the foreseeable future, emigrating looked like a very attractive option. Bondi Beach would suit him just fine.

'Mom, I'm meeting Debbie to go and see Connie's cat, 'cos she's away in Spain, so I won't be home when you get in from work. It's fine with Dad.' Melissa left a message for her mother. She'd tried to phone her, but it had rung out before going to her voicemail. She must be at a meeting; it was all she seemed to do these days: work and sleep.

She flung herself down on the bed and stared at the ceiling. Sarah had asked her to go to Dundrum to hang out at the shopping centre with her cousin who was visiting from England, but Melissa hadn't been in the humour. She knew they'd want to go to have something to eat at some stage, and she just couldn't do that right now. She couldn't risk slipping back. She had to keep focused on losing the weight, seeing as the scales were giving her such positive results. She'd pretended to have bad periods.

Melissa wasn't telling fibs about feeling ill. She really didn't feel well. Her stomach was tied up in knots, and she didn't know if it was because she wasn't eating, because she was making herself

385

vomit when she did eat, or because she was worrying about what was going to happen to her parents. She got up and pulled her weighing scales from under the bed and carried them out to the terrace. She never put the scales on top of her bedroom carpet; it affected the reading. She stood on them and gazed at the small red screen that showed a loss of one stone five pounds. The only thing she had control of: her weight loss. It afforded her some small comfort from the worry of her parents' rift and life in general. Her stomach rumbled and went into spasm. She was starving, but that was a good sign. It showed she was strong. Virtuous. In charge. The buzz of empowerment reinvigorated her. She went down to the kitchen and poured some lukewarm water from the kettle and squeezed some lemon juice into it, and sipped it slowly as she went back to her room. The tartness of the lemon made her wince, but she persevered, and the sharp pangs of hunger faded to a gnawing ache.

She needed to buy new jeans, as she was constantly hitching hers up these days, a satisfying reminder of how much weight she was losing. She studied her reflection critically. Yes, she definitely needed smaller jeans, but she still had a good way to go before she got *really* skinny. If Debbie hadn't texted, she might have changed her mind and met up with Sarah and her cousin after they'd eaten and then gone shopping, but she wouldn't have time now, if she was meeting Debbie at 6.30. She was so looking forward to seeing Connie's adorable little cat. She'd always longed for a pet, but Aimee wouldn't have one in the penthouse, saying it was no place for an animal.

When she hadn't heard from Debbie after Connie had gone to Spain, Melissa had wondered had her half-sister forgotten their plan to drive out to Greystones. Getting the text earlier had lifted her glum spirits. If anyone understood how she was feeling, it would be Debbie. After all, she'd gone through her parents' divorce and survived it. Melissa couldn't let on to Barry and Aimee that she'd overheard their horrible argument, but she might confide in Debbie and see what she had to say about it. She went back into her bedroom and began to try on a selection of outfits for her jaunt in her half-sister's sporty soft-top, turning this way and that to observe her figure from every possible angle.

'So, Ian, I'm giving you a month's notice, as required.' Aimee handed over a crisp white envelope. 'And I'll be taking my annual-leave entitlement, which works out at three weeks and two days. I'll spend the next few days going through my schedule with Rhona – I think you'll agree she's the most experienced one to replace me until you fill the position.' She couldn't help enjoying the moment: shock followed by dismay registered on Ian's thin, fake-tanned visage.

'Wha . . . what do you mean you're resigning? You can't resign; we're up to our eyes. You have half a dozen major-league events in your diary,' her boss stuttered.

'I can and I just have,' Aimee said coolly.

'But why? What's going on?' He jumped up from his chair and walked around to her side of the desk. Two dull red spots appeared on his cheeks under his orange tan, and his little walnut eyes glimmered with panic. Aimee was convinced he'd had Botox; his forehead was as smooth and unlined as her own. Today, he was dressed from head to toe in black; almost priest-like, she observed as he stood in front of her. Black jeans, black Armani shirt, and a black cashmere pullover draped over his narrow, wire-hanger shoulders. He stuck his hands into the back pockets of his Dolce & Gabbana jeans and stared at her in disbelief.

'You know, Ian, I've made big bucks for your company, especially in the last year, and you haven't even had the decency to offer me a raise. The best you could do was to send me an email telling me to take a great big bow,' she added dryly.

'I've been meaning to get around to it,' he blustered. 'It's just been so busy. Now calm down and sit down, and let's take a moment to discuss your raise. You know I couldn't run this company without you.' He gave her a sweet smile, cocking his head sideways in a boyish manner, a mannerism that invariably melted any woman it was directed at. Aimee was unimpressed. She'd long since grown impatient with his poor-little-me-I-just-can't-manage-by-myself act.

'What are you offering?' she asked out of curiosity, to see how far he'd go to keep her.

'Um . . . an extra five thou?' He arched a plucked eyebrow hopefully, and then saw the look of disdain on her face. 'Plus a new company car,' he added hastily. 'Maybe seven,' he amended when he saw her turn to walk away. 'Come on, Aimee, you owe me, big time,' he bleated. Aimee came to a dead stop.

'No, Ian, *you owe me*. And, you know something? You never appreciated what I did for you or this company, but one of your clients did, and he's made me an offer I simply can't refuse. Double the salary I'm getting here, a top-of-the-range car and, even more important, an employer who appreciates my capabilities. I'm going to be MD of his company. I'd never have got the chance to run my own company with you. Ian, you get handed things on a plate. I've had to fight for every rung I've climbed up the ladder. I've brought this company and myself on to the top rung and, FYI, one thing you need to know for further reference: when you hire my replacement, patronizing, flowery emails are a big no-no. Money talks.'

'Listen to yourself,' Ian vented, all pretence of being lovey-dovey gone with the wind. 'You're beginning to believe your own publicity, just because you've had a taste of what it's like to work for the mega rich. It was me and my contacts that got you where you are. I gave you your big chance, and this is the thanks I get – being left in the lurch without a backward glance. So, let me guess – it has to be Roger: he's been going on and on about how wonderful you are. Has he got into your panties yet? Because that's where he wants to be.' His thin lips were drawn back in a sneer, and hostility oozed from every pore.

'Really?' Aimee gave him a withering look. 'Well, don't be jealous, honey. If he's your type, there're lots more like him out there.'

'I beg your pardon? How dare you, Aimee Davenport!' Ian was apoplectic. Little flecks of spittle flew in the air.

'Oh get over yourself,' Aimee threw over her shoulder as she marched out the door. Five measly thousand was his first offer, chickenfeed, for the amount of business she'd brought to his company the last year. And it was offered begrudgingly. He hadn't a hope of keeping her with that sort of attitude.

She knew she was being a real bitch, and she didn't care. She began to clear out her files. She'd had enough of men pushing her around; it was good to hit back, even if wimpy Ian was a less than perfect target. He'd been disgusted at her innuendo, but it served him right for his nasty, scurrilous little remark about Roger. She shuddered. Sex with Roger was a revolting thought; their relationship would be a purely business one, and she felt he knew that very well. Ian was just being his usual bitchy self when things didn't go his way. She was almost glad he'd lowered himself to make such remarks because, when she screwed him by taking half his clients with her, she wouldn't feel at all bad.

Her phone beeped, signalling she had a message, and she picked it up from her desk. Her lips tightened when she listened to what Melissa had to say. What did she want to be going off to Greystones with Debbie for? Why did she want to be getting so closely involved with Connie and her half-sister? Hadn't she managed perfectly fine without them all these years? It was bad enough that the pair knew about her pregnancy almost as soon as she'd found out about it herself, she bristled. She was so bitter, volcanically angry and resentful these days. Those dark, seething emotions had consumed every cell and fibre of her. She was going to give Barry a piece of her mind about that when she got home later. If Ian was a less than perfect target for a tongue-lashing, Barry was just the one for it. With any luck, he'd get sick of her bitchiness and run back to Saint Connie because, right now, as far as Aimee was concerned, the other woman was more than welcome to him.

CHAPTER TWENTY-FIVE

'Hi Connie, how are things? How's the holiday going?' Barry asked, as his ex-wife answered her mobile phone.

'Fine, lovely.' Connie sounded surprised to hear from him.

'I just wanted to let you know that Melissa and Debbie are going to drive to Greystones later this evening. Debbie texted her, so she's thrilled. Debbie will probably call you later. I'm delighted about it, Connie, and I just wanted to thank you again.'

'Ah, that's great, Barry. I'm delighted myself, thanks for letting me know.' There was genuine warmth in her voice, and he felt a sudden longing to be with her, to pour his heart out to her and tell her all his woes.

'I suppose Aimee told you we met Juliet on the flight over, and we've been spending some time with her. It looks like she and Ken are headed for the divorce courts,' Connie said conversationally.

'You're joking!' He couldn't hide his astonishment. Ken was a pompous boor, but he'd never figured he'd go the divorce route. 'Is there someone else?'

'Who'd have him? He's obnoxious. Juliet asked him for a divorce, did Aimee not tell you?' Connie was surprised.

'Are you serious? She's hardly spoken two words to me these last few days. It looks like Ken and Juliet aren't the only ones heading for the divorce courts. Aimee's talking about divorcing *me*. I'll be looking for a place to stay; you might have to put me up,' he said mournfully.

'What?' Now she was the one to be astonished.

'She says she wants a divorce. She's like a briar. She really doesn't want this baby, you know. I'm at my wits' end, Connie. I don't know what to do or say. We've been having fierce rows. I feel she hates me. It's horrible. The atmosphere at home is glacial, to say the least.' It all erupted out of him, and it was such a relief to share his burden with Connie. She had always offered him such comforting solace when they were together in the early years of their relationship, before he'd felt trapped by marriage and walked away from her. Now, more than anything, he realized what a fool he'd been to let her go. There was nothing abrasive about his ex-wife, not even in their worst moments. 'What should I do?' he asked, glad that he had someone to worry about him.

'I don't know. Things might calm down, it's the shock of her pregnancy—'

'It's more than that,' he said dolefully, looking for

succour. 'It's all work, work, work these days. She doesn't spend any time with Melissa. Hell, she doesn't spend any time with me,' he moaned, enjoying feeling sorry for himself.

'Look, Barry, you have to sort things, you've got Melissa and the new baby to think of. You need to talk to Aimee when she's more amenable. Don't let it slide,' Connie said earnestly, and he could have hugged her for her concern.

'Thanks,' he said gratefully. 'At least I have you to talk to. Give Karen my love, and have fun. I'll keep in touch. Bye, Connie.'

'See you,' she replied, and hung up.

Barry sat at his desk and felt as if a load had been lifted off his shoulders. He wasn't on his own any more. Connie would be there for him, no matter what happened, and knowing that made life so much more bearable.

'For God's sake,' Connie muttered irritably as she slipped her phone into her bag and stared out to sea. She was lazing on a lounger, in a garden fringed with bougainvillea, wisteria and flowering shrubs, overlooking a small, crescent, golden beach. She'd taken a lounger to one of the palm trees on the verdant lawns that rolled down to the sea, content to be alone. Karen had gone into La Cala to pay her taxes, and Connie had been up to her eyes in the latest Lee Child novel when Barry had phoned her.

Could he have not kept his sorry tale to himself until she'd got home? And what was it with him telling her he might need a place to stay? She shook her head as she massaged sun-tan lotion into her arms. Did her ex-husband really think that he could assume she'd put him up if he and Aimee divorced? He could think again. She wasn't getting involved, she told herself firmly. It wasn't her problem.

She picked up her novel and tried to get back into it. Jack Reacher was a very sexy character, and she'd been enjoying her book and feeling thoroughly relaxed until Barry had ruined it for her. It was so typical of her ex-husband to unburden himself and offload all his problems on her – and typically selfish to do it while she was on holiday. Why did he think, after all these years, and after him walking out on her, that she'd be interested or even care that he and Aimee were having problems? Had it been the other way around, and she was in a relationship break-up, would he have been so quick to help her out, if all had been well with him and Aimee? As far as she could see, Barry would always feel she'd be at his beck and call, until she had a man of her own. It was a pity there weren't a few Jack Reachers waiting in the wings. That would put a halt to her ex-husband's gallop. Some relaxing holiday this was turning out to be, between Juliet and Ken's episode and now this.

Connie lay back against her lounger and closed her eyes, feeling the heat of the sun on her limbs. The sea soothed her as her thoughts drifted and lethargy infused her. The heat of the early evening was less intense and stifling than it had been earlier.

The balmy breeze whispered through her hair and, in spite of herself, her body sank into lassitude and her eyelids drooped. Jack Reacher reminded her of someone, she thought indolently, trying to remember whom. A strong, handsome, tanned face with a pair of deep blue eyes flashed into her mind. Oh yes, she thought, remembering. Drew. Very Jack Reacher. She couldn't imagine Drew looking for comfort or a place to stay from his ex-wife. Drew Sullivan was a man who stood on his own two feet. It was a pity Barry couldn't be more like him. Emotional blackmail would be well and truly wasted on Drew, from what she'd seen of him, thought Connie with a little smile, as her book fell from her hands and she fell into a languorous doze.

'Oh, hi, Drew. Fancy running into you here. What are you doing in town?' A petite blond woman stared up at Drew Sullivan, her green eyes raking him up and down, missing nothing.

Drew felt a jolt of shock as he gazed down at his ex-wife, Marianna. They were outside the AIB in Wicklow. She was at the ATM, and he had just left the bank after making a deposit.

'I still bank here,' he said stiffly. 'I didn't know you were in town.' He hadn't seen her since Katy's wedding, but she still looked as if she'd just walked out of a beauty parlour, all perfectly coiffed hair and lashings of make-up. She placed her money in her leather wallet, and he noted her blood-red nails. She'd got those talons deep in him once, and bled him dry.

'Dad took a heart attack; I flew in the day before yesterday. I'm just going up to the Blackrock Clinic with Mama, and I needed some cash.'

'Sorry to hear that,' Drew said politely. Privately, he couldn't give a hoot about his ex-father-in-law's heart attack. He certainly wouldn't be attending that old buzzard's funeral if and when it happened.

'I guess I'm gonna stay a couple of weeks. Perhaps we could have dinner some night and catch up?' Marianna suggested, slanting a sultry glance up at him.

'Busy time of the year for me; horses foaling and all that,' Drew said crisply. The last thing he wanted to do was to have dinner with her.

'Oh, you don't have to make a firm commitment, Drew,' his ex-wife drawled. 'I was just suggesting a casual meal some time; surely you don't spend your whole life in the stables? You must have some free time?'

'Indeed I do, Marianna. I'm my own boss now, so I can come and go as I please,' he said pointedly, hooking his thumbs into his jeans and staring at her.

'So what's the big deal about dinner then?' she murmured seductively. Drew almost laughed. She hadn't changed at all over the years. Still fluttering the eyelashes when she wanted something. She still showed off her boobs, too, and they'd been enhanced, to say the least, he observed, as his eyes slid over her décolleté. They looked like two round balloons. He wondered if he stuck a pin in them would they pop. 'Well,' she said huskily, noting the way his eyes roamed over her, 'what's the big deal?'

'No big deal. As I say, I'm a bit tied up at the moment. Hope your dad's OK. See you around.' He raised his hand in farewell and strode towards the car park, leaving her standing looking after him. Just his luck to bump into her, he thought grimly, as he headed towards SuperValu to do some grocery shopping.

Marianna came home every summer, but he always had some warning when she was coming because the girls would mention it in their emails. He usually shopped in Greystones while she was around, and did his banking early in the mornings, knowing he wouldn't bump into her before eleven. She'd never been an early riser. Wicklow was a small town, too small for comfort when his ex was home. It drove him mad that she expected him to be friendly and accommodating. Had the woman no conception of the grief she had caused him? He had missed his daughters' childhood and missed being a big part of their lives because of her selfishness. Some things you could forgive and some things you could forget, but that loss was too deep-rooted to do either, and some day he was going to tell her to get lost and not be annoying him, thought Drew angrily as he flung bananas and oranges into his trolley, and made his way along the aisles scowling ferociously.

Marianna Delahunt stared after her ex-husband as he marched away from her without a backward glance. He had aged so well, she acknowledged admiringly as she put her wallet in her handbag and followed him into the car park. He was striding along ahead of her and, if she wanted to catch up with him, she'd have to run, he was walking so fast.

He was so fit and healthy, and his blue eyes had lost none of their intensity. When he'd stared down at her, there was no warmth in his gaze, just cold, disdainful hostility. Marianna sighed. She remembered a time when his eyes had been hot with desire and those long, hard legs of his had imprisoned her beneath him. Sex with Drew had been fantastic. It probably still would be, she thought wistfully. Edward, her second husband, had become paunchy and flabby as he'd grown older. There was no flab on Drew – he still had a six-pack to be proud of and muscles in his arms that would be the envy of many a younger man.

She frowned as she compared her ex to her current husband. Edward fell way short, she thought angrily. He was carrying on behind her back; she knew it, and she didn't care. What did that say about their marriage? As long as he paid for her lifestyle, he could do what he liked. She knew whom he was carrying on with, too. Kendra Duvall was a divorcee, fifteen years younger than Marianna, and equally blond, pert, petite and Botoxed. Nevertheless, Kendra's husband, Marshall, had dumped her for a twenty-year-old bimbo, and she'd taken him to the cleaners and got a very healthy divorce settlement.

Marianna and Edward were in the same golf club

as the other couple, and they socialized in the same circles. So not only was Kendra blond, pert and petite, she was now wealthy in her own right and on the look-out for a new husband. Edward was managing her investments and, it seemed, looking after her emotional and sexual needs as well. Marianna had found receipts for perfume, and jewellery from Harry Winston's, which she'd never received, in one of Edward's suit pockets when she'd been sending it to the dry cleaner's. That had alerted her that her husband was up to no good.

From then on, she'd kept an eye on his cell phone and his credit-card bills. One number kept coming up on his cell phone, and she'd written it down and phoned it from a call box in the local mall one hot August afternoon.

'Halloo.' Kendra's unmistakable clipped Connecticut tones came down the line. Even though she'd anticipated it, it still gave Marianna a shock. She put on a false New York twang, said, 'Ronng numba,' and hung up. When Edward came home, she said casually, as she placed a steaming fish-chowder starter in front of him, 'I met Francine Crammer today, and you know how she's such a gossip? She tells me Jamie Van Horan is leaving her husband for a much younger man, and Kendra Duvall is seeing someone new and Francine thinks he's married, because she won't spill. It doesn't surprise me – she walks around with her tits hanging out and her skirts up to her bony little ass. She's such a tarty trollop, wouldn't you think?'

Edward had turned a deep shade of maroon, reminding her of an over-ripe tomato, and muttered something about not being interested in Francine Crammer's silly gossip before bending his head to his chowder and eating as though his life depended upon it. When she told him she'd booked herself into an expensive spa for a full day of luxury treatments, he'd said, 'Fine, fine,' without any of his usual comments about belt-tightening and cutting down on frivolous extravagance.

From that day on, she had spent as she wished, and spend she did. And from that day on, she had moved out of the marital bedroom into Katy's old one, and she hadn't had sex with him since. 'Your snoring keeps me awake,' she'd said, as she carried her possessions across the landing.

'We can't have that,' Edward had said dourly. 'You need your beauty sleep.' He'd paid for that snide remark with a brow lift and collagen treatments around the eyes and lips.

She didn't miss not having sex with Edward. It had grown boring and mechanical on both their parts, and she was always glad when it was over and he had hauled himself off her to his own side of the bed. There was no cuddling, like in the early days of their marriage, no lazy chatting and teasing, just a turning on his side with his back to her and, five minutes later, deep, rumbling snores and, on a bad night, several loud, stinky farts.

What would sex be like now with Drew, Marianna mused as he turned right into the

SuperValu car park that lay at right angles to the one in which she was parked and disappeared from view. Was he seeing anyone, she wondered, unlocking her father's Merc, reversing out of her parking space and heading towards Brittas to pick up her mother.

She'd given up quizzing the girls when they came back from their holidays with him because, as they'd grown older, they'd become even more loyal towards him. They'd always loved him fiercely – not even distance had dimmed that. 'Why didn't you stay in Ireland, so we could have seen more of Dad?' Erin had asked her once, and she'd been hard put to answer her daughter without showing herself in a bad light. Marianna shook her head almost unconsciously. All that was water under the bridge. Why couldn't Drew accept that? Why did he continue to treat her as the most loathsome creature, as something that had crawled from under a stone? Well, this trip it was going to be different, Marianna vowed. This time, for once and for all, her ex-husband was going to put the past behind him, and she would do everything in her power to make him remember what it was about her that had made him fall so hard for her in the first place. A rare sparkle lit her green eyes. If Edward could play away from home, so could she, but for her it would be more like *coming* home, and Drew Sullivan didn't know what a treat was in store for him. She hadn't had sex in more than a year, and she was ready for it and *how*. Just thinking about it made her hot, and she sighed with pleasure, remembering some of the delicious things her ex-husband had done to her when they were madly in love and the world was their oyster.

CHAPTER TWENTY-SIX

'Hey, you look cool,' Debbie smiled as her half-sister hopped eagerly into the car beside her.

'Thanks, I bought this top in Zara a little while back, and Mom bought me the combats in Milan two years ago, and they never fitted me but I can fit into them now. Mom goes to Milan a lot, to trade fairs for work,' Melissa explained as she settled in beside Debbie.

'Right. That's handy for getting cool gear, they're fabulous. You're losing weight for sure. I need to lose a few pounds too.' Debbie patted her little round tummy.

'It's easy – just stop eating and it falls off,' Melissa advised.

'Easier said than done. I'm starving. Will we get a Chinese for supper?' Debbie suggested.

'Oh . . . OK,' Melissa agreed, sliding her D&Gs down off the top of her head and settling them on her nose. The sun had come out, and Debbie had the roof down, and she was hoping against hope some of her classmates would see her swanning around in the Audi soft-top. It was *so* cool.

They drove along towards the People's Park and, as luck would have it, Wendy Collins and Selena Armstrong were strolling along on the opposite footpath, chatting animatedly.

Melissa sat up straight and gave a casual little wave. Wendy stopped and looked twice before waving back, and then they had driven past. Melissa glanced in the side mirror, but couldn't see if the two were looking back or not. She would have loved to turn her head, but that would have been too childish. Wendy was OK on her own, but when she was with Selena she was totally bitchy. Still, at least, she'd been seen. Driving around in a sports car was better than hanging around in the People's Park for sure. Let them see that she was as super cool as they were.

'So how's the holliers going?' Debbie asked as they drove past Teddy's ice-cream shop along the seafront, the breeze making her hair blow back from her face.

'OK,' she sighed. 'It's pretty boring, to be honest.'

'Make the most of it,' laughed Debbie. 'I'd give anything to have three months off. Are you going anywhere with Dad and your mom?'

'I don't think so,' Melissa said slowly. 'Debbie, can I tell you something – and promise you won't say anything to anyone?'

'I promise.' Debbie flashed her a look of concern. 'Look, why don't I pull into the car park here and we can talk? Is everything OK?'

'No,' Melissa said, and her lip wobbled.

'Hold on, just let me park,' Debbie said hastily, manoeuvring into a space and pulling the hand-brake up. 'What's wrong?' She reached out and took Melissa's hand. It was very cold, she noted.

'I heard Mom and Dad having a terrible row, and Mom wants a divorce when the baby's born, and I'm really scared. And I just wonder has Dad found someone else. And you're the only one who would understand 'cos you've been there.' She burst into tears, sobbing her heart out, not caring that people walking along the promenade could see her.

Debbie gazed at her in dismay. This was totally unexpected. How would she handle it? If Barry and Aimee were going to divorce, Melissa was in for a very hard time, no question. She took a deep breath. 'No, I'm sure Dad hasn't found someone else. Really, Melissa,' she said, injecting as much reassurance as she could into her voice. 'Look, maybe they were just having one of those rows that people have. Me and Bryan have them all the time,' she fibbed.

'Do you?' Melissa took off her sunglasses and wiped her eyes with the back of her hand, smearing eye shadow and mascara across her cheeks.

'Here, have a tissue,' Debbie offered helpfully. 'Sure we do. I think Bryan wouldn't mind a divorce right now, because he's pissed off with me because I'm telling him we have to stop spending money and start paying off our credit-card bills. In fact, we're going to have to get rid of this for something smaller,' she confided.

'Really?' Melissa exclaimed, as the knot of worry that had held her prisoner since she had overheard her parents' row seemed to dissolve.

'Yeah, we owe a lot after the wedding. So look, don't panic, people say things in anger that they don't mean at all.'

'But they're hardly talking. It's horrible at home. And Mom's not happy about having a baby, I don't think.'

Debbie made a face. 'I can kind of understand that,' she said slowly. 'If you haven't planned to have one, it can be a shock – I'd be horrified if I got pregnant right now – but things will settle down and she'll get used to the idea, and then things will calm down between her and Dad.'

'Do you think so?' Melissa studied her half-sister's face earnestly, trying to see if she was just being kind or if she really believed what she was saying.

'I do,' Debbie said confidently. 'The thing is not to worry. I used to spend my time worrying about Mum when I was your age. I used to lie awake in bed imagining this disaster happening or that one, and none of them ever happened, so it was just a complete waste of time.'

'Really! I do that, too, all the time.'

'Well, stop it,' Debbie instructed firmly. 'You just go and have fun with your friends and forget about worrying about your parents – they can look after themselves, trust me on that.'

'Oh! Right, OK. Hey, thanks – it's such a relief to

be able to talk to someone who knows. I didn't like to say it to Sarah, even though she's my best friend. I wouldn't like her to think there was anything wrong at home.'

'That's what sisters are for so, if you've any worries, you can tell me, and don't be making yourself miserable.' Debbie gave Melissa's hand a squeeze.

'But you won't tell Dad what I said?'

'Of course I won't, you ninny, and you don't tell Bryan what I said,' Debbie warned.

'Of course I won't, you ninny,' Melissa echoed, and they grinned at each other.

'Right, let's get to Greystones and see Miss Hope. I've brought her a treat of chicken pieces that I kept out of the wrap I had for lunch.'

'And I brought her some cat-food treats,' Melissa said happily, feeling as if a load had been lifted off her shoulders. 'I just can't wait to see her, she's the most beautiful little cat I ever saw.'

'I have the latest Duffy CD – will we play it?' Debbie suggested, starting up the engine and edging out into a gap in the traffic.

'Deadly,' Melissa agreed, as her half-sister slid the CD in and music filled the air. They broke into a rousing rendition of 'Warwick Avenue' as they zoomed off towards Dalkey. The wind blew their hair off their faces, and they let their worries float away in the evening breeze.

Debbie watched from the kitchen sink as Melissa, outside on the deck, tickled Miss Hope under her chin. She was washing up after their Chinese supper, scraping the remnants of their meal out of the aluminium cartons. Melissa hadn't eaten half hers, she noted, and then she looked at the scraps more closely. Her stomach gave a strange little lurch and she gazed at the carton in dismay.

Melissa's crispy chicken looked half chewed, and Debbie realized, as she poked it with a fork, that that was exactly what it was. Dread and fear wrapped their tentacles around her as it slowly dawned on her that her half-sister was chewing and spitting out her food. No wonder she was losing weight so rapidly. How long had she been at this, and what else was she doing to keep her weight off? Was she in the first stages of anorexia? she thought, thoroughly shaken at her discovery.

She'd felt so sorry for her in the car park when she'd blurted out her fears. Debbie had got a shock there too. Although she'd encouraged her half-sister not to worry, hearing that Aimee was looking for a divorce was a bolt from the blue. Despite the fact that she had no time for the woman and it wouldn't bother her in the slightest if she never met her again, Debbie wouldn't like Melissa to go through what she'd gone through as an angry, worried teenager: all the worrying she had done over something she had no control of, all the misery she'd endured. Melissa was obviously experiencing the same sort of emotions, and Debbie felt for her. Although she appeared cool and sophisticated, it was all a façade. She was a real child at heart, Debbie thought with a sudden surge of affection. Who would ever have thought she would end up worrying about her half-sister, she thought wryly, remembering all the years she'd loathed the very mention of her.

She scraped the chewed-up food into the bin and wiped the counter with a damp cloth. What should she do? She might mention it to her dad to keep an eye on Melissa. But she wanted to be careful. If Melissa felt she'd discussed her behind her back, she might never confide in Debbie again. She'd ask Connie what to do when she came home from her holidays, she decided. It was imperative that Melissa had someone to talk to because, for all her confident words, Debbie wasn't at all sure that Barry and Aimee wouldn't end up divorced and, if that was the case, Melissa would need someone she could trust more than ever, and Debbie would like that someone to be her.

'I love you, Miss Hope.' Melissa buried her face in the cat's inky soft fur. She purred like a train and flicked out her little pink tongue to give Melissa a lick. Melissa tickled behind her ears, and the purring became even more ecstatic. If only she could get a cat, Melissa thought wistfully, gazing into Miss Hope's green eyes.

Still, at least she could come and visit Miss Hope, and it had been fun driving down with Debbie. It had been great, too, to confide in her. Having an older sister was deadly. She'd never realized what a comfort it could be. Debbie seemed quite sure that her parents wouldn't divorce, that it was only a row that would pass. She would know – she was married, too, and even she and Bryan had rows.

The best thing of all was that Debbie had complimented her on her weight loss. All her hard work was really paying off. It made starving herself worth it. She'd been a bit horrified when Debbie had suggested the Chinese, but she'd managed not to eat most of it by discreetly chewing and spitting. Later, when she got home, she would make herself puke, even though she didn't really like doing it. Making herself puke was wrong, it was bad for her body, but eating crap food was even worse, and stern measures had to be taken. But she wouldn't think about that now. She was having too much of a nice time. All in all, it had been quite a good evening, Melissa decided, kissing the top of Miss Hope's furry head and receiving a reciprocal and very welcome lick back.

'You had no business telling Connie I was pregnant, Barry Adams, and you never told me you'd given Melissa permission to drive down to Greystones with Debbie.' Aimee launched into her attack the minute Barry walked in the door. Unusually for her, she was home first, having been reluctant to spend more time than necessary with a sullen and furious Ian.

'Ah, gimme a break, Aimee, I'm not in the mood to listen to you yakking on,' Barry snarled as he dumped his briefcase in the hall. 'For your information I didn't tell Connie that you were pregnant. I wouldn't dream of it, knowing how you feel about her. Melissa let it slip when we bumped into her and Debbie in Dun Laoghaire the morning you took the test. She's just a kid. She was excited, and out it came.'

'Well, you could have told me she knew. She went and told my mother, and she's in a sulk because I hadn't told her about it, and the whole bloody world knows, as far as I can see.'

'Yeah, well, these things happen,' he snapped. 'Deal with it.'

'You know the way *I* want to deal with it,' she yelled, incensed at his attitude.

'If you had *really* wanted to have a termination, you'd have had it, no matter what I said, so stop blaming *me*, Aimee, and stop being such a walking bitch while you're at it.' He raised his own voice, safe in the knowledge that they could fight in peace without Melissa overhearing them.

'And know that you'd have it hanging over me, judging me? And never knowing if you'd tell Melissa? No thank you, Barry.' She was white-faced.

'I wouldn't do that. What sort of a bastard do you think I am? I'd never lay that on Melissa's shoulders.' He was stunned at her accusation.

'But you don't mind what you lay on mine, do you, Barry?' she accused bitterly. 'I'm the one with most to lose in this scenario, but you don't care.'

'I do care, if you'd let me, goddamnit, but you

412

weren't even going to tell me, were you?' he challenged.

'I don't know any more,' Aimee muttered, suddenly weary. She sat down on the sofa as dizziness overcame her.

'Are you OK?' Barry looked at her in concern. She was as white as a sheet.

'What do you care?' she retorted, putting her head in her hands.

'I do care,' he said, all the anger ebbing out of his voice as he saw how pale she looked. 'Lie down, and I'll get you a drink of water.' He eased her gently back against the cushions, and she felt too sick to resist. Moments later, he was at her side, raising her up and holding the glass to her lips. She sipped the cold water and lay back against the cushions.

'Do you want me to call a doctor?' he asked, taking the glass from her and sitting beside her.

She shook her head. 'I didn't get time to eat lunch today; it's probably a dip in blood sugar. I'll get something to eat in a minute.'

'Ah, Aimee,' he groaned. 'That's not good for you. You've got to take care of yourself, for your own sake as well as the baby's. Will I make you an omelette, or some toast and scrambled eggs?' he offered.

'OK, some toast and eggs,' she agreed, closing her eyes. She lay on the sofa, listening to him move around the kitchen. For the first time in a long while she'd seen a little of the old, kind, supportive Barry.

Fighting was so exhausting; she didn't have the energy for it any more, and it was easier to let him cook her something than to have to bother herself.

She'd fallen asleep, and he had to rouse her. She sat up sleepily, suddenly famished as the smell of hot, buttery toast and creamy yellow scrambled eggs garnished with a sprinkling of parsley made her mouth water. He'd added some strips of smoked salmon to the plate, and she ate with relish, noting how attractively he'd presented the tasty meal on the TV tray: a linen napkin folded neatly, extra toast in the rack, a small ramekin of capers and olives on the side and a glass of milk.

'Thanks,' she said gratefully when she'd finished.

'Cuppa?' he asked, taking the tray from her.

'I'd murder a glass of wine, but I suppose a cuppa will have to do,' she said, kicking off her shoes and swinging her legs back on to the sofa. It was nice being looked after and mollycoddled. Her phone rang, and she slid it out of its designated pocket in her bag. It irritated her, watching women scrabbling about in handbags for their phones; she always knew where hers was. She saw with surprise that it was Ian. Maybe he'd had a rethink and was going to increase his offer, she thought smugly. And rightly so. But unless it was mega bucks, she was leaving *Chez Moi* for good. It would be good to hear him grovel though.

'Hello,' she said coolly.

'Aimee, it's Ian. Don't bother coming back to-morrow. I'd prefer not to have you in the office.

414

You'll be paid until your notice is up. I'll take over your client list myself.'

'I do have some personal items in my office,' she pointed out icily, caught completely off guard. 'And I'd like to say thank you to the team.'

'Your possessions will be couriered over to you, and I'll say your thanks for you,' Ian said snootily, and hung up.

Aimee stared at the phone. So Ian was playing dirty, and she was being locked out. Well, she could play just as dirty. Wasn't it just as well she'd taken copies of all the files she might need, plus a copy of the entire client list and all their contact details? She knew that, if she went to log into her work files, the password would have been changed and she wouldn't be able to access them. Ian would have seen to that.

Aimee lay back against the cushions. She had her PA, Miranda's, personal phone number on her mobile. She had plans for her. Miranda had been a first-rate PA, calm in a crisis and thoroughly dependable. She hoped the offer of a good salary increase would induce her to move to Hibernian Dreams. Lia Collins, one of the secretaries, had an excellent phone manner, and Aimee felt she would do very well in reception. First contact and front of house was so important, and Lia would be perfect in the job.

'How are you feeling now?' Barry asked as he came back into the lounge with a mug of tea and a Tunnock's teacake for her.

'Better,' she said. 'Thanks for the meal.'

'Could you not tell Ian you're pregnant, and maybe he'd give you extra help or something,' Barry said tentatively.

'Right now, Ian would stab me in the back if he could get his hands on me,' Aimee said, amused at the notion of her erstwhile boss trying to make life easier for her.

'Why, what's wrong with him?'

'I resigned today,' Aimee said slowly. 'I got that big job offer in spite of being pregnant. I'm setting up a new company for Roger O'Leary and a partner of his. I'm going to be the MD after all. Fair dues to Roger – even knowing that I'd have to take maternity leave didn't put him off.'

'Oh! Congratulations. Well done, you deserve it,' Barry said awkwardly.

'Thanks, it's going to be hard work, and I certainly won't be taking a long break once I give birth. I hope to be back at work within the month.' Aimee yawned.

'But what about the baby?' Barry protested. 'Are you going to breastfeed this time?'

'Absolutely not.' She shuddered. 'I didn't with Melissa. And, as for the baby, Barry, you wanted it, *you* look after it,' Aimee said firmly, and closed her eyes, glad she had made *that* crystal clear.

Barry threw his eyes up to heaven and marched out of the room, grim-faced, their temporary truce well and truly over.

* * *

416

'Home sweet home,' Juliet muttered as the taxi crunched the gravel behind her and she rooted for her key. Ken's car wasn't there. A small mercy, she thought dejectedly. She'd decided to fly home and get herself sorted. It had been almost impossible to get into relaxation mode again after her confrontation with Ken. Her thoughts kept racing as she played various scenarios out in her head. In her heart and soul, she knew that if she stayed living with him, very little would change. If she wanted to live life on her own terms, she'd have to get a place of her own, even if they didn't go as far as divorcing. But if Ken decided to be insufferable about it all, she would get herself the best lawyer she could find and fleece him, she vowed as she walked into the silent house and felt that old familiar miasma of oppression smother her.

She'd phoned Connie and Karen to let them know that she was flying home, and they'd made her promise to keep in touch. She intended to. Their blossoming friendship was one good thing to come out of the sorry saga, and she was extremely grateful for all their help and support.

Ken had moved back into their bedroom, she noted ten minutes later as she unpacked her case. Well, he could move right back out again, she decided, picking up his pyjamas and dressing gown and walking across the hall to the guest room with them.

It was almost dark when he got home, and she guessed he'd been golfing. 'So you're back,' he said coldly as he saw her at the kitchen table with a mug of hot chocolate in front of her.

'Not for long, Ken,' she said quietly. 'We can do this the hard way or the easy way, it's entirely up to you.'

'And what do you mean by that?' he said brusquely, taking a can of diet tonic water out of the fridge.

'I want a place of my own, Ken. I don't care if we divorce or not, but I'm leaving and, if you don't give me what I want – a place to live and a decent allowance, plus a share of your pensions – I'm going to get a divorce lawyer and go the whole hog and it will cost you a hell of a lot more, and you'll probably end up having to give me a hell of a lot more too. I'm not a mean person, Ken, you know that, and I'm not a money-grabber, but I'll do what I have to do unless you agree to my terms.' She said her piece calmly, confidently and firmly, knowing that, if she showed any sign of weakness, she was a goner.

'Now listen here, Juliet,' he blustered, 'this is ridic—'

She stood and held up her hand. 'I've said what I had to say. You decide,' she said, and walked out of the kitchen.

She was sitting in her dressing gown, the bedroom door closed, when she heard him come up the stairs. She heard him pause and, then, to her surprise, knock. Usually, he barged into the room.

She swallowed and her stomach was spasming with nervous tension. 'Yes?' she managed.

'I don't want you to leave me. I'm sorry if I've offended you.' Ken stood ramrod straight just inside the bedroom. He looked tired, careworn. His thick white hair needed a cut, she noted, back in wifely mode. She felt a flicker of sympathy for him and then realized what she was doing. She couldn't afford to go back down that road.

'I need to live my own life for a while, Ken,' she said tiredly. 'I want to concentrate on my needs before I get too old and decrepit to enjoy the things I like to do. We don't have to divorce if you don't want to. We can just separate.'

'But I need you. You know how to run my life. It always runs so smoothly when you're here. Like clockwork. And the house is lonely when you're not here. Please, Juliet, reconsider,' he said hoarsely, and she knew for him even to admit that much was a huge effort. She knew, too, that it was now or never. It was her last chance to make a fresh start.

'Look, Ken, I don't *want* to run your life, I want to *live* mine and that's why I have to go. It doesn't mean we won't see each other. We can have dinner occasionally, go to family events together, but I can't live like this any more. I'm sorry.'

He stared at her in disbelief, his blue eyes clouded with shock, the lines on his forehead drawn together in a perplexed frown. 'But I provided very well for you. You never wanted for anything. Has it been that bad?' he demanded truculently.

'You have no idea,' Juliet said bitterly, twisting the cord of her gown between her fingers.

Ken exhaled a deep breath. His shoulders sagged in defeat. 'Do what you want, Juliet, but I'd prefer if we didn't divorce – if that's all the same to you,' he added, with a touch of sarcasm.

'That suits me fine. Goodnight, Ken.' She turned away from him so that he wouldn't see the tears that were sliding down her cheeks as sadness mingled with relief that one part of her life had ended.

Chapter Twenty-seven

'Will we go for a cheap 'n' cheerful dinner tonight, seeing as it's payday, and have a chat about making a start on sorting our finances?' Debbie ventured as she applied her eyeliner and caught Bryan looking at her ass in the mirror. They hadn't had sex for a while, and she guessed he was feeling randy.

'OK,' he said sulkily. 'Where do you want to go?'

'The early bird in the Talbot 101, or Mario's?' she suggested.

'Might as well meet in town, if we're going for the early bird.'

'101 then.'

'Right, see ya there around six thirty,' he agreed, picking up his mobile phone before heading downstairs.

'OK, I'll book a table,' she called cheerfully, glad that there was a thaw of sorts.

It was typical, though, she thought twenty minutes later as she stood swaying on a crowded Dart. She had had to make the first move. God knows how long the 'silence' would have lasted if it had been left to Bryan. As long as they had been together he had never been the one to make up. It was just the way he was, she supposed. He'd been spoilt rotten as a child and, even now, Brona Kinsella couldn't do enough for her much loved son. She should have her parents-in-law over to dinner one of these days, although she'd much prefer to have Connie. The train slowed into Tara Street, and she was pushed and shoved towards the exit before escaping on to the crowded platform.

Caitriona was going around the desks with the wages slips as Debbie hurried into the office. Even though Judith was out sick, none of them liked to be late, fearing that Caitriona would think they were taking advantage. 'Hi, hon,' her acting boss greeted her cheerily, 'your envelope's on your desk.'

'It's spent already unfortunately,' Debbie sighed, pouring herself a cup of chilled water from the cooler. She didn't even bother to look at her payslip, as her phone rang and someone on maternity leave began to bombard her with questions about tax relief.

It was a busy morning, and she was kept going, delaying her tea break until she had sorted a particularly complicated job-sharing query. Debbie drank her coffee and scoffed a Twix, wishing Connie was home so she could talk to her about Melissa.

Idly, she tore open her payslip and looked at the figures in the various columns. She glanced at her net payment, and her jaw dropped. She scanned right, to the top of the column, and saw that her gross figure and annual salary figures had increased. How come? She looked at the figures again, thinking it was a mistake. But no, she worked it out that the amount tallied with what her increment would be, had she got it when she was supposed to have. Had HR decided to give it to her for some reason? Should she say nothing, and take the money and run, so to speak? She was just leaving the canteen when Janice Harris, who ran HR, walked past her.

'Um . . . Janice, I got extra money in my salary this week. Do you know anything about it?'

'Oh hi, Debbie, yeah, I meant to say it to you. Judith rang me from the hospital and asked me to make sure you got your increment this week. Does it add up OK? Is there a problem?' she asked matter-of-factly.

'No . . . no . . . it's fine.' Debbie was gobsmacked. 'Er, did you say Judith rang up about it?'

'Yep, she felt she shouldn't have withheld it, and I agree with her. You do a good job, Debbie.' Janice smiled at her.

'Thanks, Janice and um . . . if you're talking to Judith, tell her thanks too.'

'Will do,' the other woman said.

Debbie couldn't believe it. Judith Baxter had phoned from her sickbed to get her increment paid. She'd been sure the other woman would knife her if she got the chance after the altercation they'd had in the hospital. Maybe taking her courage in her hands and confronting Judith with her unacceptable behaviour would be good for both of them in the long run. Today was turning out much better than she'd expected. Debbie's heart lifted as she walked back to her desk.

An unexpected pay rise, a conciliatory dinner with her husband, an olive branch from her detested boss – and her mum would be home at the weekend. Life was looking up again. She sat at her desk and began to work out which of their debts her increase would go towards paying off first. It had to be the car, but she was only going to tax it for three months, because they weren't keeping it. She'd had a look at a few used-car ads. A second-hand Ford Focus wouldn't be a bad buy, but how would Bryan feel, driving around in one? Wouldn't really suit the image of successful businessman around town, but life wasn't all about image and, if they wanted to avoid being declared bankrupt in *Stubbs Gazette*, they had to start downsizing, and that was the be all and end of it.

Bryan lay wide-eyed in the dark listening to Debbie's even breathing as she slept curled up against him. They had gone for an early-bird dinner, and she'd been all excited about getting her pay rise. When he'd suggested they buy a bottle of bubbly to celebrate at home, she'd nixed the idea, saying the extra money was earmarked for the car tax.

Things were bad when they couldn't even buy a bottle of bubbly, he thought glumly, wishing he could go asleep. As they'd drunk their coffee after their meal, she'd suggested totting up what they'd earned that week and allocating certain amounts for their various bills. By the time they'd covered everything, there was damn little left. Just enough to cover food, petrol and Dart fares. He had about eighty euro to last him until payday. He'd often spent eighty euro in the offie. The convertible was going to be traded in for some Dinky or other, but the extra money wouldn't be going into their pockets, it would be paying off bloody debts.

Debbie had been so relieved that they'd finally knuckled down to addressing their financial issues. They'd opened a bottle of red wine when they got home and made love and she'd fallen asleep, happy.

Bryan sighed deeply. Was this to be the pattern of his life? Working to pay off debts, a cheap meal and a bottle of wine and a shag on a Friday night? A life of grim, unremitting boredom. He wasn't going to be able to hack it, he just knew it. He loved Debbie, it was hard not to love someone who loved you wholeheartedly, and she had, up until now, given him a free rein to indulge his carefree lifestyle.

Getting married was the biggest mistake he'd ever made. He should have taken the out Debbie had offered him before their wedding, when his reservations had begun to show. He'd had the chance, and he hadn't taken it, and now he felt trapped, as he'd never felt before. It was almost dawn before he finally fell into a fitful sleep, which afforded him no comfort at all.

* * *

Her grass needed cutting, Connie observed as Debbie drove them up the drive on her return from Spain. She'd do it some afternoon next week after work. Work! It was hard to believe that her holiday was over and she was starting a new job. Still, it was nice to come home, and she was dying to see Miss Hope. As if reading her thoughts, a black streak shot down over the garage roof, and the cat stood standing at the front door meowing in greeting. Connie raced out of the car and picked up her little pet, delighting in their joyful reunion. 'It's lovely to come home to someone,' she said to Debbie as her daughter lugged her case into the hall.

'You came home to me,' Debbie said indignantly.

'Yeah, but you'll be leaving me,' Connie teased. 'Miss Hope and I will grow old disgracefully together.'

'Well, you certainly don't look old. You look fantastic. You got a great colour.'

'I walked on the beach a lot early in the morning or in the evenings. It was scorching over there.'

'I've loads of news for you, Mum. Why don't you have a quick shower and get into a tracksuit, it's feckin' freezing today. I'll have supper ready when you come down,' she offered.

'OK,' agreed Connie. 'I don't know what it is about airports, but you always feel manky after travelling.' Upstairs, her bed looked really inviting. She yawned as she pulled off her white cut-offs and black T-shirt. At least she had everything ready for her early start the next morning. Her new uniform,

426

a dress, as requested by Mrs Mansfield, was hanging on the back of the door, and her white cap and shoes were on top of the chest of drawers.

She was tired after travelling but the holiday itself had thoroughly refreshed her, and she'd enjoyed every minute of it – apart from the nasty little episode with Ken Davenport. She wondered how Juliet was getting on. She'd give her a call some time in the week.

Twenty minutes later, she was sitting down to a tasty supper of prawn salad, coleslaw, tomatoes, peppers and nutty brown bread.

'Scrumptious,' she murmured appreciatively, as she chewed a succulent fat prawn.

'Got them in Cavistons,' Debbie said, pouring each of them a mug of tea.

'So what's your news? Are you preggers?' Connie asked after she took a welcome slug of tea.

'Wash your mouth out,' Debbie admonished. 'No, I'm not. But Melissa and I came down to visit Miss Hope, and she was very upset and told me that Dad and Aimee were talking of getting divorced. What do you think of that? She overheard them having a row.'

'Ah, the poor little moppet, that's horrible for her,' Connie exclaimed. 'As it happens, your dad told me about the divorce thing, he rang me to tell me that you were bringing Melissa down. He was really chuffed about that. And he mentioned about the divorce and told me he might be looking for a bed and a place to stay,' Connie said dryly.

'Oh crikey! What did you say to that?'

'Nothing, absolutely *nothing*,' Connie retorted, and Debbie grinned at the vehemence in her voice.

'It will be a bummer for Melissa if they do get divorced, although it wouldn't bother me a bit.' Debbie cut a slice of tea-brack and slathered it with butter. 'Do you want some?' she offered.

'I shouldn't. I ate all round me on holidays – that's why I did so much walking. I don't want to gain even more weight,' Connie demurred.

'Talking of weight, Mum, something awful's come up, and I don't know how to deal with it. I need your advice,' Debbie said earnestly.

'What's that?'

'I think Melissa's developing an eating problem. She's lost loads of weight, and we had a Chinese here last week, and she was chewing and spitting out her food. I saw it when I was clearing up afterwards. I didn't actually notice her doing it, and that's even more worrying, that she's practised at it.'

'Are you sure? Maybe she didn't like it and was too polite to say?' Connie put her knife and fork down, dismayed.

'I don't think so. And I want to be really careful here, because she's starting to trust me, telling me about the row and everything, so I don't want her to think I'm talking about her behind her back. She'll never tell me anything otherwise and, I know it's hard to believe after the way I've been towards her over the years, but I'm actually beginning to feel protective of her,' Debbie admitted sheepishly.

'Ah, Debbie, that's wonderful to hear,' Connie said warmly. 'It's something your dad and I have always wanted for you both. Blood is thicker than water at the end of the day, and a good relationship with a sister is a great blessing.'

'We had a really nice time, actually. We sang our heads off the whole way down. What should I do about it, Mum?'

'We'll keep a good eye on her. I'll invite the two of you down to dinner next week and we'll see if it happens again and, if it does, I'll have a word with your father about it,' Connie suggested.

'OK, that's a good idea. Thanks, Mum, you're the best. Now tell me all about the holidays. Did you meet any fine things?'

'Sure did,' grinned Connie. 'There was a nudist beach not far from where Juliet lives – but wait until I tell you the news about the Davenports!' Connie exclaimed as she got up and refilled the kettle to make another cup of tea.

It was after eleven before Debbie left, and after midnight before Connie fell asleep. At least she didn't have a long commute, she comforted herself, as she stood at her breakfast counter, showered and dressed, at 7 a.m. the following morning gulping hot tea.

There was a foggy mist when she set off. It was almost autumnal, she thought in dismay, even though it was only the beginning of August, hating the thought of dark mornings and short days. She pulled her little blue cardigan on and made her way to her new job.

The back door was open and she let herself into the kitchen. Fiona, the night nurse, was making porridge. Jessie had introduced them before she went away on holidays.

'Hi Connie – look at the colour of you, ya lucky thing,' Fiona greeted her. 'I'm just making the porridge for Mrs Mansfield; she always has it in bed with tea and toast at eight thirty. Then you'll help her wash, or bathe if she prefers, help her dress, give her her medication and, basically, that's all the nursing duties that are required. Her Parkinson's is not too severe. She reads her paper and does her crossword – but she'll need you to fill in the clues for her – and then she has lunch around twelve thirty and her meds again. Sometimes she has a walk, sometimes she likes to go for a drive down to see her horses, or she might go for a nap, depending on how she's slept. It varies, and then Jessie comes in at two, and off you go. She's a great patient really, but she does like her routines and is most particular about taking her medication at the correct time every day. Just remember that, and you'll do fine,' the other nurse said reassuringly.

'It's weird wearing a dress and cap again,' Connie remarked as she took the mug of tea the other girl offered. 'Trousers are so handy.'

'I know, but she can't stand nurses in trousers and blames the lack of the veil and cap for all sorts of bugs, including MRSA,' Fiona laughed. 'She has some funny little notions, but she's as sharp as a button, and woe betide anyone who thinks

430

otherwise.' She gave the porridge a final stir. 'Right, I'm off. Good luck on your first day. I think you'll enjoy it,' she said. 'Make yourself at home – there's plenty of food in the fridge if you want a bacon sanger or anything. You met Rita, the housekeeper – she'll be in around eight fifteen. Just have Mrs Mansfield's breakfast up to her at eight thirty sharp.'

'No problem,' Connie said cheerfully. If this was to be her routine, it would be a doddle compared to the backbreaking shifts she'd often endured, and well worth the drop in pay. She was right to go part time, she assured herself; she'd worked hard all her life and, now that Debbie was reared and the wedding was over, it was time to take life easier.

The morning passed quite quickly, by the time breakfast, bathing and dressing were over and Mrs Mansfield was settled at her crossword. Her new employer had a lively mind, and they'd had some interesting discussions.

'Now Connie, I look at the crossword first and, when I'm ready, I'll ring the bell and you can fill in the clues I can answer. Then I'll have a look at the more difficult ones and call you again. Go down now and have your tea break and make sure Rita gives you one of her scones. They're very, very tasty,' Mrs Mansfield instructed.

'Thanks, I will and, in the meantime, if you need me, ring your bell,' Connie said kindly.

'I don't believe in having my nurses as slaves to the bell,' Mrs Mansfield said firmly. 'I'm not in my

431

dotage yet. And the shakes aren't too bad, so have your tea and enjoy it. I'm very pleased with you; I knew we'd get on well. Just put the cat on my knee before you go, I always concentrate much better when I'm stroking her.'

Connie gently lifted Mittens, a little marmalade tabby, on to her patient's lap and saw a smile of contentment spread over the old lady's face. 'Go, go.' She waved Connie away gently and settled back to peruse her crossword, which was securely placed on a reading frame.

'Connie, tell Drew our lives won't be worth living if he doesn't call up and see her ladyship,' Rita said the minute she walked into the kitchen.

'Oh hi.' Connie smiled at the tall man who was leaning against the doorframe, arms folded. 'Our lives won't be worth living if you don't go up and see her ladyship,' she parroted obediently. 'I thought Friday was your visiting day.'

'I couldn't come on Friday. But I did ring her. One of her horses foaled, so I took a photo of it and said I'd drop it in when I was passing by. I'm in a small bit of hurry, and she'll want me to have tea with her, and I don't like refusing her,' Drew explained.

'''Cos you're a big softy,' Rita teased.

'Don't listen to her, Connie, I'm as hard as nails. Did you have a good holiday? You've a good colour.' Drew's eyes lingered over her, and she wished she were a stone lighter.

'The weather was fabulous,' she sighed, at what was now almost a distant memory. 'I heard it rained a lot here; the grass was up to my ass when I got home.'

'And have you a big garden?' He arched an eyebrow at her, his blue eyes studying her intently.

'Big enough for the old crock of a lawnmower I have. I'll have muscles like Popeye by the time it's cut.' She poured herself a cup of coffee, thinking how tanned he was without even leaving the county, let alone the country.

'Where do you live? You're local, aren't you? I have a John Deere that mulches, so there's no emptying involved. I'll throw it in the trailer and do it in jig time for you?' he offered.

'Ah God no, I wouldn't put you out,' Connie exclaimed, flustered.

'You won't be putting me out at all,' he said crisply. 'Give me a time that suits, and your address, and I'll be there. Who knows when I might need a splinter removed, or a wasp sting or worse, and you can return the favour.'

'Are you sure?' She was mortified, cursing herself for having mentioned it in the first place and having exaggerated the grass's growth in the second.

'Certain.'

She told him the address, and he pulled a piece of paper out of his jeans pocket. 'Give me your mobile number, just in case anything happens that I can't make it,' he ordered. She rattled it off, conscious of Rita grinning at her as Drew wrote it down.

'Better go. Here's the photo for Mrs M.' He

handed her a colour photo of the most adorable jet-black foal.

'Oh it's gorgeous!' Connie exclaimed.

'Drop by any time to see her,' Drew invited. 'I'm sure you'll be bringing herself to visit anyway.'

'Drew, you'll have to go up with it. You know the way she's mad about you,' Rita insisted.

'The foolish woman.' He grimaced. 'I'll go up for five minutes, but no tea, no matter what she says,' he warned.

'Why don't you give me your mobile number, and I'll ring you after ten minutes and you can pretend there's an emergency at the stables,' Connie suggested.

'Brains as well as beauty, a rare combination.' He smiled and wrote his number down for her. 'Five minutes, max,' he cautioned sternly.

'Aye aye, sir,' Connie saluted, amused at his bossiness.

'Sorry,' he apologized. 'But I am in a rush.'

Mrs Mansfield was delighted when she heard Drew had called. 'Bring up tea and scones,' she instructed Connie when she showed him into her sitting room.

'Now, Mrs Mansfield, this is just a flying visit, I'm in an awful hurry. I just wanted to drop you in a photo of the foal,' Drew said firmly as he bent his cheek for her kiss. He was a kind man, and gentle with the old lady, Connie thought approvingly.

'Sit down there now and tell me all the news. The tea will be here in a minute,' Mrs Mansfield instructed, as pleased as punch. Connie made her way back down to the kitchen, grinning inwardly at the look of pleading Drew had thrown her. Rita had the tea made, the tray was set, and a plate of buttered scones was at the ready. 'It won't take him five minutes to scoff one of these and drink a little cup of tea,' she declared. 'Do you want to bring them up?'

'No, you do it – don't forget I've to ring him to let on there's an emergency.'

'Are you sure? I think he fancies you,' Rita said wickedly, eyes twinkling.

'Ha ha, I think *you*'ve a vivid imagination. You go,' Connie said, as she topped up her coffee.

'We'll see,' said Rita smugly as she lifted the tray off the counter and hurried out of the kitchen. 'I bet he'll ask you out.'

'Don't hold your breath,' Connie called after her. She sat down at the table and stretched. The morning was flying, she thought, as she glanced at her watch. It was great to think she'd be finished in a couple of hours. The rest of the afternoon was hers. Should she try and cut the grass herself, so that when Drew called she wouldn't waste his time? It would be a bit churlish if she did, she supposed. What on earth had made her open her big mouth?

'He's going mad up there,' Rita chuckled. 'You better make the phone call in a minute or so, or he'll never speak to me again. He's always in a rush, that fella.'

Connie took her phone out her bag and dialled the number he'd written down for her.

'Hello?' His voice came strong and clear down the line.

'You've an emergency at your stables. What it is I'm not sure exactly, you can make it up yourself,' she said, trying not to laugh.

'Thanks very much, I'll be right there,' he said briskly, and hung up.

Two minutes later he was in the kitchen. 'Thanks for the tea, Rita. Thanks for the phone call, Connie. Have you decided what day suits you for me to cut the grass?' He looked at her.

'Tomorrow? Wednesday? What suits you?' she hedged.

'Tomorrow's fine. Two thirty. See you then. Bye, ladies,' he said, and then he was gone, striding out to his jeep and glancing at his watch in barely suppressed exasperation.

'A man in a hurry,' Connie murmured.

'He's never any other way. He's a workaholic, if you ask me,' Rita remarked, chopping vegetables at high speed.

'And who'd want to be involved with one of them?' Connie drained her mug. 'Not me for sure.'

What on earth was wrong with him, going around offering to cut strange women's lawns, Drew pondered as he drove along the narrow road that led to Mrs Mansfield's. Surely he had enough work of his own to be doing. His offer had popped out almost before he'd known it. He could see Connie was embarrassed. He should have kept his big mouth shut. Drew sighed as his mobile rang and the Bluetooth clicked in.

'Drew, it's Marianna.' An unwelcome voice crackled down the line.

'Yes, Marianna, what is it?' He could hardly conceal his impatience or his distaste.

'I have a favour to ask. As you know, my dad's in hospital, but Mama needs the car tomorrow, she has to see a chiropodist. Would you be able to drop me up to Blackrock, and she'll drive up later? I wouldn't ask, only that he's seeing his cardiologist tomorrow and he's asked me to be there.'

For crying out loud, leave me alone, woman, Drew wanted to roar at her, but he suppressed the impulse and said stiffly, 'I'm very tied for time tomorrow. I'll pick you up at eight thirty sharp. Take it or leave it.'

'Thanks, Drew, that's wonderful. You're the best,' Marianna gushed.

'Eight thirty then,' he reiterated, and hung up. She had such a nerve, he fumed. How he wished he could have told her to get lost. But she was the mother of his daughters and she was in a fix, and he'd been reared to do a good turn if someone was stuck. That was it, though, he swore as he drove into the stables, to see that the farrier was already there.

'Sorry for keeping you, Mick,' he apologized. 'I got delayed. I called into Mrs Mansfield's with a photo of her new foal, and of course she had to offer me tea.'

'I hear there's a fine-looking new nurse started

437

out there this morning. The postman was telling me all about her. Divorced, too, but I'm not fussy,' the old bachelor cackled.

'News travels fast, Mick.' Drew followed him into his own horse, Marino's, stall.

'Would I have a chance, d'you think?'

'Don't ask me – what do I know about women only that they're trouble,' Drew said grumpily, stroking his horse's neck as the farrier held its hind leg up for inspection.

What would she wear for her trip to Dublin with Drew? Marianna flicked through the items in her wardrobe. Something smart, elegant and sexy. The sun was shining, for once, she noted as the early morning light filtered through the folds in the net curtains. Why her mother wouldn't get blinds she could not understand.

She took out a pair of red linen trousers and a floral halterneck top and tried it on. Bit too casual if she was meeting a consultant, she thought regretfully. Red was good on her.

She tried on a pair of white trousers with a black cami and white jacket. Perfect, she decided. She could slip off the jacket in the car, and he could have the pleasure of looking at her perfect, pert boobs. She was so glad she'd had them done. They'd started to droop and, as they had drooped, so had her spirits. Middle age would be held at bay come hell or high water was her motto, and Edward had plenty of money.

She applied her make-up with extra care,

smoothing the foundation over her serum, admiring her collagen-enhanced lips as she did so. She wondered, yet again, had Drew a woman in his life. He hadn't brought anyone to Katy's wedding. But that had been ages ago. Marianna expertly applied a set of false eyelashes. She didn't look a day over thirty-five, she congratulated herself.

Her ex-husband arrived at eight thirty precisely and beeped on the horn. That was a bit rude. Marianna frowned. Surely he could have knocked at the door and said hello to her mother.

'Morning,' he said as he leaned over and pushed open the door of the jeep for her. She tried not to wrinkle her nose as she stepped up into it. It was mucky and dusty, although he'd obviously wiped the black leather seat for her. White was not the ideal colour to be wearing in Drew's jeep.

'Thanks so much for this.' She tried the effusive-gratitude tack.

'You're welcome.' He hardly gave her time to fasten her seatbelt before he was racing down the drive, staring straight ahead.

'So what have you got on today that has you so busy?' she asked chattily.

'This and that,' he said offhandedly.

'What time do you have to be back?' she persisted, eyeing him from beneath her lashes. His jaw jutted straight out as it did when he was annoyed, she remembered.

'I'm dropping you off and coming straight back.'

'Oh dear,' she sighed. 'I was hoping you could

stay until after the consultant's been. If I get bad news about Dad I'll be devastated.'

'What time are you seeing him at?' Drew flashed an irritable look in her direction.

'Two. I thought we might have a bite of lunch together beforehand, and then I'd see what's up.'

'Sorry, I can't stay for lunch. I've made an arrangement with a friend of mine. She's expecting me at two thirty,' Drew said flatly.

'Oh . . . is she a good friend? Are you seeing someone?' She couldn't contain her curiosity, and this was a perfect opportunity to ask the question casually.

'Marianna, my business is my business, and your business is your business. I've no desire to know about your life, and I've no desire to tell you about mine. Let's leave it at that.' He was so cold still. So bitter.

'I was only making polite conversation,' she retorted.

'No need,' he said curtly, as he overtook a combine harvester.

Marianna bounced up and down on her seat as he flew over a pothole and hoped she wouldn't lose her breakfast as well as her chance to win her ex-husband over. Now she was going to be stuck up in Dublin hours too early. And her plans for an intimate lunch and a chance to draw him back into her life had come to nothing.

She tried several times to make conversation as they sped towards the city, but he gave terse, monosyllabic answers, and she desisted eventually, knowing she was banging her head off the proverbial brick wall. And he *was* built like a brick wall, she thought admiringly, noting his lean, flat stomach and the muscles in his arms and shoulders. The familiar musky clean scent of him when he'd leaned across her to pick up the phone that she'd knocked out of the hands-free with her handbag had brought back vivid memories of how, in the early days of their marriage, he would grab her as soon as he was home from work and kiss her with a passion.

She couldn't remember the last time she'd been kissed with a passion, she thought disconsolately as the traffic became heavier and they slowed to a halt at Cornelscourt. They'd be at the clinic in another ten to fifteen minutes, and she'd have lost her chance. What could she do? Marianna racked her brains. A gift voucher. She'd get him a gift voucher to thank him for the lift and drop it over to him in the stables. She'd never been there, and it would give her the chance to have a look around. The girls were always raving about his house and the view from their bedrooms. Perfect, she thought happily. The gift might defrost him a bit. Because defrost him she would, this summer, Marianna decided, as Drew yawned behind his hand and pointedly ignored her.

CHAPTER TWENTY-EIGHT

Connie groaned as she got stuck behind a tractor-load of hay on the windy road that led from Mrs Mansfield's towards Greystones. She wanted to be out of her uniform before Drew got to the house and have time to freshen up. This time of the year, getting stuck behind farm machinery and tractors was inevitable, but it was a nuisance all the same. Her fingers did a tap dance on the steering wheel as she slowed to a crawl.

Ten long minutes later, the tractor took a left turn, and she picked up speed again. Her eyes widened as she drove down the narrow road that led to her house and saw Drew's jeep already there and the front lawn cut. He was leaning against the gate pillar, on the phone to someone, and he waved when he saw her pull up behind him.

'Afternoon,' he said, sliding the phone into the top pocket of his shirt as she got out of the car. 'I was hoping this was the right house; otherwise someone I didn't know at all was getting their grass cut. I got here a bit early, as the morning didn't go as planned.

If you let me in the back, I'll get on with it.' He was all businesslike.

'Sure. It looks great. Thanks a lot.' The front garden looked so neat and tidy compared to how it had looked when she'd left for work that morning.

'You're welcome,' he said politely, but she could tell he wasn't in good form and was in no mood for polite chitchat or banter. She went into the house and out the back, but he stayed outside until she'd opened the side gate for him.

'Would you like a cup of tea or a beer?' she offered.

'I'll cut the grass first, if you don't mind,' he said, pushing the big mower behind her, along the side of the house. 'Lovely garden, Connie,' he said admiringly, gazing around at all the flower-filled pots and the profusion of blossoming shrubbery.

'It is when it's not a jungle. I hope to spend more time working in it now that I'm nursing part time,' she explained, tucking a wisp of hair behind her ear.

'Right, I'll get going,' he said, not wasting a minute.

'I'm just going inside to change out of my uniform,' she said, a little thrown by his terse manner.

'Work away,' he replied, before positioning the lawnmower and starting it up. She watched him from the bedroom, standing back from the window so he wouldn't see her. He worked methodically, hardly breaking his stride to turn the awkward machine. He looked grim as he marched up and down, and she hoped he didn't feel she had

443

expected him to cut her grass or that she'd been hinting that he'd do it. She made a face. Men truly were from Mars; there was no dealing with them. She'd been looking forward to him coming to cut the grass, hoping to get to know him better and have a laugh with him. She liked his sense of humour, but there was certainly little of it on display today.

She undressed and changed into a pair of taupe Bermudas and a sleeveless lilac shirt. The weather had changed yet again, and today the northerly breeze had given way to a south-easterly that was warm and humid. She slipped a pair of loafers on to her feet and vacillated over whether to freshen up her make-up. She didn't want Drew to think she was making a play for him. She compromised by spraying the merest hint of D&G Light Blue on her wrists and neck, and running a brush through her thick auburn hair.

He had the grass cut in ten minutes, and she had the kettle boiled when he was finished. 'Tea or beer?' She stuck her head out the back door as he trundled past with the lawnmower.

'Ah, you're grand. I'll head off.'

'Have a cup of tea at least. I'm very grateful to you, for cutting the grass,' she protested.

'Well, a quick cup then. A mug if you have it, or are you into china cups like Mrs M.?'

'Nope, I like a big mug of tea,' she assured him. 'Are you hungry? Did you have any lunch?'

'Ah, I'll get something over at the stables,' he said diffidently.

'I've cold corn beef and homemade beetroot, and pickles and cheese.' She raised an inquiring eyebrow at him. He was standing with his thumbs hooked into his jeans, with not a flicker of a smile, the lines around his mouth deeply carved, giving him a stern countenance, his eyes lacking their usual teasing glint.

'Well, as long as it's no trouble. Are you having some?' he queried.

'Yep, I didn't bother eating at work today, because Rita doesn't know when to stop piling food on your plate, and I'm going to turn into an elephant if I'm not careful,' she grinned.

'I'll put this away so.' He indicated the lawnmower.

'I won't poison you,' she said, a trifle acerbically, and was rewarded with a brief grin and a shake of his head. Connie moved swiftly around her kitchen, carving the meat and plating it up attractively. 'There's a loo in the hall if you want to wash your hands,' she said when he came and stood at the back door.

'A bit of good clean muck never harmed anyone, but I suppose I should for manners' sake.' He smiled at her, the tension easing out of his face as he went out into the hall. 'So how did your second day at work go?' he asked as he came back into the kitchen.

'Grand. Mrs M.'s a nice woman to work for. It's a lot easier than what I have been doing,' Connie said, feeling inexplicably shy.

'She's a lady. She reminds me of my mother – that's why I like her. She's of that generation – you know, the sort that were real ladies and would help out a neighbour if they could, and always did the "right thing" by people.'

'Is your mother still alive?' asked Connie as she put the plates on a tray containing dishes of beetroot, pickles and wedges of cheddar.

A shadow crossed Drew's face. 'No, she died a few years back. I miss her,' he said simply. 'My dad died fifteen years ago. Are your parents alive?'

'Yes, they are. My dad's great; my mother's a bit of a briar. We don't get on so well. She disapproves of me being a divorcee,' she confessed, lifting the tray to bring it out the back.

'Let me take that,' he offered. 'I take it we're eating al fresco?'

'Might as well make the most of the fact that it's not raining. We ate out all the time in Spain. I love eating out here,' she said as she followed him to the table with the teapot, mugs and milk.

'So you'd a good holiday?' He put the tray on the table, and the two plates of meat where she'd set places for them.

'Terrific.' She nodded, as he sat down and she poured the tea. 'But then I came back to find out that my ex-husband and his wife may be divorcing, and he's looking for a bed and a place to stay, and he thinks he's going to get it here. And then, Debbie, my daughter, told me that she thinks my ex's daughter's on the road to developing an eating disorder. So it's back to real life with a bang – even though my plan, once she was married, was to let everyone fend for themselves and just look after myself.'

'What age is your ex's daughter?' Drew asked as he buttered a slice of brown bread.

'Thirteen, fourteen this year. She's a good kid. Her mum, Aimee's, a real career woman, and she's got unexpectedly pregnant and isn't happy about it. I think it's put a huge strain on the marriage. I don't know. Why can't they get on with it and keep me out of it?' she moaned.

'*Exactly.*' Drew lowered his forkful of meat. 'My ex-wife's home from the States, and she had the nerve to ask me to bring her to the Blackrock Clinic to see her father this morning because her old bat of a mother wanted to go to the chiropodist and she needed the car. As if I give a hoot about her or her bloody corns,' he said sardonically. 'Marianna wanted me to wait with her until she'd spoken to her father's consultant in case she got bad news, as if I gave a toss about him either.' He glowered. 'That old walrus cleaned me out of it when we divorced. He's a solicitor and, by God, he took me for every penny I had. If it hadn't been for the girls, I'd have fought him tooth and nail.' Drew couldn't hide his anger. 'And she wants me to have dinner with her? I ask you.' He was so indignant his eyes were blazing. 'She took my daughters away from me, and my mother's grandchildren from her – and my mother grieved the loss of them as much as I did –

and Marianna expects me to be all over her when she comes home. She makes me mad as hell.'

'So that's why you were rampaging up and down the garden looking like you could murder someone,' Connie murmured, relieved that she knew what was behind his bad humour and that it had nothing to do with her.

'Was I that bad? Sorry. It had nothing to do with you.' He gave her an embarrassed smile.

'It's understandable. At least I always had Debbie. Her father made the choice to go to the States. I could never understand how he could leave her, even though he eventually came back to Ireland.'

'You get on well enough with him now, though, if he's asking you for a bed,' Drew remarked as he wolfed a wedge of red cheddar.

'Not *that* well,' she said dryly. 'Barry seems to think I'm only waiting for him to come back to me and all will be forgiven and we can start over.'

'And would you like him back?' He didn't beat about the bush; his blue eyes studied her intently.

'Absolutely not,' Connie retorted.

'Don't you mind living on your own?'

'I have my cat.' She grinned as Miss Hope rubbed up against her leg. 'Do you?' she countered.

'I have my dog and my horses.' He leaned back in his chair and smiled good-humouredly across the table at her.

'Can you ever see yourself having dinner with your ex?'

'*Never*,' he said emphatically. 'If the girls want me

to have a family meal, I do it for their sakes, but me and Marianna on our own? Hell will freeze over first. If I never saw the woman again it wouldn't bother me.' He shrugged. 'You probably think I'm heartless and unforgiving.' He gave her a wry smile.

Connie shook her head. 'No, I don't. Some things are too hard to excuse. I'm sure I'd feel exactly the same if I were in your shoes.'

'I don't know. You have a kindness about you, Connie, that I just don't have,' he sighed.

'You're very hard on yourself, Drew,' she said quietly. 'I don't think I'd have coped if Debbie had been taken from me.'

'It's different for a mother,' he observed.

'No. Not at all. Many fathers love their children equally as much. I always feel terribly sorry for fathers who have to give up living with their children because of divorce. And I feel very sorry for grandparents; they're often forgotten about. It's incredibly painful all round. Your path was very hard, and you've done really well from what you've told me. Your girls have a great father; you should be proud of yourself.'

'Thanks. My mother said something like that to me just before she died. But she was biased. I appreciate what you've just said, Connie,' said Drew gruffly.

'You should listen to what your mother said and take it to heart. She knew what she was talking about,' Connie assured him. 'And I really mean that.'

Almost of their own volition, their hands reached across the table to each other and, in that brief, silent gesture, a new friendship was born that would last a lifetime.

'I got this for you, Melissa, it's just a little gift. I thought you might like it.' Connie smiled at Barry's daughter as she handed her over two small boxes.

'Hey, thanks, Connie, that's, like, so kind.' The teenager jumped to her feet and gave Connie a hug that pleased her hugely and which she returned with great warmth, noting that Melissa had indeed lost a lot of weight.

'Open it,' she urged. Melissa wasted no time pulling apart the lid of the smaller parcel first, under the amused gaze of Debbie and Connie.

'Oh, she's gorgeous! Oh cool, Connie, I love her,' she exclaimed as she held up a little crystal angel that sparkled in the sunlight. She turned her attention to the second box, and her eyes lit up as she opened it to reveal a shiny, ceramic black cat with green eyes.

'Oh, Connie, she's deadly. Random present, thank you very much for thinking of me.'

'Thank *you* very much for being so kind to Miss Hope and coming to visit her when I was away.'

'Oh, that was no trouble,' Melissa assured her. 'Debbie and I had good fun that night.'

'She's got a good voice – Duffy watch out,' teased Debbie, and Melissa giggled.

'OK, let's have supper,' Connie suggested,

and saw a flicker of tension cross Melissa's face.

'I already ate before I came, so just something very small for me,' she said hastily.

'Sure, no problem,' Connie said easily. 'I made a homemade lasagne and Caesar salad for us.'

'Oh, I love that,' Melissa exclaimed, forgetting herself.

'Me too,' said Debbie, pulling out a chair at the kitchen table and plonking herself down beside her half-sister. 'This is nice, a girls' night.' She smiled at Connie. 'It's great to have you home, Mum. I missed you.'

'That's nice to know,' Connie replied, as she spooned out a helping of lasagne for Melissa.

'Excuse me, I just need to go to the loo,' Melissa said ten minutes later as they were eating their supper.

'Use the one in the hall if you like, it's handy,' Connie said, as alarm registered in Debbie's eyes.

'I bet she's making herself sick, Mum. It's horrible – what are we going to do?' Debbie whispered, utterly dismayed as she strained to hear.

'I'll have a chat with Barry. Just act as normal when she comes back,' Connie sighed. She'd done agency nursing in a hospital that had an eating-disorders unit, and she'd found it extremely difficult nursing the young girls who were intent on starving themselves to death. Once anorexia got its claws into you it was very difficult to beat it. If something wasn't done to help Melissa, she was on the slippery slope to a very tough, hard, miserable life. Why hadn't Barry or Aimee copped it before now? What was wrong with the pair of them? Melissa was the most precious gift in their lives, and she wasn't even on their radar. Connie felt like driving over to Dun Laoghaire and tearing strips off them. But that wouldn't help anyone, least of all Melissa.

She smiled at the girl when she came back to the table, cheeks flushed, eyes bright. 'I started my new job last Monday,' Connie said, to distract from the meal. 'And my new patient, Mrs Mansfield, owns several horses. One of them's had a foal, and I'm taking her to see it tomorrow. The man who owns the stables brought her a photo of it. It's a gorgeous little thing. Completely black, with a white star on its forehead. She's going to call it Frisky, because Drew, that's the man I was telling you about, says she's always kicking her heels up and racing around the paddock.'

'Oh, I'd love to see her. Do you think I could come and see her some time?' Melissa said eagerly.

'I'll arrange that for you, no problem, if it's OK with your mom and dad,' Connie assured her.

'Of course it will be, I'll be with you,' Melissa said matter-of-factly, pushing a leaf of lettuce around her plate.

'Isn't she superb!' Mrs Mansfield's eyes were bright with pleasure as she leaned on Connie's arm and fed an apple to her new foal.

'She's a dote,' exclaimed Connie, gazing into the foal's chocolate-brown eyes, which stared back at them both, so innocent and friendly. The mother, a fine-boned brown mare called Swift, neighed proudly as she chomped on the carrot Drew had just fed her.

'So you're pleased then?' He smiled at the elderly lady, who beamed back up at him and patted him on the shoulder. 'You did well, Drew. They're both so healthy, and a credit to you.'

'Look at her movement and her outline and the way she carries herself. She'll be a fast one, and excellent for dressage, I'd say – she loves the lime-light already,' he observed.

'I think I agree with you there – she knows she's a star.' Mrs M. was in complete accord and obviously knew a lot about horses from the discussions she'd been having with Drew. 'The girls will be as pleased as Punch when they see her; they're back from Florida next week,' she said, talking of her grand-daughters, who were away on holidays. 'Make sure they do plenty of mucking out; they're getting too used to the good life,' she instructed, sitting down on the fold-up chair Connie had opened up for her. 'Now, go show Connie around, seeing as it's her first time here, and let me talk to my darlings.' She held another apple out to the foal, who whinnied excitedly.

'We'd better do as we're told,' Drew laughed, as he led the way back to the yard, where a farrier was shoeing a horse and a stable girl was grooming a big, black gelding.

'Drew, could I ask a favour?' Connie said slowly.

'Sure. If I can do it for you I will,' he said agreeably.

'You know my ex's daughter that I was telling you about?'

'The one with the eating problem?' He nodded. 'How can I help?'

'She was over for supper last night, which she got rid of halfway through the meal. Anyway, I was telling her about Frisky. Could I bring her to have a look at her some afternoon next week? I won't bother you or get in the way,' she assured him.

'You won't bother me, and you won't get in my way, and you can bring the world and his mother to visit Frisky,' he said, smiling at her, his eyes full of warmth.

'It might take her mind off things and give her an interest. She's going down a very hard road. I've nursed kids like her, it's the pits.' A lump came into her throat and tears brimmed unexpectedly in her eyes.

'Don't get upset, Connie,' said Drew hastily. 'Come into my horse's stall, for a bit of privacy.' He opened a half-door, where a massive brown horse whinnied softly in welcome. 'Hello, boy, good boy,' he murmured, patting his horse's rump as Connie rooted for a tissue in her bag.

'Sorry.'

'Don't be – why wouldn't you cry at something like that?' he said kindly.

'Oh, Drew, her parents have no idea what's in store for her. I could smack them. Can they not see what's going on under their noses?' she said angrily, bursting into fresh tears. She'd spent the night tossing and turning, worrying about Melissa.

'Shush, don't be upsetting yourself,' he said awkwardly.

'Sorry, sorry,' she apologized, sniffling. 'It's just she's a nice kid, and there's something lost and forlorn about her sometimes.'

'I know, but she's lucky to have you and Debbie. Don't forget that,' he reminded her as she blew her nose. 'Are you OK?'

'Yeah, just a bit mortified,' she admitted, managing a wobbly grin.

'Don't be daft, didn't I unburden myself yesterday?' he said wryly.

'So there's a pair of us in it.' She wiped her eyes.

'Yeah,' he agreed, giving her a quick, unexpected hug.

She rested her head against his chest for the briefest moment as his arms tightened around her, as if it were the most natural thing in the world. They stepped back and smiled at each other.

'Do you like my horse?' he asked. 'This is Marino. Marino, this is Connie. Do you ride, Connie?'

'Tragically, neither men nor horses for quite a while,' she murmured, and he guffawed.

'Did you ever horse-ride?' he amended, laughing again.

'When I was very young. I wouldn't inflict myself on a poor horse now – tragically, also, as you can see, I'm no longer a twig.'

'You're a fine hoult of a woman, as they say in the country.' He grinned at her.

'I'm not sure if that was a compliment or not,' she retorted, 'so I won't comment.'

'It *was* a compliment. I'm just out of practice and, if you'd like it some time, I've a lovely placid mare called Fuchsia who'd be perfect for you until you get more adventurous,' Drew said firmly.

'They're very big,' she demurred, looking up at Marino, who was standing gazing at her as Drew began stroking his neck.

'Not at all, no bother to you. I'll look after you,' he promised. 'And by all means bring your ex's daughter any time you want, Connie. You'll always be welcome here,' he said.

'Thanks, Drew. I feel very welcome.'

'Good,' he said succinctly, leading Marino out into the yard. 'I'm going to bring this fellow over to the paddock. Mrs M. always likes to see him. Come on, I'll show you how to lead him so we can start you getting used to horses at least,' he teased, and she laughed.

Mrs Mansfield shaded her eyes against the glare of the sun and saw Connie laughing with Drew over in the yard. A smile flitted across her fine features. 'Excellent,' she murmured to Swift. 'Excellent. Just what he needs.'

CHAPTER TWENTY-NINE

'Hi, Connie, you look terrific. The holiday did you good.' Barry leaned over and gave his ex-wife a kiss on the cheek, as his eyes roved appreciatively over her, noting the golden glow of her skin and her bright, clear eyes.

'Thanks, Barry, and thanks for seeing me,' Connie said quietly. She was sitting outside a small seafront café in Bray, to where she'd taken the Dart to meet her ex-husband.

'So are we on a date?' he flirted, delighted with this unexpected meeting. She'd been very mysterious on the phone, just saying she needed to see him to discuss something.

'Don't be silly, Barry,' she said crossly, waving at a waiter to serve them. She had fierce PMT and wasn't in the humour for his jocularity.

'Just joking – lighten up, Connie, I get enough gloom and grief at home,' he growled.

'Sorry,' she apologized. 'And, Barry, I'm sorry also to have to tell you there's more of that in store for you. Debbie and I are both convinced that

457

Melissa is suffering from an eating disorder. Debbie caught her chewing and spitting her Chinese the night they came down to see Miss Hope, and the evening before yesterday, when she had supper with me, she went into the loo halfway through the meal and made herself sick. You've got to get her seen to,' Connie said bluntly.

The colour drained from Barry's face. 'Ah no, you couldn't be right. She eats at home fine,' he protested.

'Come on, Barry, when do you ever eat meals together? I'm not mistaken; I saw the puke spatters around the rim of the loo. And look how much weight she's lost.'

'Surely that's puppy fat falling off. Remember Debbie used to be a bit plump in her teens?' he argued, desperate not to hear what she was saying.

'Barry, listen to me. Melissa's in trouble, and you and Aimee need to put aside your differences and get her taken care of before this gets any worse. I'm telling you, if this takes a hold of her, she could die. Do you understand what I'm saying here? If this is allowed to go untreated, and Melissa goes the whole hog with it, she will starve herself, her periods will stop and her fertility will be affected. She could develop osteoporosis and damage her heart, before her body starts eating itself. Lack of potassium can bring on a heart attack. Look what happened to Karen Carpenter. Not even force-feeding will save her. In hospital, those girls encourage each other to starve themselves. When one of them dies, they applaud her for it, wishing it was them. Barry, it's horrific, and you've got to do something about it.'

'Jesus, Connie, stop – you're frightening me,' he protested.

'I want to frighten you, Barry. This is your daughter's life we're talking about. And you cannot let on that I spoke to you, or say anything about Debbie knowing what she was doing. She is not to know that we alerted you, under any circumstances. She needs someone to confide in at her own pace, and Debbie is very anxious to be there for her.'

'God Almighty, Connie, I . . . I . . . don't know what to say . . . or do.' He was ashen.

'Look, I'll suss it out and get some names for you, but just be aware of what's going on, will you?' she said sympathetically. 'I know St Vincent's have a unit, and there's one in St Pat's; I'll get you the relevant contact numbers. You need to talk to your GP, too. I'm really sorry to have to be telling you all of this, Barry, but it's imperative you act now. I'll call you tomorrow when I have some information for you.'

Barry put his head in his hands.

'Look, she'll have plenty of support, we're all behind her,' Connie said gently. 'It's better to deal with it now, before it becomes too severe.'

'This is a hard burden, Connie,' he groaned. 'I don't know if I can carry it. Aimee wants a divorce. I don't know what's to become of us. I need you more than I've ever needed you.'

'Well, this time you have to carry your burdens,

Barry. You can't run away from Melissa the way you ran away from Debbie,' she said sharply. 'And I'll help you all I can, but I have my own life to lead, please don't forget that.'

'I won't – but promise me you'll be there for us.'

'I'll be there,' she sighed. 'Just start dealing with Melissa; the divorce can wait until she's sorted. I'm sure Aimee will see that when you tell her what's going on with your daughter.'

'All Aimee can see is me me me,' he said bitterly. 'How do I deal with that?'

'Barry, I'm not a marriage counsellor,' she said exasperatedly. 'My advice to you is to go home and tell her what I told you and take it from there.'

'That's easy for you to say,' he griped.

'Look, this is not all about you or Aimee, this is about Melissa.' Connie was losing patience fast. 'And, by the way, she knows about you and Aimee discussing divorce. She overheard you having a row, so bear that in mind as well.'

'Oh, for God's sake!' he exclaimed. Could this evening get any worse, he wondered, sick to his stomach. 'Who did she tell about the row?' he muttered.

'Debbie. But at least she felt she *could* tell her. That could send her into a downward spiral too,' Connie warned. 'You might need to talk to her about it, she was very upset, Debbie said.'

'OK, I hear you,' Barry retorted as the waiter came to take their order.

'Just tea for me, please,' Connie said.

'Same for me, please, and a scone,' Barry ordered. 'Are you sure you don't want anything?' He looked across the table at her.

'I'm not hungry,' she said sombrely.

They sat in silence until their teas came.

'Sorry. I shouldn't be taking it out on you,' apologized Barry as he poured her tea.

'Forget it, I just want Melissa to be OK,' Connie said.

'Is that what you think? That I ran out on Debbie?' he said gruffly.

'Didn't you?' She didn't see why she should let him off the hook.

'I suppose so, if you want to look at it like that.'

'Look, there's no point in crying over spilt milk, just be there for Melissa, no matter what happens. Not everyone's lucky enough to be given a second chance, Barry, so take it,' she urged.

'What's it like to be perfect?' he said bitterly.

'I'm far, far from perfect, that's unfair, Barry,' she flared, hurt.

'Well, stop judging me,' he muttered.

'Oh, grow up, Barry. For crying out loud, I'm not friggin' judging you. Look, I'm going. I know this is hard for you and, believe me, I don't want to be involved, but I like Melissa very much and she's the only reason I'm here. I'll call you tomorrow with the information I get. See you.' She grabbed her bag and stalked off without a backward glance, furious.

He didn't call her back and, if he had, she wouldn't have gone. She glanced at her watch. If she hurried, she'd catch a Dart to Greystones earlier than she'd planned. She could see the train in the station, and she ran as fast as she could, collapsing in a breathless heap on the seat when she got into the carriage. She wheezed; she needed to get fitter. Walking on the beach was all very well, but she'd have to put in more of an effort and do some aerobics or something.

She could murder Barry Adams, she thought as the whistle blew and the train rumbled out of the station. Just because she was the bearer of bad news, she was not the baddie. Typical of him to turn it all around to himself, doing his poor-me act. He and Aimee would want to get their respective acts together, or Melissa was going to slip through their fingers.

She was in a thoroughly grouchy mood when she got into her car in the car park in Greystones a while later. She was driving along past Tesco's when a familiar jeep beeped at her, and she saw Drew observing her quizzically. She pulled in further up the road, and he parked behind her and got out.

'You look as grumpy as I did the other day,' he said mildly when she rolled down the window and he leaned on the door with his forearm.

'I just met Barry and told him about Melissa,' she explained.

'Did it not go well?'

'Oh, it's a long story,' she sighed. 'What are you doing in Tesco's at this hour of the evening?'

'Ran out of dog food. Nothing for his brekkie. Do

you want to come for a drink and tell me the long story?' he asked diffidently.

'Are you sure you want to hear it?' She looked up at him, noting the way his black chest hair curled at the V of his shirt just below his throat. She liked chest hair on men. Bryan got his waxed so he'd look like David Beckham, Debbie had told her once. There was no comparison between Bryan and Drew, or Barry and Drew, she thought as he stared down at her. He'd a nice mouth, too, a firm mouth, she thought, with a sudden longing to be kissed and cuddled and comforted.

'I like long stories,' Drew said solemnly, but his eyes were twinkling.

'I'm not very dressed up,' she murmured.

'And I am?' He arched an eyebrow at her, and she laughed. 'You look fine to me. Where do you want to go?'

'I've cold beer in the fridge at home, I got it in for you the other day when you were cutting the grass,' she said impulsively.

'Perfect. I'll follow you.' He straightened up and tapped the roof. 'Drive carefully.'

'I will,' she said, happy that the evening wasn't going to be a total disaster.

'And when did she tell you this?' Aimee demanded.

'She asked me to meet her in Bray earlier. She didn't pull any punches either, Aimee. This is serious. I've told you what Connie said could happen.'

'Oh, Connie, Connie, Connie. I'm sick of Connie,' Aimee muttered.

'She's probably sick of us too,' he retorted. 'She told me she'd have some information for us tomorrow. Places and people we can contact.'

'Maybe it's just a phase Melissa's going through,' Aimee said, grasping at straws.

'I don't think so and, another thing: she heard us arguing and knows we've used the "D" word. She's very upset about it; she told Debbie about it.'

'For God's sake, do they know *all* our business?' Aimee snapped, irately.

'Well, they seem to know more about our daughter than we do, and what does that say about *our* parenting skills?' he shot back.

'And you want us to have another child?' she said bitterly.

'Look, this is getting us nowhere, Aimee. We need to focus on Melissa for the time being. Do you agree?' He stopped pacing up and down the lounge and stood in front of her.

'Yes, I suppose you're right. It's scary, though. Kathryn Lawson's daughter has been in and out of hospital for the last three years, she's like a walking skeleton. She only weighs six stone.' Aimee's face crumpled, and she started to cry.

Barry sat down beside her and put his arm around her shoulder. 'Look, we'll deal with it together. We'll put our own issues on hold and be there for Melissa until we have her sorted. What do you say?'

'OK,' Aimee sniffled, thinking that this was the worst year of her life, new job notwithstanding.

'And . . . err, Connie suggested we don't let on she or Debbie knows anything about this or has mentioned anything to us. Connie feels Melissa needs someone she can trust, and she seems to be bonding really well with Debbie,' he said hesitantly.

'I suppose it makes sense, although I wish they weren't involved,' Aimee said sulkily.

'In fairness, I think Connie wishes she wasn't involved either. She has her own life to lead.'

'Why, what did she say?' demanded his wife. 'She doesn't have to be involved. We can take it from here, tell her, thank you very much.'

'No, no,' he said hurriedly, thinking Aimee was such a powder keg these days. 'She was apologizing for being the bearer of bad news and having to lay this at our door, but she felt she had to,' he pacified.

'Oh . . . I see. I suppose it wasn't easy to tell someone their daughter has a problem like anorexia,' Aimee conceded. 'That's if it is anorexia.'

'Something's up, Aimee. She *has* lost a lot of weight and, looking back, she's stopped eating treats with me when we go for coffee on Saturday mornings, and she never eats with us here. She's always saying she's had something earlier,' Barry pointed out.

'I never even noticed,' Aimee muttered, tears starting to fall again. 'What kind of a mother am I?'

'You're a good mother,' he said stoutly. 'We lost our way for a bit. We'll get back on track with her.'

'I hope so, Barry. Anorexia and bulimia and all those things are very hard to deal with. I'm scared.'

'I know, me too. But we'll deal with it together, OK?'

'OK,' she agreed.

They heard the front door open, and Aimee went to draw away from him, but he pulled her back. 'United front,' he whispered as their daughter clip-clopped down the hall.

'Hi, Muffin. Where were you until this hour? Your mother and I were just starting to worry about you,' Barry said lightly.

'Were you?' Melissa looked inordinately pleased to see them together on the sofa.

'It's getting dark earlier these nights,' Aimee said, patting the sofa beside her. 'Where were you?'

'Hanging out with Sarah.' Melissa flopped down next to her mother.

'Listen, I was just thinking – you know this new job I have? Well, I've three weeks' holiday to take. How about we head off somewhere for a few days? Barry, would you be able to manage that?' She looked at him.

'For my ladies, anything is possible.' He smiled at them. 'Where will we go? It would be a relief to get away from this disaster of a summer.'

'Any suggestions?' Aimee looked at her daughter, noting the gaunt hollows in her cheeks and the dark circles under her eyes. She felt sick with terror. How could she have missed what was under her nose?

Melissa's eyes lit up. 'I'd love to go to

Disneyworld in Paris?' She looked hopefully at Aimee.

'How about Disneyworld for a day, shopping for two days and a few days in a hotel in the south of France so your mom can relax and put her feet up?' Barry suggested.

'Savage, Dad. Can we, Mom?' Melissa's eyes were sparkling.

'Let's get on the internet and book.' Aimee held her daughter's hand tightly.

'What have I let myself in for?' Barry groaned, but he leaned down and lightly kissed the top of his wife's head, and then gave Melissa the biggest hug he'd ever given her as they trooped into the dining room to gather around Aimee's computer.

'Look at the time, Connie – it's well after midnight.' Drew stared at his watch in surprise.

'It only felt like an hour.' She yawned and stretched. It was a sultry night, and they had sat out on the deck and she'd lit candles and Chinese lanterns to lend some atmosphere.

'You're easy to talk to.' He smiled at her.

'You're pretty easy yourself,' she complimented back.

'I can't remember the last time I talked so much. I don't usually spend hours chatting. You have a knack of drawing people out.' Drew stood up reluctantly. 'I had a lovely evening, Connie, thank you,' he said quietly.

'On one can of beer,' she laughed.

'It was the company.'

'I had a lovely evening, too. Thanks for listening to my moans about Barry and Aimee. It was great to get it off my chest.'

'Any time. Make sure to bring Melissa to visit Frisky.'

'I will. Thanks, Drew.'

'I guess I better go.' He leaned down and gave her a kiss on the cheek.

'How chaste,' she teased as she stood up.

'I'm a shy country boy.' His eyes glinted in the moonlight, and he turned her face to him, stroking her jaw with a long, tanned forefinger before leaning towards her, his intention unmistakable.

'Are you sure you want to? Maybe I was being forward,' she said hastily.

'I love forward women,' he said huskily, and bent his head and kissed her, lightly at first, with soft butterfly kisses which were gentle and tender, then, more deeply, with a passionate, hungry kiss which she returned ardently.

They drew apart breathlessly. 'I thought you said you were shy,' she murmured, pink-cheeked.

'I am,' he assured her. 'Maybe if we kiss again, I'll get over it.' He wrapped his arms around her and kissed her soundly for a second time before resting his chin on the top of her head and holding her tightly to him. She leaned her head against his chest and listened to his heart beating beneath her cheek. It was the strangest feeling. She felt that she'd come home.

'I'm going to go now,' he whispered against her hair, 'because, if I don't, it's more than kissin' we'll be doing. And I want us both to be comfortable with what we're doing and where we're going.'

'Well, you better go quick then, because I like what we've been doing up until now, and I'm very comfortable,' she said slowly, wishing he would stay but knowing that what was happening between them was too important to rush.

'Me too,' he said, kissing the tip of her nose. 'You sleep well, Connie, I'll see you soon.'

'Night, Drew.' She stroked his cheek. 'I'm so glad we met.'

'Me too,' he said. 'Very glad.'

They walked arm in arm around the side of the house to the front gate, and she stood waving him off with a grin the size of a melon slice on her face. She felt a surge of wild joy. It had been a long, long wait, but she knew with certainty that she and Drew Sullivan were going to be together for the rest of their lives.

Drew drove into his driveway and patted his golden Labrador, Tusker, who stood up lazily and pattered down the steps of the veranda that ran the length of the house. His tail wagged ecstatically, and he looked at his beloved master with total adoration.

'Hello, boy.' Drew bent and tickled the dog's ears, let himself into the house and headed for the kitchen. He took a bottle of beer from the fridge, opened it without even bothering to put on a light

469

and headed back to the veranda to sit down in the rocking chair. Tusker curled up beside him as Drew stretched his legs, and took a swig from the bottle.

He smiled, thinking of the past evening. Who would have ever thought that he'd meet a woman like Connie? He'd known the minute he'd laid eyes on her that she was special. He'd felt completely at ease in her company. They had so much in common and, best of all, she had a sense of humour that matched his own. They 'got' each other. It was amazing. He felt as though he'd known her all his life. How rare was that, Drew wondered, to meet another human being and, in such a short space of time, to feel a connection that touched mind, body, soul and divinity? He'd wanted to make love to her and spend the night with her, but he wanted to be absolutely sure it was what she wanted; he didn't want to take advantage. He was no monk – he'd been with women since his marriage broke up – but this was very different. Lovemaking would come in its own good time. He would woo her, Drew decided, as well as teaching her to ride. The clouds had thinned and parted, and a cluster of stars shone brightly in the inky darkness. A shooting star streaked across the firmament. 'Thanks, Mam.' He raised his face to the sky. 'I couldn't be happier.'

Chapter Thirty

'Mrs Baxter, how are you?' It was Mrs Meadows, the woman who'd shared a ward with her a few months ago. They smiled at each other in recognition in the corridor of the private clinic they both attended. Lily had come for an eye check-up, and Mrs Meadows had been for her six-monthly visit to see her geriatrician. 'A lovely man, indeed, and very hand-some. Not like the rip I went to for my heart trouble recently,' she informed Lily, holding open the door for her. 'How are you getting on, Mrs Baxter?' She settled into step beside Lily as they walked down the long driveway to the main road.

'Well, it's been a hard enough time, Mrs Meadows,' Lily explained. 'My daughter, Judith, was in a bad car accident and nearly died. She's still in hospital but coming along grand.'

'Well, God help you!' Mrs Meadows exclaimed. 'Are you in a hurry home or would you have time for a cuppa? We're so close to the Botanics, and it's a fine day.'

'Do you know, that would be a treat.' Lily was

delighted with the invite. Although the other woman didn't know it, Moira Meadows had been her great inspiration, the one who had shown her how a positive attitude and a degree of bravery could enhance and enrich a life. Had she not met her, Lily felt sure she would never have had the courage to change. When she'd heard her talk about living on her own with not a bother, and not allowing herself to become dependent on her sons, Lily had felt ashamed, thinking of how she'd clung leechlike to Judith. Moira Meadows had been a shining example to her, although she would never know it.

Twenty minutes later, the pair were sitting at a window table, sipping tea and eating hot buttered scones with jam. It was a rare, glorious sunny day, and the windows of the refurbished palm house sparkled in the afternoon sunlight. The tropical border was ablaze with colour, and they had decided to go for a walk after their repast. Judith had told her mother not to come visiting because of her appointment with the eye specialist, so Lily was in no rush home.

Mrs Meadows listened intently as Lily described the events of the past couple of months, confiding how nerve-wracking it had been to live on her own at the beginning and how daunting to venture back into the outside world.

'Well now, aren't you wonderful, Mrs Baxter?' she praised. 'And hasn't Judith's accident been a blessing in disguise for you both? There you are, getting on with your life, setting Judith free, and now she'll have a whole new life ahead of her with her own roof over her head and independence. It's a strange thing, but I've often found that sometimes, what seems like a terrible hardship can be a most valuable gift.'

'Well, do you know? When you look at it like that, I have to say you're right, Mrs Meadows. I'd never thought of it that way before.' Lily nodded in agreement, enjoying her chat with the other woman immensely. 'And why have you to see a heart specialist?' she asked, feeling it was rude to spend the whole time talking about herself.

'I need a stent put in,' Mrs Meadows declared. 'But I can tell you one thing, the fella I was sent to was the rudest little ornament I ever met. If there's ever anything wrong with your heart – and I hope there won't be – never go to a fella called Davenport. When I think of the impudence of him, it galls me, Mrs Baxter. Galls me. But I gave him his answer, I can tell you.' Her eyes shone triumphantly at the memory, and Lily listened avidly, marvelling at her companion's pluck.

'What happened?' she inquired, taking a ladylike sip of tea. Mrs Meadows needed no second urging.

'In I goes to his posh office – my son insisted on me going private, even though it costs an arm and a leg,' she explained. That wouldn't be Tom, Lily thought sarcastically, but said nothing, and Mrs Meadows continued. 'Hello, doctor, said I, holding out my hand to shake his – good manners, like,

473

Mrs Baxter.' She looked at Lily for affirmation.

'Indeed,' said Lily.

' "I'm not a doctor, I'm a professor," said yer man, a big tall fella with a head of white hair on him and a nose like a crow's beak. But I had the measure of him while he was there, looking down his snout at me.

' "You're not a doctor?" said I. "Oh dear!" I was being sarcastic, of course.'

'Of course,' tittered Lily, wishing she could be so outspoken.

' "I *am* a doctor but I'm a professor, my good woman," he snapped, just like that. "My good woman," he called me, in a very sneery tone of voice. Something was surely biting him that day, but he picked the wrong woman to give impudence to,' declared Mrs Meadows.

'He certainly did, he was a foolish man indeed,' smiled Lily, enjoying the tale.

' "Now my good man," said I, "if I'm paying you 180 euro – and that's an exorbitant amount, if you don't mind my saying so – that means *I'm* employing *you* to provide *me* with a service and, as your employer, the one who pays your wages today, I expect to be treated with courtesy, manners and respect. However, I don't like the look of you, or the manner of you, so I won't be having you. Good day to you, *professor*," said I, emphasizing the *professor*. And then I walked out,' she said proudly. 'I hope he's still picking his jaw up off the floor. The cheek of him! Some of them are like little tin gods, Mrs Baxter, and need taking down a peg or two, and I'm just the one to do it. They won't treat me like dirt.'

'Indeed, and you're absolutely right: they forget who pays their wages, so they do. Well done. I'd love to have seen that.'

'You have to stand up for yourself, Mrs Baxter. No one else will and, from what I've heard, you're doing a fine job of it. Now, you'll be lonely when Judith moves out, so why don't we exchange numbers and we could meet for a cup of tea every so often? I don't live too far from you; I'm just up the road off Griffith Avenue. And, do you know, a few friends and myself go to the bingo twice a week in Whitehall. Have you ever been to bingo?' Her blue eyes were as bright as two little diamonds as she stared across the table at Lily.

'Ah, no – the crowds, you know,' she murmured as her heart gave a little flutter.

'Now, don't worry, we always sit by the door because Evelyn, one of the women, is a bit claustrophobic. But, sure, look, come with us one night and see how you feel. It's great fun,' Mrs Meadows urged.

'We'll see,' Lily hedged. Some steps took more courage than she possessed.

'I'll show you the ropes, don't worry,' the other woman said cheerfully and, once again, Lily marvelled at, and envied her, her passion for life.

It was after five before she got home, and she inhaled the unmistakable smell of new paint. Jimmy had done a lovely job on the house. He'd painted the hall, the stairs, and the landing and bathroom as well as her sitting room after he'd finished the bedrooms, and he hadn't charged her a fortune. It was worth every penny to have the house looking so well. It was fresh and clean, and it shone like a new pin from the thorough cleaning she had given it. Judith was coming home the following day. Jillian was going to collect her from the hospital and stay for the night, so the small guestroom was all ready for her, with the bed made up and brand-new towels rolled up neatly on the chair for her.

Lily had bought three sirloin steaks for the dinner; sirloin steak was Judith's favourite meal. She'd cook fried onions with it, and creamy mashed potato. She'd bought a pavlova from Thunders, another favourite of her daughter's. And she had another surprise that she herself was looking forward to.

Tomorrow was going to be a momentous day. It would be strange having Judith back in the house again after all this time. Who would have ever thought that Lily would get used to living on her own? Now, she didn't get out of bed two or three times a night to check that all the windows and doors were locked, as she had in the early days of Judith's hospital stay. Neither did she jump at every sound on the street. These nights she said her prayers and went asleep and slept better than she had in years.

She had enjoyed the day so much, Lily thought as she lay in drowsy contemplation of its events, having said her prayers. The unexpected meeting with Mrs Meadows and the tea and walk in the Botanic Gardens had been a wonderful treat. They had strolled along admiring the glorious herbaceous border and had crossed the river to admire the marvellous profusion of blooms in the formal rose garden, with its sundial right in the centre and the weeping willow dipping its graceful branches almost into the river that rushed and roared over the falls beyond the hedge.

She hadn't been in the Botanic Gardens since Ted had died, and it brought back poignant but comforting memories. She would look forward to meeting Mrs Meadows again. She had written her number down in her telephone book – but she baulked at the notion of playing bingo in a crowded hall. That would be a step too far. She knew her limitations, Lily decided, rearranging her hairnet and settling down to sleep.

'Post for you, Judith.' Margaret, her favourite nurse, waved an envelope at her as she walked into Judith's small room. 'I see you're all ready to go. Well done, and take it easy now. Don't take on too much – let your body and mind recover and get plenty of rest,' she advised.

'I will,' Judith promised. 'I'm going to stay with a friend of mine for a few weeks, she lives near a lovely lake.'

'Well, let's hope the weather improves and we get an Indian summer, because it's been a disaster, hasn't it?' The nurse took her wrist and began to check her pulse.

'I suppose it didn't matter to me because I was in here, but it's back to real life now.' Judith turned the letter over, wondering who it was from.

'How do you feel about that?' Margaret asked. 'You've been in hospital for quite a while. It will be hard to adjust, so don't worry if you find it all a bit overwhelming,' she said reassuringly.

'I suppose the worst thing will be getting behind the wheel of a car again – I'm dreading that,' Judith confessed.

'Well, don't rush it, take it all in easy stages,' the nurse advised, taking Judith's temperature for one last time.

When she was gone, Judith sat in her chair by the window and opened the envelope. A thank-you card fell into her lap, and she wondered why would anyone be thanking her. *She* was the one who had many people to thank, and the previous evening she had spent a good hour writing her thank-you notes. She opened the card, a pretty one with a little bear holding a bouquet, and read:

Dear Judith,
I just wanted to thank you for arranging for my increment to be paid. It was kind of you to do it from your hospital bed. It came as a very welcome surprise last payday.
I hope you're feeling much better. We heard you're

*getting out of hospital, so the best of luck and I hope
that your recovery goes well.
Thanks again,
Sincerely,
Debbie Kinsella*

What an unexpected surprise, thought Judith, pleased that Debbie had gone to the trouble of writing. It was extremely decent of the girl after all Judith had put her through, she thought with a pang of guilt. Not many would have done it. Debbie had gone up another few notches in her estimation, Judith decided as she reread the note. Maybe it was a good omen, a sign that both of them were moving on and making a new start. Judith would hold that thought. She tried to quell the collywobbles she was feeling.

What would it be like living at home again with her mother? Would old ways resurface, and would Lily become dependent? Would Judith feel stultified and resentful, or would it all have changed? Did Lily really mean it about putting her name on the deeds, or would that go by the wayside once things were back to normal? Was getting a place of her own just a pipedream?

Judith took a few deep breaths. This was the start of her second chance: she would not ruin it by negative thinking, she told herself sternly, putting Debbie's thank-you card in her handbag. She stood up, wandered over to the mirror at the small sink, and retouched her lipstick. Her hair was streaked with grey and badly needed a cut and colour; she had it coiled up on her head, and she couldn't wait to make an appointment with her hairdresser. Her cheeks were pale and sunken, but a few days of sunshine and fresh air would sort that, she assured herself, noting how loose her trousers were. This small room had been her haven from the world, but it was time to go and pick up the reins of her life again. Soon, Jillian and her mother would come to collect her. She would do her very best to put on a brave face and try not to let them see how apprehensive she was, Judith promised herself, blotting her lipstick with a tissue.

'I'll wait here until you come back. I'm sure Judith would much prefer to have Jillian collect her than me. I brought some cream cakes to welcome her home.' Tom plonked a square white box on the kitchen table.

'I don't know what time we'll get home at,' Lily said, quite vexed, but trying hard not to show it. Tom had arrived minutes ago, offering to collect Judith when he knew very well that Jillian was doing the honours. She couldn't very well throw him out of the house, Lily thought crossly.

'The place looks great. How are you, Jillian? Long time no see,' he said chattily, sitting down at the table.

'I'm fine, Tom,' Jillian said politely.

'And you like living in culchie land?' He chuckled at his little joke.

'Love it,' she said evenly.

'Just excuse me a moment if you don't mind,' Lily said. 'I want to get my jacket and a clean handkerchief.'

Tom threw his eyes up to heaven when she left the kitchen. 'Still uses handkerchiefs, wouldn't use a tissue to save her life.'

'A lot of old people do. My mother does, and they're always scented with lavender.' Jillian wanted to say 'you pillock', but she refrained, admirably.

'So Judith's going to stay with you for a while?' Tom changed the subject.

'I hope so,' Jillian agreed.

'Umm . . . I'll have to keep an eye on Ma then, she's come to depend on me a lot. I got the place painted for her,' he boasted. 'Have to keep it in good nick; we don't want it falling around her ears. And it needs to be well kept when the time comes to sell it.' He looked at Jillian over the rim of his bifocals, reminding her of Alex Ferguson, as he chewed gum relentlessly, his jaws working like pistons.

'Are we ready, dear?' Lily appeared at the door, looking serene.

'We are if you are.' Jillian smiled at her.

'Tom, put those cakes in the fridge, and make yourself a cup of tea if you wish, and be sure to wash your cup. I want the place to be ship shape when Judith comes home,' Lily instructed.

Tom stopped chewing. 'OK, Ma,' he said slowly. 'If you want to give me a ring when you're at

Griffith Avenue, I'll make a pot of tea,' he offered.

'Oh, it's not tea we'll be drinking,' Lily said gaily as she followed Jillian out the door.

What on earth did his ma mean by that? Tom resumed chewing as he heard the front door close. He made his way into Lily's sitting room to watch their departure, noting how attentive and kind Jillian was, holding the car door open for his mother and helping her to adjust her seatbelt. He had made his offer to collect Judith knowing full well that Jillian was going to do it, and in the certain knowledge that it would be refused. No sooner had the car disappeared out of sight than he hurried back to the kitchen to shove the cakes in the fridge. It was immaculate, and smelt clean, he noted, not like their fridge freezer at home, which was always sticky and grimy with mouldy cheeses and out-of-date ham turning green and curling up at the edges.

What was Lily doing with a bottle of Moët in the fridge? Jillian must have bought it, he surmised, noting the green bottle lying on its side. He slammed the door shut and raced up the stairs two at a time, finally getting the chance he'd been looking for. He couldn't believe his luck. After all his scheming to get a key, and having to pay to have the bedrooms painted, to no avail, today, his mother had just left him alone, without a thought, to poke around to his heart's content. How strange life was, he reflected as, a touch breathless, he reached the top of the stairs.

Lily's bedroom door was half open. He couldn't

believe it. He hurried into the room, sniffing the faint scent of powder and lily-of-the-valley perfume. He stood and took a deep breath. Four big drawers in the chest. Two dressing-table drawers, a bedside locker and her wardrobe. Lily's papers could be anywhere, even stuffed in old handbags on top of the wardrobe. He must make sure to put everything back *exactly* as he found it so as not to raise his mother's suspicions. When he'd found what he was looking for he'd have a rummage through Judith's stuff. Might as well see what little secrets *she* had stashed away while he was at it. Brimming with anticipation, Tom set to his task.

'Have you to get shopping?' Judith asked as Jillian parked the car on double yellows outside a small group of shops and offices not far from home.

'Just get out, Judith, and open the door for me like a good girl,' Lily ordered crisply from the back seat. She'd insisted that Judith sit in the front seat with her friend on the journey home.

'OK. Where are you going?' Judith extracted herself from her seatbelt and opened the front door.

'We are going into Mr Martin, Judith. He has everything ready for us to sign on the dotted line. It won't take five minutes, he said. Jillian's very kindly offered to wait. She knows all about it – we planned it when we knew you were getting out.' Lily was so excited her eyes were dancing.

Judith burst into tears, remembering her unworthy thoughts in the hospital.

'Now, don't cry, for goodness' sake,' her mother protested in dismay.

'Get in there, Judith, and do what your mother tells you,' Jillian said sternly. 'And hurry up, here's a warden. I'll do a circuit.'

'Ma, are you sure? I don't expect you to do this,' Judith said earnestly as she limped slowly alongside her mother to a dark-red door with several gold plates on the side of it.

'I know you don't. But the sooner we do it the better. Your brother's at home waiting for our return and no doubt having a grand old root around – but he can root all he wants, because I have everything he'll be interested in in my handbag, and I've locked your door. So he's wasting his time and, by the time we get home, you'll be on the deeds, and there won't be a thing he can do about it.' Lily smiled smugly. She was getting just as good as Mrs Meadows for asserting herself, she decided, peering for the buzzer and pressing it confidently, unaware that her daughter was looking at her almost in awe.

The ould bitch had locked Judith's room. She must have known he'd go prying. There was nothing of any interest in her own room, although he'd gone through it meticulously. He wasn't staying here to have tea and cakes and listen to women yattering; he had plenty of other things to be doing, Tom decided, bitterly disappointed and thoroughly disgruntled.

'Have to go, got a call from work,' he scrawled on

the back of a flyer he found on the mantelpiece. Lily and Judith were in cahoots, it was clear, and the pair of witches was keeping him in the dark. *And* they'd had their bedrooms painted for free, paid for with his hard-earned money. It was the last penny of his either of them would ever see, Tom swore, as he let himself out, slamming the door behind him.

'I never drank real champagne before,' Lily confided as she held out her glass for a top-up. 'Well, we had Babycham at your father's and my wedding, but that's not real champagne like this. I thought it would be a great treat for us and something to make this a special oosasio— ossio— occasion.' She gave a tipsy little giggle, her cheeks rosy, her eyes bright and giddy.

'Drink up there, Mrs Baxter,' Jillian grinned, filling up her glass. 'And you, too, Judith.'

'To Judith. A dear daughter and now a woman of property.' Lily raised her glass a little unsteadily before taking a gulp, laughing when the fizz tickled her nose.

'To you, Mother, for your kindness and bravery. I'm so grateful to you and so proud of you – well done.' Judith clinked her glass with Lily's, almost overwhelmed.

'And to a very special occasion,' Jillian toasted, as mother and daughter embraced affectionately, faces wreathed in smiles.

CHAPTER THIRTY-ONE

Melissa crushed half a Weetabix into a dish and poured just enough milk to dampen it. She was going to visit the stables with Connie in the afternoon, and she didn't want to feel faint. She'd have the other half with an apple for her lunch before she got the Dart to Greystones. Her mom was in the dining room working on her laptop and making calls, and Melissa knew better than to disturb her. She strolled out on to the balcony and sat at the wrought-iron table, eating very slowly. She was starving. Once she'd found out they were going on holiday, she'd cut back big time so she wouldn't look like an elephant in her bathing togs.

She was worried, though: it seemed her parents had copped that she was dieting. In the last few days, Barry had been cooking dinners and insisting that she eat with them and, once, when she'd left the table immediately after the meal to go and throw up, she'd found him waiting outside the door for her.

'Are you ill, Muffin? Did I hear you getting sick?'

he'd asked, even though she'd done it as quietly as she possibly could.

'No, Dad, I'm fine, I was just clearing my throat,' she fibbed, hoping that he believed her. She sighed as she ate another little spoonful. She'd leave her dirty dish in the sink so that her mom could see that she'd eaten breakfast. The other half of the Weetabix was wrapped up in clingfilm in her handbag.

In two days' time she'd be in Disneyworld, and then Paris, and then the south of France. They were staying in a posh hotel very near where Johnny Depp and Bono had villas. Bono had had Brad Pitt and Angelina Jolie to visit; she'd read it in a magazine. Imagine if she saw any of them – she could take a photo on her phone. How cool would that be to show off when she went back to school in September? It was such a relief they were going abroad; she wouldn't feel out of place when the other girls in the class were talking about their trips. Sarah was very worried; she was only going to visit her cousins in Cork. Her mother had had to stop working to take care of her grandmother, who was ill, and they weren't even going to get to Spain for a week.

'Hi, darling, are you eating breakfast? What are you having?' Aimee interrupted her daydream and came and sat beside her at the table.

'Weetabix.' Melissa showed her the empty bowl with the damp bits clinging to the side.

'Darling, I just want to say, it's all very well keeping fit and losing weight, but don't lose too much.

It's not good for you, and I need you to be on top form to help me when the baby comes.' Aimee reached across and squeezed her hand.

Her mother looked tired. She had circles under her eyes, and she was quite pale. It was so strange to have her at home all day, even though she spent most of it working. Melissa and Sarah felt constrained by her presence; usually, they had their music on fairly loud, or played Wii tennis, yelling at each other when they got a point. Aimee always wanted to know where they were going and who they were seeing and, after the heady days of freedom earlier in the holidays, it was like a bucket of cold water dousing them having her mother there 24/7.

'Are you looking forward to the holiday?' Aimee asked, raising her face to the sun's welcome rays.

'Yeah – it's a huge surprise. I wasn't expecting it,' Melissa said.

'Me neither. I thought it would be your mid-term in October before we got away. Having the time off before I start my new job is a real bonus.'

'And it's great Dad's coming too,' Melissa slipped in, watching her mother's reaction.

'Wonderful,' Aimee agreed heartily. Was she a bit too hearty, Melissa worried. 'It's going to be lovely to relax as a family. We should make the most of it.'

'Are you really glad Dad's coming? I heard you having a row,' she blurted.

Aimee looked startled and a little embarrassed. 'Oh, darling, every couple has rows, and we're no different. Forget about it. Dad and I have,' she said dismissively, waving her hand as if to brush away an unwelcome topic.

'Really?' Melissa persisted.

'Yes, really.' Aimee grimaced.

'Mom, will you be bringing your BlackBerry?' Melissa fiddled with her spoon.

'I have to, darling. There's a lot going on for me just now, setting up this new company, but I'll only check it every so often. I promise.'

'Umm,' Melissa murmured. She'd heard that one before.

'Honestly,' her mother assured her. 'Now, what do you think? I'm getting a new company car—'

'Oh, can you get a Merc or BMW sportscar?' Melissa was thrilled.

Aimee made a face. 'A sportscar is much too girly for the image I've to portray, far too frivolous and silly and, besides, what use is it in the appalling weather we've had? How often do you get to put the roof down?'

'Well, a big Merc or BMW then,' Melissa said, disappointed.

Aimee shook her head. 'Darling, every Tom, Dick and Harry has a Merc or a BMW nowadays. I was thinking of getting a top-of-the-range Lexus actually.'

'*Boring.*' Melissa made a face.

'No, darling, a Lexus makes a very subtle statement. It *oozes* class. It's not a car for airheads, if you know what I mean. A woman driving a top-class

Lexus is at the top of her game and not to be trifled with, and that's the image I want to portray in my new job.'

'I love Debbie's soft-top,' Melissa said wistfully. 'Except they can't afford it any more, and they're going to get something smaller.'

'Really?' said Aimee, not in the slightest bit interested in whether Debbie and her husband could afford their soft-top. 'Well, darling, that's tough, but my new job pays very, very well, and we are going on a serious spending spree in Paris, you and me.' Aimee smiled at her and got up from the table.

'Deadly.' Melissa grinned. 'Hey, Mom – you know the way I'm going to visit the stables with Connie to see Frisky today?'

'Yes.'

'Could I get a horse some day?'

'I'll talk to Dad about it,' Aimee said slowly, thinking if they got their daughter a horse it might take her mind off dieting and give her something else to think about. It would also be good to drop it into conversation. *My daughter's crazy about her horse, she's never at home . . .* It would be a fine social investment as well as an interest for Melissa. 'It might be good for you to have a horse; you'd get plenty of fresh air,' she added.

'Oh cool, Mom, cool. Only three girls in the class have their own horses.' She jumped up and hugged Aimee excitedly.

Aimee hugged her back. 'You need to be fit and

healthy to ride horses, so maybe have some brown bread or toast with your Weetabix every morning,' she suggested.

'I *am* fit and healthy, Mom.' Melissa's eyes slid away from her mother's gaze.

'Well, that's good to hear,' Aimee said. Her phone rang, and it was with the greatest relief that Melissa watched her go to answer it. She just hoped that her mom and dad would get off her back about food. If they didn't, it would take all the fun out of going on holidays and getting a horse. It would give her something else to worry about, and she didn't need that.

'There's only one Weetabix gone out of the box; I counted them last night.' Aimee kept her voice low so that Melissa wouldn't overhear her phone call.

'And she's definitely making herself sick. When we come back from France we'll bring her to the doctor. Might as well let her have a bit of fun first. I've been reading the literature Connie emailed over. Scary stuff, but she's given us names and contact numbers so we can decide what's the best route to go when we've spoken to the doctor,' Barry said wearily. 'Do you want to ask your dad for advice? Maybe he could get her seen to quickly?'

'Absolutely not,' Aimee retorted vehemently. 'I don't want him to know anything about it. He'd think that it was a terrible weakness of character, and I won't have him looking down his nose at her. It's bad enough that he looks down his nose at me.'

'He wouldn't be like that surely,' Barry protested.

'I'm not giving him the chance.'

'OK then. It was just a thought.'

'She asked me about getting a horse. She's going to some stables with Saint Connie to see a foal today.' Aimee studied her reflection in the dining-room mirror and noted that she could do with a Botox treatment. She wouldn't be able to have that while she was pregnant. She'd have a forehead like a walnut shell by the time she had the baby, she thought dolefully.

'Don't call Connie that,' Barry said irritably. 'She's been very good to Melissa.'

'Umm . . . Well, anyway, I told Melissa I'd talk to you about it, and I told her that she'd have to be fit and healthy to be riding horses.'

'Good thinking. I'd buy her a stableful of horses if it would sort her out,' Barry said morosely.

'I know. Anyway, I have to go, I've another call on the line,' she fibbed. 'Bye.'

'Bye, and Aimee . . .'

'Yes?'

'Don't forget to eat something yourself.'

'I won't,' she sighed, before hanging up. Food was the last thing she wanted, but it behoved her to eat for the baby's sake. It was bad enough having to worry about one sick child without worrying that she was harming the one she was carrying by not taking proper nutrition. Heavy-hearted, she walked slowly back to her desk and tried to immerse herself in the challenge of setting up a new company.

Barry gave a wry smile as he put the phone down. It hadn't even cost Aimee a second's thought to entertain the idea of buying and keeping a horse. She hadn't told him what her new salary was. They weren't back that close yet. Still, at least they were rowing in the same canoe and putting on some sort of a united front and, for that, he was thankful. Maybe the holiday away would do them good. *He* needed a holiday for sure.

He picked up his mobile to ring Connie. He'd been rude to her the other night. Hurt and anger had made him lash out; he should apologize. She didn't have to bring Melissa to that stables this afternoon; she was going out of her way to be kind, and he should acknowledge it. He dialled her number but, to his disappointment, it rang out, and he didn't leave a message. He'd catch her again later, he decided, as he Googled anorexia and clicked on a website that caught his attention.

Tight black jeans, Manolo slingbacks and a clingy black vest top that showed off her pert boobs and toned arms to perfection today, Marianna decided as she surveyed the contents of her wardrobe. She was just back from Dublin having visited her father, and she was changing to drive over to Greystones with Drew's gift voucher. She'd found the address of the stables in the phone book, Googled it up and read his most impressive website. Drew had done well for himself since their divorce. He'd built up a thriving business, and the testimonials were top notch.

She'd bought him a hundred-euro voucher for Avoca Handweavers. If he didn't like the household or clothing departments, he could use it in their garden centre. It gave her a twisted sense of satisfaction to be spending her lying bastard of a husband's money on Drew. Not that *he* really deserved it, she thought irately, inserting gold hoops into her ears. Her ex hadn't even bothered to lift the phone to inquire after her father. That was bad form. Drew *was* his ex-son-in-law, after all, and, surely, he must, at this stage, realize that, when her father was negotiating her divorce settlement, he was only doing what any good father would do.

Marianna sighed. Her father was going to have to have a triple bypass, so she would have to spend a significant amount of time at home this year. It would be nice to have Drew onside to provide a bit of diversion.

She applied her make-up, including her false lashes, and added extra lipgloss. She studied herself critically in the full-length mirror. No, she really didn't look a day over thirty-five, and her gym work and lipo had really paid off, she thought with immense satisfaction, wondering how he'd be able to resist her. Humming, she made her way downstairs, took the Merc's keys off the mahogany hall table and click-clacked down the marble steps of her father's Edwardian pile, bursting with anticipation.

* * *

494

'Nice dress,' Drew murmured, as Connie got out of the car.

'Thanks.' She smiled, wishing she could kiss him. She was wearing a fifties-style green and white halterneck floral sundress that showed off her curvy figure and golden tan, and a pair of white espadrilles.

'Drew, this is Melissa. Melissa, this is Drew.' She introduced the teenager, who had come around from her side of the car and was standing shyly by the bonnet.

'Very nice to meet you, Melissa.' Drew looked at her kindly and shook her hand firmly.

'Hi,' she said quietly. 'Cool stables.'

'Thanks; it's a good place to work. Do you want to see Frisky?'

'Oh, yes please,' she said eagerly. 'My mom said she'd talk to my dad about getting me a horse,' she confided.

'Well, if I can give you any advice, you know where I am,' he offered, leading them over to the paddock where Frisky and Swift were standing together nuzzling.

'Oooohhhh, she's gorgeous, isn't she, Connie?' Melissa cried out with delight as the little foal pranced up to the fence.

'Want to give her an apple? She loves them, and Swift loves carrots.' Drew smiled at Connie, his eyes warm and admiring.

'Sure.' Melissa took the apple from him, and Frisky whinnied joyously and stuck her head through a gap in the fence and chomped on the apple Melissa held out to her. 'Ooohhh, Connie, thanks so much for bringing me,' Melissa said, ecstatic, as she stroked the beautiful foal.

'How about I get one of my stable girls to introduce you to all the horses and show you around?' Drew suggested five minutes later after Frisky had taken off for a gallop around the paddock, kicking her heels exuberantly, watched by her proud mother.

'Is that OK with you, Connie? You're not in a rush, are you?' Melissa asked politely.

'No rush, go and enjoy yourself,' Connie urged.

'Triona,' Drew called, and a young woman in dusty boots and navy jodhpurs came out from one of the stalls and hurried across the yard. 'Triona, can you show Melissa around and introduce her to the horses?' Drew smiled at her and plucked a piece of straw out of her hair.

'Sure, no prob. Come on, Melissa, we've some fabulous horses,' she said enthusiastically. 'We'll grab some carrots and apples, and they'll love you.' Melissa needed no second invitation and hurried along beside her guide, eager to make the animals' acquaintance.

'I might be getting a horse,' they heard her say.

'Oh cool – I'd *love* a horse of my own,' Triona replied with heartfelt longing.

'Thanks, Drew, I really appreciate your time, and Triona's,' Connie said as they walked over to a bench at the side of the end stall and sat down.

'Don't thank me. Just sit here and talk to me and

let me feast my eyes on you.' He grinned at her, their arms and knees touching as they sat snugly beside each other.

Connie laughed. 'I'm doing a bit of feasting myself, mister. That shade of blue is lovely on you. It brings out the colour of your eyes.'

'Would you give over, woman,' Drew chuckled, half mortified, unused to compliments. Their eyes met and they burst out laughing. 'It's a lovely afternoon, want to go for a walk on the beach later on, and have a bite to eat – or is Melissa with you for the night?' he invited.

'No, I'll be dropping her to the Dart. I should be back home by seven.'

'Pick you up at seven thirty?' He arched a black eyebrow at her.

'You're on.'

'What's the dress code?'

'Speedos and a dickie bow,' she teased, and he laughed.

'Helen Mirren-style bikini for you then, madam,' he retorted, and she grinned up at him, loving their banter.

A maroon Merc drove up the wide, tree-lined drive and Drew shaded his eyes against the sun to see who it was.

'Oh hell!' he cursed, his face darkening as he recognized the driver.

'What's wrong?' Connie asked, seeing a blonde in tight jeans and impossibly high heels totter over the gravel towards them.

'It's Barbie, aka my ex,' he scowled.

'Drew, hi.' Marianna beamed. 'I hope you don't mind me coming unannounced.' She gave Connie a quick once-over. 'I just wanted to thank you so much for driving me up to see my dad – although I thought you might have phoned to see how he was,' she pouted.

'Skipped my mind, Marianna, how is he?' Drew said coldly.

'He has to have a triple bypass, the poor darling. I guess I'm going to be here quite a lot this year.' She gave him a sultry smile. It wasn't returned. 'I'm sorry – Drew's forgotten his manners.' Marianna turned to Connie. 'I'm Marianna Delahunt, his ex-wife?' She held out a delicate, manicured hand and gave Connie a limp handshake.

'This is Connie Adams, a very dear friend of mine,' Drew said curtly, dropping an arm around Connie's shoulder and drawing her close. Connie nestled in against him, and Marianna's eyes narrowed.

'I don't think I've heard of you,' she said snootily. 'Our daughters keep me up to date on all the news from home.'

'Really?' Connie said politely. 'I know *all* about you.'

Drew spluttered, and tried hard to keep his face straight.

'Could we have a few words in private, Drew?' Marianna said icily.

Connie made to move away, but Drew held her hand tight.

'Fire ahead, Marianna. My time with Connie is precious, and I don't like to waste it.' He eyeballed his ex-wife, hostility crackling in the air between them.

'Oh! Oh! Well, I just wanted to give you a small gift – you know, to thank you for bringing me to Dublin.' She took an envelope from her Gucci bag.

'Not necessary, but thank you,' he said tersely, slipping it into the back pocket of his jeans without looking at it.

'Lovely place you've got here. The girls are always raving about the house,' Marianna said chattily, trying to recover her poise.

'It's not bad, and I'm glad they like it and feel at home here, because it *is* their home, obviously,' said Drew pointedly. 'Now, if you'll excuse us, I've some important business to talk to Connie about. Thanks for the gift.' He put his arm around Connie's waist.

'Oh!' Marianna was rattled. 'I wonder could I use your loo?' she rallied.

'No problem,' Drew said. 'Avril!' He called another stablehand, who was grooming a chestnut gelding. 'Would you bring this er . . . lady . . . over to the loo there, thanks. Just follow Avril, and she'll show you where to go. Mind your shoes,' he added, 'there's a lot of muck around, it's been a wet summer.' His eyes glinted with amusement, and he glanced at Connie, who was trying hard to conceal her mirth.

'Forget it, I'll hang on,' Marianna said, attempting to hide her fury.

'Suit yourself.' Drew shrugged.

Trying to keep her dignity, and her balance, Marianna teetered across to the car. She pulled her oversized sunshades down over her eyes, reminding Connie of a bug-eyed cartoon character. She started the engine, spun the wheel and scorched down the drive.

'You're awful,' Connie chided.

'Excuse me . . . "I know *all* about you"?' Drew mimicked. 'That was priceless.'

'How could you marry someone like that?' She looked up at him, perplexed.

'Shy, horny young men do harebrained things,' he said ruefully.

'And what do shy, horny older men do?' She tucked her arm into his.

'Come in here, and I'll show you,' Drew said, leading her into Swift's stall and kissing her passionately.

'Oh God, Sullivan, you're a great kisser,' Connie sighed a while later as she nuzzled in against him.

'You're pretty hot yourself, Adams.' He smiled down at her, holding her tight.

'Isn't it amazing? I just feel so comfortable with you. I feel as though I've known you for ever. It's weird.'

'Not weird,' he said firmly. 'It's right. Everything feels just right. We're right, the time is right—'

'Oh, stop talking and kiss me again,' she urged, drawing his head down to hers.

'You're incorrigible and a—'

He never got to finish, as Connie raised her mouth to his and silenced him with a kiss that just went on and on.

How dare they? How dare they laugh at her? Tears of rage spurted from Marianna's eyes as she drove out of Drew's stables. He was a bastard, a complete and utter bastard. Who did he think he was? He was only a Wicklow clodhopper. How *dare* he treat her with such disrespect and contempt? *And* in front of that Connie woman, with her real tan and freckly nose, and hair that had never seen peroxide. She looked the earthy sort, like Meryl Streep in *The Bridges of Madison County*, or Jessica Lange and Susan Sarandon in their later years. Voluptuous and sexy – no wonder Drew couldn't take his eyes off her; he was probably getting more action in a night than Marianna had had in years. It just wasn't fair. And they looked so comfortable together, so in tune and companionable. He'd never been like that with her. 'Comfortable' was not an adjective she would ever have used to describe her relationship with Drew. Once, she would have classified 'comfortable' as boring. But there was nothing boring about Drew and that woman. They were into each other in every way, it was unmistakable, and she envied them with every fibre of her being.

Marianna rooted impatiently for a tissue. She'd been so sure he wouldn't be able to resist her. She hadn't let herself go. She was still the same size she'd been when she'd married him. She was toned and supple, not like that woman he was draped all over. *She* was a woman in her prime, Marianna assured herself, as she blew her nose and wiped her eyes.

Well, no one treated her the way her ex-husband just had, and that Connie one would have the smirk wiped off her face, because Marianna Sullivan Delahunt didn't give up that easily, and that was something Ms Earth Mother was going to discover over the next few months, Marianna vowed, as she blew her bobbed nose once more and headed for home.

Barry glanced at his watch. Ten to seven. He was restless and edgy. Aimee had picked up Melissa off the Dart and they'd gone to the pictures in Dundrum, and he was at a loose end. Melissa had been as high as a kite when she'd phoned him on the train back to town. She'd raved about the stables and the horses and the foal, and begged him to let her get a horse. It was so good to hear the excitement in her voice, and he felt hugely grateful to Connie. He went into the bedroom and took the small painting of Greystones he'd bought for her from the top section of his wardrobe where it lay bubble-wrapped under some sweaters. Picking up his car keys, he hurried out of the apartment and took the lift to the basement. The worst of the rush-hour traffic would be over; it wouldn't take him long to get to her place.

He stopped at a florist on the way and bought

two dozen yellow roses. He needed to apologize to his ex-wife, and nothing said sorry better than roses. His heart lifted as he turned off the N11 on to the slip road. He needed to get back on track with Connie, needed her reassurance and companionship on this long, bumpy road ahead of him. He drove fast, looking forward to a good chat once his apologies were over.

Barry frowned when he saw a dusty black jeep parked outside her house. Who owned that, he wondered, pulling in behind it. He was just about to get out of the car when the front door opened and a tall, fit, grey-haired man came out, followed by Connie. They were holding hands, and she was laughing up at him, looking more radiant than he had ever seen her. She was wearing a pale-lilac sleeveless summer dress with a bodice top and a skirt that fell in soft folds down to her ankles. She had a pink pashmina draped casually around her shoulders, which emphasized her golden tan. She looked fabulous. His heart clenched in pain as he saw her reach up and stroke the man's tanned cheek.

Barry almost couldn't breathe. He'd lost her. After all these years, he knew she was no longer his safety net. He was stunned. He wanted to cry. She saw him and looked surprised. Barry composed himself, with difficulty, and got out of the car.

'Hi,' he said, handing her the roses. 'I just wanted to thank you for all you're doing for Melissa . . . um . . . sorry about the other day.'

'That's OK, Barry,' Connie said easily. 'There was no need for the roses.' She took them and looked up at the man. 'Drew, this is Barry, my ex-husband, Melissa's dad. Barry, this is Drew, a very dear friend of mine.'

'Hello.' The man greeted him and held out his hand politely. Barry extended his own, and Drew shook his hand in a strong, and very firm, grip.

'Nice to meet you. I should have called, I suppose.' Barry glanced at Connie. 'You look as if you're on the way out.'

'We can do it another time, Connie,' Drew said.

'No, Drew, we've made our plans, Barry won't mind. Sure you won't?' she said firmly.

'Go right ahead, just wanted to say thanks.' Barry spread his hands, in a casual gesture. He really wanted to kick the man in the goolies and tell him to stay the hell away from Connie.

'Have as good a holiday as you can, Barry. We'll talk when you get back,' Connie said kindly, as she slipped her hand into her companion's.

'Will do. Cheers,' he said flatly, and walked back to the car.

'I'll put these in the house, Drew, won't be a sec,' Connie said, taking her keys out of her bag.

'No rush,' said Drew, and leaned nonchalantly against the pillar and gave Barry a salute as he drove past the jeep and reversed in Connie's drive.

'Arrogant bastard,' muttered Barry as he geared up and sped down the road. He could at least have taken his jeep to a carwash if he was going on a date.

The painting lay on the front seat, unopened, a taunting reminder of his loss. His heart was as heavy as lead. He felt like crying. He was on his own now, with a pregnant wife who wanted a divorce and a daughter who was starving herself to death, and the woman he'd always thought he could depend on, and run to, was turning her back on him. Well, he wouldn't let that happen, he decided. He and Connie had a bond that no one could sever.

Maybe this was only a fling and the bastard would break her heart, and she'd come running to him for comfort. He'd be there for her with open arms. *Then*, she'd appreciate him. Barry glowered as he caught sight of the black jeep in his rear-view mirror, closing the gap between them.

'He still holds a torch for you,' Drew remarked as they followed Barry's Merc to the end of the road.

'Well, I don't hold one for him.' Connie shrugged. 'And it's only in the last year or so that he's wanted to get close again. And the reason for that is that life with Aimee's become difficult, and he can't hack it. He was always the same when things got tough. Bryan, my son-in-law, is *exactly* the same, and I can't see him staying the course with Debbie. And that's being realistic. She married the same type of man I did, and it's not going to be easy for her.'

'You have to let them get on with it,' Drew cautioned.

'I know.'

'And you can't take on the burdens of the world. You have your own life to live.'

'I know that too.' Connie smiled at him, as Barry's car turned left and she and Drew turned right to get to the beach. She glanced in the side mirror and saw the other car disappear around a bend. The man at her side was a far different kettle of fish to her ex-husband. He took what life threw at him and got on with it.

'What are you looking so serious about?' He looked over at her.

'Nothing, nothing at all,' she said lightly. 'I'm looking forward to our walk.'

'Me too,' Drew said. 'Your ex is gone, and I don't expect to see mine tripping along in her high heels on the beach. We're safe.' He grinned.

'Perfect,' Connie declared. 'Absolutely perfect.'

EPILOGUE

Judith felt a singular sense of wellbeing as she lay in a candle-lit room filled with the perfume of burning incense and the sound of Enya playing softly in the background. Her body felt completely relaxed after an Indian head massage and a reflexology session. Jillian had booked the treatments for her as a surprise. It was the first time she'd ever had either, and the sense of relaxation that followed them was a whole new experience, one she hoped she'd be having again. She was going to start giving herself little treats every so often. She deserved them, she decided. Jillian was in the room next door having a hot-stone massage; Judith was going to try that, too, in the not-too-distant future.

She was feeling so much better in every way, Judith thought drowsily as she lay under a snug quilt and tried not to fall asleep. She had spent a week at home with Lily before taking the train west to stay with Jillian.

It had been strange at home with her mother. The whole energy of the house was different. And it wasn't just the excellent painting job that freshened everywhere up. It was Lily who had changed so much. She was in charge again. Her house was her own, and Judith found it a novel experience to have her mother making decisions about what they'd eat and when, or even to be watching TV with her mother in her sitting room, something she'd rarely done before her accident, preferring to go up to her bedroom and watch it there. Lily was now a member of the library, and the two of them had walked the short distance to it on Judith's second day home. Lily had had to slow down to accommodate her daughter's pace. What a turnaround, Judith thought, following her mother through the big heavy doors and hearing her greet the girl at the desk with a cheerful, 'Hello, Aileen.'

At home, Judith's room gleamed like a new pin and smelt delightful, the scent of the sage and lavender Lily had placed on the windowsill to counteract the smell of new paint perfuming the room. It had been wonderful to sleep in her own bed again, but even her room seemed different, as though it was no longer hers. She was being fanciful, Judith knew; she was now named on the deeds of her mother's house, but it was as if the house she'd lived in, unwillingly, for so long was saying goodbye to her. It was time for her to go and be free. When she got back to Dublin, she was going to buy a new car and start looking for a home of her own.

Lily had waved her off in the taxi urging her to

have a great time with Jillian, a sight Judith had never ever expected to see. Truly, Lily had come into her own, she reflected, stretching luxuriously. She wondered what her mother was doing. She'd ring her when she got home to Jillian's.

Judith's eyelids drooped and she floated off to sleep, more relaxed than she'd been in a long, long time.

Lily's heart was thumping. Her palms were sweating. She swallowed hard. She was half afraid she might take a turn.

'Two fat ladies, 88' came the call, and she nearly fainted with excitement.

'It's me,' she squawked. 'I've got all the numbers.'

'Well done, Lily,' Moira Meadows declared, delighted. 'Full house. Now didn't I tell you you'd enjoy yourself at bingo?'

'Beginner's luck, Moira,' Lily beamed. They were now on first-name terms.

'Not at all,' said Moira's friend, Joan, 'I think you're going to be a lucky player.'

'Do you think so?' Lily said delightedly. She hadn't had such fun in years. It was very exciting. And Moira had been so kind to her, encouraging her and showing her the ropes. And she liked Joan, a small, plump woman with tight, grey wire-brush-permed hair and apple-red cheeks, too. Joan was also a widow.

'I do,' Joan affirmed. 'I think you've a long bingo career ahead of you.'

'Will you come back for a cup of tea?' Lily invited as they left the crowded hall an hour later.

'Well thank you, Lily, I'd be delighted,' Moira said.

'I would, too, if it's no trouble,' Joan agreed, tying a red headscarf with two galloping horses and horseshoes on each corner under her chin to protect her perm from the damp evening air. It was her lucky headscarf, she'd told Lily. She always wore it to bingo.

'No trouble at all,' Lily declared firmly.

She was making the tea when the phone rang. It was Judith.

'Hello, Ma, how are you? How are things?' her daughter asked with a cheerful lilt to her voice.

'Things are fine, Judith, but if you don't mind, I don't have time to talk at the moment. I'm just back from bingo, and I'm making a pot of tea for my friends,' Lily explained. 'I'll ring you back . . . and Judith, you'll never guess – I won. Isn't it great? You'll have to come some time. Bye bye, dear.' Lily hung up, glad that her daughter sounded so well. The trip to the west would do her all the good in the world, she reflected, arranging slices of lemon cake and a selection of chocolate rolls on her best china plate to serve to her new friends.

Debbie stood back and admired her handiwork, wiping her hands on a rag tucked into her jeans pocket. What a warm, rich colour the claret was compared to the cold blue that had decorated their bedroom. She was painting the wall behind their bed claret and the rest of the room a rich cream. She'd been dying to change the colour since they'd moved into the house. Now at last she was making the room their own.

Bryan was going to help her later. He was just having a quick drink after work. She was sure he'd like what she'd done so far. It was great to be doing up the house at last. The difference a lick of paint and new colours made. She could get a cream duvet set and dress it with a rich burgundy throw and a couple of burgundy pillows to accessorize. She'd get them in the sales. Simple but effective.

She hummed to herself as she resumed her work. She felt much less stressed than she'd been when they'd come back from their honeymoon. Things were settling down again, and she loved being a married woman with her own home, she thought happily, dipping her brush in the paint and covering another patch of the detested blue.

Bryan inhaled the second line of coke and waited for the rush to hit. 'Hello, old friend,' he muttered as the drug took effect and he felt his old exuberance return. He was supposed to be at home painting, but one of the girls was leaving and an impromptu party had broken out in the office, and they were all going to go to the Harbour Master's for a couple of drinks. One of the lads had sold him some coke, and he'd slipped into the loo to get reacquainted with his drug of choice. He'd send Debbie a text and tell her he'd be home later. She'd be pissed at him he knew, but he needed a night off for good behaviour, he'd bloody earned it. A night on the tiles was a far more inviting option than painting bedroom walls as far as he was concerned.

'Come on, you guys, let's party,' Bryan urged as he stepped back into the office to celebrate the weekend with his workmates.

'I think this will do very nicely,' Juliet said to the estate agent as she walked around the bright, airy, ground-floor, two-bedroom apartment in Blackrock. It was her second viewing, 'I'll take it.'

It had a lovely private terrace overlooking the well-maintained grounds, facing south-west, so she'd get the afternoon and evening sun. It was just a short stroll to the shops and the Dart. It was a station away from Aimee on the train and just up the road in the car. It was perfect.

Ken had agreed to sell the villa in Spain, which would more than cover the cost of the apartment, so he wasn't being too financially stretched, even though he was moaning that he wouldn't get the optimum price. He would still get a lot more than what they'd paid for it, Juliet had pointed out. Once he'd seen that she was very serious about leaving him, he'd become quite subdued, like a balloon that had fizzled out of air. He'd bounce back, she told herself, once he'd got over the shock of her going, but going she was, and the sooner the better. It was as though she'd been released from a cage.

Mid-sixties was still a relatively young age, and she had lots of things that she wanted to do.

Juliet felt ridiculously happy as she wandered about looking out through the windows and letting the place wrap itself around her. She felt very much at home.

Ken sat flicking TV channels but not seeing or absorbing anything that flickered past his eyes. He was tired. And he'd come home to no dinner. A note from Juliet had said she'd gone to look at an apartment, and that there was cold cuts and salad in the fridge if he wanted them.

She'd seen a few places and hadn't bought any of them; no doubt this one would be the same. It was just a notion she had, and he had to appease her, he supposed as he wandered out to the kitchen and opened the door of the fridge. She wouldn't really leave all the comforts of a big detached house to go and live on her own in a poky apartment, Ken assured himself, pulling out a cold chicken leg and munching it while he put the kettle on to make himself a pot of tea.

Debbie was sizzling as she washed the paint out of her brushes and flung them into a bucket. It was just after ten and, despite several messages and texts to Bryan's mobile, he hadn't got back to her. He'd gone on the piss. She knew it. Why could she never depend on him? He'd promised her he'd be home to help her paint. He'd been with her when they'd bought the paint, and he'd been enthusiastic about the colours. She'd felt he was finally starting to take more of an interest in doing up their home. Now, she felt like crying.

Her phone rang, and she grabbed it off the kitchen table. She let it ring for a while, not wanting to seem too eager when she saw his number flash up. 'Hello,' she said coldly. She'd see what he had to say before she launched into a rant.

'Debbie, it's Stuart. Bryan's taken a bad hit, he's been taken to the Mater. You better get over there.'

'What!' she exclaimed, aghast, recognizing the voice of one of Bryan's workmates.

'Look, we were just walking up the quays to Kev's gaff, and he took some sort of a convulsion and we called an ambulance. I'm just telling you, you should get over there. I have his phone and wallet.'

'Right, right,' she muttered, stunned. She grabbed her bag and the keys of the car off the top of the phone table in the hall and raced out the front door. She thought she was going to puke with apprehension. How could Bryan have been so stupid, she fretted as she drove like a maniac towards the East Link, mentally plotting her route past the Five Lamps and up the NCR to the Mater. The traffic was light, but it seemed as though every set of traffic lights was red. She parked on a sidestreet off Dorset Street, ran into the grounds of A&E and up the ramp into the entrance, which was manned by security guards. A prisoner from the nearby jail, handcuffed to a warder, limped ahead of her, slowing her progress. She managed to sidestep him and slip into the A&E as someone on the other side of the door buzzed to open it and let themself out.

It was controlled chaos – old people in chairs and patients on trolleys along the sides of the big central desk; ambulancemen waiting for their patients to be admitted so they could reclaim their stretchers before their ambulances were once more equipped to race off into the night to bring back another human cargo. Cubicles, some with curtains drawn, others open, all full. She was about to ask for Bryan when she saw him, spread-eagled on a trolley, his clothes stained with puke. He was conscious. 'Hey, babe, sorry about this. Took a bad one,' he slurred. 'Had my stomach pumped. I've to stay for a couple of hours just to make sure. Glad you're here, babe. I don't want to be here on my own.' He lifted his hand to take hers.

Debbie stared down at him. Anxiety turned to ice-cold fury. 'I'm not staying. You can get a taxi home or get one of your druggie friends to drive you. And then you can go to hell,' she exploded, turning on her heel. She made her way past a cluster of relatives surrounding an elderly man in a wheel-chair, grey-faced as he took great gasps of oxygen. How dare her good-for-nothing husband take up a trolley when someone who was really sick needed it? How dare he expect her to stay in that hellhole with him, holding his hand and probably his head after leaving her in the lurch for the evening? How dare he treat her like a doormat?

'No more,' Debbie muttered as she hurried back to the car. She had a good mind to keep driving until she got to Greystones and spend the night and even the weekend at her mother's. But Connie would want to know why, and Debbie had no intention of telling her about Bryan's shameful episode.

She couldn't go running to her mother every time something bad happened. She wasn't a child any more. She'd married Bryan in spite of Connie's misgivings. She was going to have to deal with her own problems. And if Bryan thought he was going to treat her like dirt, he was in for a rude awakening. From now on, he was on probation. One more stunt like that and he was out, Debbie vowed, and she got into the car and drove home.

Bryan blinked rapidly and tried to focus. Was he hallucinating? Had Debbie just told him to go to hell? He felt weird; it was a really bad trip. Surely his wife was concerned about him? He could die; people had died from dodgy drugs. She couldn't have walked out on him and left him alone in this dreadful, noisy, stuffy place. The bright, fluorescent lights hurt his eyes and were giving him a headache. He closed his eyes and immediately felt dizzy. Nausea washed over him and he groaned as his stomach heaved and he began to barf. Debbie had abandoned him in his hour of need. So much for better or worse. Some wife she was.

Aimee yawned as she stood at the baggage carousel

with Barry and Melissa, waiting for her luggage. She'd enjoyed her holiday and the feel of the sun on her limbs. It had been a relief to get out of wet and windy Ireland. And now they were back to miserable weather again. It had been cold walking down the jetway to the terminal, and it was cloudy and raining outside.

She'd done the family-holiday thing now, she thought with relief. She and Barry had even had sex one night, and she'd enjoyed it, because she hadn't had it for ages. But now she wanted to get back to work. She wanted to have as much done as she possibly could before the baby was born. Hibernian Dreams would be up and running in the next couple of months as far as she was concerned.

She smiled at Melissa. Her daughter had a good tan, which took away that dreadful pallor she'd had before they came away. 'Good holiday, wasn't it?'

'Yeah, it was great, Mom. Have to go to the loo, I'm bursting,' she said. 'Don't forget: my case has a pink ribbon on it, if it comes before I get back.'

'I know it,' Aimee assured her.

'Where's she off to?' Barry shouldered his way through the group waiting for their luggage to join her. He'd gone off to get a trolley.

'The loo,' Aimee said, peering along the carousel as the cases started arriving.

'You don't think she's being sick, do you?' Barry frowned.

'No,' Aimee said. 'I thought she did fine on holidays.'

'It's hard to know. We'll bring her to the doctor anyway. We need to be vigilant.'

'OK,' Aimee agreed, spotting her Louis Vuitton.

'And you'll have to go for your scan too,' he reminded her.

'For God's sake, Barry, I know,' she said irritably. 'I'll sort it next week. Let's get out of the airport first.'

Could he just not leave her alone? Going for scans and hospital visits was a bloody nuisance; she wanted to leave it as long as she could. Did her husband not realize just how busy she was going to be? She scowled as she hauled her case off the carousel and dumped it on to the trolley with a lot more force than was necessary.

Melissa made herself quietly sick in the small cubicle. There was so much noise with hand-dryers and flushing loos, no one would hear her, she assured herself as she got rid of the unwelcome food. She was sure she had put on a ton of weight when she was away. It was time to get serious about getting it off again.

She emerged into the crowds milling around the toilets and made her way to the sink. It *had* been a good holiday, she reflected as she washed her hands and held them under a dryer. Her mom and dad had been like their old selves, and they'd even hugged one day. They'd been very watchful of what she ate, and she'd seen them looking at each other when she protested about eating dessert and starters. It was bad enough eating a main course.

A thought struck her: it was clear they were concerned about her, and it was as if they had joined forces again. If she kept them concerned about her weight, they'd be so focused on her they wouldn't end up fighting and talk of divorce would fade away. That would be excellent, Melissa decided. It was a win-win situation. By controlling her weight she'd be keeping the family together. She couldn't think of anything better. It was a challenge she would embrace eagerly, she decided, as she noticed with dismay how round and fat her cheeks had become the week she'd been away. The first thing she was going to do when she got home was weigh herself.

Barry's phone beeped, and his brow furrowed as he looked at the message.

Can't contact the bastard. Hasn't been seen around the club in the last few weeks. Not looking good. Derek.

Bloody hell, thought Barry, a dark, turbulent tide of anxiety washing through his veins. SecureCo shares had plunged, there was talk of the company going under and Jeremy Farrell had gone to ground. Derek Holmes had sent him a text wondering if Barry knew of his whereabouts and explaining the reason why he and several club members were anxious to contact the elusive stockbroker. Barry hadn't heard a peep from him. What a welcome home from his holidays.

But perhaps Jeremy was on holidays, too, and

that was why no one could contact him; it wasn't beyond the bounds of reason. People went abroad on holidays, he reassured himself silently. All would be well. Jeremy was too wily a fox to back something that was going to fail, even in these rocky economic times.

Barry watched his wife dumping her case on the trolley and sighed. Back to normal, he thought gloomily. The holiday had been a truce of sorts, but the battle of real life had just re-engaged, and it was disheartening. The south of France had been a pleasure. They had lazed around the hotel and pool, gone to Nice and Monte Carlo, read and swam and totally relaxed after the exhaustion of Disneyworld and shopping in Paris on hot August days.

Aimee hadn't been as relaxed for months. They'd even had some decent sex, which was totally unexpected. It was as though by unspoken consent they'd left their problems at home and cocooned themselves in their Riviera bubble. But the minute they'd touched down in Dublin, the BlackBerry was out and she was all business again.

He glanced at his watch and yawned. Gone eleven thirty. Another three-quarters of an hour to get home. An air-traffic controllers' strike had delayed them a couple of hours. Flying was a nightmare these days. It would be nice to sleep in his own bed, and at least he didn't have to get up for work the next day. Coming home on a Friday was a good idea always.

He thought of Connie and wondered how she

was and what she was doing. No doubt she was on a date with that man. *Don't think about it*, he told himself as Aimee pointed out Melissa's case and he grabbed it. Maybe he'd send her a text to say they were home, he mused as he waited for his own case to come around. A text couldn't harm anyone, and he wanted Connie to know that he was thinking of her. She'd appreciate it, he assured himself as he took out his phone.

'Are you sure this is what you want?'

'Couldn't think of anything else I'd like better,' Connie said as she led Drew up the stairs. They'd gone out for a meal in a local restaurant and she'd invited him back for a drink. She thought she heard her mobile phone beep, but she didn't care. It was probably one of those messages to tell her her inbox was full. She was always forgetting to delete her messages. Debbie and Bryan were painting their bedroom; her daughter would hardly be ringing her at this hour of the night.

Hand in hand, she and Drew walked into her bedroom. She was longing for him to make love to her. Now, finally, her life could be all about her and this wonderful new man who'd arrived into it like a precious gift from the universe. The rain was lashing down on to the Velux window, adding to the cosy feel of the darkened room, and they turned to each other eager for what was to come.

They were hungry for each other, their hands fumbling at buttons and zips before, freed from the encumbrances of clothes, they pressed against each other, hands sliding, caressing over bare skin. How lovely it was to have a man's arms around her again. Connie sighed with pleasure as she kissed Drew's neck and throat before finding his mouth again. The first time was fast, frenzied, and both cried out when release came, burying their faces into each other's necks and gasping for breath.

'I love a horny man,' Connie smiled in the dark, tracing her fingers down the long length of his spine.

'And I love a horny woman,' Drew laughed, leaning up on his elbow to look down at her. 'Sorry about the rush. It's been a while.'

'Don't be. It was deeply, deeply satisfying,' she purred. 'I couldn't have waited myself, it's been a while for me too.' She smiled, staring into his eyes. 'I have to tell you something, though,' she confessed. 'Barry and I did it once before Debbie's wedding. It was a one-off. You know the way things happen . . .' She trailed off. 'Do you mind?'

'Why should I, Connie? Of course I don't, as long as you won't be doing it again,' he teased. 'Then I might have to go and shag Marianna.' She laughed against his shoulder.

He bent his head and kissed her tenderly. 'This time we'll do it slow,' he promised, sliding his hand along the curve of her waist to cup her breast.

'Whatever you say,' Connie murmured as the delicious quivers began again, and kissed him back with enthusiasm.

Later, entwined in each other's arms, drifting off to sleep, Drew said drowsily, 'I'm falling for you, you know that, don't you?'

'Right back at ya,' Connie said sleepily, kissing his cheek as his arms tightened around her before she fell fast asleep, snuggled in against him.

ACKNOWLEDGEMENTS

Be truly glad. There is wonderful joy ahead.
1 Peter 1:6

For all the wonderful joys and gifts I've been given
in my life, I give thanks. And for the gift of this book
as always, I thank Jesus, Our Lady, Mother Meera,
St Joseph, St Michael, St Anthony, the Holy Spirit,
White Eagle, all my Angels and Saints and Guides,
and my Beloved Mother, who is now with them.

To my much-loved family, who are always there in
good times and bad and whom I love dearly – I am
truly Blessed.

To all my friends, who continually offer love and
support, but especially to Aidan Storey, who has the
biggest heart and who minds me so well and makes
me laugh. To Alil O'Shaughnessy, who counsels,
consoles, listens to moans, and edits superbly! To
Tony Kavanagh, one of the funniest, and most
talented men I've ever met. To Deirdre Purcell, for
the truly relaxing holidays. To Pam and Si Young,

for all the loving, inspiring emails that lift my heart. To Cathy Kelly, a most dear and cherished friend who, with kind and generous Fiona O'Brien, helped me in a most wondrous way at a lovely 'elbows on the table' lunch. To Ann Barry, Anita Notaro and Claudia Carroll, always on 'candle lighting' duty; and to Breda Purdue and Ciara Considine, who've seen me through many ups and downs, as has Geraldine Ring, even though she's always giving out to me! To Marian Lawlor, a wonderful friend and neighbour. And to Sylvia and John in Mi Capricho, who are kindness itself.

To Dr Peter Boylan, who listened and made such a huge difference to my quality of life – a caring physician, as well as a great gynaecologist. Thanks so much, I'm in your debt. I was told you were the best, and you are. And to Averil Priestman, who was always so warm and kind when I went for my appointments. To all in Unit Four in Holles St Hospital who took such good care of me. Huge thanks.

To the doctors, nurses and staff of the Cremore Clinic, who look after my family and me with such diligence and kindness.

To Dr Joseph Duggan and Trish, who take such care of my dad.

To dearest Francesca Liversidge, great friend and great editor who is always looking out for me, and to Jo Williamson, who is always reassuring no matter what the problem. It would take another book to thank all the team, in Editorial, Sales &

Marketing, the Art Department . . . The list is endless but I really appreciate all you do, so to everyone in Transworld, Transworld Ireland and to Simon, Helen, Dec, and all in Gill Hess and Co, for all the hard work and constant support, mega thanks.

To Sarah Lutyens, dear friend and agent, who is so calming when I'm in a tizzy, and to Felicity, Jane and Daisy also, for their commitment and hard work.

To Edwin Higel and all my colleagues in New Island for their on-going commitment to Open Door. Onwards and upwards.

And finally, a very special thanks to all my dear readers who have bought my books down through the years. It's hard to believe *City Girl* came out nineteen years ago. Thank you all so much for the support and many kind letters you've sent me. I hope you enjoy this one, and may your lives be as greatly Blessed as mine has been.

Forgive and Forget

Patricia Scanlan

There's nothing like a good wedding . . . to start world war three!

And that's exactly what's going to happen if Connie Adams, the mother of the bride, can't smooth things over between Debbie and her dad.

He's hell bent on bringing his stuck-up second wife and their sulky teenage daughter to the big day, but Debbie would rather walk up the aisle of a supermarket than have *them* at her wedding.

It's the last thing Debbie needs right now – her boss is making her life hell and she's starting to suspect that her fiancé's getting cold feet . . .

So will they all live happily ever after, or are the whole family heading for divorce?

Reasons to love Patricia Scanlan:

'The ultimate comfort read'
GLAMOUR

'More fizzy fun from the Irish bestseller'
YOU MAGAZINE

9781848270152